D0122753

A SINGLE EYE

A SINGLE EYE

Susan Dunlap

CARROLL & GRAF PUBLISHERS
NEW YORK

W

A SINGLE EYE

Carroll & Graf Publishers
An Imprint of Avalon Publishing Group, Inc.
245 West 17th Street
11th Floor
New York, NY 10011

AVALON
publishing group incorporated

First Carroll & Graf edition 2006

Library of Congress Cataloging-in-Publication Data is available.

ISBN-13: 978-0-78671-850-4
ISBN-10: 0-7867-1850-1

9 8 7 6 5 4 3 2 1

Interior design by Susan Canavan
Printed in the United States of America
Distributed by Publishers Group West

FOR MARYLOU DIETRICH

A SINGLE EYE

CHAPTER ONE

O

It was the perfect day for the gag. Ten minutes from now was going to be the perfect moment; the sun would gush over the east wall to create a golden backlight for Kelly Rustin and me as we did leaps from high mesa to high mesa, across the canyon. This was her first stunt; the one she'd always remember.

The far side was a broad ledge of rock, a no-brainer landing. Our take-off point, a wind-baked peninsula, stuck out over the wooded canyon like a pointed foot. "Just for you, Kel," I'd said, "in case you need a little kick." She was nervous, of course, but no way would she admit it, and I was working triple-time to keep her from letting worry eat into her concentration. In the stunt business double-checking the wire and the carabiner is your life; distraction will kill you. But this was an easy gag; no one was going to die here. It was a stylish stunt that would show Kelly's great lines in the air and my "yikes" landings. We only had time for one practice run, then one shot. That one shot had to be perfect, for the movie, for me, but most of all for Kelly.

Almost covering the take-off mesa was a giant yellow crane with a hundred-foot arm holding our wires. Hoisting the crane up here had taken twenty guys and hadn't done the forest trails any good. Its feet were so close to the edge that the cameramen were hanging off the side in a basket to give Kelly and me room for the run-up to the leap.

"Eight minutes," the second unit director called. "Last run-through."

We moved to the start marks. Kelly attached her wire and checked it just as I had taught her. I hooked mine. We double-checked each other. "Break a tooth," I said. Her father was a dentist. She shot me a smile, but never took her eyes off the leap point. I couldn't help but be proud of her.

"Go!"

Kelly ran, kicking up scree with each step. A fan blew her long blond hair out straight behind her. When she hit the leap point I started after her. I hit the edge and pushed off into a glide out over the abyss. I didn't look down, not because of the two-hundred-foot drop—heights aren't my fear—but to focus on camouflaging the "hold" moment when the wire took my weight. I sailed feet up, arms out, *flying* onto the wire with no telltale jerk, holding the pose till I could make out individual pebbles on the far mesa. I pulled up knees to chest, swung my feet hard forward onto the dump spot, windmilled my arms, did a lurch-and-sit, and pushed off into a lope across the mesa.

"Cut."

I skidded. The wire jerked me back.

"Great job, everyone. Get back to the start marks. Two minutes till sunrise."

I walked back to the edge of the shelf. I'd hit the dump spot perfectly; my lurch-and-sit was the best I'd ever done, I could feel it. I looked at Kelly; she was rerunning the gag in her mind just as she should be, but the corners of her mouth twitched. She knew she'd been on mark. She was holding off her smile till the final take was in the can, but I couldn't resist grinning for her. She'd been a wad of terror coated with a crust of bravado two weeks ago when she auditioned; only I had been sure she had it in her to be a great stunt double. In a quarter of an hour everyone on the set would be patting her back and insisting they knew all along.

The cable jerked me up like a crate on a container ship and swung me back to the start side. Kelly landed next to me, rechecked her wire, then stuck her hand in the goo pot and fingered the stuff through her hair.

"On marks," the director called.

I checked my wire again, then Kelly's. On my next job *I'd* be the second unit director.

"Break another tooth?" She almost managed to hide the quaver in her voice.

"A bicuspid."

"Camera."

A thread of sun broke over the eastern wall.

"Action."

Kelly ran, scree shooting from her feet, hair straight out behind her.

The front crane foot slipped over the edge.

She hit the edge and leapt into the air.

I poised to go.

The crane swayed. The arm jerked Kelly off trajectory. Behind me the director gasped. Kelly had momentum. She could still pull it out. We had to get the shoot *now*.

The sun flooded over the mountaintop; its searing light threw the world into slo-mo. Sparks shot out from the top of the crane arm; the wire snapped. *Kelly's* wire. Slowly, as if sailing, Kelly hit the side of the canyon wall and bounced. And bounced. And bounced. Like a wad of paper, opening more with each hit. Stunt doubles know how to curl and roll. Kelly wasn't curled, wasn't rolling; she was flayed out.

Noise shot up, people screaming, metal grinding.

I skidded to a stop at the mesa edge, still on my wire. "Lower me down."

"The crane won't hold."

"I only need a minute. Send me down fast. *Now!*"

I didn't wait for an answer. I leapt into the canyon. The wire spun out. I eyed the wall for holds.

Below, branches snapped. Kelly screamed.

The wire jerked hard, smacking me headfirst into the rocky wall. Blood dripped in my eyes. I kicked off. "Faster!"

For an instant I hung in air, then fell free seventy, eighty feet before the wire caught hold. There was no sound from Kelly below, no scream, no moan, no "I'm okay." Shrubs and trees poked out toward me from the walls.

"Trees," a guy yelled from above. "Kelly's in the trees below!"

The wire jerked, spinning me around. For the first time, I chanced a glance down—I'm not afraid of heights—into the top of the thick woods on the canyon floor.

The wire ran loose again. Before I could react, I shot down through a canopy of leaves and branches into a forest. The leaves blocked out the light. I couldn't get my breath.

"Help me!" Kelly moaned. "Oh, God, I can't move my legs!"

Panic cut through me.

I grabbed the wire and yanked hard three times. "Pull me up." I tried to yell, but no sound came out.

The wire snapped to a stop and then slowly lifted me up through the branches. The fronds grabbed for my head and arms. Sweat covered my face, poured down my back. Bile filled my mouth. I was going to wretch.

"Darcy?" Kelly moaned. "Darcy, I can't move. Help me!"

The muted light hit my face again. I was out of the canopy. I stared straight up, to avoid catching sight of the tree-covered walls. I swallowed hard to push down the bile. "Kelly's at the bottom," I yelled. "Send the medics." I swung myself into the wall, grabbed onto an outcropping, unhooked, and gave three yanks.

Kelly shrieked.

I went stiff. "The medics are coming, Kel. Hang on!"

"Darcy!" she wailed. "Don't leave me down here!"

"I gave the medics my wire."

"Darcy!"

I clung to the outcropping above the tree line and didn't move, didn't look down. Sweat poured down my face, my back, my legs. My hands shook. My heart slammed against my ribs. Kelly's screams reverberated, filling the canyon.

I looked down, into the trees. The green swam. I couldn't breath. I shut my eyes and clung.

I didn't dare look down again, into the trees where I could not make myself go.

○

Two weeks later the air was cool in the Ninth Street Zen Center, still, and so silent it hushed my own jumble of thoughts. In the white-walled meditation hall, round black cushions perched atop black rectangular mats. Two students bowed to each other before settling on their cushions and pivoting to face the walls. My shoulders relaxed, my breath flowed more easily, and, as always, I felt, in a way I couldn't explain, at home.

But before I could enter the hall, a finger tapped my shoulder, a head nodded toward the *dokusan*—interview—room. Inside, the *Roshi*—esteemed teacher—waited.

His summoning bell rang. I opened his door.

Yamana-roshi sat perfectly still, a small Japanese man in brown robes, on a brown mat in the small white room. On the altar beside him lay offerings to the Buddha: flowers, incense, and candle light. The candlewick had been trimmed too short and the flame threatened to fail, but Yamana-roshi did not turn toward it. It would last or it would die.

I bowed to the Buddha. I bowed to Yamana-roshi, and to my black cushion before sitting cross-legged on it and swiveling to face him. The ritual was like a soft hand on my shoulder. The two-foot by three-foot mats under our cushions almost touched, symbolizing the spiritual intimacy of the *dokusan* interview. My knees were inches from his; his face was calm. Normally, he would wait for me to pose my question. Then he would sit silently till the right reply, perhaps a *koan*, arose in his mind. To us Americans, koans are paradoxical tales from another time and another culture. But Yamana-roshi would choose one that paralleled my life, perhaps one like *You are on the top of a hundred-foot pole. How do you advance?* Carrying the riddle in the back of my mind, I might see my next step differently. I might *see* differently.

Buddhism is a religion; Zen is the practice of looking into yourself, peeling off layers till you find your essential emptiness. I had entered here before and held out my life like a ball of string and, each time, he'd found a strand to pull so I could begin the unraveling. Now he sat in front of me, legs crossed, hands together.

"Roshi, I hope—"

"You hope. When is hope?" he asked, reminding me that our goal is to experience the present, not create pictures of a future. The Japanese language is without inflection and Yamana-Roshi had transferred that even-weighting to his English. There was no rise of the voice to hint that he questioned my assumptions, to demand I explain how my life could be anchored in a future reality I had just made up.

Word was that he had once been stern and I could imagine him years ago as a middle-aged man, his eyes narrowed in irritation at bowing done carelessly, rituals ill-performed by students who bristled at the discipline. His square face and prominent cheekbones would have given him the look of a taskmaster and his beginner's English left listeners to their own judgments. But time had loosened the skin over those bones and transformed his frustrated grimace into an accepting half smile. Despite his age his forehead was smooth, and no squint lines bracketed his eyes. He wasn't searching outside to spot answers.

From the altar, curls of incense rose, widened, and vanished between us.

I smiled. "Roshi, my hope is about two weeks of zazen. I'm going to a sesshin!" The words tumbled out; I hadn't realized how desperate I was to tell him. "The sesshin, it's in the woods, back in California. Two weeks long. I just got the acceptance letter. I leave on the red-eye—at the crack of dawn tomorrow!" I was leaning forward, to spot his approval a millisecond sooner.

A little smile brightened his face. He didn't speak, as if to let us both savor this moment. Zen practice is to be present in the present, and I was particularly glad of it now. Yamana-roshi wouldn't mention how long he had been encouraging me to do a multiday sitting at some other Zen center where I wouldn't be the work leader or the head server like I was here, where I couldn't spend my meditation time thinking about assigning tasks or allotting serving pots, all the while convincing myself I was sitting zazen. Nor would he bring up the excuses I had raised every time there had been a notice of a suitable sesshin: there was a call for stunt doubles who could do high-fall gags; I had just landed a job; I'd just finished a job; my apartment was being painted; it was winter; it was summer. In a long sesshin I was afraid I'd see myself for what I was, or worse yet, that I wouldn't.

Still smiling, he looked up, caught my eye and said, "Ah, jumping in with both feet!" Jumping in with both feet was one of the quaint Americanisms that amused him, the making of a great coup out of the easiest way. "Harder than jumping in with only one foot?" he had demanded in delight the first time he'd heard it. "Than with no foot?"

"You mean belly flopping?" I'd said, and he had laughed open-mouthed.

I smiled now, basking in our shared amusement.

But Zen masters don't speak frivolously.

"You're right: once I make up my mind to do something, I'm in whole hog." *Whole hog* was another of his favorites. "But I had to this time. Two weeks ago the wire snapped in a stunt. My friend, the girl I had lobbied for and trained, broke her leg and three ribs and punctured her lung. She fell into woods. She was terrified, and the pain . . ." I had to stop to breathe. "I was thirty yards above her. She was screaming. And I couldn't make myself go down into the woods for her. Suddenly everything turned strange; top was bottom and I was in a whole other place, black, airless, no way out. All I could do was panic!" My back was clammy. I swallowed hard. "Roshi, that's happened before, the sweat, the panic, the other place . . . but it is never going to happen again. So, I'm jumping in with both feet. I hunted around for a sesshin in the woods, and redwoods are as big as woods come, right?" I blurted the last before my bravado failed.

On the altar the candle sputtered, sending a wave of dark across his face. He said, "This is not why we sit zazen."

"I know, Roshi. But I have to do this. I hope—"

"Hope is not now. Hope is—"

I thought he would say hope is throwing yourself into a future that you've made up and ignoring the reality of the present. But he didn't. He said, "Hope is a trap. Be aware of that when you enter sesshin. *'Do not judge by any standards.'* Do not set standards to judge yourself before you begin; do not hope. Even when you jump with both feet." He nodded, as if to acknowledge my propensities, and said, "Fear will arise. Feel it in your body, observe your thoughts. Nothing more."

Many times he had told me that fear was nothing more than thoughts and sensations. "Nothing more." Many times I had repeated those words in the safety of the city and been too panicked in the woods to even recall them. But this time was different. I believed him. I was ready to test it out.

There was a small teacup on his right. He lifted it with both hands, drank, and put it back. "Who is the teacher?"

"Garson-roshi, your former student!"

"Ah, Garson," he said, brightening. "He is a deep teacher. A man of big heart, like you, Darcy. Very good for you." He nodded slowly, as if to acknowledge a deeper connection. "Garson is like you. He keeps hidden from himself. He will help you see what you do not want to see, perhaps what you do not expect. It is a great chance for you."

His hand reached for the brass bell beside him, and hovered above it. In a moment he would lift it. Outside the door, the waiting student would poise to move at hearing the soft rub of tongue against metal. He would hope for the firm ring calling him, just as I was intent on forestalling it, in solidifying Yamana's approval.

I said, "I heard that Garson was leaving the monastery. This'll be his last sesshin. All his students must have heard; I was lucky they left any room for me."

"Leaving?" His question hung, the word uncolored by anything behind it. And yet, I knew him so well, my beloved teacher, that I tensed.

"In my acceptance letter Garson said he was leaving at the end of sesshin. The sesshin will be in honor of a student named Aeneas. That will be a focus different than what I'm looking for, but it'll still be valuable for me to do the sesshin in the woods and . . ."

I stopped. Yamana-roshi was sitting still as before, but he wasn't listening. In *dokusan*, the teacher gives the student his full attention. He listens not merely to the words, but to everything behind them. I had never seen his attention waver at all. Even when I ran into him on the street his mind never wandered. For him to be distracted here, in *dokusan* . . .

Yamana-Roshi raised his head, looked at me in a way I couldn't assess. His hand, still poised above the bell, didn't move. No sound broke the stillness. When he spoke, his voice, always soft, seemed like words in a dream. "This sesshin may not be for you. You—"

"Roshi, I have to go!"

"There could be difficulties—"

"You said this was a great chance for me. Garson is leaving. Roshi, this is my only chance!"

No reaction was evident on his face or in his body. He sat utterly still, eyes downward, face impassive. He wasn't toting up pluses and minuses; I didn't know what his process was. Nor could I understand his sudden balking about my going to the event he had urged me toward, in the place I would have to face my fears, with a teacher even he had said would be good for me. The only sound in the room was my own breath. I tried to sit as still as he and failed. My jacket rustled as I shifted, strands of my curly hair tickled my neck. A waft of incense—dry, acrid—passed over my face.

"The student at the monastery, Aeneas, disappeared," he said.

"Disappeared?"

"No one reported seeing him since, since six years."

"Do you think he's . . . dead?"

"Could be dead. Could be in Paris. What is known is he disappeared," he said, pulling me back from speculation. He lifted his hands and settled them back as they were. He started to speak and stopped. His pallid face colored in a way I had never seen in this self-possessed man. Finally, he said, "Garson is my dharma brother, student of my teacher. When he was in Japan I was his guide. With problems he telephoned me. He is wise, a man of deep compassion. But now . . ."

"Roshi, hearing my friend scream in agony, that was the worst. But this fear of mine is ruining my life. I have to deal with it now!" My hands clenched into fists, fingernails digging into palms. "I work in a field as macho as they come; I can't be saying I'm scared. I live three thousand miles away from Hollywood, so I don't keep having to make excuses to avoid a party in a producer's house in a wooden canyon, a hike in the Sierras, an easy job in the mountains. I live in the city so I never have to see a forest. I can't admit the truth, even to people who aren't in the business, not even to my friends here in the zendo, because they might inadvertently say something to someone who knows someone in the business. My whole being is a lie. Roshi, I have to do this sesshin, in the woods. This is the right time; it won't come again. I can take care of myself." My heart was pounding. I inhaled as slowly, as long as I could manage. "But if you say not to, I won't go."

Yamana-roshi nodded almost imperceptibly, but I knew that with my willingness to trust him I had passed through a gate. The candle sputtered; the shadows turned his face dark, but he seemed not to notice. When he raised his head any softening of age was gone. He looked out through eyes ringed with sadness, but his voice brooked no dissent. "Go, but do this: tell Garson I know what he is planning and he must not do that. Tell Garson I am sending this message with you."

"Why—"

He grasped the bell and lifted it with such balance it made no sound. "Darcy, keep an eye open." "An eye open" was another of the quirky American expressions that amused him, the single eye saving half the ocular effort. But there was no humor in his voice now. "Be alert," he said, and rang the bell.

Questions flooded my mind. But the interview was over. I bowed to him, fluffed the cushion for the next student, bowed to the Buddha, and opened the door and left. The next student, a pediatrician with an office down the block, stepped inside. I didn't know what Yamana-Roshi had been thinking a minute ago, but now, he wasn't thinking of me at all; his whole attention would be on the pediatrician.

Tell Garson I know what he is planning and he must not do that. What could that mean? A student disappeared six years ago. Why was that such a big deal? After gearing up to go to sesshin, students rarely leave, but it does happen that a guy can't deal with sitting in front of a blank wall hour after hour, or a woman gets fed up and stalks off. People leave zendos; people leave Zen practice. No one hears from them again. They don't get entire sesshins in their honor. And roshis a continent away don't send desperate messages.

Tell Garson I know what he is planning and he must not do that.

I needed to talk to Yamana, but he had said all he would. And the red-eye waits for no woman.

CHAPTER TWO

O

You can get a cab at any time of night in Manhattan, but hailing one at 3:30 A.M. and carrying a suitcase, a duffel bag, and a dog is like a reality show challenge. Duffy is a proper Scottish laird, but he's still a small black dog with a big head, a loud bark, and teeth that would be at home in the mouth of a wolfhound. I had finally backed him into his carrier and given him my iPod. He'd either like the music or the taste.

When we got to LaGuardia, the iPod was intact and Duffy was a happy hound. I let him out and checked my bags at the curb. "And the dog?" the baggage handler said, readying another label.

"I'll carry him on."

"Dog's too big for under the seat."

"He's fine."

The clerk gave me a you'll-be-back shrug.

But I was ready. If Duffy had been advertised on one of the used-dog Web sites his story would have read: "Previous owner moved to a place that doesn't allow pets." His owner had been his handler, who had departed a location shoot in the sheriff's car. I had inherited Duffy.

Intelligence in a dog is a mixed blessing in apartment life, but in an airport crisis it can't be beat. Duffy is smart, and he loves to be onstage. He even has a S.A.G. card.

I paused outside the automatic doors to ticketing, bent down toward him eye to eye, my long red curly hair to his cropped black, and said, "Go small, Duff."

He backed into the carrier, wriggled and curled. By the time he finished he was half his usual size. He had even mastered a way of putting his paws over the end of his snout that gave him the look of a cropped-nosed dog in prayer. I credit his former handler, who must have made many quick departures with hardly enough time to check luggage. I breezed through check-in, and as soon as I settled him under the seat I unzipped the carrier. It's against the rules, but, of course, I let him stick his head out; and, of course, he invited conversation as he eyed the aisle and the window-sitters' carry-ons as if they were unexpected deliveries to Balmoral.

United Airlines Flight 733, La Guardia to O'Hare, Monday, Nov. 10, 6:00 A.M. EST.

"I'm going to a two-week meditation retreat," I said in answer to the dental technician, who was heading to Chicago for his trade show. He was midtwenties, and larger than the seat that squeezed him. He had glanced at Duffy and moved his feet almost into the aisle.

"You mean 'stare at the wall' stuff?"

I nodded.

"All day long?"

I nodded.

"No C-SPAN, no MTV?"

I nodded.

"Not even radio? Or . . . or . . . even newspaper?"

"Nope."

"Or . . ." he seemed to be grasping for a level of diversion even less entertaining.

I spared him. "Or talk. We don't talk."

"Not talk? How can you go all day without talking? I mean, like, suppose there's something you've got to say?"

"You wait."

"But two weeks? How can you—that's crazy." Immediately he saw he'd been rude, and he grinned in a manner that must have eased the late delivery of dentures and crowns. "I mean that in the nicest possible way."

It wasn't till we started the descent into O'Hare that the woman on my other side lost her restraint. "I'm sorry," she said. She looked to be around my age; like me, she was wearing blue jeans and a sweater. "I couldn't help overhearing when you were talking about the meditation place. Is that Zen Buddhism?"

"Yes."

"Excuse me for asking, but, well, tell me this. Why? I mean what's the point of all that meditation? I mean, what do you get out of it?"

I swallowed and plowed ahead. The traditional Zen answer is: 'Nothing. You don't get anything because you already have everything; it's just that you don't realize it—yet.'"

"Oh," she muttered and turned to the window.

My next seatmate was about ten years older than I—late forties. On the tray table, her laptop waited, nagging. She wedged her feet between briefcase and a bulging shopping bag. "Guilt gifts," she said. "It's so hard to leave Jake and the kids, even when I'm one of the speakers at the conference. What about you? Where are you headed?"

"A meditation retreat."

"Can I come?" she asked, and laughed.

My oldest brother, John, met my plane. I was the youngest by far of us seven Lott children. I might be a grown-up with a successful career, but in the eyes of my family my job was still me just swinging from the roof and going to the movies instead of doing my homework. John wasn't surprised about the meditation retreat. Buddhism is common in San Francisco, though not in our family. Like my middle brother's cave-diving or my oldest sister's collecting commemorative salt and pepper shakers, it was an odd enthusiasm the family had accepted. What he said was, "You're doing it *where?*"

"At the Redwood Canyon Monastery a couple hours north of Santa Rosa. You don't need to take me, John. You've got a job. The Greyhound will drop me."

"Redwood Canyon, north of Santa Rosa. The *woods?*"

I took a deep breath. "Yes."

"*You're* going to the woods for weeks? The fear thing is that serious?"

"Yes," I forced out.

John sat open-mouthed. He started to say something and then rejected it.

"What?" I demanded, knowing it couldn't be the standard 'woods' comments; they had all been made many times over many years. My fear had been a joke in the family, but a gently handled one, as befits a failing of the baby. Mom had once referred to the older kids as her German shepherds, the policeman, the lawyer, the doctor, the journalist, and the teacher. Me she'd labeled a Labrador puppy.

"Well, Darcy, I guess Duffy's the one with the sense. He'll be halfway to China by the time you get back."

"Starting his dig from San Francisco'll be a real boon."

"Mom's fenced in the roses, had the butcher on the alert for a bone bigger than Duffy himself, and we're putting up directions to the Sierras for all the raccoons." John grinned, but there had been another hesitation before his comment and I could read behind his cop's face to the unnerved brother. I wanted to say, "I'll be fine in the woods, John. Why this sudden worry?" But somehow, I, too, hesitated. Instead, I took his shift of topic as a statement of support, gave him a big hug, and hopped out in front of the Greyhound station. As I unloaded my bags, John pulled Duffy into the front seat. I stuck my head in the window and Duffy braced his stubby front paws on my shoulders, laid his head on my shoulder and moaned. It was trick he had learned for a B-movie role, but it never failed to make me tear up. I swallowed hard, nuzzled his snout, and then the car pulled into traffic and I was left covered in sweat and an inch from fainting.

Six hours later, the Greyhound slowed and I jerked awake. Outside were tall trees, lots of them. I shivered, then jumped out onto the macadam. Still thinking of John, I forced myself to stare into the spaces between the redwoods and pines.

The chill afternoon fog was gusting in, already blocking the sun. The back of the Greyhound bus was growing smaller. In moments, even that was gone. Woods loomed to the left of me, woods to the right of me, woods in front and in back of me. The briny air hinted that the ocean was beyond the line of cypresses across the blacktop, but I had no idea how far. I couldn't believe I'd gotten myself into a situation where I was standing on Route One, "the coast road," as the bus passengers had called the *main* road here, and it was a deserted two-laner. And this was the safe spot. From here I was heading into the woods, to a monastery where a student had disappeared. I was going there to tell a roshi I didn't know not to do what he was dead set on doing.

I was crazy.

A rattling sounded in the distance. Another bus? I'd take it. Even if it was headed the wrong way, I'd leap aboard and the blacktop and the monastery and the woods would be a nothing but a bad memory. I grabbed my bag and turned just as not a bus but an old Ford pickup rattled to a stop beside me.

CHAPTER THREE

O

I'd been in vehicles far worse than this decrepit Ford pickup when I was doing car chase gags—cars with every door held by breakaway wire and seats set to eject, trucks on timers to ignite—but in those stunts I'd prepared for the dangers. Anything could be inside this old wreck. Doing gags, I never panicked; now I could barely beat back the fear. The trees or the stranger? I made myself stand still, and waited to see who sat behind the wheel.

The passenger door crackled open and I smelled the interior of the truck before I actually saw it—the stench of mud and wet wool, and—oddly—chocolate. Then I saw who was leaning toward me—a funny-looking old guy in a dark wool sailor's cap, gray hooded sweatshirt and jeans. "You're headed for the zendo, I assume?" he asked me, in a husky voice that matched the rich, chocolate smell. When I nodded yes, he grinned the way strangers had when I was a copper-haired child. And there was something about the old guy's grin that made me grin back at him, albeit tentatively.

"Yeah. To the zendo."

"Well," he said, "it's nine miles. If you slog on foot, you'll get there in a few hours, depending on your hiking skills. If you ride with me, it'll be forty minutes."

There was no way I was going to make it nine miles into those woods by myself. Given a choice between a guy who could be a serial killer and the woods, I'd take my chance with the guy. On location shoots, I'd fended off way bigger than he, with way bigger egos. "Thanks," I said, and climbed up into the cab—into the outer reaches of sesshin. The door clanked shut on New York, on my family in San Francisco, even on Duffy. Now reality was sesshin, the roshi here, and that student who had disappeared. With luck, this old guy in the cap would chat away, the news would be good, and the monastery would be on a hill so I could use my cell phone to call Yamana-roshi.

The engine groaned, shrieked, and gurgled all at once as the truck turned onto the dirt road. The cab was wide, the seat a bench upholstered in duct tape. In the bed, things rattled and thudded, and since the driver hadn't offered me the option of stowing my luggage there, I had wedged my Rollaboard in the foot well and plunked the duffel on top like an already-sprung air bag. That left me with my back to the door and my legs dangling over the luggage, playing footsie with the gear stick. Still, I was safe behind a windshield. One of the tricks I've learned when riding past the woods is to focus only on the glass, blur my vision, and pretend I'm in the shower.

As the truck jolted eastward I leaned back and had a good look at the driver. He seemed to be bald under his wool cap, and his worn gray sweatshirt hung loose. He was probably a short man anyway, but it's always hard to tell when a guy's sitting down. In this big truck he looked like a doll—thin, angular, except for his calloused hands. But when he turned toward me, the whole doll image shifted ridiculously. Every one of his features was too big: his eyes were a light hazel—almost yellow—

his brows brown and bushy, his cheekbones so high they seemed in danger of spiking those yellowy eyes, and his lips full and wide as if stretched from years of laughter. I liked that. The doll he reminded me of now was Mr. Potato Head. A narrow Idaho with all those big features.

The truck hit something, maybe a rock, and jolted to the side. The Rollaboard rattled.

He shot a friendly glance at it. "What've you got in there? You planning to dress for dinner at *sesshin*?"

Dinner at sesshin—retreat—is gruel, eaten in silence as you sit cross-legged on your cushion in the meditation hall. What would my airplane seatmates think of *that*? "That's probably the sea cucumber lotion—for knee pain."

"You've got a lot of clanking there. How much knee pain are you planning on?"

I always packed enough salves and liniments to coat the bodies of every stunt double on the set. I'd been in the checkout line at the Rexall before I reminded myself I wasn't in charge on this trip. "Just a precaution. But I figured you couldn't buy it out here, so I got a few extra bottles in case anyone else needed them."

He said something but the truck lurched and I didn't catch his words.

I braced my knees against my duffel.

"Don't worry. The ruts are so deep you'd need a crane to make it over the edge. I'm Leo, by the way." He stuck a hand in my direction, eyeing me appraisingly, smiling again at my copper waves of hair.

I shook his hand quickly. "Darcy Lott."

"You're from New York, right?" His attention was back on the road now. "You're the one who left on two days' notice. How'd you pull that off?"

"Magic."

"So that's what you've got in that suitcase, rabbits."

"And a top hat to wear to dinner in the zendo. Actually, I cleared my calendar so—"

"Calendar? You a therapist?"

I laughed. "Not hardly. Wrong side of the couch." His head was cocked for the rest of my self-description. Everything about Leo screamed "trustworthy." I did trust him—as much as I did anyone. But not enough to chance revealing my profession and my fear. I fell back on the generic, "I organize."

"What is it you organize?"

"Anything."

He grinned at me. "Anything, huh? Okay, then strut your stuff. Organize my truck."

I'd doubled an actress playing professional organizer in a chick flick a few years back; I could fake it now. I glanced at the dashboard, a memoir-in-disposables of his last month or two. "Too easy. You find me a luggage rack for the back and let me throw out probably most of what you've got in the glove compartment, and get a container for your collection of plastic forks up here on the dash, and that'll get us halfway there."

"They're sentimental forks. From drive-throughs all the way to Canada."

I picked up a brown number with two surviving tines. "Please! Do you think you're the first guy who tried to rationalize his clutter? I suppose these six dead tubes of poison oak cream are sentimental, too."

He let out a guffaw.

"A professional's motto is: The client's taste is always good. Despite the distressing aesthetics, we can create a very fine display case for these fine forks. We'll affix it on top of the dashboard so you can enjoy your collection every time you drive. And the best part is if you get hungry on the road—"

"Yeah, and build me in one of those picnic baskets with plates for eight to go with them."

Now I was into my role whole hog. In my mind this ancient cab, this receptacle for the extraneous unpart-withable of Leo's life, had already become a rolling office, with a bench seat. "We'll add a little fridge so you can keep your chocolate cold, and a hanging drawer for the rest of the stuff behind the seat—"

"There's no chocolate— Oh, the cacao beans. They're not behind the seat; they're in the bed. *Criollo* beans, the finest cacao in the world, I'm told."

"Really? Do we get cocoa at night here?"

"In your dreams, girl. The *tenzo*—the cook—makes gourmet chocolate for sale. That's what pays for our gruel."

This was not unusual, I knew. Many monasteries, whether Buddhist or Catholic, have to bring in money from guest fees or the sale of some suitable commodity. There's a Trappist monastery in Kentucky that sells wonderful fruitcake and bourbon chocolate fudge. A moment passed in cocoa dreams, then he reached over and nudged my arm. "Occasionally, *occasionally*, you might get a cup of cocoa. It'll be worth the wait."

I smiled. This easy bantering was what I liked in a man, no matter his age. The wipers cleared half-inch stripes, leaving most of the windshield an Impressionist haze that veiled the trees. This rain was going to make it a lot easier for me to live here; maybe I would go the entire fortnight without ever having to see a tree clearly. Feeling oddly content in the cluttered cab of the old truck, with the funny old guy driving, I leaned against the seat back and tried to get a handle on him.

"Are you going to the retreat, too?"

"I am."

"You go a lot?"

He smiled, as if at some small, private amusement, but then merely nodded.

"You probably live around here, right? For a while now?"

Again, he only nodded. I'd always heard that backwoods types are leery of revealing too much about themselves to strangers, but his reticence didn't seem unfriendly, so I pressed on.

"A long while," I heard him murmur.

"Then you're just the man I want to talk to—"

"Lucky for you." He glanced pointedly around the cab.

"Right." I laughed. "So, tell me, what's the monastery like? And the roshi?"

Leo's hands tightened on the steering wheel, his small amused smile faded, and suddenly he seemed to be watching for every rock and dip on the road.

"The monastery?" he said with sudden formality. "The property is forty acres surrounded by forest. This road loops around the edge. The nine-mile portion; it makes a good transition to the monastery. There should be twenty-six people at sesshin, four residents, and the rest will be people like you who've flown in from all over. The schedule is standard for American Soto Zen centers. We start at five A.M., sit forty-minute periods separated by ten minutes walking meditation, three periods before breakfast. That's breakfast in the zendo—"

"But no formal dress?"

He eyed me again. For a moment I thought he was annoyed, or just confused, but then he shifted his glance to my suitcase that did *not* hold the evening gown, and grinned. "Then there are three more sitting periods, lunch, break, work period, three sitting periods, dinner, break, sit, sit, sit, snooze, if you haven't been doing that on and off all day. The sesshin director, Rob, has been around for years. There's no one better. He's the Buddha of detail, so competent he doubles as *jisha*."

"*Jisha?* The roshi's assistant?"

He nodded, barely skipping a beat. "The cook—even his gruel is

great! We grow some of our own vegetables, and there's the little chocolate business to bring in money. What else? Hmm. You sleep in a cabin
or a dorm. Bare bones. Have *dokusan*—interview—with the roshi—"

"Garson-roshi. Tell me about him."

The catch in my voice surprised me. It jolted me back to the reason I
had come to this sesshin, to study with this teacher. *He is like you. Keeps
hidden from himself. He will see what you do not want him to see. It is a great
chance for you.* If Garson-roshi was going to see into me, I damned well
needed a heads-up on who he was. As for the guy who disappeared, I
knew better than to ask directly. Students are protective of their teachers.
Leo wouldn't tell a woman he'd met half an hour ago about what could
well be his teacher's lowest moment. More likely, he'd clam up altogether.

I hedged, "Garson was here in the beginning, right?"

The steering wheel was big and thick. Leo tapped his fingers slowly,
as if taking careful aim with his nails. Even amidst the clatter of the truck
and its contents, the sharp clicks were unnerving. He let his gaze rest on
me a shade too long. "We don't have much time to talk. I want to hear
about *you*, Darcy."

The truck jolted again and forced his gaze to the road. I clutched my
pack in front of me, only partially to keep it from bouncing. Did he know
about me, my work or my dumb fear? How could he? I hadn't mentioned
either on the application. To everyone here I was tree-neutral Darcy
Lott, self-employed.

So, then was he just avoiding my question? Or did this sweet old guy
have more on his mind? There's an intimacy about any sesshin; romances
bloom, die, and can be long buried before the end. You think when you
come to sesshin it'll all be spiritual, but twenty-six people in the woods
for two weeks are still twenty-six people in the woods. I eyed him anew
over my pack. Nothing about him offered an answer; he was just a funny,

cute old guy in a knit cap trying to shepherd an old truck along the road. A guy, but maybe not so old as I'd assumed. I'd been judging him by Manhattan standards. Life out here was hard on skin, and sitting zazen could be murder on knees. He was probably no more than ten years older than I and there was definitely something intriguing about him. But that didn't matter, because the last thing I needed in my two weeks here was getting involved with a man, "cute and intriguing" notwithstanding.

"You okay, Darcy?" Leo's hand was on my shoulder.

I jumped. "Yeah. The truck bouncing around; it scared me. We don't drive dirt roads in Manhattan."

"We're almost halfway there. Around the bend there's a path to the monastery, about a mile long. You could walk. But the road's not that bad, right?"

He smiled. I could tell he knew I was avoiding and covering, and something about the way he let his hand linger made me uneasy about leaving him with questions to gnaw on. I had to give him something.

"Okay, here's the thumbnail. I am the youngest of seven children. My oldest sister, Katy, works for a news organization now, Janice was known as 'the nice one' growing up, the youngest, Grace, a doctor. My oldest brother, John, is a police lieutenant, the next one's a lawyer—he's Gary—and Mike, the youngest, the one closest to me in age, is gone. I was always the little kid puffing out my chest and scrambling to keep up. By the time I was in ninth grade, even Mike was in college. Grace was in medical school. The others were married, buying homes, having children, succeeding in their lives. It was like everything had been done, you know? Like books read and shut. I wanted to rebel, but Mike had done that one. I wanted to live somewhere exotic but Gary had spent two years in the Peace Corps in Ethiopia and written us so often we knew the townspeople by name. I wanted . . . In the end, I realized that, rather than knowing where I fit into the picture, I just wanted to know who I was. And then I just wanted to *know* for myself without some authority giving me its truth."

"You didn't tell them that, did you?"

I shook my head, "Oh, yeah. I bored them all to death, even dragged one sister into the zendo for the longest forty minutes of her life. It says a lot about what a gracious, decent person she is that she didn't stalk out." Suddenly I laughed. "It also says her legs went numb."

"Arrogance," he said, seemingly as much to himself as to me, "the Zen disease. It shows how ignorant we are."

"About life?'

"That, too. I meant, about Zen."

"But, I have to say for my family, strange as they think 'Darcy's Zen thing' is, they don't bug me about it. My brother met my plane, and Mom is keeping my dog for two weeks so I can come here."

I felt a pang of loneliness thinking of Duffy, who had been ecstatic to be in Mom's backyard, which would soon be little more than a hole with just his black rope of tail showing above grass line. I was sorry there'd been no time to see Mom. I wished I could tell Leo about them all and the baseless fear that had brought me here. It had been a silly childhood fear, probably born of nothing more than a family day in Muir Woods, each of the older kids assuming the other was watching the little one, all of them forgetting me for an hour or so. If I hadn't screamed "till her face matched her hair," the incident wouldn't have become family legend and the cause of death of a succession of Christmas and birthday bonsais. I wished I could laugh with Leo about whichever well-meaning sister came up with the bonsai idea, not to bring a touch of life to my apartment but because she figured that my seeing the little tree die would show me I was in control. But I couldn't tell him, anymore than I could chance letting a hint about my fear out to anyone. I drew back into the corner of the cab.

The truck flopped into holes and rattled its way out. I shifted my luggage and braced my knees against the outer pocket that held sweaters. A soft low sound came from Leo's side of the cab, like he was starting to hum. It was a moment before I realized he was gearing up to ask the question.

"So you're an organizer?" he said. "A professional organizer? That's what you do for a living? You have your own business?"

I stiffened. But I hadn't told him about my fear. So, then there was no need to hide my job. In a burst of relief, I said, "I'm not really a professional organizer, organizing is just a small part of my work. I've got the world's best job: I'm a stunt double, in movies. I love it. I've loved it since I was a kid climbing out my window. I was nine when I figured out how to get to the tree and down. When my brother John spotted me, he cut off the limb by my window. I was so mad . . ."

Leo was grinning.

"But here's the thing"—my words tumbled out powered by the joy of talking gags and of not having to watch what I said—"I started out intent on escaping, but soon it was the escape itself that was the kick. Figuring out how to do it, and then doing it. There were times I got out and walked back in the front door just so John would make it harder for me. John's a big-time control guy, so making it hard was what he liked to do. When I was older I'd sneak out, across the roof—"

"John couldn't cut the roof off, huh?"

"Just what I told him!" I caught Leo's eye and we laughed. "Then I'd go to the movies, not for the show but to watch the stunts. For me, second unit directors were like football stars were for Dad and my brothers. And when we got a VCR with slo-mo I was in heaven. I was also a huge bore in family gatherings. Well, you can probably imagine by now."

Leo was still smiling.

I sat, enjoying our easy connection. I busied myself looking at him, at the dashboard, at my luggage, as if we were floating along in the Bay rather than driving between gigantic trees.

After a bit, I said, "You were going to tell me about Garson-roshi."

"First tell me about your teacher in New York."

My family, my job, and now my teacher: Leo was stalling. I didn't want to think what that meant. And it was hard to pass up the chance to coo about Yamana-roshi.

"Yamana-roshi came to New York because his American students insisted they could never keep up their Zen practice at home without him. That was thirty years ago. Yamana-roshi was forty-five years old. He spoke about six words of English. His students hadn't given a thought to how to support him. He lived in a tiny studio that doubled as the zendo, got mugged four times in his first two months, survived on rice for years. After morning zazen, when his students went to work, he was alone till evening zazen, day after day. In Japan he had a temple in his ancestral village. Its picture is on his wall. Once, he had a chance to go back there— five or six years ago—that was before I knew him—but something happened to keep him here. Now he's too old to travel."

Yamana-roshi! I squeezed my eyes shut against the flood of longing. I felt as if I had walked into exile just like he had. I had to swallow before I could speak again, and then the words came more slowly. "He's still in the zendo every morning, still gives each of us dokusan every week, and even though he has never mastered how to hail a cab, he can see into our hearts."

Leo's face stiffened. I couldn't read his expression enough to figure if he was annoyed, or something else.

"Was I telling you more than you wanted to know? I guess I went on a bit long. It's just that I, well, I have such respect for Yamana-roshi. And, well, love. But I'm sure you feel the same about your roshi here."

He didn't respond at all, just kept staring ahead with the same glazed expression. I thought he muttered *six years ago* to himself but I couldn't be sure.

Then he said, "The roshi here . . . Okay, I'll tell you about him, but it won't be the same kind of story, not by a long shot. You may be sorry you came."

My stomach clutched.

"The general take, early on, was that the roshi had 'a lot of promise.' He was one of those rare Westerners who could sit in full lotus easily. Never moved. He gave off the air of seriousness. He had a good memory. He could quote obscure Buddhist scriptures. Promise. Lots of promise. So they sent him to Japan to study. More promise. A certain type of personality does well in Japan. In the monastery there, sitting in full lotus for long periods won him a certain acceptance. He learned to be contained. And he learned to drink. Alcoholism wasn't uncommon among Japanese masters. In their controlled environment, on the monastery grounds, it was quite manageable. Just a different type of consciousness. But it didn't translate well to this country."

Leo hesitated, tapping his teeth softly, as if weighing whether to give me the full explanation. He inhaled shallowly, and before he spoke, I knew I'd be getting no more.

"So when this piece of land was given for a monastery, and when people realized how far out into nowhere it was, they were only too glad to exile the roshi here. Other than burning down the forest there wasn't much damage he could do."

Zen in American isn't organized like the major Christian sects; no one could force him to go anywhere. But I could imagine the abbots of his lineage making an argument he couldn't sensibly refuse.

"And that all happened before the student disappeared, right?"

He slowed the truck and turned toward me, his shaggy eyebrows scrunched in surprise, or maybe distress.

"Darcy, I don't . . ."

I felt terrible. This sweet man! But I had to know. I looked pointedly at Leo and waited.

"Okay. Thumbnail. The student, Aeneas, was here almost from the beginning. He was meticulous in his work; he was a mimic with perfect pitch, memorized all the chants in Japanese, and could sit zazen without moving for longer than I have seen anyone sit. Abbots and teachers from Japan came for the opening ceremonies. When they left Aeneas was gone. We assumed he went with them. Recently we learned he didn't. No one has heard from him."

"What do you think happened? Is he dead?"

Leo looked straight ahead, but he wasn't concentrating on the road. "What I know is there's been no word from him since the opening."

"So he could still be here. His body, I mean, if—"

He clutched my shoulder again. "Darcy, this is wild country. A man could stumble into a ravine and never be found. He could get a ride to the coast road and hitch to Canada. He could get in a fight with a friend and be dead."

I gasped.

"I'm not saying that to shock you, or because I know the answer. The last time I saw Aeneas was the day of the opening and as far as I know no one has heard from him since."

The admission had deflated him. I wanted to reach over and touch his arm to comfort him. "It must have made being out here the next years all the harder."

He nodded.

I took a breath and asked the question I needed answered, the one Yamana must already have asked. "And Garson-roshi, what did he do?"

His smile faded, replaced by a tight mouth and sharply drawn cheeks. I had the feeling I had posed the kind of question a nice man couldn't answer honestly. He seemed to be considering each word.

"The roshi did nothing. The roshi was too involved in his own regimen of Samurai sitting—zazen hour after hour, day after day, in a desperate attempt to deal with his personal disgrace and disappointment. He was under the illusion he was *really practicing*, aiming for a concentration that blocked out everything, when what he was really doing was isolating himself and shirking his responsibilities." Leo started, as if he heard the disgust in his voice and was shocked by it, or more likely by the fact of having revealed so much to a newcomer. "So, to answer your question, Darcy, he chose to ignore any questions about the Japanese abbots taking Aeneas with them. But this was his monastery; he should never have put himself in a position where he could be uninvolved."

The bitterness of his condemnation shocked me. "Do you really despise him that much?"

Leo winced. "No. There was a time, a long period of time, I would have said yes. But now, no. Everyone is doing the best he can. A lot of times that best doesn't seem very good, but it's their best under the circumstances. Look at you, for instance. Here you are, heading to a monastery you know nothing about, right? Run by a roshi you wish you knew nothing about, right? Instead of packing thick sweaters and heavy rubber boots you fill your suitcase with ointment in case strangers' knees hurt. Not very good, you could say, but it's the best you could do, right?"

I shrugged. I liked Leo, felt an intuitive trust in him; but about Garson-roshi, I desperately wanted him to be wrong. The whole thing had the ring of story-not-over. "But since then Garson's changed, right? He—"

The truck shot to the left. A red tree was sticking out into the road. I braced for the crash. Leo yanked the wheel; metal scraped but the truck kept moving. The windshield-blur was gone and I saw all the trees as *trees*. The blood-red Japanese maple stood in front of deep green red-woods and pines. I jammed my eyes shut against the looming great trees. I had to gasp to breathe. I tried to picture something safe—anything—green and yellow ducks on Mom's old plastic shower curtain. Sweat coated my face, draped my shoulders. I dug my fingers into my pack; the harsh broadcloth scraped the tips. I swallowed, and swallowed again. I made one of those little glucking noises getting myself under control. Leo must have heard that.

He assured me, "When we get the road paved, we'll take out that maple. Rob's opposed to changing the road, but paving only makes sense."

It was another minute before I could open my eyes and swipe at my forehead with my shirtsleeve. When I did open them, several surprising things happened, and so fast they took away what little breath I had left.

First, a man pulled open the passenger door, startling the hell out of me. "You trying to kill me, Leo? You could have run me over!"

I hadn't even noticed the guy until now.

Leo leaned over, in front of me, almost eye to eye with the stranger. "Well, if you're going to stand in the middle of the road just behind a curve, you might expect something like this to happen. I nearly killed Darcy and myself trying to avoid you, you know."

"That little maple would hardly kill you."

Leo gave no response, and when I glanced at him, he looked as if he didn't think the point worth arguing. For me, that tree wasn't little; for me, it loomed.

The man Leo was staring back at was tall and straight-backed, with an angular face that could have been called handsome, imperious, or just cold. He wasn't wearing a priest's robe—no sane person would in this mud—but even without it, there was no question in my mind that this was the roshi himself. I had to admire Leo sounding so unintimidated by him.

Then I got my next shock.

The tall, fierce roshi grabbed hold of me and pulled me out of the truck.

"In back," he commanded, with a jerk of his head toward the flatbed of the truck. "I need to talk to Leo."

My heart was thumping; sweat was still making sticky rivulets down my back, and I wasn't anywhere near to coherent thought yet. If I had been, I would have told him to go to hell, roshi or no roshi. But the trees had turned me back into a quivering four-year-old. Humiliated, I stumbled toward the bed and began to clamber over into the back. I was so undone by the trees, by the near-accident, by *him*, that I couldn't find words, couldn't think, only knew I had to get out of the woods. I wanted to huddle next to the big bag of cacao beans and cover my head, but I mustered enough pride not to let this guy, this jerk of a roshi, see me that way. I sat on the bag and stared in the only safe direction—through the rear window of the cab. This panic was exactly what I'd been afraid of. No. Worse, way worse.

Leo turned around and gave me a grin and a wink. I didn't expect that; I thought he'd be taking this wretched encounter as seriously as I did, and his nonchalance made me feel even more stupid. His gaze held mine for a long moment, as if he was waiting for me to tell him somehow that I was okay back here. I managed a nod of false heartiness, even added the jaunty little hand wave that had once fooled a director as I raced out of a location set. Leo started the truck and checked me again in the rearview mirror. I nodded again, but found myself clinging to his gaze like a lifeline. The truck rattled on slowly.

The roshi rapped on the window. He must have meant for me to move away. Not hardly! I couldn't even look to the right or left for fear of what I'd see. My hands were shaking so, I could barely hang onto the cacao bean bag. If anyone in the stunt community ever heard about this— I couldn't worry about that, not now. I focused on what was happening in the truck. Yamana cared about this roshi; there had to be good in him.

The roshi turned to Leo. His words were muted under the clatter of the old truck, but whatever points he was making he emphasized with sharp raps on the dashboard. He paused. Leo nodded. He leaned in toward Leo and spoke and rapped again. I was so close behind I could see the taut lines in his jaw as he spoke. The man was close to regal; the forward thrust of his head when he spoke, and the ropes of tension bulging out of his throat when Leo laughed, scared me.

This couldn't be the deep teacher Yamana remembered; Yamana must have realized he had changed over the years, changed so much he was going to do something dreadful. No wonder Yamana had given me the warning.

The truck swerved sharply to the left. I grabbed onto the cacao bag with both hands. It was all I could do not to vomit. I couldn't think.

I didn't look through the window anymore, I just stared down at the burlap. All I wanted to do was get out of here, out of this truck, out of the sesshin, out of the woods.

But even in the deepest moment of panic I knew I couldn't walk away, not from my own fear, not from Yamana-roshi's instruction. *Tell Garson I know what he is planning and he must not. Tell Garson I am sending this message with you.*

I would tell him, but I couldn't imagine how I was going to stop him.

CHAPTER FOUR

O

The truck veered sharply, but I didn't see where it was headed. Suddenly I could barely breathe; sweat coated my body. It was all I could do to just hang onto the burlap bag.

Metal banged. The door slamming jolted me to attention in time to see the roshi jump off the running board and stride away from the still-moving truck. With each long graceful stride he looked every inch the great pooh-bah.

The truck jerked and stopped. The burlap bag slid backward into the tailgate. I risked a glance into the distance. No trees in sight. We were in a parking area. Beyond was a grassy area the size of a football field, slanting up a rise to a round wood-shingled building I took to be the zendo. People were hurrying across the grass in various directions. I glanced at my watch. 6:15! The first sitting was at 7:00. No wonder everyone was rushing.

The driver's door opened and Leo eased out back first, bracing his arms on the roof and door to lower himself. Even so, he had to try three times to get his foot to the ground, as if the drive had crunched his lower back and it was painful to stretch his leg and put weight on it. His entire weight didn't look like much. I jumped off the side of the truck bed, intent on racing around to help him to the ground. But I almost smacked into him pulling down the tailgate.

"Leo, what are you doing?"

"I've got a hundred-thirty-pound bag of cacao beans. You were incidental on this trip, girl. It's these beans that were the paying passengers." He patted the truck like an old friend. "Now, go on and find yourself a cabin. I'm going to run this bag up to the cook."

"On your shoulders?"

"On that wheelbarrow that's been waiting right there." He reached over to a rusted red barrow, and stopped. A van pulled into the parking area. Men and women jumped out and headed up the knoll. "You better get moving, Darcy. Accommodations here are first come first served, and for even the first it's no night at the Ritz."

Sweet man! He was the one thing I'd be sorry to leave here. I took him by the shoulders—he wasn't much bigger than me—and eased him aside.

"I can handle the cacao. Just point me to the kitchen."

"You don't—"

"Hey, you know I'm a tough broad, right? So move it, you hear!"

He laughed. His face relaxed slowly back to his usual quizzical look, as if he couldn't be sure he'd laughed quite long enough, or if he'd asked everything he wanted to know or—It was that ever-present *or?* that summed up his normal expression. But now he passed through that and sighed as if he'd weighed and made a key decision.

"Okay. That way, up the hill."

Before I could get my hands on the bag of beans, he had turned and yanked it into the barrow. The move must have taken every bit of strength he had. I put my hands proprietarily on the barrow handles. The air itself suddenly seemed still and thick, as if it were cementing us both to this pivotal moment.

I took a breath and said, "Leo, I'm trusting you not to mention my work to anyone. I hope you trust me."

His eyes closed a moment; he seemed to be considering longer than necessary, certainly way longer than polite. My stomach went cold. But it was too late to gulp back my secrets.

I swallowed, and said, "I have to be straight with you. My teacher, Yamana-roshi, was very worried about the roshi here, and now that I've seen him I can understand why."

"What did he say?" he asked warily.

I hesitated. I couldn't tell Leo Yamana's private message to the roshi. But I had to get Leo's assessment of this guy.

"He said your roshi here was a deep teacher, that he would see into me." I wasn't even looking at Leo. I was afraid his face would be blank, walling me out. "But it's been years since Yamana saw him, and I would never ever say Yamana-roshi was wrong, and yet, well . . . I dropped everything to come . . . I can't work with a man like that, who'd yank me out of the truck so he'd have more room to wag his finger at you."

Leo stared at me. Then his bushy eyebrows shot up, his mouth sprang open and he guffawed.

"Leo?"

"You thought he was the teacher here?"

"He's not?" Who is he, then?"

"Rob."

"Rob, the roshi's assistant?" Just how appalled I was came through my voice.

Leo laughed again.

The *jisha*—roshi's assistant—is the one closest to the roshi himself. It's he who watches over the roshi's schedule, reminds him when he's falling behind. He brings the roshi his coffee in the morning, checks with him last thing at night, and is in and out of his quarters ten times during the day. If the roshi ponders, he's the one in front of whom he ponders. If the roshi questions how things are going in the zendo when he's occupied giving dokusan, it's his assistant's assessment he trusts. And when students are desperate to see the roshi in dokusan and the line seems endless, it's up to the assistant whether he tells the roshi, gives the student an encouraging pat on the shoulder, or does nothing at all.

"How can Rob be the jisha?" I demanded. "He's the last person . . . How come the roshi didn't choose you, Leo? When people come to a wild place like this, they need someone like you they can count on, someone who cares about them."

A woman rushed past us toward the knoll. The final words chanted at the end of each sesshin rang in my head: *Time swiftly passes by and with it our only chance.*

"If he's not the roshi, then who . . ."

Leo started to answer but I knew before he got the words out. "Omigod, Leo, it is you, isn't it?'

Leo nodded. "Me."

Relief washed over me. Then delight. And then I was just pissed. "Why didn't you tell me?"

He shrugged. "You had questions needing answers. You couldn't have asked the roshi."

His answers about Garson-roshi, about *himself*— It was *himself* he'd been so hard on. I'd have to rethink everything he'd said.

Another clutch of students hurried by, one of the men pausing for a "Hello, Garson-roshi. I'm looking forward to this sesshin."

It was Leo I had to deliver Yamana's warning to. Suddenly, it would have been worlds easier to give the warning to self-absorbed Rob. But Leo, how could Leo be planning anything Yamana-roshi considered so dangerous? I wanted to look away, to be no part of this message. I maintained my gaze.

"Leo. Yamana-roshi didn't send me to this specific sesshin. He has recommended your sesshins in the past. When I told him I was coming he thought it was exactly the right thing for me . . . initially."

"But?"

"But when he heard you were leaving and that this sesshin was going to be in honor of your student, Aeneas, he said to tell you that, that—" I swallowed, then repeated the words verbatim. "He said, 'Tell Garson I know what he is planning and he must not do that.'"

Leo didn't move, not his body, not his expression. He looked neither chastened nor surprised. Whatever his reaction he was not reflecting it back on me. He stood there in the failing light of the November evening; he could, I realized, have been Yamana-roshi. At this moment he wasn't Leo, he was the roshi.

Then he turned back to the wheelbarrow. "Time's short. If you're going to take that bag of beans up the hill and get into the zendo by seven, you're going to have to make some tough-broad moves with that wheelbarrow."

"Leo—"

He seemed to draw into himself and become not exactly larger but majestic in a way Rob had not. He said, "You don't contradict the teacher." Then he grinned, as if switching back from roshi to Leo, as if nothing had happened. "Since you're Yamana's student, I'm giving Rob a new job assignment. You'll be my jisha."

"Your assistant! How could you—?"

"You don't contradict the teacher. If Yamana trusts you, so do I."

I started to speak and realized I couldn't get words out. And shouldn't, for that matter. This, too, was not all that surprising, at least not in the context of Zen. Masters can be inexplicable. Ours not to wonder why . . .

"Darcy, when you dump that bag of cacao beans, see if you can get the cook to make me a cup of his fine cocoa. I'll just have time for it before we get to the zendo."

My head was spinning. I was glad to have something as concrete as pushing a load up a hill to anchor me to reality.

"And Darcy?"

"Yes?"

"Have him make you a cup, too."

O

Leo, Garson-roshi, slumped back against the truck bed. It was the New York student's trust that got to him. She should be able to trust him, it was the least she should expect, to trust that her teacher wouldn't put her in danger. But had he done just that?

He had given the wheel of dharma a big turn when he set up this sesshin—his last sesshin. His students each had an opinion as to why he was suddenly leaving Redwood Canyon Monastery with no future plans for either it or himself. The skeptical, he was sure, assumed he was back on the bottle, the hopeful hoped that, after his long exile in the woods, he'd been offered a city post he couldn't mention yet; the wiser focused on Aeneas and figured after six years things had finally caught up with their teacher.

A man is being chased by a tiger. He runs as fast as he can, as long as he can. He comes to a cliff. He skids to a stop. The tiger is bounding at him. What can he do? He spots a vine dangling over the cliff. He lowers himself over the edge and lets out a sigh of relief.

The sound echoes back at him, louder, angrier. He looks down. At the bottom of the cliff is another tiger. The man clasps the vine tighter and looks up. Sure enough, the first tiger is still there. But now that tiger is gnawing his vine.

Leo, Garson-roshi, sighed. He knew the story well; he'd used it as the basis of lectures many times. But not till this instant had he seen the parallel to this sesshin he had set up. What happened to Aeneas had loomed over Redwood Canyon Monastery's opening ceremony. It had stood beneath every event at the monastery, created an unnamed anxiety in each one of his students whether or not they realized the source. As for himself, it had thrust him into a life of self-deception, at first blatant, then ever more subtle. He had spent the last six years avoiding looking at the vine.

The man eyes the tiger above, the tiger below. He hears the vine cracking apart. At that moment he looks a bit to the right and spots a ripe red strawberry. He plucks it and plops it in his mouth. How sweet it tastes.

Leo pushed himself away from the support of the truck and straightened up. He had to be every bit as aware as the berry eater if he was going to lead his students though this sesshin. It was the last thing he would do for them. Darcy, Yamana's student from New York, was the final piece of the plan, the outsider he could trust.

The sentence with which he had ended all those lectures echoed in his head. After describing the tiger below, the tiger above gnawing at the vine, and the man tasting the strawberry, Leo had paused, grinned, and added, "Of course, then the tiger ate him."

CHAPTER FIVE

O

I t had been all I could do not to leap forward and throw my arms around Leo. Leo's being the roshi was beyond my greatest hope. Leo, the roshi who would provide a great chance for me. He wasn't only deep, like Yamana-roshi said, but he was also, well . . . just Leo, the goofy-looking guy in the truck. How bad could problems be in this place with a sweet, thoughtful guy like him in charge?

With a burst of happy energy I gave the wheelbarrow a great shove and headed it uphill, for Leo. It was admittedly strange, this surge of affection and devotion for a man I'd met only an hour ago. But I really felt as if I'd known him—or had he known me?—forever. I pushed that barrow with all my strength, for both my old teacher and my new one.

I'm in good shape—I can get called on a day's notice for a wall-climb gag that's all arm strength, so I don't dare slack off at the gym. But this loaded barrow weighed more than I did. It was all I could do to get traction on the slick path, find a safe moment to shift my grip, and keep the thing moving so it didn't come banging down the hill and run me over in the process. I hit a rock or something. The barrow lurched; the cacao bean bag pitched; and I had to flatten myself across the load to keep it from thumping to the ground. My hands slipped on the handles: my shoes slipped on the path. I didn't dare stop: I'd have had to call a tow truck to start up again. I almost missed the kitchen door and had to do a classy five-point turn with the barrow to head it in the right direction.

Inside the kitchen, three people were lifting, lugging, shoving, trying not to smack into each other in the tiny space and succeeding none too well. Feeding twenty-six people for two weeks is a big job. At the beginning, with all the raw food assembled, sesshin kitchens tend to look like warehouses. A tall, wispy-thin blond woman was jamming about thirty heads of lettuce into a restaurant-sized refrigerator. A short, serious guy in his late twenties, head shaven, was stashing apples under a table. A girl, a few years younger, honey-haired, plump in a way that looked sweet to probably everyone but her, was carrying cauliflowers to a bin one head at a time. The cartons of cauliflowers stood on the counter and I was surprised no one pointed out the disadvantage of her method. She kept stopping, touching the apple-stasher's arm, murmuring things I couldn't hear. He nodded brusquely as if the dictum of silence were already in place.ˈ

I've been in my share of sesshin kitchens before sesshins. It's always as if everyone's hopes, plus their unnamed fears, have materialized in the lettuce and apples, the lines of milk cartons, the cauliflowers. Workers are scurrying to compress all the perishables into one refrigerator; they're talking about their inbound flights, bemoaning the loose ends at home, throwing anchors to their normal lives. Paradox reigns: those are the lives they've come to sesshin to see through but suddenly are terrified of losing.

I didn't know any of these people, and yet I knew these circumstances intimately. The setting, here in the woods, was the last that would have comforted me, but the underpinnings of sesshin were so familiar they gave me a feeling of "home." I was an old hand at sesshin preparation, and as such I wanted to put an arm around the girl's shoulder and give her a hug of encouragement. It would be a hard two weeks physically and mentally. We'd all come here to cut loose from our moorings. I watched as she touched the boy's arm again and he gave another curt nod with his monk-shaven head. There was no way to assure her that she was not the mooring he would be cutting.

"You here to help?" the tall blond woman called out as she stacked boxes of green-tea bags. At sesshin, it doesn't matter if you're a waiter or a CEO, groceries need putting away and toilets need cleaning.

I glanced at the wheelbarrow and said to the woman, "I just brought up the cacao beans for the roshi. He would like a cup of cocoa. He figured I might get a cup, too."

"Take them up to the next door. You're in the peasant half of the kitchen here; you want the next door, the regal chocolate preparation parlor." She laughed. "Barry!"

"Huh?" a man called from the better half of the kitchen. I executed another classy turn and shoved the barrow up five yards and into the next door in time to hear the blond woman call to him, "You're supposed to give this woman some cocoa."

"What, Maureen? Who says so? I don't have time to be making cocoa now."

"Roshi says so." She winked at me. "The woman hauled your beans up. It's the least you can do."

"I said I don't have time. The way it's been raining the last few weeks I'll be lucky if the road holds out till Thursday and I can get out to . . ." His voice trailed in the fashion of one who's walled himself in with his own worries and is startled to find someone else's words actually breaching that wall. He looked from Maureen to me, then his eyes lighted on the barrow as if it was Santa's sleigh. "My beans are here! My *criollos!*"

I couldn't keep from smiling at the big guy's kid-like glee. He was in his midforties, and twice my size, with bare muscled arms I would have killed for on those wall-climb gags. His black monk's robe had sleeves hooked back at the shoulder for work, and those big arms were already hoisting the hundred-and-thirty-pound bag up onto a metal table that looked uncomfortably like one on which I'd once seen an autopsy. His face was round, his head shaved so close I couldn't have guessed the color of his hair. His eyes I couldn't make out at all. They were only for the beans. He stood planted like a huge solid Buddha in the center of the altar. And, from what I could tell, that altar was his chocolate kitchen. I breathed in the wonderful aroma of dark winy chocolate.

"Oh my God, I must've died and gone to Hershey."

"Hardly," Barry muttered contemptuously. "I do not create *milk* chocolate."

I, who owed many happy moments to Hershey's with Almonds, was silenced.

"Standard American chocolate!" he huffed, as he poured the beans out onto the table. "These are *criollos*, the most prized cacao beans in the world. What I create will be seventy-two percent cacao."

Sounded good to me. Any percent chocolate was more percent than the usual sesshin fare. Surely he wouldn't be shipping off for sale all of that fine chocolate. Surely there would be the occasional short-weighted bar, the tainted truffle. While he made the roshi's cocoa, I leaned back against a counter and took in this decidedly unusual kitchen, really two kitchens in one. Not exactly before-and-after. More like for-richer-for-poorer. Here in the richer half the windows were high up and even with white walls there was something dark and cozy about this room with the giant man and his hulking, old-fashioned machines. I could just imagine hauling them out here nine miles on the rutted road from the highway!

And when I took a sip of the half-cup he offered me, I just sighed. It was like Irish coffee but a million times better—thick, dark, with a touch of sweetness, a bit of liquor flavor.

"Oh, I really have gone to heaven. Barry, can I just stay in here for the whole sesshin? I'll cart *you* up and down the hill."

He turned to me and smiled as if I'd cooed over his first-born. "I make it special for Roshi. And that cocoa is from the old powder, only half *Criollo* beans. But this new batch—"

"By which, he means, don't figure you're going to get another cup," Maureen commented from her end of the kitchen. "The rest of us get cocoa very occasionally, as a great treat, but not the roshi's special cocoa. So enjoy."

Zen teaches us to be in the moment and a moment of the Roshi's Special Reserve cocoa was just the one to be with. I stepped outside and sat on a bench between the kitchen doors and looked over my steaming cup at the people strolling across the knoll and at the great trees beyond. It says something about the illusory nature of fear that the forest didn't seem so bad now that I had a cup of cocoa in hand. But sitting here wasn't walking into the woods. I had arranged my life so that the possibility didn't arise.

I sipped slowly, trying to focus entirely on the taste. But the woods teased and jeered. I'd survived the ride in the open bed of the pickup; maybe this was the time I'd get over my childish fear. Slowly I raised my eyes and stared at the line of trees at the far side of the quad a quarter mile away. No reaction! I took a long relieved swallow, finished the cup, and with bravado turned to the trees just beyond the kitchen. My stomach lurched, my gaze went blurry. The cocoa cup jolted and I had to grab to keep from dropping it.

". . . way to the cabins?"

I breathed in thickly, slowly, so the movement took all my attention.

"Are you okay?"

"Oh, sorry," I said, in a voice that couldn't have sounded as constricted to her as it did to me. "Maureen?"

The blond woman from the kitchen nodded. "I wanted to make sure you knew the way to the cabins."

"I was just . . . Thanks, yes, it'd be great if you pointed me there. Let me take my cup into the kitchen," I said, grabbing for time to pull myself together.

When I came back outside, with the roshi's thermos in hand, Maureen was shifting her wraith-like body from one long thin leg to the other. She was as dissimilar to bear-like Barry as two people could be. Like a young gazelle's, her feet seemed to hit the ground solely so she could spring off. As soon as we were clear of the building, the wind smacked our faces. It was one of those damp winds that chill you so slowly you don't realize it till you're iced to the bone and you feel like you'll never be warm again. The down jacket that had been a burden as I pushed the wheelbarrow was now barely adequate, but she, in tan drawstring pants and a black short-sleeved T-shirt, seemed oblivious. Goose bumps bloomed on her arm but they might as well have been body paint for all the attention she paid. She turned toward me and the fading light showed spidery lines around her eyes and mouth, sun scratches. She wasn't as young a gazelle as I had assumed. A bit older than I. Forty probably. And yet, as she bounced from foot to foot, she seemed years younger, lithe, free.

"Tell me how things work here."

We headed across the knoll. "Parking lot, where you arrived, is down there to the right. Meditation hall—zendo—is that round dome up to the left. Whole place is like a baseball diamond, only much bigger. Cabins are first base, zendo's second, kitchen's third. The office is home, and the parking lot, well, imagine the shortstop between third and home. When we built the zendo having it at the top of the quad, near the top of such a steep hill, seemed wonderful. But I'll tell you, uh—"

"Darcy."

"Maureen," she said, apparently not registering the number of times I'd heard it. "There are plenty of mornings when I'm headed up there in the dark and rain at quarter to five, that I wish we'd had the humility to put it in the middle."

"So you live here all the time?" *Don't they ever let you off the Styx, Charon?*

"The whole six years, since the beginning. I was here the first summer, before the Japanese roshis came for the official opening."

Dusk was edging toward night and a heavy mist was beginning to gust. I pulled my down jacket tighter around me, glanced over at Maureen shifting foot to foot, blond hair tossing, the wind flapping her T-shirt over her pert nipples. Clearly she had plenty still to do before sesshin started and no time to chat.

"You've been here since the beginning," I said. "You must have known everyone then, Rob, Leo, and, well, Aeneas—"

She jerked back, looked down at her T-shirt, yanked at the hem. "And Barry, too. You're wondering about Barry's kitchen, right? How come the rest of the place looks like a scout camp and Barry's chocolate kitchen could be in the Saint Francis Hotel?"

Aeneas was sure a sore spot. She hadn't seemed jumpy until I mentioned his name. I was dying to ask what she thought his disappearance meant. But she wasn't likely to tell me any more than Leo had. So I made do with seeing where she'd go with her detour about the kitchens.

"Yeah, how come the differences?"

"Because Barry's gourmet chocolates sell for a bundle and he gives the money, at least most of it, to the monastery. At that level of 'gourmet,' his old world machinery makes a big difference. Rob paid for those machines, plus the generator in the kitchen and the running water in the bathhouse, which was probably way more important to him." She laughed awkwardly, and I silently added: *Tight ass that he is.*

My silence seemed to unnerve her even more and she said quickly, "That's okay. Rob can laugh about it now, when he has to. Early on, one of the students went into town and made six copies of his picture, framed them in those cheap paper frames and hung them in the place of honor over each toilet. We all bowed to him before and after."

One of the students? Aeneas? Or herself? I didn't ask what privileges Rob got in return for his money, but there was just enough of an edge to her voice to make me sure there were some. Life in a monastery is like a family and "Mom loves you best" isn't just for kids. Now the regal bully who yanked me out of the truck so he could wag his finger at the roshi made sense. If he owned half the place, no wonder he was so put out when Leo fired him as jisha. That had to be what caused that brouhaha in the truck. There was one question I wanted to ask about this Rob, but I couldn't bear to. Instead I asked, "Where'd a resident get the money for exotic chocolate machines and good plumbing?"

"Resident? Oh, Rob wasn't a resident. Back then he was still a partner in a San Francisco law firm. It was before he even moved to town up here. He's only been full time here for a year or so. This'll only be his second winter."

Only his second winter! Did the imperious Rob have a clue that he was lower tier?

Maureen shot a glance over her shoulder, as if sighting last-minute tasks. "I have to get—"

"But why?"

She turned back to me, her shoulders suddenly hunched against the cold she hadn't noticed before my question.

"Why would Rob spend all that money on a place he didn't even live at for years?"

"For the good of the monastery."

"Generous," I said in a tone that conveyed how little that word fit the man who had dragged me from the truck.

"Because he knew he *would* come to live here . . . eventually."

Now things fell into place, into appalling place. "Because," I said, "he's the one slated to succeed Leo when Leo leaves. After this last sesshin."

Maureen crumbled forward. Her eyes went opaque, as if my words had knocked out the light behind them. She was shaking now, perhaps from the cold. She turned and strode away, not like a gazelle at all.

$$\bigcirc$$

A great ball of loneliness filled Maureen Heaney's chest. It choked out her breath. *The last sesshin!* Why? Was Roshi leaving here? Was he closing down the monastery? What was he doing? A small cry erupted from her; she stopped, startled. Why wouldn't he tell her what he was up to? He had always confided in her. It had been she he'd eyed when he made a joke, she who'd brought him juice on mornings after, she who'd celebrated with him when he'd got sober. She who protected him. And now . . . nothing.

And Rob? No, that she couldn't think about at all.

She kept moving, overrunning the grounds, as if distance could lessen the pain. The chill air slapped her face, her bare arms, T-shirt–clad chest. How had she ever survived this isolated life? Ask her seven years ago if she'd like to live in the woods with three strange men and she would have laughed. She wasn't a nun, she'd had lovers and planned to have lovers, but in other ways she lived closer to the life of the convent than any other. The garden here, it was all hers. When she'd planted the lovely red Japanese maple, no one questioned the location, and no one offered to help. She liked that. And the feel of muscles on her back, her butt, her thighs and arms from that work. You'd never find it in a Zen book, she thought, but years of hard work and practicing being aware had made her sex life a whole lot better . . . when she had any sex life.

Now she couldn't imagine leaving here. She loved setting off through the woods at sunrise, walking long and without plan, till she collapsed. She was strong, a runner, a dancer still in every stride, and it was always close to noon before that moment of welcome exhaustion came. She napped, then ate, and she set about finding her way back to the monastery. In her early years here she had gotten lost and the thrill of fear was part of the experience.

Now, after six years, there was little to surprise her. But for the first time in years she felt fear again. This time it wasn't a game; there was no thrill, only dread, confusion, things swirling out of control.

Six years ago she'd made a choice. Maybe if she had done the right thing then . . .

CHAPTER SIX

O

I liked Leo; I liked him a lot. I really hoped that this last sesshin of his would be everything he wished for. As his jisha, I wanted to give his students the best access to him, to shield him from all distractions; I wanted him to be able to see into his students, to make their last sesshin with him here important. *Keep an eye open*, Yamana-roshi had said. *Be aware!* I'd do my best. And if the kind of problems Yamana-roshi foresaw arose, I would spot them.

It was already twenty to seven. I was cutting this close. Thermos of cocoa in hand, I took a deep breath and knocked on Leo's cabin door.

It swung open.

For a moment I thought I'd got the wrong place. The cabin looked empty, really empty except for an oil lamp, a narrow two-drawer dresser and a futon. The whole room—bare wood walls, no plaster—was the size of a one-car garage. The lamp sent dim waves of light over the bare floor and bare walls. Oil lamps cut the dark enough so you don't stumble over a book, but only a fool would try to read that book. It was a moment before I noticed the brown-robed figure beside the futon.

"Leo! I hardly recognized you!"

"Sensei," he corrected.

I must have flushed neon red. "Or Roshi?"

He grinned and held out his hands for the cocoa, like a kid.

"This should be the worst mistake you make! I just don't want you to get into bad habits already. People aren't sure what to call the teacher. A lot of students don't even know what roshi means."

Sensei means teacher. But roshi is more. People assume it's an administrative title, like abbot, or a rank, like lieutenant colonel. But roshi is a title of respect given by a teacher's students. It signifies a teacher who has experienced enlightenment and also one they trust can teach them.

I nodded, still not quite recovered from my gaffe. It was cold in the cabin. Roshi poured from thermos to cup and held the cup between his hands, warming his fingers while savoring the aroma. The oil lamp sent deep shadows over his face, making his eyebrows bushier, the points of his high cheekbones sharper, and his mouth wider. Exaggerating his already exaggerated features gave him an aura of almost mystical authority.

He motioned me to the cushion across from him. I plunked my jacket on a hook, gave my head a shake—a mistake that sent the cold condensed mist down my hair onto my shoulders and back—and sat. I stared at the hem of his *okesa*, the sari-like rectangle of brown silk hand-sewn together from many smaller rectangles, all cut from the same original cloth. The okesa would have been stitched by his students, silently repeating a mantra with each stitch, squinting to make sure the stitch matched every other stitch in height and spacing. The sewing of a teacher's okesa was a coming together of the community, a visible sign of support, indeed, of love, from the students. It was too dark in here to spot a frayed hem or block of stitches come loose, to guess how tattered his support had become.

"Leo—Roshi—if I'm going to be any help to you I need to know what's going on now. What is it you're trusting me to keep an eye out for? Is it Rob?"

He nodded, and for a moment, I really thought he was going to explain. What he said was, "These first few days of sesshin will be dead simple. I want everyone in the zendo all the time. I won't give *dokusan* interviews till later."

I'd been around Zen long enough to understand his tacit answer to my question: *Don't presume. I am not the old guy in the truck now. I'm the teacher. I set the rules. I'll tell you what I want you to know when I want you to know it.*

I was almost sorry now I'd had that ride with him and formed that picture of a nice old guy with a quirky sense of humor, the kind of guy I'd share a glance with when things got too-too in the zendo. Leo would have told me his worries and suspicions straight out. But a master of Zen teachings, a roshi, was different. *Do not seek after enlightenment, merely cease to cherish opinions*, the teachings say. A roshi does not utter an offhand opinion, much less a mere suspicion.

I was impressed, but, dammit, I was also frustrated. Still, I've had a lot of experience swallowing frustration. In stunts I create the illusion of near-death; I'm not about to let it become reality. I may postpone, but I don't give up.

I looked at Leo and postponed.

He was all Zen master now in his formal brown robes. "When we approach the altar in the zendo, do you know how to handle the incense, Darcy?"

"I think so."

"Rob will be my jisha tonight. Just watch him."

I nodded.

"Okay, then. Tomorrow morning we sit zazen—three periods like I told you—do the service, and eat breakfast. After lunch we have work period. Your job is to get me my newspaper."

I laughed.

He didn't.

"I'm serious. I'm the boss; cocoa isn't my only perk. One of my students pilots a helicopter for the fire watch. He knows how attached I am to my newspaper"—he nodded, acknowledging his un-Buddhalike attachment—"and it's his gift to drop it in the meadow, *almost* every day. On the days he doesn't, disappointment is his gift. I accept either."

We hadn't passed any meadow. A chill shot down my back. Did he mean I'd have to walk through the woods to this meadow of his? This had to be a hoax, the kind of thing that would amuse Leo, the guy in the pickup truck. But nothing about him looked amused now.

"But—a newspaper? Dropped from what, a hundred yards? It'd be in shreds."

"No, Darcy, it would be in a padded container, a red one, like the pizza deliveries use, only this one's a tube. I have another student who owns a mailing service." He sipped his cocoa.

"It's already starting to rain. No one's going to be flying around here."

"Rain might stop. You don't know. Don't assume. Either way, it will be good for you to learn the path before the weather gets any worse. You go back along the road we came on till you pass the bridge, and that red Japanese maple that juts out into the road, the one you were so sure I was going to plow into, right?'

He'd paid that much attention to me, even when he was driving. He wasn't the kind of man who would blithely send me into the woods. Was this a test? Didn't Leo understand?

"Then you take a left. The path is right along the river. It's about a mile long."

"A mile! In the woods! In this weather?" Horror rang from my voice. I should have told him about my fear. Could he know somehow? Was this a test? Yamana-roshi must have told him about me. Didn't Leo understand?

The answer to my fears wasn't as simple as telling me to walk through the woods. I tried to think. My head was in chaos. I had to swallow twice so my tongue didn't stick to my palate. "Yamana-roshi must have told you about my—"

"He didn't *tell* me anything. He sent a message."

"A message?"

"Darcy, we don't have a phone here. You're lucky I was in town yesterday to pick up messages at all." He started to sip his cocoa, reconsidered, and checked his watch. "His message said: 'I am sending my cherished student. Pay attention to her.'"

The muddle in my head was worse. The woods; I couldn't—His *cherished* student! How could I disgrace him? But the woods, I couldn't— I could tell from Leo's brusque sigh as he considered and again rejected his cocoa that he was through humoring me.

There was no time for me to explain the depth and reality of my fear; anything I blurted out would sound superficial, and hysterical, or just plain untrue. I needed to see through *the Roshi* and recapture my buddy in the truck. Desperately, I tried a line that had worked for me on a weekend visit with friends near Lake George.

"I'm a city girl; I know the woods are full of dangers. Walking in alone, it's like asking for a separate canoe in *Deliverance*. Anything could happen. Crazed survivalists. Bears, cougars . . ."

"Cougars wait all year for a tasty New Yorker."

"No, listen, I'm not kidding. I don't do woods."

He was laughing.

"Leo! You'll just have to find someone else to—"

He lifted his cup and poured the cocoa on the floor.

I stared, stunned into silence.

He refilled his cup from his thermos and sipped as if nothing had happened. He sat there in his robes, his gaze downward: 0% Leo; 100% Roshi.

I was so shocked I just stared. I looked at him with fury, but I was damned if I was going to give him the satisfaction of seeing my panic. It took all my restraint, but I waited, forcing him to make the next move.

A full minute passed. The aroma of cocoa, wasted cocoa, filled the room like thick, noxious smog. Finally he pointed to a corner cabinet. "The cleaning supplies are in there."

I said nothing. I did not bang the door open, or slap the rag on top of the brown puddle as I started to mop it up. I didn't dig my fury into the floorboards with each push, not did I bang or even leave open his outside door when I took the sodden rag out to rinse in the rain spitting off the gutter.

I am no stranger to choking back anger. Movie sets are aflame with egos, and the *first* in Me first is never the stunt double. But even considering the provocation now, it was frightening how furious this man made me.

"One thing to watch out for," he said.

One thing? Just one? But I didn't say that.

"Once you leave the road, the path forks in half a mile. And you remember, I know my forks." He paused, watching me till, in spite of everything, I almost smiled at the thought of his collection of plastic utensils and the two of us laughing about them. Then he flashed a grin. "The right tine goes uphill to the fire-watch tower." He paused, looked me square in the eye and said, "It would be a mistake to take that."

I started to speak, but he put out a hand. "After tonight's zazen, Darcy, give me about ten minutes—I like to get in the bathhouse before the late-night rush—then meet me back here and we'll talk about tomorrow."

He didn't say *don't bang the door on the way out*, not quite. He certainly didn't say he'd reconsider about the walk in the woods, but that door seemed open. After all, he had mentioned the paper not arriving some days and the gift of disappointment. Still, I hated the thought that gift would be coming from me.

As I walked down his steps into the thick gray of evening, it shocked me how quickly the light had vanished. In the dusk the valley seemed narrow and deep. I pulled my jacket tighter around me against the cold rain. My feet splatted with each step. I almost didn't hear the sobs as I passed another cabin.

Maybe I shouldn't have stopped. In sesshin we face our own problems alone. We don't speak, don't make eye contact, don't give encouraging pats on the shoulder, don't offer distractions. The support we give one another is that we, too, are facing ourselves silently moment after moment, day after day. But sesshin hadn't quite started and I did stop long enough to see the girl who had been hauling individual cauliflowers in the kitchen. She was sitting on the steps under the porch roof. Her long honey-colored hair was wet, her face was blotched red. "I can't—" she muttered. "I just can't."

I sat down next to her on the step and said nothing. Two weeks is a long frightening time.

She wasn't looking at me. It didn't matter who I was. She was already alone with her fear. "I hate it here. And Justin, he's so fucking gung ho. He won't even talk to me. And I just know I'll never ever be able to do this. I can't—" she turned to me, tried to swallow and ended up coughing. She blurted out, "I'm so damned scared."

I put my arm around her shoulder and could almost feel her fear flowing into me. For a moment I just felt sick. "I've come to sesshins for years. I've never started one without being scared. We're here to find out what's real and to see through what isn't. We could come out fundamentally changed. It's scary, real scary—"

"But it's different, for me. No one's as scared—"

"Sure they are."

"Are you?" she asked pleadingly.

All I had told her about sesshin would be a lie if I lied. "Yes."

There was a little crinkle by the corner of her nose as if she couldn't decide whether to pout or laugh.

In for a lamb in for a sheep, or whatever livestock. I was leaving myself no choice but to face my fear. I forced a grin. "I'll bet you the first cup of cocoa we get, winner take both. And you can be the judge. But I have to warn you you're on very slippery ground here. You on?"

I freed her shoulder and shifted right, leaving a little space between us.

She ran a finger over the rough denim of her jeans, back and forth, as if moving from her fears to mine. Her pouty mouth said she knew no one could be as terrified as she was. But was she sure enough to deny herself the one special treat we'd get?

I was just about to take pity on her when she surprised me. "I'm afraid I'll go stir crazy in the zendo. I'll start screaming. I'll make a fool of myself, the roshi will scream 'Amber, get out of my zendo,' and my boyfriend will be so disgusted he'll dump me. And that'll just be tomorrow."

I let out a laugh. "Amber, the contest is over. You win. None of that will happen. But you still win."

"Huh?" She looked almost disappointed by her easy victory. "But what was yours?"

I shrugged.

"Tell me," she said, sounding like a pleading little sister. Then she dared me. "Double or nothing if you give in to it."

I could tell, she, too, wouldn't give up; she'd postpone. "Okay. It's the woods. Here I am in the middle of the forest and I'm terrified of the woods."

She stared. Then she snorted. I had intended to cheer her up—I'd revealed my deepest secret, or at least the most damning part of it—and here she was laughing so hard she could barely sit up. It was almost insulting. Still, it was nice to have a buddy at sesshin. Amber wasn't Leo, but she'd do. By the end of sesshin, I'd find a way to assure her discretion; I'd have to.

I almost missed the sound cutting under the bubbling of her laughs. The clappers. Wood hitting wood, and again, and again. The timekeeper had been standing on the zendo steps striking together polished blocks the size of blackboard erasers. By now he'd be walking toward us, or toward the kitchen, or the parking lot, ready to hit the clappers again, to signal students at the farthest corner of the property.

"The clappers," I said to Amber. "Ten minutes till sesshin starts. You're already closer to that extra cocoa."

Her lips quivered in what I took as an attempt at a smile. "Yeah. If I survive the zendo and the trees don't grab *you*."

I had meant to comfort Amber, but oddly that little interchange lightened my own steps and made me feel a part of the place. I walked more easily toward the zendo and when I passed the regal Rob, the jerk who had pulled rank in the truck and then sat in the cab wagging his finger at Leo, I even smiled. After all he wasn't the roshi, not even the jisha anymore.

He motioned me off the path behind a bench. Before now, I hadn't taken in quite how tall he was. I was staring at his chest. I looked up and caught him glaring at my copper curls the way strangers had at Mom's red frizz, like it made the head beneath incapable of linear thought.

"You had something to say?" My sharp tone must have startled him. It startled *me*.

He cleared his throat, then covered his mouth with a hand. "As the sesshin director," he said, "I need to know Roshi's plans. You can meet with me each morning after breakfast. Come to where I caught the truck this afternoon."

Where you *pulled me out of* the truck this afternoon, I thought. "A meeting half a mile down the road? What are we, spies?"

He breathed in through his teeth. "We don't want to disturb people."

The clappers struck again.

"I'll take it up with Leo."

He hunched toward me and for an instant I thought he was going to grab my shoulders like he did in the truck. Then he straightened to almost military erectness and ordered, "Go ahead, ask Roshi. He'll tell you to meet with the sesshin director."

He was right, and what really got to me was that it wasn't for the reasons he assumed. I'd have bet my cocoa and Amber's that if I went to Leo to complain about meeting *anyone* on the road to the woods, Leo would just laugh. There was no way I'd let Rob see me cringe at the sight of trees. But there was no way out.

"Right then," Rob said smugly. "Tomorrow at the beginning of work period."

I could have laughed. "Sorry. Can't. I have to get Leo—*Roshi's*—newspaper from the meadow then."

"No problem. We can talk on the way." He turned and strode across the knoll toward the zendo, black robes flying out behind him as if he were a pirate ship in full sail.

Monasteries have buildings; sesshin directors have use of rooms. Teachers meet with sesshin directors. A sesshin director doesn't set up a rendezvous with an underling to find out the topic of the next day's lecture and the dokusan schedule. Not unless he knows the teacher is making a point of not letting him know. And that would be stranger yet. In all the sesshins I had sat, nothing like that had ever happened. It would be like the president planning a summit and not telling his chief of staff.

Whatever Rob was going to ask me or tell me was something I could not afford to miss. I had thought the last thing I wanted to do was walk through the woods to get Leo's newspaper. I'd been wrong. The last thing was to head in among the trees to meet the guy whose job I had usurped. And that was just what I had to do—somehow.

CHAPTER SEVEN

O

The clappers sounded again, wood on wood but cutting like a bell through the thick wet air. No longer the three preliminary hits that meant there was ten minutes to get to the zendo. Now the roll-down had begun, with strikes frustratingly slow to begin with but picking up speed steadily. *Move toward the zendo. Sesshin's about to begin.*

Cabin doors opened. Two women with blue umbrellas hurried across the path. A man in a dark green slicker came out of the men's dorm, stopped dead and rushed back inside, as if an item left behind now would be lost forever. On the path a tall man put his arm around a woman's shoulder and whispered urgently, then he kissed her ear and both of them smiled nervously. Three women passed by, wrapping thick shawls around their own shoulders. They ambled across the grass, one grabbed the others, stopped, and all three laughed softly in the rain before they moved on. The knoll filled with people, some college-aged to some fiftyish and one man who looked almost seventy. The clappers sounded again, an odd melodic ring of expectation. I felt the draw of silence, of clarity—and an excitement. It was the same thrill—chill—as stepping into the funhouse where anything could happen, anything could change.

And yet the roiling in my stomach was deeper than it had ever been when I handed my ticket to the arcade master. I never began a sesshin without this terror, never knew precisely what I was afraid would pop up. A clear mind is like still water; would I see down to the murky bottom of memories, find more than I wanted to know? Would Leo and Aeneas and Rob crowd out those memories? Would I be able to figure out what was going on here in time to save Leo from whatever he planned, whatever Yamana-roshi had warned him not to do? Or maybe, just maybe, would I actually give up thinking for long enough to just sit zazen?

The clappers stopped. Silence resounded. The smush of rubber soles on wet grass created a background beat. The rustle of sleeves against windbreakers sliced through. Then the clappers began again, oh so slowly, strike after strike calling: *Come. . . . come. . . . come now!* I started up the hill as the clacks came quicker, echoing in my chest like a heartbeat. Around me people moved faster in the deepening dark. We walked, mostly silently, but with a whisper here and there, up the knoll to the zendo, up the five wide wooden steps to the covered porch outside the round shingled building.

On the porch, people slid off shoes and stowed them on the shoe rack, a bookcase for footwear. Still in the running shoes I'd flown out in, I balanced on one foot and yanked at my shoe, reversed the process, then placed the pair on the rack. The cold from the wooden porch spread through my socks as I moved into the line of entering students. Outside the door I paused, my stomach tightened, then I took a deep breath, bowed, and walked inside, into sesshin.

The zendo was a dome. The black cushions, *zafus*, were in the center of two-foot by three-foot black mats, *zabutons*, lined up on *tans*, twenty-inch high platforms, that nestled against the curved wall. When we all turned around and sat facing the wall, as we would do most of the time, it would be slanting inward toward our heads. But for now, this first period, we faced the center of the room, making an incomplete circle along the wall, the inner edges of our mats almost touching.

In the open end of the circle stood the altar, a highly-polished teak block about three feet high, topped by a statue of a Buddha. The dim glow of oil lamps on either side threw odd shadows across it. *Light and darkness are a pair*, says the eighth-century Chinese poem, the *Sandokai*. One does not exist independently of the other. On one side of the altar, a candle flickered seductively, sending swaying shadowy arms from the flowers over the statue of the Buddha onto the walls beyond. The sweet, woody smell of incense drifted and disappeared.

I found my seat, halfway between the door and the altar along the right wall. I bowed to the cushion, turned and bowed to the room and the community of people here, about to undertake this hard half month, each of us moving in the cocoon of our own fears and fantasies, yet with a calmness of purpose. Normally, the serenity of this communal beginning comforts me, but now, here, it served only to highlight Maureen's edginess and Rob's extreme demands. Why were the two people who should have been most settled going into sesshin the most unnerved?

That moment passed, and on the far side of the altar the roshi's entrance door creaked. In his formal brown robes, Leo stepped into the oil-lit room. Rob followed, holding a smoking stick of incense. His step was sure; his black robes barely swayed. He paused before the altar and bowed slightly, extending the incense. The flickering light of the oil lamps reflected off his polished skull and sharpened his chiseled nose and cheekbones. Next to tall, elegant Rob, Leo looked like a gnome.

Leo—*Roshi*—accepted the proffered incense and placed it in the middle of a bowl of compacted ash that sat in the center of the altar. He bowed before the altar and walked to his seat beside it. A soft, sweet bell rang. Despite his unsteady steps and unprepossessing shape, there was a dignity in his demeanor. I caught myself looking right at Leo and smiling proudly like a parent at a school play. I felt ridiculous. But for an instant when he looked around the room his gaze paused at me.

With all his robes inside robes, a priest's settling onto his zafu is always a long process of yanking cloth and tucking cloth and general robe-futzing. But Leo was so brittle it took him a good half minute just to cantilever himself onto the cushion. It was too painful to watch. I was glad anew I'd hauled the cacao beans up the hill for him.

Now that the bells had rung, the first period of *zazen*—meditation— had officially begun. The time for watching was over. Hands were to come together in a *mudra*—palms upward, left resting on right, thumbs lightly touching—eyes were to be open, gaze turned downward, attention on the flow of the breath. Nothing else was to be moving. Stillness in body leads to stillness in mind.

I breathed in slowly, felt the breath flow out, smelled the incense and the wet wool, heard the clatter of rain beginning on the dome, felt the wisps of exhaled air that connected me to my seatmates. There was something so lush about the first minutes in the zendo when everything and everybody was fresh and eager and glad to be together. Pain, exhaustion, frustration, and anger would follow, but right now the novelty connected us all. I had lived in ten different places in sixteen years and the only place I felt at home was in the zendo.

The forty-minute period was half over when Leo cleared his throat and began to speak. "I'm going to tell you about Aeneas, and why I didn't do this sooner." He cleared his throat. "Someone said to Suzuki-roshi, who brought Zen from Japan to San Francisco, 'Define Zen.' Suzuki-roshi answered, 'Things change.'"

Leo took a breath and though it was hard to tell in that half-light from the oil lamp, I could have sworn he had a hint of a smile on his wide mouth when he repeated, "Things change." Then he sat silent so long I wondered if I had hallucinated his words. To my left, Amber recrossed her legs in a flourish more indicative of impatience than pain. I glanced up at Rob, Maureen, and Barry, across from me and took in their still, calm postures. As senior students, monastery residents, they were assigned the seats closest to their roshi. Rain tapped on the curved roof; the oil lamps barely flickered. I was about to let my eyes close when Leo went on.

"We hear, *Things change*, and we immediately assume that refers to cosmic things. *E* equals *MC* squared. Solids become liquid; matter becomes energy; life becomes death. We can accept that; tuck it in a corner of our minds to be pondered sometime later. Life becomes death: well, that's not so comfortable, but it's not a real problem, at least not for years. Ice becomes water isn't so bad, either—unless it's summer."

He grinned, but none of us reacted. The new people were probably too nervous, and those of us who had heard other teachers give talks understood that this offer of humor was a ruse before he dug into his real point. We didn't want to be suckered.

"But we don't like change," he continued. "Change around us reminds us that *we* change, that we are not the solid substance we like to believe we are. We are nothing but stuff that changes. Maybe not even stuff, but just change. We like to come to sesshin and settle into the solid, reliable rules that make us feel safe, secure, unchanging, right?" He looked at Rob, Maureen, and Barry. "Right?"

He laughed. They smiled. And I was glad to let their aplomb reassure me. "Nothing but change" was not a way I wanted to see myself, not at all.

"I've been here a long time," he went on. "Six years. When I came, there was only land and trees"—he shot a smile at Rob—"and poison oak. When Rob first got here he thought he'd stumbled into the asylum with a lunatic in charge. Poor Rob. He was about to abandon a flourishing law firm in San Francisco to study with a teacher of great promise. What he got was a guy consumed with his skin. All I could do was try not to scratch . . . and scratch. I had poison oak so often I felt undressed without it."

People did smile at that, though I suspect a good proportion of us were hoping he'd say he had gone on a tear to rid the place of every leaf and stem.

"Of course there was no way to avoid it. You do what you can—take this pill, use that ointment—but when you have to clear the land and the land's full of it, it gets you in the end. And everywhere else." He waited a beat. "I had taken the hardships in Japan as a challenge and an honor of sorts. They were foreign, exotic hardships and I knew they weren't going to last forever. Then I came home and screwed up big. And this place was my exile. So here I was out in the woods with my life turned upside down and, to add insult, with poison oak." He started to scratch his arm, looked down at it and shrugged. "I have never hated anything or any place so much. If there had been any possibility of anything else—But I'd already burned every bridge and I was stuck. I knew if I left here I would be leaving my Zen practice. I knew—" He paused to look slowly around the room. There was no hint of a smile. Those oversized features on his face made him seem larger than life. "I knew if I left here I would die."

A shiver shot through me. I had to control the urge to reach out to him.

"So I stayed and led sesshins like this and cleared the land and built the cabins you sleep in and this zendo you're sitting in and the kitchens and the bathhouse and tried not to scratch and did scratch, and tried to sit here on the cushion and see my thoughts and just let them go and sit without thought and I didn't succeed with that. And it all went on for years. When I had a bottle of scotch or sake I'd escape into it. If there'd been a steady supply I'd have escaped constantly. But there was never enough of anything here, even escape. Right?"

He glanced in the direction of the senior students, but none of them managed a full nod in return.

"People came to study. I never asked anyone why. No one's reasons could be less lofty than my own. Or more desperate. Anyone who chooses this demanding practice has his reasons. So we cleared and built and sat. Last year it rained every day all winter long. The road flooded out in October and stayed flooded and by February we were boiling ferns and rationing oatmeal. Then, finally, the sun came out and everything burst into bloom. Everything, including the poison oak, and, alas, me." He actually winked at Rob and now Rob did manage a watery smile that seemed unsuited to his regal face.

"Now I itched so much that I knew if I scratched I wouldn't have any skin left. The road was still out. So there was nothing to do but sit and think about scratching. I kept wishing to be that statue of Shiva with the hundred hands, you know?"

He flung his hands so fast in so many directions he did look Shiva-like.

"And I knew all about poison oak. Each time I got it I grasped at a new hope—that this time it would be different, a milder case, that I'd developed an immunity, a tolerance, a thick skin, that my practice would give me a serenity enhanced by B vitamins and I wouldn't itch so much. But I knew the truth: poison oak doesn't let up for weeks. I had no reason to hope for anything better. And suddenly at this worst of all moments, with every inch of my skin itching, my mind went blank. No thoughts. For the first time in all the years I'd sat. No thoughts. Just itch. But not even itch, just sensation. Itch and not-itch. Just this moment, not the beginning of three miserable weeks. You get what I mean here?" The candle shimmied and tossed out a shadow that landed momentarily on his brow. "I wanted to let go but I couldn't. Not till the gift of the poison oak. The great gift."

He looked around the room, but no one returned his gaze. It was too expensive a gift.

"Facing change in your skin is easy. Even in your body, hard as that would seem if you lost a leg, still that's easy. Easy compared to the notion of finding your mind different, your ideas new, and the very way you think altered—of 'you' changing. We devote our lives to protecting ourselves from change. But one way we change is by facing facts. Being honest with people and with ourselves." Pointedly, he looked at me, as if to say, *You wanted it. Here it is.* "I'm about to be honest."

My breath caught. Beside me Amber stirred. I had the sense she had been on the verge of dozing, but she was wide awake now.

Leo said, "This sesshin is in remembrance of a student, Aeneas, who disappeared. For years I wanted to believe that nothing was any different than before. But the truth is: that incident changed everything. One of the changes was that I chose to believe nothing changed, because I was so intent on protecting this place and protecting myself."

He leaned forward almost intimately.

"Now I'm going to tell you what happened. There were eight of us here then: Rob, Maureen, and Barry,"—he nodded toward them. They returned his nod, but stiffly. "There was a woman; Anna, I think her name was. And three men: Dusty, Max, and Aeneas. It's Aeneas I have to talk about. He was twenty-four then, a sweet man who could sit every period in an entire sesshin and never move, who would do any job and never complain. It was a rough winter, and people got on each other's nerves, but Aeneas never argued with anyone. It poured for weeks, people got fed up and went home, but Aeneas stayed and worked on whatever there was to do. If there wasn't work, he listened to the tapes of the

Japanese chants. By spring he was pitch-perfect in every one. He was the Zen poster boy."

Leo closed his eyes and sat silent. But there was an uneasy unstillness about him that seemed to vibrate through the room. Rob and Maureen were no longer merely listening but staring at him, as were the people down the row from them. And Amber, next to me, had stopped squirming and was dead still.

"If Aeneas had an impairment in his ability to judge, well, it wasn't a problem—that's what I thought then. It's what I wanted to think."

Leo let his gaze lower. The zendo was electric with tension. Leo inhaled slowly, and when he spoke it was to the middle of the room where no one was sitting.

"Then Aeneas up and left. I heard he had gone to Japan to study with Ogata-roshi or Fujimoto-roshi, the Japanese teachers who came to the official opening here. I was hurt he hadn't told me, but I didn't want to think about that. I wanted to sit zazen.

"Aeneas never wrote me to explain, nor did the roshis in Japan. I assumed that showed what disgrace I had brought to Zen in America and, reflectively, in Japan. For years I thought Aeneas and Ogata-roshi and Fujimoto-roshi were ignoring me, but I couldn't write to them because I couldn't bear to have them snub me—because, you see, that would have forced me to have to change. I didn't want to change; I wanted to sulk—in a dignified manner, of course. I wanted to sit zazen, not to become aware but to escape. Understand? Pretend-zazen."

A gust of wind flickered the oil-lamp light and I couldn't tell whether the hollow look on Leo's face was a reflection of the six years of hurt or just the play of shadows. He looked around the room and I should have followed his gaze, but I couldn't bear to come upon a damning face. Leo took a deep breath and exhaled open-mouthed.

"I know, you expect better of a teacher. I can't offer you better; I can only tell you what is. A month ago, after my last bout of poison oak taught me about change, I screwed up my courage and wrote to the Ogata-roshi in Japan. Here's what I found out: Every one of the ideas I had held as truth for the last six years was fantasy. Every single one. Got that? No truth. Aeneas had never been in Japan at all. All I know is that Aeneas vanished when the visitors left." He put up a hand as if to stop questions. "All else is speculation. Fantasy, theorizing. But don't worry or make up your own fantasies. There's nothing to suggest either that Aeneas left or that he did not leave. All we know is that we don't know. That is reality."

The air crackled with the tension. The senior students couldn't hide their shock. Rob sat, hands in mudra, eyes lowered, but his shoulders were hunched halfway to his ears. Barry, the bald chocolate cook, was staring at Leo with the intensity that I was staring at him. And Maureen looked like she was about to be sick. Even Amber was learning forward, as if this place had suddenly gotten way more interesting than she could have hoped. Justin, Amber's boyfriend, was staring intently at Leo. I couldn't assess that reaction, though; he'd been staring as intently at the vegetables in the kitchen an hour ago.

But the tension stopped there. On the far side of the room, the three women in shawls were nodding, and the man in his seventies showed no reaction at all, as if the disappearance of some guy a half dozen years ago was ancient history. I glanced around quickly. None of the people I had seen hoisting suitcases off the van looked stunned or panicked. One man was visually examining his skin, his attention still caught in the danger of poison oak. It was like parallel universes here, one unmoved, one of which had had the mats pulled out from under it.

Was this what Yamana-roshi had warned Leo not to do? *Tell him I know what he is planning and he must not do that.* I stared at Leo, willing him to return my gaze.

When he looked up, it was to acknowledge each student, as his gaze moved slowly around the circle. I waited for my turn, but his contact was closer to a pat on the head than a meeting of the minds.

He took a breath and said to the group, "You had a right to know. And you have a right to leave if that's your decision. The van that brought you is still here and the driver will take you back to town right now if you choose. Do what is right for yourself. Make your decision now. Once the van leaves it won't be back for two weeks.

"But if you stay here don't waste your time entertaining yourself with fantasies about Aeneas. We've got two weeks of intensive sitting to do. We each have our own demons in our past. Don't search for them." Now he did glance over at me. "The issue isn't in the woods; it's within ourselves. Just sit zazen. Things change every moment; be aware. Whatever is important will come up. Don't turn away. Do not let yourself escape."

A bolt shot through me: anger, hope, fear, trust, outrage? I couldn't name it, couldn't even ballpark it. The only thing that was clear was that Yamana or not, Garson-roshi had a plan and he was dead set on seeing it through to the end.

CHAPTER EIGHT

O

It's amazing how quickly a zendo empties out after the last bell, as people's attention shifts from noticing their breaths to wanting to get into the bathhouse before there's a line, into bed before someone blows out the oil lamp. Small comforts swell into great needs. No one had accepted Leo's offer of leaving sesshin.

Traditionally, in Japan, the monks sleep on the zabutons they sit on during the day. But Americans are too big to curl up on their mats. So only some students sleep in the zendo, and those sprawl over three mats. But whoever was assigned to sleep in here tonight wouldn't be spreading out his sleeping bag for a few more minutes.

The altar candle had been extinguished, but the sweet smell of incense endured. I felt almost weighted to the floor. There is something wonderful about being in the zendo alone, like standing at the nave of Chartres watching the sunlight pour down through the great rose window. Well, on a smaller scale. But the oil lamps still shone their own subdued suns on the Buddha. I paused in front of the altar where the roshi had bowed. I bowed to the Buddha—life as it is in this moment—and felt the silence of the room, the air brushing my face and hands, the connection between the Buddha, the bow, and me. And I felt just the tiniest bit a fraud. Skepticism was what had lured me to Zen to begin with. I couldn't imagine ever being without it. I bowed again, but now the movement seemed entirely fake, and I headed silently to the door.

My hand was on the latch before I noticed the voices outside, whispering. Leo had postponed the normal rule of silence; they didn't have to whisper. I hesitated. One voice was a man's but I couldn't guess whose, the other a woman's.

"Aeneas!" she said. "Why couldn't Roshi just let him go?" Her voice was fuzzy, but panic sharpened her last words.

"Aeneas!" Disgust flooded the man's muted voice. "Leo has no idea what he's opening up. He could destroy this place."

"He could *be* destroyed."

I stood frozen, hand still on the latch. The woman was Maureen. I recognized the timbre she'd had when she asked me if I was okay this afternoon, only now it was much lower, flowing up from the depths of dread. I leaned toward the edge of the door, desperate to hear the man contradict her. The floor creaked. I jolted back. But it was too late. Shoes slapped fast down the porch steps.

I yanked open the door, jammed my feet into my running shoes, and nearly skied down the steps. I did slide halfway across the mud-slicked path. But Maureen and the man were gone. The rain was coming thicker, turning people into dark blobs, drumming on my jacket, covering all other noise. I felt like I'd gotten up in the middle of the night in a strange room where I couldn't find the light and my ears were plugged up. People passed by me like ghosts wafting toward the bathhouse, drawn by the pale yellow light. It was only by dint of flailing arms that I kept myself right end up long enough to make the turn outside the bathhouse toward

Garson-roshi's cabin. Was he thumbing his nose at the danger, or did he not even know?

I skidded past two tall men waiting under the overhang for the toothbrush and toilet crowd to thin. My foot caught on something, anchoring me.

". . . snore," one of them was saying.

"Yeah, and you're not the only one. You can count on that," the other guy whispered, with volume enhanced by irritation. "I went to a sesshin in San Diego. There they've got a snore room."

"What?"

"Yeah, all the snorers are stuck in one room. And I'll tell ya, when you wake up in the middle of the night it's like you're in the middle of a volcano."

"Bet you didn't tell that to your wife?" The first guy was laughing.

"You got that right. She'd be callin' me Vesuvius Jack."

I righted myself and hurried on over the path and up the roshi's steps. I knocked on his door, hearing the thumps of my fists nearly drowned out by the drumming of the rain on his roof, the tinkling of a rivulet running off it somewhere, and my own panting.

The door did not open. I leaned closer, squinting my ears for sounds of thick-socked feet shuffling stiffly across the cold wood floor. All I could hear was the rain.

A spike of panic shot through me. Where was he? It wasn't like he'd discovered he was out of fudge ripple ice cream and had run to the deli. I banged, waited half a second, and pushed open the door.

No one was in the cabin. Leo's oil lamp stood in the middle of the floor, illuminating a sheet of paper. *Darcy*, it said, *you're sleeping in the cabin nearest here. Go back to the bathhouse and take the first path to the left. See you at 4:45 A.M.*

Sleep? How could I even think about sleep?

I hurried outside, but in the minute I'd been in his cabin the paths had emptied. Wind snapped leaves, rain splatted against my face. Trees that had been distant earlier were closing in. I started toward the bathhouse.

Leo emerged from the men's side, bracketed by two men whose names I didn't know. When he spotted me, he pointed to a path to the left and kept going, as if there was no danger, no danger *he* had created.

"Leo," I began as I came abreast of them.

"Tomorrow."

"But—"

"Tomorrow," he insisted as if teaching manners to a rude child.

"Fine," I muttered to myself, my embarrassed, frustrated self, and headed in the direction he had pointed.

I hadn't given a thought to where I was to sleep. Had I done so I would have guessed the dorm, the repository of last come last served. A wave of gratitude replaced my panic. And relief. A tsunami of relief. Leo *did* consider the results of his actions. At least sometimes.

My questions would keep till tomorrow. Four A.M. would be here all too soon.

I needed to get to bed, and before I could do that there was the cabin to find, toothbrush to unearth in my duffel, stuff to unpack, and clothes to lay out so I could leap into them in the morning.

I made a left at the bathhouse and hurried back across the slick path to my cabin. Rain licked my face but not as hard now; trees kept their distance. Still, I was glad to step inside.

The first thing that struck me was the stillness, protected as I was now from wind and rain and dripping cold. Next was the stench of wet wool, but even that seemed a welcome indoor smell. The cabin was the same size as the Roshi's, but filled with two futons and multiple suitcases it seemed like a cell. Amber was kneeling on her futon and rooting in her suitcase, yanking out things like a golden retriever after a buried bone. Her clothes covered her futon, the floor between hers and mine, and had spilled over onto my suitcases, but I didn't care. It was like I'd stepped off the set of a horror movie back into the lunch wagon.

"I'm glad it's you, here," I said, as I held my raincoat outside and gave it a final shake.

"Yeah, me, too. I'd hate to be bitching to a stranger." But she stopped pawing a moment and looked up at me with a small smile that said more than she had put in words. She extricated a rust red sweater thick enough to have been petrified. "It's fucking freezing in here. I didn't bring enough stuff to wear to bed."

"Couldn't you put that sweater over your nightshirt?"

"No, listen, I know about layers, but I mean if I wear everything in my suitcase it's not going be enough."

I snickered.

"What?"

"I can picture you, in sweater over sweater over sweatshirt, and all the pants you own, and you in your sleeping bag like sausage stuffing so I'd have to squeeze you out of it in the morning."

She grinned. We didn't know each other well enough to share a giggle yet.

"There's a basin over there and a pitcher. You know, so you don't have to make a special trip to the bathhouse just for your teeth."

I nodded, picturing a me holding my teeth in my hand as I ran to the bathhouse. *That* I didn't bother to give voice to. I was so tired, so light-headed from relief I almost lost it, though.

In the dim oil light Amber was blurry, as was my own suitcase and duffel. I set about positioning the bags in the two-foot space at the end of my futon. Normally, at a sesshin there's a good bit of setting up the first night, but tonight I'd make do with the barest necessities. And even that wasn't going to be any snap. I'd been so rushed in New York I had tossed in sweater on top of pillowcase on top of water bottle. I knelt and began to yank like Amber, pulling a deep-forest-green sweater with one hand and charcoal corduroy pants with the other, then a yellow towel, a brown shark cartilage bottle, a white flannel nightshirt, another shark cartilage bottle, another sweater, till Amber's hooting caught me.

She was doubled up on her futon, amidst her pile of clothes, just as, I realized, I now was on mine. The room looked like a teenager's dream. I started to laugh, too. And when we got ourselves under control, I thought maybe we were good enough friends to giggle together. She must have had the same thought. She sat up, pulling on pajama bottoms.

"Darcy, you said you were scared of the woods. How come?"

A gust of wind slashed the side of the cabin. In its wake the rain seemed to stop dead a moment, then let loose with an extra bucketful. I pulled a black wool turtleneck out of my duffel and lay it on top for morning. I reached for another garment and then stopped. I could feel the shadow of gooey orange panic, more a shame-filled memory of it, an almost dead panic smothered under layers of other stuff. I'd known the instant I opened my mouth about the fear thing to Amber that I'd be sorry; I just hadn't realized how sorry and how soon. But, too late for regrets. I pulled the sweater around my shoulders and sat to face her. *The truth?*

I was sitting *seiza*, on my heels, as I had sat facing Yamana-roshi when he warned me against a reality I had made up. Against letting fiction pass for truth. I pulled the sweater tighter. The truth, but maybe not all of it.

"Amber, I don't know why I'm afraid of the woods. When I was four my older brothers and sisters lost track of me in Muir Woods and no one found me for hours."

Amber wriggled to face me. "That's it?" she demanded, as if she'd paid for a double feature and seen only a trailer.

"You wanted rapists and cougars?"

"Well no, but jeez, Darcy, that's like *nothing*."

"I'm sorry for your loss," I said, but she missed my sarcasm.

"I mean, how can you have made such a big deal about it all these years when it was, like nothing?"

I was folding my green sweater to lay atop the black pants. I slammed it down. "The stupidity of a fear does not make it better. Don't you think if I was going to be so jerked around by a fear I would rather have it caused by some dramatic, brave, interesting or at least not embarrassing reason?"

"More than an hour in the park? Well, yeah!"

"Thanks."

This time there was no missing the sarcasm.

"Oh, sorry." Then she giggled again. "I guess that was pretty bad. Justin says I've got a big mouth. Guess he's right."

She slumped and looked so chastised I felt worse for her than myself.

"It's okay, really. My woods-thing, it's just so, well, undignified." I reached over and nudged her shoulder. "But don't let this go to your head, roommate. I'm still planning to score your first cup of cocoa."

She grinned and I grinned back.

I turned to my pile of sweaters and pants, and started folding, focusing on each item as if I'd be quizzed on the appearance of each stitch in every sweater. The cabin was cold, just as it had been in the woods that long-ago night, or so I assumed.

I wriggled down into the sleeping bag, and stared into the dark, worrying, not about the woods all those years ago but about words on the zendo porch: *Leo has no idea what he's opening up. He could destroy this place. He could be destroyed.*

CHAPTER NINE

O

L
eo Garson-roshi blew across the top of the oil lamp globe and the flame died, leaving the cabin in darkness but for the candle on his small altar. He knelt in seiza, knees together, buttocks resting on feet and softly chanted the *Maha Prajna Paramita Hridaya Heart Sutra*, the sutra at the heart of Zen practice. At its end he surprised himself by going on to chant the *eko* which followed it in the morning service. His voice was a whisper, almost inaudible to himself. But he listened as he spoke, letting the words flow back into him, and seeing anew how strongly they applied to this sesshin.

"What we pray is . . . to save all sentient beings from the world of suffering and confusion;

"to encourage us to continue our practice even in adversity;

"to avert the destruction of fire, water and wind, and the calamities of war, epidemic and famine;

"and to keep forever turning the wheel of the *Dharma*."

He bowed low, rocked back on his heels and stood in one movement.

No man controls the wheel of the Dharma, but he had given it a sharp turn when he forced the issue of Aeneas. The wheel didn't stop till all the

Dharma played out. Dharma, he reflected, is a term with multiple meanings: the cosmic law of the world, the teachings of the Buddha and Buddhism, the general state of affairs of normal life. Garson-roshi had considered the teachings when he decided to make this the last sesshin here. But now Leo wondered if he had given enough thought to the affairs of normal life, to cause and effect. The wheel of the Dharma was turning. No man controls the wheel of the Dharma, no man slows it down, turns it away from its path. Every hand is on that wheel, everyone spins it and is spun by it.

CHAPTER TEN

O

TUESDAY

Ten after four is a revolting time of morning. The best you can do is move before you think about it. Move and move fast. The room was icy. I slid into black wool slacks, black turtleneck, dark green sweater, and black raincoat. Outside, rain banged down, bounced up from the steps, off from the roof. There was no sound but the rain, because everyone else was still in bed. There was no light at all. The macadam path from my cabin to the bathhouse was a water channel and I almost skidded into the bathhouse wall before I grabbed the door and swung myself inside. I had been up at this hour on location sets, but there the second unit director and the entire stunt crew were discussing the first gag; conversations buzzed as the wardrobe, makeup, first unit director, the gaffers, and other crew guys worried over weather, timing, breakage. And the smell of coffee drew us all to the "lunch tent" with warmers of eggs, sausage, muffins, pancakes, and endless coffee.

Here, I poured myself coffee and stood in the silent empty kitchen.

By the time I got to Leo's cabin with his cocoa, it was too late for questions. He poured a cup, inhaled that wonderful chocolate aroma and drank. There wasn't even time for him to finish before he handed me the incense stick. Outside, the clappers had already given the warning three hits. Now the roll-down had begun.

I stashed the incense under my raincoat and walked behind him—past groggy students hurrying to the zendo porch—to the back door of the zendo, the teacher's entrance. He must have guessed we'd be late. As soon as I took off my shoes he handed me a note and whispered, "Read it later."

I was dying to pore over the note, but even if I'd had time the light was too dim, and I was already worried that the incense would be too damp to catch fire. Normally we would have lit the incense stick at the altar in his cabin and carried it to the zendo, marking the union of the teacher's practice with the community's practice. Now I hunched under the porch roof protecting the matches from the sluicing rain. When I had lit the incense, shaken out the flame, and watched the smoke curl uncertainly upward, Leo nodded and I opened the zendo door.

The zendo was in shadows but for the pearly glow of oil lamps on the altar and the sharp flame from the thick candle. Leo walked slowly across the wood floor, the balls of his feet touching first so that each step had the soft, full sound of intent. He stopped at the end of the mat before the altar and made a standing bow.

Later, I wished that I had savored that moment of him there, bowing in our stead, all of us assuming we were safe, our only worry the pain in our knees.

I walked behind him to the side of the altar, the floor so cold that my feet lost their traction and I had to concentrate on each step as if I was walking in roller skates. He moved around the mat until he was right in front of the altar, took the incense stick from my outstretched hand, and planted it in the small round bowl before the Buddha.

The smoke from it wafted past my nose, the pungent smell connecting this first full day of sesshin with so many others I had sat. Suddenly I thought of Aeneas. Had Aeneas felt this bond when he stood in this spot inhaling this incense, not knowing he was about to vanish like the smoke?

As I walked to my seat the note crackled in my pocket. But the chance to read it didn't come till after three zazen periods, the service, and breakfast. As everyone else on the porch stuffed their feet into their shoes and hurried to their cabins for a precious hour of rest, I pulled out the paper and read. It was the last thing I wanted to see: "Get my newspaper during break."

A mile through the woods! My stomach went to mush, my whole body was clammy. I stuffed the note in my pocket and strode toward Leo's cabin, launching spray with every step. At 7:30 A.M., night had thinned to a sort of dawning, but the rain kept everything gray and was already spreading damp up under my sweater, icing my back. Leo's thermos stood outside his door, on the steps. I knocked. No answer. The thermos stood by my feet. Was this Leo's—*Roshi's*—way of saying: Don't argue with me? Or had he just stepped out and left his thermos?

I took a deep breath, grabbed the empty thermos and headed for the kitchen, my last stop before the woods. Every gag in every movie was wrapped in fear. Every time, I pulled off the wrapping and reached inside for what would make the stunt work. Some gags I tore into, some I approached by layers of research, others by days of practice, some by combinations. But I never balked. Except when it came to the woods. Already I could feel my body tightening, my shoulders going hard, my neck turning into a choke collar.

When I pulled open the kitchen door the smell of cocoa struck me anew, but now it was tainted by Leo's spilling incident, though not so much that I'd have refused a cup if Barry offered. The room had cooled, the heat replaced by the rattling of what looked like a long tin box large enough for a six-year-old to slide through. It was spitting beans into a bucket and Barry squatted next to the bucket staring into it like it held little brown nuggets of gold.

At the far end three or four people—the dishwashing crew—bustled around the sink, shifting great wooden serving bowls, running hot water. They were all in green aprons, but aprons can only do so much. By the end of the sesshin, sleeves and shirt shoulders would be dotted with Clorox stains.

I shook my head and again the rain pelted off my hair. My raincoat had been fine for New York, with cabs and umbrellas. There I hadn't considered a hood; now I would have traded my chance of enlightenment for one. I stood a moment in the warmth, watching Barry watch the beans, wishing I could be as entranced with anything here as he was with those little brown pellets, putting off the trek through the wilderness.

I dribbled a bit of coffee into a cup and said, "How's it going?"

Barry nodded thoughtfully. "I'm only doing a small batch, but I'm cutting it close, getting it done by Thursday. The roasting went fine. These beans only need forty-five minutes. And the winnowing—well, you can see I've got half a bucket of nibs already. The shells are over there. Maureen will be glad to get them for the garden. I'll have the nibs into the melangeur this morning—"

"Melangeur?"

He pointed to what looked like a 1900s washing machine, the kind with two thick hand-operated wringers on the top. "They'll be in there for twenty-four hours."

"Washing?"

He jolted back and looked at me like I was an idiot, and I could see that a *criollo* and its melangeur were not suitable topics for levity.

"Grinding. Stones are solid granite. Best surface in the world for creating a smooth paste. Aztecs used them."

I nodded, but he didn't look up. He was nearly talking to himself.

". . . got to conch and temper and set the chocolate in molds. There's barely time. If the road holds out. So little time. If anything goes wrong . . ."

The last thing Barry needed was me here.

"Oh. Sorry," I muttered and started for the door.

"Hook."

"Hook?"

"On the left."

On the hook on the left there hung one of those parkas like you see in pictures of Arctic explorers, not as heavy, and without the fur all around the face—we are Buddhists after all—but with a hood that was virtually a front porch. It stuck out so far it shielded my coffee when I drank. The coat hung halfway down my shins and even with rolling the sleeves I couldn't get my hands entirely free.

"It's *your* coat," I said out loud. I felt like I was inside a bear, and it felt real good.

Barry nodded, then looked away quickly as if he might be embarrassed by the effusion of thanks I was on the verge of offering. It was his only coat as far as I could see, and a huge gift to a stranger. If I tripped and tore it, he'd be soaked every time he went outside.

I swallowed hard and was almost glad that his preoccupation kept me from finding the right words of thanks. I gave him a quick squeeze on the shoulder and stepped outside.

Even in the parka the cold was a shock after the toasty kitchen. I made my way across the parking area toward the road, rain drumming on my roof and as thick as a plastic shower curtain in front of me, turning the trees into a dark green blur. I walked cozy, like a kid in a snug and secret hiding spot. It wasn't till I'd reached the road and turned right that the drawback of the parka struck me. It blocked out sounds and any hope of peripheral vision. Bears and cougars along the path could fight over my tastier parts and I would hear nothing.

The road was muddy. Those deep ruts that had kept Leo's truck from bouncing over the edge were now puddles. But the ridge between them was surprisingly wide and firm. The green blur of trees along the sides made a wind break, and the great branches I didn't want to start thinking about held off the rain as long as they could and then dropped their load on my head. I walked stiffly, tensed up, waiting for the next deluge, hunched against the sight of the bridge and the red Japanese maple that would signal the path into the woods. The great coat shifted with each step and I realized the weight was only on one shoulder.

Not weight. A claw! I let out a scream. I'd forgotten about the rendezvous with Rob.

But it wasn't Rob; it was a stranger, a small, soaked stranger, with a lopsided grin. "Hey, hold it down, woman. I'm not Dracula."

"You could have fooled me." I spun around on the narrow ridge and ended up grabbing the guy's arms to keep from falling.

"Nice. Real nice!"

He was about Leo's height, with a mat of dark curly hair. The guy looked like a cat who'd fallen in a vat overnight, a grumpy cat ready to spring. And yet, even under all that water, he seemed "pet quality"—not the cat who'd curl up on your lap, but the one who leaps from floor to top shelf, knocks off a bowl in the process, and then stares down at you knowing his cuteness will save him.

"Who are you?" I said.

"Who's asking?"

I pulled myself together and announced, "The roshi's assistant," as if I had held the job for years instead of hours.

"You got a name, Assistant?"

"You going to answer my question?"

I was smiling now. The man, whatever his name was, was stockier than Leo, and younger, and . . . a New Yorker, no doubt about it. He had one of those accents that instantly endear him to other displaced New Yorkers. He sounded born-and-bred enough to tell Bronx from Brooklyn from Queens.

He must have taken my musing for pressure. He shrugged. "Okay, okay, Assistant. Gabe Luzotta here."

"From where in New York?"

Now he smiled. "Bronx originally, Upper West Side now. You? You live in the city?"

I nodded.

"Who do you sit with?"

"Yamana-roshi."

"Lucky you. I sat with him a while, but I don't recall you there."

"I've only been in New York two years. I flew in for sesshins with him before, but I couldn't make it to them all."

He nodded, agreeing with himself. "Okay, then. I was before your time."

"Sesshin's already started," I said, sure I hadn't seen him in the zendo.

"No diff. I'm going to sleep through the first three days. I've gotta be the most worn-out Zen student in a fifty-mile radius. First my plane gets held up in La Guardia. Then I miss the connection in O'Hare and have to wait six hours and thirty-seven minutes, keeping watch over all my stuff, so I can't even hit the john. So I get to SFO, and would you believe, the damned rent-a-car place has lost my reservation and it takes another hour to straighten that out."

I started to speak, but he was on a roll.

"So I snag the car and head out on the freeway and all of a sudden I'm heading over a bridge, going east! Would it kill the great state of California to mark its roads so you can get where you're going? I had to hunt up another bridge to get back to my road—all this in a monsoon yet— and when I finally get here and turn onto this road, I can see I need pontoons. So, Assistant, I drive so slow I'm like some guy's granny. And even with that the car sinks—like slurp!—halfway in. So what'm I gonna do, right? I gotta hike. That or wait for spring. But I figure I'm over halfway, so there's like three miles to go. Three miles. Sixty blocks, right? That's nothing. Chelsea to the Museum of Natural History, right? Do you know how long that took me? The whole fucking night! Mud and rain. You wouldn't believe it! You ever been in a pool where they got those water walkers? Well, I'll tell you, I got a lot more sympathy for them now."

"Maybe Rob will give you a day off."

"Rob? Rob Staverford? Is that uptight asshole still here? Oh, great, and by now the asshole's in charge, huh? What is he, sesshin director?"

"Yup." Giving up any attempt at restraint, I said, "So you've been here before?"

"Oh, yeah. On and off since the beginning. Whenever I can get free."

"From?"

"Deadlines. I'm a writer. But don't tell everyone. It makes people nervous; they always think I'm writing about them."

"Are you?"

"Not hardly. Writing about a bunch of silent guys in the woods doing nothing but sitting in front of a blank wall? Like there's a big market for that! Nah, I do magazine pieces. Like for the *New Yorker*."

"Really?" I said, impressed. "Politics? Medical? Food?" Considering where we were meeting, I added, "Religion?"

He winced. It was a small wince, and he covered almost immediately. A person who wasn't used to watching nervous actors for telltale winces might have missed this one. *Don't ask me if I'm afraid of heights. Oh, god, I should never have let on! I want to do my own stunts, without a double!* those winces said. *Don't ask. . . .*

He was grinning now, looking like the cat caught over the broken bowl. "Well, one piece for the *New Yorker*. But I keep hoping, so when you come up with hot topics, call me. In fact"—he stretched back up to his full height, which was a couple inches more than mine—"call me anyway when we both get home. We'll go out for a cappuccino after evening zazen."

Quite the smooth shift. But I didn't say no. I wriggled as if to reclaim my balance as I tried to grasp the tail of memory of that story. There had been some *New Yorker* story years back before I came to Manhattan; something to do with religion but not religion itself. Some problem with it.

"So, Assistant, what are you doing standing out here like the doorman?"

I gave him a salute, as if I'd been focusing on him. But the two of us standing here reminded me that it should have been Rob here with me. It had been odd enough that he'd insisted on a rendezvous this morning, and odder yet that he apparently blew it off. But here was Gabe, the one person not averse to speaking ill of his fellow Zen students.

"Gabe," I said, and smiled, "what do you know about Aeneas? You were here when he was, right?" I was guessing if he hadn't met Aeneas, he'd have made a point of finding out about him.

"Why do you ask?"

"Roshi's talk last night. He said Aeneas vanished and was never heard from again."

"Really. What else did he say?"

"Nothing. And *I* was asking *you* the questions. What do you know about Aeneas vanishing? I mean, why wasn't it a big deal back then? How many Americans do Japanese teachers lure off without the courtesy of a mention to the local teacher? Leo said he didn't write to them, but why didn't he—"

"Because, Assistant, Aeneas's departure wasn't the embarrassment, even him running through the grounds wearing Leo's robe and waving a gin bottle wasn't it."

Waving a gin bottle didn't sound like the obsessive Aeneas. "What then?"

"The Buddha."

I waited, half expecting him to quote some familiar koan.

"The statute of the Buddha. The Japanese teachers brought an antique Buddha as a gift for the opening of the monastery. Someone stole it."

"Someone stole the Buddha?" I couldn't restrain a laugh. "I mean, how tacky is that?"

"Well, yeah." He was grinning. "Later, Roshi said there's nothing that can't be replaced, well, except for something someone didn't want to admit to begin with." He shrugged as if to say he had digressed. "But lemme tell you, Assistant, no one was laughing at the time. It was a huge giganto embarrassment. Garson-roshi had a spotty past; he'd been on the sauce in Japan and here. The Zen establishment had gone to a heap of trouble to find a place for him and then to get the Japanese masters over here, to give the monastery their blessing. For something so, like you said, *tacky*, to undermine it was unthinkable."

Gabe yawned, a movement of rolling shoulders, face scrunched in all directions, mouth open so wide it dwarfed his face. "Listen, Assistant, I'm dying here. I got to get something to eat before I hit the zendo."

He started to maneuver around me, avoiding the soggy vehicle tracks, then stopped as if he'd forgotten something. He focused on me and his eyes narrowed. I had the sense he was rubbing the possibilities of me between his fingers. The last thing I wanted was him gnawing on why the roshi's assistant was standing around at the edge of the woods.

"Gabe, you've got like no time at all to stash your stuff, tell Rob you're here, plus snarf something from the kitchen. Go!"

He hesitated, but stomach triumphed. He gave my shoulder a friendly nudge and trotted off.

I had qualms about Gabe, but he was the bratty kind of guy I like. I'd lied to him about the time, but he'd forget that. Like me, he'd be pleased to have a new buddy. We come to sesshin to be alone with our own practice. We do it in a group because we'd never make ourselves follow a 5:00 A.M. to 9:00 P.M. schedule alone at home. But as soon as we get here we start making friends to protect ourselves from the terror of being really alone. Amber had done it with me, and I with her, Barry, Maureen, Leo, and now Gabe.

With Gabe gone the forest took form before me, and in this protected area under the branches I could make out thick trunks of redwood, swaying branches of live oak above and fronds of fern below. Quickly I looked down. Walk! Step forward! Just a step onto the path, into the woods! I had to do this; it was my job; it was my practice; more to the point, it was my life.

Beneath the bridge, water was already running fast, though low in the trench back toward the zendo grounds. The bed was much deeper than I'd assumed, the banks littered with boulders. I didn't want to consider how full that stream would get if the rain kept up or how easy it would be to crack your skull if your truck skidded off the bridge. I jerked my gaze back up to the bridge, to the thick stone wall that formed a low railing, wide enough to sit on. Stones protruded irregularly, like a ledge in Muir Woods. My eyes blurred; sweat coated my face and neck and stuck my sweater to the sides of my chest. I crossed the bridge carefully, as if the stone railing would suddenly collapse and pull the bridge and me down with it. Once over it I spotted the red Japanese maple Leo had nearly hit and the path beyond.

I turned toward the path, but I couldn't—I just couldn't make myself put a foot on it. I walked back and forth on the road, up to the red Japanese maple and back from it. I goaded, I threatened. I thought of Yamana-roshi, of the stunt coordinating I would never be able to do with this paralysis of fear, of all the years of protecting my secret, of telling it to Amber, the last person to keep it. I heard Kelly Rustin screaming from the bottom of the canyon. Tears mixed with the sweat on my cheeks. I stared, not at the trees but at the water tumbling white under the bridge, then slowly rotated my gaze upward. I tried to feel, and lost the feeling in both my feet. I just couldn't walk into those woods.

My face was flushed under the hood, my body spiking from sickly hot to icy chill and back. My right leg ached in the three places it had been broken. For years I had gone after the highest high falls, the most dangerous car explosion gags, the scariest of the scary. I thought I had learned to rein in fear. But here, all that was useless; I was helpless.

When I checked my watch, forty minutes had passed since I left the kitchen. I was still standing by the red maple. I could have cried. I'd let down Leo, and Yamana-roshi, too. In a few minutes, break would be over and we'd be back in the zendo again. How would I tell Leo, or would I tell him? I could just say the weather was too bad for flying and his paper hadn't come. That was probably the truth anyway. It wasn't as if he needed a newspaper to keep himself occupied now; he'd be in his cabin preparing his lecture. The paper could wait till tomorrow; I could get someone else to go tomorrow.

Confess? Lie? I couldn't decide. In the end I stumbled back into the zendo and sat facing the wall, feeling the turmoil in my stomach, listening to the degrading thoughts that heckled me. Feeling like shit.

Amber sat beside me, her crossed legs twitching, her hands moving when they weren't supposed to. But to me she was a comfort.

It took me all three periods of sitting to see what I'd known all along: I had to go to Roshi's cabin and admit the truth. Roshi would replace me as jisha; but I more than deserved that.

When the bell rang, I lifted myself off the cushion slowly, bowed to it, bowed to the room, walked out as slowly as if I was still pushing that hundred-thirty-pound bag of cacao beans up the hill. After my confession, I would still see the roshi, of course. I'd see him in the distance at the altar, talk to him as roshi in dokusan. But he'd never grin at me, talk about tines, never be *Leo*. God, I would miss Leo.

I pulled on my boots, walked through the pelting rain to the roshi's cabin. I didn't even bother to knock, just pushed open his door and stepped in.

"I'm sorry, but I—"

Leo lay dead still on top of his comforter. There are a lot of things I should have noticed, but what sticks in my mind is his bare feet—blue and stiff—sticking out of his brown robe.

Chapter Eleven

O

Leo!" I screamed. "Leo! Omigod, Leo!" He looked so small, so gray, so dead. I was shaking him by the shoulders, by his *cold* shoulders. His head wagged like a string mop. "Oh, Leo, if only I'd come straight here instead of going back to the zendo. Leo, don't be dead. Leo!" I screamed.

"Shh."

His hazel eyes opened only a slit and he looked as if he was spending all his strength accomplishing that.

"I'll get you a doctor. Do we have a doctor here? We can drive the truck to town, to a hospital—"

"No!" he forced out in a voice that was more air than sound.

I put my hand on his forehead. It was clammy. That comforted me, not that I know anything about medicine. When you grow up the youngest, your goal is never to let on you're sick, lest you be drowned with advice.

"Leo, I'm useless. I've got to get you help."

"No!"

"What's the matter? Is it your heart? Chest pains?"

"Fever."

"Fever! You were fine this morning."

"Fever."

"I have to do—"

"Do nothing."

"Leo!"

"Roshi!"

His eyes opened slowly, deliberately, as if he was cranking the lids. But his gaze seemed to flow from his intent, not from his frail body. He didn't repeat the word, the gaze did it for him, embodying the first moment he insisted I call him Sensei or Roshi, the moment he poured the cocoa on the floor, and this moment.

I was crouching awkwardly next to him, one knee on his futon, the other somewhere in the air. Common sense said: You know Leo doesn't merely have a fever; get this man to a hospital. Zen tradition said: Roshi is in charge and you are his assistant. Later I would look back on this moment and know that no matter which decision I made, I would regret it.

He didn't move. His breath was ragged, his clammy face gray as if he'd thrown up.

"Roshi," I repeated.

He gave the slightest of nods. He looked so small lying there, like a scrawny old dog, barely able to snap at the hands trying to help him. I wiped the sweat from his forehead, asked if he wanted another blanket, spread it over him. Only then did I remember those blue feet of his, still sticking out into the icy air. I clasped one between my hands. The sole was stiff with cold, the skin lank between the bones. I pressed the sole against my stomach for warmth and rubbed the other side. When it finally had a vague pink tinge, I pulled the blankets down around it.

He murmured something. It had the sound of profundity. I leaned closer. "What, Roshi?"

"Other foot."

I almost laughed with relief. Then I set about massaging that foot. I'm sure I rubbed it longer than necessary, from thanks and the joy of being here with one manageable thing to do.

"What about sesshin? What do you want me to tell people?"

"Fever."

"What about your lunch? I'll ask Barry to make you some broth."

"No!"

"Isn't there someone in sesshin who's a doctor or nurse? Maybe they could—"

"No!"

That clearly meant: Don't ask anyone about me.

"You know, Leo, stubbornness is an unattractive quality in the sick."

He didn't answer.

I hadn't been able to watch his face from this vantage point, but when I tucked his other foot under the covers, I could see he was sweaty again. His eyes were closed, either in sleep or in an effort to silence me. I had the unreasonable urge to shake him awake again, not to ask him anything but because the act of talking to him staved off the fear that he was sicker than he was letting on and that I was colluding in making things worse. Things that are no big deal in the city can be deadly in the woods.

I didn't want to leave him alone, and I didn't want him sick in this freezing cabin. I sat on the edge of his futon listening to his labored breathing and made myself a list of what needed to be done, so I could make only one trip out.

1) Get some kind of light food from the kitchen.

2) Get wood to make a fire.

3) Tell Rob there'd be no lecture today.

I wiped Leo's brow again, put on my raincoat and was almost out the door when I remembered his cocoa thermos. His cup was about a third full, just as he'd left it before five A.M. The cocoa was cold, of course, but I had skipped lunch to rush over here, and as long as Leo wasn't going to drink it anyway— I lifted the cup to my mouth.

"No!"

I stopped, embarrassed, furious, and then dead scared. The aroma of the cocoa was strong enough that I wouldn't have noticed the slight smell of burnt almonds—cyanide—not till I'd drained the cup.

My fingers went stiff. The cup slid slowly through them and smashed on the floor. Brown liquid bounced over the floorboards, onto my shoes as I stood paralyzed, watching.

I croaked out, "Roshi, this is poisoned. I've got to get you to a hospital. Medevac, there's got to be a helicopter service. They can alert the hospital and—"

"No!"

"This is *poison*. You're going to die!"

"Am not," he said, sounding like a toddler, a very weak toddler. "Four hours. Book: you live four hours, you're okay. I'm okay."

"What book?"

He didn't answer. This time there was no question that he was faking sleep. His eyes were twitching closed, his breathing was shallow and ragged, and then suddenly he'd lunge for breath and then start the cycle over again. I had the feeling he had saved his last little bit of energy to watch over me and the cocoa and now even that little bit was gone.

"Oh, Leo," I murmured with such a shock of gratitude.

There are different characters of roshis; some are intellectual pointers and prodders, some are quiet men—and now women—who teach by example, but the best ones are the ones who care so much that everything about their lives is a teaching.

But that didn't cut my panic. He was so sick. How could I not call the paramedics? *If you live four hours!* It had been almost five hours by now. Clearly, Leo had researched this. He didn't seem to be getting worse. It defied common sense, but I had to trust him. Sort of.

I bent down and scrubbed up the cocoa once again. This close, the bitter almond smell of cyanide cut through the chocolate. I thought I could catch other smells—whatever was in this cup could as easily have been a potpourri of poisons as straight cyanide. Fortunately there had been less than two inches of liquid in the cup. I stood up, opened the door, and washed the rag in the water dripping off the entryway roof, rung it out, and gave the floor another wipe.

I had stood right here and watched as he filled the cup and drank two thirds. Surely he'd smelled the cyanide? I would have smelled it as soon as I'd swallowed the first mouthful. I probably would have noticed the taste. And Leo, who was familiar with this cocoa, definitely would have spotted the difference. He should have noticed it before he took the first sip. Of course, he knew the cocoa was poisoned.

"You knew you were *being* poisoned," I said to his sleeping form, "and you drank it anyway. Are you crazy?"

Crazy is a term that has been used for roshis over the years. Crazy in the sense of not following standard logic. But what would make him do a thing so crazy as drinking poison?

"Leo!"

He didn't even shift. I stood staring as anger, frustration, and just plain bafflement fought for control of me.

Two things were obvious: Number one, no one dribbles cyanide into cocoa by mistake. Leo was poisoned intentionally; and number two, the monastery wasn't located where a killer could drop in, do a little poisoning, and catch a cab on home. It was just us Zen students here, and one of us was willing to spend two weeks facing the wall, sitting with a hatred so great that he had tried to kill the roshi.

Right now that student was sitting in the zendo, cross-legged on the cushion, his hands together in front of a gut so roiling with anger that he could scream, except he couldn't scream. He couldn't escape. All he could do was sit there period after period, day after day, tasting his bile and worrying about being discovered.

"Like he won't try to kill you again." I stared down at Leo's gaunt shoulders sticking out from beneath the blankets. "And next time he'll learn by his mistake. He's got half a month. Did you consider that, Leo, when you decided to drink down his cocoa and make yourself sick? What were you thinking?" My voice was cracking. I didn't know whether I was more angry or panicked. "Are you letting him play out his resentment, his fury, his self-absorption, whatever it is—play it out in your body? Or have you just been facing a blank wall too long?"

I don't think he registered my words, but if he did, he chose to give no sign. He just lay there as the most appalling connection of all came clear to me.

"Leo," I said, my throat suddenly so dry I could barely speak, "Aeneas was murdered, wasn't he?"

Leo slept on. There was no need to wake him.

Aeneas created a disturbance at the opening ceremony six years ago. Right after that, he disappeared. Recently, Leo had discovered Aeneas had never left with the Japanese contingent after the opening, and Leo immediately planned this sesshin in honor of Aeneas. Now Leo had been poisoned.

Speaking of Aeneas, Yamana-roshi had said, "Could be dead."

Had to be dead.

This sesshin in honor of Aeneas was what Yamana-roshi warned Leo against. Leo ignored the warning and he had been poisoned.

My throat was so tight I had difficulty breathing. I inhaled slowly, willing calm, failing. I needed to call—but there was no phone here. I needed to send for the sheriff- and tell him what? My conclusion about Aeneas? The sheriff would remind me there are a hundred places to die of exposure in the woods.

I started another long, slow breath, and gave up halfway, gasping. No wonder Maureen and Rob were on tenterhooks. But Barry, in the kitchen where—suddenly, I felt so cold I didn't even shiver—the kitchen where the poisoned cocoa came from. How could I be sure it wasn't Barry who—

"Of course, it wasn't Barry," I muttered, talking to myself now. I remembered his surprised, grateful smile when he'd realized I had carted his beans up the hill for Roshi. "If I told Barry what happened he'd turn over heaven and earth to find whoever did this to his Roshi."

A numb iciness took hold. I didn't shiver, nothing that positive. I felt utterly alone. Much as I longed to trust sweet Barry, or even puppyish Amber, I couldn't trust anyone, not with Leo's life.

There was an extra zafu here in the cabin and I sat on it, letting the shock settle into reality. Killed. Poisoned. The cold seeped through the floor, up my spine. Leo lay on his side, nothing moving but his heaving chest. He was breathing through his mouth like his nose was clogged and his throat was stuffed with cotton. I don't know how long I watched him, ten minutes, half an hour? He didn't change and I took some tiny comfort that he wasn't getting worse.

A book lay open to the story of the Sixth Patriarch. I picked it up, but was too jittery to concentrate. I knew the story, though. The Fifth Patriarch asked his students to write a poem so he could judge who was qualified to succeed him as head of the monastery. His long-term best student wrote four lines beginning with a reference to the tree under which the Buddha sat in meditation and was enlightened:

The body is the bodhi-tree
The mind a clear mirror on a stand
Polish the mirror continually
So not a speck of dust distorts it.

But an illiterate monk saw the error in the poem and had someone write for him:

There is no bodhi tree
No mirror or stand
Fundamentally nothing exists
No place for dust to land.

And so the young monk became the successor, the Sixth Patriarch.

The tale seemed so "Leo," with the in-your-face young monk saying: Wrong, wrong, wrong, so there! But I was a novice, mine was the most superficial of readings. What had Leo been pondering when he reread the poems? Last night he had been talking about the illusion of time. Was he thinking here of the illusion of mind? Or was he remembering the end of the story, that after the success of his poem the young monk was sent into hiding lest the best student's supporters kill him?

I studied Leo, but all his sleeping body relayed was that he was shivering. I grabbed my raincoat, stepped outside, and locked the door.

"What are you doing?"

I started. From the bottom of the two steps Rob glared. We stood frozen, me in my panic about Leo; he, I couldn't guess why. With his chiseled features and startlingly French blue eyes he should have made my stomach go queasy, mine and every other woman here. Another time, with another personality, perhaps he would have. He stretched out a hand for Leo's door key.

"You were supposed to meet me this morning."

I just stared. Rob and his demand for clandestine conference seemed so trivial now.

"And you've got no business gossiping with Gabe Luzotta. This is sesshin. You're the jisha; you're supposed to be setting an example, not wallowing in chatter."

Chatting with Gabe Luzotta had been a lifetime ago. Had Rob been watching? Listening? That was the least of my problems. I took a deep breath and another, this time with more success at forcing calm. I focused on what needed to be done. Not only could I not trust Rob, I had to deceive him big time. If I was to have any chance of protecting Leo, I had to convince Rob that Roshi was merely a bit under the weather, but still in charge. To everyone here, it had to seem that I, the jisha, was relaying the roshi's instructions. It was an impossible task—I didn't know the dharma well, and as for Leo, I barely knew him at all. I'd be making things up as I went along, trying to think like a Zen master, to guess Leo's quirks, and marry the two; I'd be grasping for black straws in the dark. And my first audience was the resident Zen scholar, the guy who had been Roshi's student and friend for six years. I fell back on asking questions, starting with the all-purpose one to cover the fact I'd been so distracted I'd forgotten what Rob had asked. "What are you doing here by Le—*Roshi's*—porch?"

"Since *you* are unwilling to confer with me, I need to talk to him. Give me the key."

"His door is locked for a reason, Rob."

"No one locks his door here."

Open access? How was I ever going to protect Leo?

"Darcy, I need to confer with Roshi about the lecture. Now."

"About the lecture. Yes." Leo hadn't lied to me. He had avoided questions and stretched the truth about his fever, but lie? No. I would try to maintain that same level of honesty and not undermine the sesshin. "There'll be no lecture today. Students need the first day just to settle in. As to tomorrow's lecture"—I almost asked, but caught myself and declared—"you'll do it."

"Of course."

I could have drooped with relief.

"What's the topic for this sesshin?"

Oh, shit. What would Leo have chosen for two weeks of lectures? The only topic I had heard was his poison oak! But there was the Sixth Patriarch.

"Lecture on the Sixth Patriarch."

It wasn't until I saw the sudden hunching of his shoulders and the tightening of his jaw that could have been from either worry or from fury that I realized I had chosen the single story most likely to put a long-term senior student on guard. I wondered if that had been Leo's intention.

Chapter Twelve

O

I stood on Leo's porch, watching the couple who had kissed before the start of sesshin last night and the man who rushed back into his cabin for something essential to take with him into the zendo as they walked across the quad now. I felt like the stranger walking into town among the unsuspectingly happy villagers in the first reel of a horror flick. They had no idea Aeneas had been murdered, or that the person they passed on the path could have poisoned Leo. When they went back into the zendo, bowed, and sat on their cushions, it could be next to the killer stewing in his own pressure cooker of emotions.

I needed to get them out of here, before the killer lost control. But there was no way. The van was gone; it wouldn't be back for two weeks. There was no phone. We were stuck, all of us here together. And Leo? Leo was sleeping the deep uneasy sleep of the sick. When he woke, we'd talk. In the meantime, the sesshin schedule went on.

In quarter of an hour the clappers would sound for work meeting, where work period jobs would be assigned. These jobs and the attitude students brought to doing them was the crossover between seated-silent-still meditation and the hassle of regular life. Some teachers called work period the most important time in sesshin. No one was exempt from the meeting, not even the roshi's assistant, who needed to find wood and figure out how to build a fire in the roshi's freezing cabin. I hadn't built a fire—ever. Growing up there had always been brothers jostling each other with wood and techniques, until the chimney collapsed in the Loma Prieta earthquake and Dad replaced the fireplace with a television nook. Now I could hardly ask anyone to help, not and have them see what awful condition Leo was in.

I ran for the shed. The macadam path was slippery; my inadequate running shoes hydroplaned and just keeping my balance required all my attention. At the shed door I skidded, caught the knob to stop myself and swung inside. Gray stripes of light slipped between the wall boards. A woodpile half filled the space—plenty to keep Leo warm till Christmas. There were a few bucketsful of twigs that would pass for kindling, but no lighter fluid. No lighter. Only matches. Matches might work for a Boy Scout, but not for a fire-novice. I checked the cans on the top shelf, and the middle, and behind them. I never did find lighter fluid; what I came across on the bottom shelf in the dark corner hidden behind a can of shellac was weed poison. Weed poison containing cyanide. I snatched the bottle, and reached for the door. I could empty it in the woods; I could brave the woods that long.

But wait! How many other garden or household poisons were here? This shed could be a bastion for skull and crossbones. Dealing with the poisoner was like guarding against terrorists; the ingredients of death were everywhere. No way to protect against them. All I could do was watch over Leo and flush out the person—his *student*—who was trying to kill him.

Knowledge of Roshi's cocoa habit and that poison would be waiting in this shed, both pointed to a long-time student, someone who had nurtured his grievance in this isolated place. Of course, anyone could have carried the poison in with him. But that still indicated an old-timer. New students don't pack cyanide along with their long johns just in case something might irritate them.

"Crazy," I heard myself saying. And then I remembered the last time I'd said that, to Leo himself. It was crazy, but the intensity of silence and isolation in a place like this can cut both ways. Zen isn't magic, particularly for someone who doesn't want it to be.

Behind me, hinges whined, wood scraped against wood. The door snapped open. I grabbed for the spade, and just caught myself before hoisting it weapon-style. My face flushed, and I was lucky the darkness of the place protected me. Gabe Luzotta was inside the door before he saw me. He started. His body outlines said "caught," but it was too dark for me to be positive. I wasn't sure till I heard the emphasis in his question.

"What are *you* doing here?"

"And you?"

"Never mind." Gabe Luzotta shrugged. "I know what you're going to say, you're the roshi's assistant."

"And you?" I repeated.

"And I'm not."

Another time I would have laughed, a time I wasn't in a shed with poison and a stranger.

"Okay, okay, Assistant. I'm hiding out. Look, I asked Rob to let me start sesshin tomorrow. 'No exceptions,' says His Assholeness. You'd think he was getting a cut of the gate here. 'Everyone else got here on time,' he whines. Shit!"

Gabe threw up his hands. His utter outrage drew me to him. The enemy of my enemy and all. Besides, Gabe Luzotta was exactly the kind of wink-and-break-rule guy I liked. It had taken me years to leash in my penchant for the scoff-rule set, at least when I was doing gags with them.

"So," Gabe went on, "when the mid-morning sittings started, I climbed on my cushion and I sat. The first period I nodded and jerked awake, nodded, jerked awake, and kept doing it till my head banged into the wall. The second period I sat as close to the wall as I could and just let my head rest."

"So you slept right through the last two periods of zazen?"

"No."

"Did Rob wake you?"

"No, my snoring did. I'm not gonna win Mr. Popularity with the guy next to me in there. If he hadn't kept poking me I'd have entertained you all."

But none of that explained why he had made a bee-line to the place the poison was stored.

"What *are* you doing in here?"

"Looking for a place to sleep."

"In the *woodshed*? Please! Why don't you sleep in your dorm like everyone else?"

"Because it's almost work period, and His Assholeness said since I showed up late I was the one who could help him with something or other, I don't know what. I wasn't listening by then because I was so ticked. And besides, I knew I wasn't going to be doing it, so why listen to the details, right?"

That was three steps below an excuse; it couldn't be anything but the truth. I had sat through those beginning periods of zazen in sesshins and snapped from dream to waking to dream and back so often in one forty-minute period it was like turning pages. I had ended those periods with the odd disoriented feeling that neither state was real.

I don't know if it was my memory or Gabe's conspiratorial shrug or

Rob's infuriating demands that made me do what I did about this special work project for Gabe.

I said, "We're adults. We don't do punishments here. That's stupid. Go to bed. Sleep through afternoon zazen. Set your alarm so you're up in time for dinner and do the evening sittings. There's no sense in your being dead on the cushion for days."

"Shall I tell that to Rob?"

"Tell him the roshi's assistant told you it was okay."

He gave my shoulder a little punch, and I only flinched a smidge.

"I owe you, Assistant."

Then he winked! Or it looked like a wink in the half-dark. I was so furious with myself I said, "Well, Gabe, you can pay up—"

"Yeah, I should've paid up by bringing you your letter here instead of leaving it on your bed."

"Letter?"

We didn't get mail here. The mail carrier didn't trot nine miles into the woods to drop in our box.

"I picked the mail up on my way from town. Figured it might soften the blow from being late. Now, maybe if I'd had a nice package for Rob—"

"You didn't happen to notice the return address on my letter, did you?"

Who could be writing me here? No one knew I was here, no one but my family and Yamana-roshi. Yamana couldn't have gotten a letter here unless he overnighted it, unless it was vital. About Leo? Or Aeneas? Leo and Aeneas? How bad would it have to be to overnight a letter?

He hesitated. "I glanced, but I was in a rush. Jog my memory."

"New York?"

He seemed to be pulling the tail of the memory out of his head.

"Omigod, San Francisco?" Mom? Something happened to Duffy?

"What's in San Francisco?"

"My family."

"Your parents?"

"Yeah."

He looked down. "No. It wasn't from San Francisco."

"You're sure?"

Gabe's hand was on the door. But now he turned back to assess me.

"Yeah, I'm sure."

I hesitated and in that moment I saw his expression shift from the upward furrowing of strategizing to the downwardly scrunched brow of one drawing back with regret. I wondered what was behind that, but I was so relieved there was no letter telling me Duffy had run into the street or choked on an anchovy—his favorite—I couldn't do anything but sigh in gratitude. It was only when Gabe shifted to leave that I grabbed the chance he offered here.

"Tell me about Aeneas's disappearance. What happened that day?"

His whole face relaxed, and he gave a conspiratorial nod and leaned back against the shelf behind him.

"Got you already, has it? Did you read up on it in blog archives before you came? Or did you hear word of mouth?"

He wasn't even embarrassed. He assumed I was on the make, like him!

"Word of mouth," I said, choosing the safer lie. "But my facts are sketchy. I mean, I have no time line."

"Oh, well, that's easy," he said, glancing around for a ledge on which to rest his arm. The musty shed didn't offer a mantel-like support, and he ended up resting his left arm, somewhat gingerly, on the shelf above the cyanide. Rain rapped louder on the roof and the reminder that we were protected from the wet gave the small damp space a cozier feel than it deserved. "All I can tell you about is the day of the opening, the day Aeneas disappeared. I only got here that morning, so I'm not reliable on anything before. By the time I got here the Japanese roshis had been here overnight. They were old, frail guys. Used to being cared for in their own temples, used to sleeping in beautiful rooms, with walls and floors."

"Not tents, you mean?" Work period was going to start any minute. I didn't have all day.

"They don't go camping in Japan. In Japan they don't have dirt."

In spite of everything, I laughed. Poor old guys.

"So everyone's rushing around trying to make them comfortable, and there's no way they're going to be comfortable. Plus they don't speak English, so no one knows what they're not comfortable about. Are they thirsty? Do they want food? The chairs are too tall, and too wobbly. If they *had* been comfortable they sure wouldn't have been after a couple hours of that."

"But—?"

Gabe nodded approvingly.

"But one of them went into the zendo to check on something and discovered the Buddha missing."

"And—"

Gabe was enjoying this, making me ask.

"All hell broke loose. In an understated Zen kind of way. I mean your first thought at a Zen monastery opening is not that someone's going to pocket the Buddha. I think Leo just assumed the cleaning crew had moved it. Barry was elbow deep in food for the reception after the ceremony, so he wouldn't have noticed unless the Buddha was in the stew. It was Rob—well, you could guess that, right?—who went ballistic searching tents, just about turning out suitcases."

He leaned toward me, a hunger in his eyes. I couldn't figure whether that hunger was for an audience for his opinions, or a source of something he'd missed.

Outside something cracked. The clappers. The first call for work meeting. I made a 'come' motion with my fingers.

"Okay, okay. Here's what happened. They didn't find the Buddha. They had to do the whole ceremony without it."

"Surely they had another Buddha, or something they'd have had on the altar before. A Zen center running low on Buddhas is like the Forty-niners running out of footballs."

"Whatever. But Roshi didn't replace it. The empty space loomed over the ceremony. People could barely watch the priests. Honest to God, it was the weirdest Zen ceremony I've ever seen."

And it must have been one of the most embarrassing, for Leo. Poor Leo. Why had he let himself be so humiliated in front of the foreign dignitaries?

"But, Gabe, the Buddha's on the altar now."

He shrugged. "My information is that it turned up later. How much later or why I don't know."

Squinting in the dim light, he peered around until his gaze landed on a suede gardening glove. He snatched it up and began pulling at one finger, as if milking off his nervous energy. I was betting Gabe Luzotta was never still. He probably even tossed and jabbered in his sleep. But this time he wasn't just futzing for futzing's sake; he was avoiding me.

"You do know, Gabe."

"Not hardly. If I—"

"You know, and you'll tell me. You're looking at this as a potential story, right? Old scandal in Zen monastery lingers for half a dozen years. It has the makings of a *New Yorker* piece, particularly if Aeneas is dead. You think he's dead, right?"

He pulled the gardening glove taut.

"I'm going to lay things out, Gabe. I'm not a writer. I don't care about the story. It's all yours. But I need to know what happened and what *is* happening at this sesshin. You will tell me."

"Or?"

"Or I'll have a word with Rob and he'll have you out at the coast road by sunset, no matter what it takes. You know he'd love to have reason to be rid of you."

On movie sets, I'd faced down professional tough guys. Some blustered, some caved, some saved face, but some swallowed hard and considered the long run. I couldn't swear to it, but I think Gabe swallowed before he let out a huge laugh. Then he punched my shoulder.

"Assistant, I knew I liked you. I just didn't know how much. Okay, you're on, but it's not going to be as free as you think."

I waited.

"You gotta share. Whatever you find is mine, right?"

"I don't—"

"This is a deal breaker. I'm not shitting you. I need documentation. Unimpeachable documentation. You gotta share what you find."

The clappers clacked right outside the door. We both jumped. The timekeeper must have heard him laughing. I just hoped the guy hadn't heard anything else. I picked up the bucket of kindling.

"Bring those logs to Leo's porch."

"Hey, I want a handshake, Assistant."

"I'll be straight with you."

He blocked the door. "That's not the same thing."

"Take it or leave it." I stuck out my hand and we shook. But to me it meant only what I'd said, and to him it meant nothing at all.

I waited a minute after he left, considering two things. The first was what I now remembered about Gabe. His name *had* sounded familiar because he had a low-level fall-guy notoriety in New York. He was like the running back who fumbled on the goal line in the playoff game twenty years ago. His name wouldn't ring bells unless the topic was hanging onto the ball. In Gabe's case the topic was unimpeachable documentation. Gabe Luzotta's misfortune had happened five or six years ago, well before I'd moved to New York, and by the time I heard the story some details had gone missing. Gabe was not the writer of the fraudulent story that spawned the major scandal; he was the poor guy who had submitted a piece on kickbacks that snagged the spectacular Chinese Temple Diamonds Exhibit for San Francisco instead of New York. The piece, a natural for the *New Yorker*, had been documented well enough to squeak by a month earlier, but was poison in the wake of the scandal. The *New Yorker* had nixed it, and then no one else dared touch it. "Paste Diamond Gabe" he'd been called. Paste Diamond Gabe been cited in definitions of *schlimazel* more than once, though I'd heard the depiction wasn't quite accurate. Poor guy. I'd felt sorry for him when I heard the story and a lot sorrier now that I knew him.

Could Gabe have been at the opening to do a story on it? Not likely; even with Leo's history, it hardly made a magazine piece. An odd coincidence? Whichever, it wasn't anything I could settle now.

The second, and more pressing thing, was seeing the group at that opening. The ceremony was planned as a big event. There would have been a group picture taken. I just hoped no one had destroyed it. Group pictures, I've noticed, illuminate the group more than the individuals. It was a long shot but what I was desperate to see was some clue about Aeneas. Why had the star student suddenly lost it that day of the opening and raced through the grounds waving a gin bottle? Was he acting out some obscure koan in which he insulted every teacher there, the elderly eminent Japanese, and his own teacher? Or had he been a diversion while the Buddha was being snatched?

I was, I realized, asking a lot for a group photo.

The clappers resounded in the distance. I had just time to build Leo's fire and slip into the work meeting on time. That would have been the wise move. Instead I slipped out, along the path to the adjoining office, and went inside.

CHAPTER THIRTEEN

O

The clappers sounded again—three clacks—as I stepped out of the shed, ran under the overhang and into the office. Six or seven minutes to find a photo from the opening ceremony, make some sense of it, and get to work meeting before Rob started wondering about me. After that, there'd be Roshi's fire to conquer. All before I could grab a minute to slip into my cabin for my letter.

The office was the size of the two-car garage I had slept above at a friend's house. Two Japanese screens—black on white with one red accent each—divided the area into a large and small room. The larger part was a surprisingly appealing space crowded with two soft and shabby leather chairs, sagging damask couch, and a heavy round oak coffee table strewn with magazines like *Wind Bell*, *Turning Wheel* and *Tricycle*, Zen magazines, but magazines, nevertheless. A huge stone hearth took up the entire end wall. It was a raised hearth, with a granite ledge in front where the cold, wet, tired, lonely, or frustrated Zen student could sit, hug knees to chest, and let his back get dry and warm to roasting. When the chill was gone, he could reach over to a little cabinet beside the hearth, grab one of the four mugs and pour himself a cup of tea from a pot heating on a hook over the fire.

Four mugs. Leo, Maureen, Barry, and, more lately, Rob. So they were the only residents. *But who were these people?* I tried to squeeze a sense of them from the room.

It was such a bare bones place, and yet the only spot of comfort in the whole monastery complex. Everything here must have taken on over-whelming importance. The arrival of each chair and rug must have been cause for celebration, with Barry, Maureen, and Rob running excitedly to the parking lot as Leo pulled up with the green leather recliner in the back of the pickup. Maureen would be the one to climb right up, plop in it, and give the thumbs up. Barry would give a great sigh of appreciation that would shake his bear-like body, and Rob—

No wait, I had the picture wrong. It would be Rob driving the truck, because it would be Rob's money from selling his law practice in San Francisco or from ongoing, much smaller legal fees up here that would have made possible the purchase of even a used recliner. And Maureen might still clamber up and plop into it, but she wouldn't be like a kid getting a gift beyond her imagining. She'd be the kid allowed to ride her cousin's new dirt bike, play with her friend's beautiful doll, sit in the chair given by the friend who would disdain her pleasure in it. Every time she or Barry sunk down, it would be an indictment of their unseemly attachment to comfort. Rob's austere patronage would forever hang over it.

I had never done without, but as the youngest I had worn clothes that had been through three sisters, and not recently. "This is a perfectly good sweater," Mom had said as she held out a woolly item out of style longer than I'd been alive. Cold or dowdy had been my choice, and I'd been cold a lot. I'd envied my only-child friends. And I'd resented each of my sisters individually as the damp wind chilled an arm for Katy, the other arm for Janice, and my whole back for Grace. There'd been days I sat shivering, ignoring the teacher in every class till lunch period, as I wholeheartedly *resented*. So I could imagine what Barry and Maureen felt.

I had wanted to come to sesshin, but by the time it was over I'd be dying to go home. The idea of living here permanently was ghastly. And living here, alone, with three other people not of my choosing—It made me want New York so much my lungs hurt. And it made me think of those four in a different light. The commitment they'd made so they could practice Zen awed me. Even Rob. Because of them, the rest of us could drop in for sesshins like this. What could it be like day after day, year after year out here? Had two of them had passionate encounters on that sagging damask couch? Screaming fights over the magazine-strewn table? Whatever, the strength of their commitment to this monastery amazed me.

The clappers sounded again. No time for speculating. I made a bee-line back into the office section and tried the central desk drawer. It slid right open, revealing nothing but pencils, pen, paperclips, letterhead, and an array of rubber bands that made me sure no incoming band had ever been discarded.

The clappers hit, softer in the distance. The timekeeper was already moving toward the meeting site.

The left-hand drawers held old schedules, lecture notes, and pages of notes I couldn't decipher. But there, under those sheets, enlarged but not framed, were photos labeled "Opening." Three of them, eight by tens. I pulled them out and glanced hurriedly at each. They looked to be of the same subjects, taken in succession the way you do just to make sure you get one shot in which no one moved. I chose the one on top, the one someone eyed last. Aeneas would be in this picture, as would the person who killed him.

The picture showed about twenty people pressing in together in three rows in front of what looked like a huge half ball that had to be the unfinished zendo. The porch hadn't been built yet and the crawl space under the zendo was visible. Sun shone bright, glistening off the shaved heads of the two elderly, tiny Japanese dignitaries in the front, a younger, larger one in the middle row, and off the long blond hair of the woman beside him. A breeze had lifted her fine hair and held it out like a bridal veil. There was a fragile, delicate, almost translucent quality to her skin and her unexpectedly bared forehead. Her dark, wide-set eyes and too-wide mouth looked tentative. I couldn't stop staring at her. Maureen. She could have been the daughter of her present self. The difference wasn't one of wrinkles or sun damage, but something hard to tether to words. When she ran across the quad yesterday her connection to the earth had appeared tenuous. A mere six years earlier she had looked as if floating on a wind current was her natural state and rarely would her feet graze the soil.

As I scanned the other figures in the photo, I realized the reason I was drawn to Maureen was that everybody in the photo had been drawn to her. Barry, at the end of a row, was eyeing her quizzically. Rob—it took me a moment to place Rob because in the photo he looked like a mix between present-day Rob and Justin—was smiling at the camera but his shoulders were turned toward her as if to allow him to shift his gaze the instant the camera shutter closed. Leo stood in front of her and was leaning toward her. And the Japanese teacher next to her stared outright, smiling like a possessive child.

The Maureen in the photo was the just-born gazelle, struggling to stand on quivering legs. All around her were hands eager to be extended, to draw her up, draw her in, to keep her in their corral. I wondered if she had been aware of the affect she'd had with that seductive combination of ephemeral beauty and need.

The clappers—

No, it was the door. It banged open. The photo slapped onto the desk. For a moment I couldn't fathom the woman in the doorway. Unable to stop myself, I did the worst thing possible: I stared at Maureen standing rain-bedraggled and rushed in the office doorway, then back at the picture of her six years earlier. My mouth was actually hanging open. I knew, in that way you can see screens of truths lined up like computer windows, that my shock was not for the reason she would assume, and that I would never be able to convince her of that and she would always think I was horrified at the aging of the startling beauty in the photo.

I wasn't. The girl in the photo was a white bud just beginning to open and the woman in the doorway, dripping and draped in an old brown anorak was the open rose. Maureen's face was still thin, her cheekbones clear, but her skin had a firmness to it. The spidery lines around her dark eyes suggested life lived, not merely hoped for, and the set of her mouth evidence of opinions developed. Her skin was no longer alabaster but the not-quite-faded tan of the outdoors woman. Her hands were not out to be held, but out pointing to the pictures. It was only then that I realized she had spoken.

When I looked up blankly, she repeated, "What are you doing with those?'

I must have blushed three shades of purple, as if she'd caught me going through her e-mail. I opted for truth, of a sort.

"I'm taking them to Roshi." And before she could ask why, I held the photo out to her and asked, as innocently as I might had Roshi sent me for the photos of the opening, "Who's who here?"

Her eyes did not widen in surprise nor cloud with sadness as they might have on seeing long forgotten pictures, but there was no way to tell whether she had glanced at them yesterday, or studied them a year ago. She ran her finger across the figures, naming names unfamiliar to me. The only ones I recognized were Leo, Rob, Barry, and Gabe, looking even brattier at that earlier age. I wouldn't have recognized Amber under one of the worst permanents in hair history, a huge, dry, blond bush. She was staring at the Japanese teacher diagonally in front of her, the roshi who was staring possessively at Maureen.

Pointing to the bald figure in front of Amber, Maureen said, "Aeneas."

"*That's* Aeneas?" I said, shocked.

The Japanese roshi wasn't Japanese or a roshi. Shaven-headed, round-faced with eyes half-closed, Aeneas blended in with the Asian roshis rather than with the Americans. From appearance he was the last person in the world to lose it after the ceremony they'd all been planning for months. I peered closer and could see that the similarity was not so much of features, but of stance, of expression, of entitlement. Now that I knew he wasn't a roshi, I assessed him differently and thought there was something of a junior high school eagerness to the way he looked at Maureen. He could have been about to raise his fingers behind her head to make devil horns, or, as easily, use those fingers to grope her.

Then I realized the mistake I had made—one any fresh viewer would. It wasn't Maureen at all who was the center of attention. It was, standing close beside her, Aeneas. Barry was eyeing him quizzically as if unsure what his motivation was. Rob was keeping watch out of the corner of his eye as if he knew only too well what Aeneas was up to. Aeneas was definitely leaning toward Maureen, but now I could see her shifting away. And Leo? Damn. I couldn't read him any better in that frozen moment than I could now. Still, whatever their individual fears, they were all focused on Aeneas.

"Maureen," I said, "you remember this picture being taken, right?"

"Yes."

"In a group photo the photographer is usually shouting, 'Bunch together, so we can get everyone in.' But you're leaning *away* from Aeneas—"

She leaned away from *me* and if expressions could lean away hers would have now. In the distance the clappers struck, or perhaps it was a branch creaking in the wind and rain.

"Maureen? What was it about Aeneas?"

". . . devil." Her voice was almost a whisper.

"Devil?" Surely I had misheard.

"You know the story of the man who buys a devil in a cage."

She jolted back again, this time from her own words. And then she was gone.

The man is in the bazaar, in Japan maybe. Long ago. A stranger is selling a devil in a cage, cheap. The man haggles a bit, but the devil is a very good buy. Smugly he pays and takes the cage, ready to leave. But the seller stops him and says, "This is a very fine devil; he's smart; he will work sunrise to sunset and never need to rest; no job is too menial for him, none too difficult. But there is one thing you need to remember: each morning when you let him out of the cage you must give him a list of tasks that will keep him busy all day long till you put him back in his cage at night. He must never have free time. He is a fine worker, and a very good devil, but he is a devil, after all."

The buyer nods perfunctorily and carries the devil home in the cage.

The next morning, the man gives the devil a list that covers an entire page: scrub the walls in every room, clean the bathrooms, prepare all meals, rake the yard, scrub out the iron pots. And the devil works steadily from dawn to dusk.

On the second day, the man gives the devil an equally long list of jobs and the devil works equally hard.

And so it goes, day after day, month after month. The man is very pleased with his devil and thinks how lucky he was to have come across him so fortuitously in the bazaar.

But one afternoon the man runs into an old friend in a bar, and the two of them get to talking of old times and drinking sake: they have dinner, toast each other, go on drinking and talking hour after hour. Night passes, and the sun rises before the man stumbles home. As he nears his house, he smells smoke. Suddenly, he remembers the devil, and the warning the seller in the bazaar gave: You must give him a list of tasks that will keep him busy all day long till you put him back in his cage at night. He must never have free time; he is a devil, after all.

The man quickens his pace, stumbling into a run, fearful for his house and what his uncaged devil has done. The smoke is thicker. He rounds the corner onto his street.

But his house sits where it had always been, fine and unharmed.

Sweating with relief, the man walks through his house, out into the back yard. There he finds the source of the smoke. The devil is standing by a fire, roasting the neighbor children on a spit.

CHAPTER FOURTEEN

O

Maureen Heaney ran stumbling up the quad. Rain lashed her face. If only she could run full out, keep running, never stop. How could she have let those words out? To this stranger? The danger Aeneas had always been. And that *she* was the one Leo counted on to keep the devil in his cage?

The panic was back! Panic like she hadn't felt in six years, not since she'd come here. This place had been her sanctuary. Now the panic was going to smother her again.

Ahead on the path a man bent to tie a bootlace. He hunched over his foot, all lumps and jagged lines of inefficiency. There was no arc of release as he stood, no rounding down to check the other boot, no music to his movement. She stopped dead. It was like she was still a dancer, like the last six years never existed, like she was still in the ballet company. She was seeing him as she had back then, when bodies were instruments and movement was all. When her life was dance. Everything she did—what she ate and didn't eat, who she talked to, watched, what classes she took, how many hours she could get to practice—all for that one hour in one performance when she could be under the lights on the stage, dancing. Everything for that magical time, the flying jetes, the perfect adagios.

But then pressures crowded her out: shin splints kept her from training; there were the new pieces she couldn't practice, the new girl with better body lines, the new artistic director, the jobs she needed in the off-season. Solos that should have been hers—snatched away. A broken tarsal bone. The new girl in *her* role. Dancers avoiding her. Classes she couldn't afford. And the director, always him. No chance to dance. Flat-footed, all of life lead-footed, foggy, hopeless.

But here, in the zendo, in the garden she'd found focus again.

Until now, with the new girl with the better jisha lines . . . and now, again, Aeneas. No, she couldn't think about him again, not now.

Her arms enwrapped her so tightly her hands grabbed not elbows but the back of her ribs. Her breath barely moved. The fog was floating around her.

She could not let herself fall apart, not again. She stamped her feet to feel the uneven macadam under them. She had to hold herself together, remember what she had learned here, and what she had to do now.

The cage was open; the devil was free now, and Leo . . . Leo was on the spit.

Chapter Fifteen

O

Maureen dashed into the work meeting even later than I. All I could think of was the devil story, and wonder who Aeneas had roasted on a spit. Maureen looked sweaty and distracted, but no one else seemed to notice. And when I tried to catch her eye, she looked anywhere but at me.

As for everyone else, they were standing, half-asleep from having been roused out of bed so early. Some were clutching coffee cups without hope. Work period is a shock to most new Zen students . It's where the rubber of meditation practice meets the road of slights and rudeness and work beneath one's station.

Everyone is expected to attend work meeting even if he is in the middle of another sesshin job. Dishwashers wiping soapy hands on aprons stand in the circle while their pots soak in the sink. The cook, already chopping cauliflower for the next meal, puts down his knife. It's not uncommon for the teacher to stop work on his next talk for the ten minutes of the meeting, or to pitch in all work period lifting rocks, sawing wood, or pulling weeds.

Because of the rain, today's meeting was inside, in the one place twenty-six people thick with sweaters, sweatshirts, and waterproof parkas could fit—the kitchen. Barry's winnowing machine had separated all the nibs from cacao bean husks and its rattling had ceased. But the washing machine-like melangeur was grinding away, and Barry was peering into the tub like a washerwoman who'd dropped her glass eye. The smell of cacao wafted alluringly through the room, and more than one person inhaled deeply and smiled.

Maureen sounded the clappers once and we all bowed together. Then she began assigning people to crews. The three women friends who had been wrapping shawls around their shoulders as they headed to the first sitting period last night made up the cooking crew: Barry was to be in charge of it. The zendo cleaners, headed by Rob, were Amber, Justin, Gabe, and the man who looked seventy years old. Afraid to find Gabe conspicuously absent, napping away under the blanket excuse I'd given him, I made a quick, nervous survey of the group. But he was standing next to Amber. *Right* next to her, poking her playfully as Maureen corrected a mistaken assignment she'd just made. Seeing Gabe made me yearn anew for my letter he'd left on my bed.

"Frank Appley, chiden," she announced, assigning care for the altar the tall sandy-haired guy who had whispered so urgently to his wife or girlfriend and then kissed her ear before they both walked nervously up the zendo steps. The two lucky bathroom cleaners, who would get to spend the next hour in a warm place, were the recipient of that kiss and a bushy-haired man whom I remembered running back to the dorm as if he'd forgotten something irreplaceable. A plump woman with blue-tinted glasses would be washing windows inside the zendo. Everyone else was assigned to a catch-all "facilities crew," which would sweep out the dorms and cabins, and do whatever ground or building work was possible in this weather. They were to report to Maureen. As for me, I was assigned to "Roshi duties," which was good because I hadn't started his fire. We'd all be at it for an hour and a half, after which we'd wash the onion or mud off our hands, change back to zendo clothes and take our seats to be served a cup of hot tea. In some zendos—*fine zendos*—"tea" included fruit or a cookie. As the group bowed before disbursing, I wondered, again, what seeds had been planted in that similar group in the photo six years ago, to flourish so viciously now.

Rob whipped out the door. Amber trailed after, dragging her feet and scowling.

"Housework!" she grumbled as I came up beside her. "Two weeks of cleaning the damn floor. Just what I'm dying to do."

I nodded. "Amber, did you see a letter on my bed? The guy you were just talking to dropped off a letter for me."

"You got a letter!" she said, suddenly all eagerness.

"Yeah."

"Already?"

"Presumably so."

"Who's it from?"

"Amber, how would I know that? Gabe just left it on my bed; he didn't read the letter. Did you see it?"

"No."

"Are you sure?"

"There wasn't any letter. It's not like we're sharing the bridal suite. I could spot a white envelope on a blue sleeping bag. I mean it wasn't like a tiny black 'we're so sorry' from the Big Buddha Bakery. Trust me, there was no letter."

"Rats," I snapped.

I had vital responsibilities here protecting Leo. My missing letter was trivial, my reaction petty. I grabbed two bowls from the cupboard, plunked them down harder than was good for ceramic ware, ladled out soup from a vat cooling on the stove, and grabbed four slices of bread. Tomorrow I would look back on my pique as foolishness. Today wasn't tomorrow. I knew this was sesshin-overreaction. I'd been enraged about trivial things in other sesshins, as if the general deprivation made even the shabbiest trinket golden. It was an integral feature of sesshin, this chance to see one's attachments in all their grasping glory. But now, as then, I didn't care. I just wanted my letter!

I hurried across to Leo's cabin. I had only been gone fifteen or twenty minutes, total, but as I stepped inside I realized I was holding my breath, lest . . . But Leo didn't look dead. For the eight hundredth time today I wished I had insisted on getting him to a doctor. I couldn't judge his symptoms. He was wheezing like a city bus, like his pipes—his nose—had become too small for the job. His skin was sweaty and off-white, as if the tan had been sucked out of it. The color had leeched from his wide lips, and his high cheekbones seemed to have sunk into his face. I wanted to roll him onto his side so he'd breathe better but I was afraid to wake him. You don't wake a sick person, right? But if they just go on sleeping—This was like choosing between door number one and door number two.

Leo continued to wheeze. The soup continued to cool. I busied myself bringing in wood and attempting to start the fire, concentrating on leaving air space underneath. It took me nearly every bit of newspaper in the room to get the logs to catch. I had the impression Leo opened his eyes once and made a soft appalled sound but I couldn't be sure. When I turned around his eyes were closed but he was facing me. I suspected I, too, had been making soft grumpy noises. But when the logs began to burn and I could actually feel the fire cut through the chill in the room I was flying high.

"If only we had marshmallows," I said aloud.

Leo's eyes flickered open. I took that as a good sign. "I've brought you soup from lunch. It's lukewarm. I could put it in your teakettle and heat it over the fire."

Leo groaned. It was the same sound as before, only louder. "Kettle's for tea."

"Okay, then let's eat it as is. You feel well enough to sit up?"

He nodded slowly. I don't know whether I was more surprised or elated. I knelt behind him and pushed him up. He was solid for a little guy. Sitting, he automatically crossed his legs, and I tucked the top blanket around him.

He asked, "How long have I—"

"—been asleep? It's work period. Afternoon tea will be in about an hour."

"You go, then."

"We'll see."

"Go," he said in his roshi voice.

I nodded, figuring I'd decide later. Now that he was upright, he looked weaker, paler. I was afraid he'd drop the soup bowl and sodden lumps of cauliflower onto his blankets.

He must have had a similar thought. He said, "Just broth."

I poured, and we consumed, he sipping tentatively, me watching him between big gobbled mouthfuls. I ate my soup, his rejected vegetables, and three slices of bread and had hope of a cookie at the end of work period. He sipped as if checking his innards after each swallow to make sure of the next bite's welcome. He was eating, but he wasn't talking.

I wanted to say, "What the hell is going on in this place? What do you *think* happened to Aeneas? Maureen called him the devil. What did Aeneas do when you took your eye off him? What were you all hiding? Not only that but what about the purloined Buddha that reappeared? And why did you leave the altar empty during the opening ceremony? And the biggie: Why did one of your own students poison you?" But shaky and stubborn as Leo looked I'd be lucky to get one answer out of him, and, I was guessing, it wouldn't be to any of those pointed questions. I waited till Leo put down his bowl.

"Roshi, you said I should be your eyes. There's a lot going on here. For instance, you've been poisoned. So, who should I be watching?"

"Watch yourself."

"Roshi, I'm not asking a Zen question, I need practical advice!"

He caught my eye and said nothing. His silence said: Zen is life as it is; what can be more practical than that? But I didn't have time to deal with that, not now.

Before I could adjust my question, he said, "You're upset. Why?"

I stared at him as if he was crazy. "You've—been—poisoned!"

"No. Something else. Something personal to you. What?"

I flushed; I could feel my face flame as red as my hair. Was my pique that obvious?

"Gabe said he brought me a letter, left it on my bed. But Amber said there was no letter. If she had seen a letter she would have tracked me down and demanded I read it aloud to her. Gabe must have put it in the wrong cabin. Now I won't get it till dinner."

"What does it say?"

I stared, shaking my head. I might as well have Amber for a teacher! "Who's it from?"

"Leo, *Roshi*, I don't have the letter. How could I know?"

He tapped his head.

I shrugged.

"Help me lie down."

I thought he meant: end of discussion. But when I shifted him back down he was dead weight and I realized how weak he really was. I tucked the blankets back around him, stoked the fire, dealt with the chamber pot, packed up the dishes, and started toward the kitchen.

People were settled into their tasks now, shaking out the mats on the zendo porch, shoveling rivulets of mud that had overtaken the paths. Work period provides new and often foreign venues in which to observe one's reactions. The path shoveler, a lawyer from Vermont, was having the opportunity to see his hour as not merely non-billable, but as a nuisance to everyone who needed to cart supplies along his path. As a member of the landscaping crew wheeled his barrow by, the shoveler was able to experience being the victim of a splashing with no recourse, legal or even verbal. In a similar position I had managed to nurture a rage for an impressive number of days, until, quite suddenly, I had realized that stopping work, stepping back, even being splashed were as much parts of the job as the shovelfuls of mud. After that, I'd viewed egotistical directors differently, taking their unnecessary demands and nuclear tantrums as all part of being a stunt double. In theory, anyway.

The Vermont lawyer stepped aside silently as a gray-haired guy with a less lowly job bustled by with his supplies. But by the time I came abreast, he let out a mighty sigh and made a show of sweeping back his shovel, sending a spray of water over his feet.

I didn't laugh, not from virtue but because I was still fuming at Leo and his bizarre reaction to my letter. My feet were smacking the wet path with each step, sending angry sprays in their wakes. The bowls rattled on the tray. At the bathhouse I stopped, took a deep breath, and determined at least to *appear* under better control. Veering toward the kitchen I walked more slowly, listening to the rain tapping on my shoulders.

Somewhere between bathhouse and kitchen it became clear just what Roshi meant about my letter. The letter could be anything! It could be an offer to change my long-distance phone coverage, to contribute to NOW, subscribe to *Harpers* for twelve dollars a year.

That was all Roshi had meant.

Or was it?

Life is illusion.

I stopped dead. A guy with his parka hood drooping low on his face smacked into my shoulder, mumbled, and rerouted himself. *Life is illusion* is one of the basic Zen tenets. I had created my own illusion, and now I was racing around acting on it. A better Zen student would have taken time to let this discovery sink in. I, alas, was not that student. I couldn't resist trying to answer Roshi's practical questions. Who did I think my letter was from? What did I think she was saying?

She was saying.

I started to laugh and then almost choked. *She* could only be my mother. Mom, why did I think it was from Mom?

But the letter hadn't come from San Francisco. Gabe had been sure of that.

I smiled. Knowing Mom she would have figured a letter mailed in San Francisco would linger a day from box to post office to main post office before even crossing the Golden Gate. She'd have maneuvered to get it to a post office north of the Gate to give it a head start. There might have been a lunch in Sausalito with my sister, Katy, inasmuch as they were going there anyway.

Two women squeezed by me on the path. I stepped off it into the mud. My running shoes squished into it; I ignored it. Mom was the only one who would worry about her tough stunt-double baby up here in this strange place. Mom worried about anyone who had to venture beyond the San Francisco city limits.

No, wait, that wasn't right. The letter in my illusion wasn't filled with worry, it bubbled with urgency, something she could tell only to me. Mom had worked hard to be a good parent to my older siblings and their success had rewarded her. But I was her child of menopause, her "joke from

God," and lots of rules got jettisoned in my upbringing. Each of my sisters had had to cook one dinner a week solo. But I got to help Mom and grump and gossip and share secrets the other kids never guessed she had. What couldn't she wait to tell me now? That, I didn't have to ask myself twice. I was smiling again. She was telling me—again—about the Big Buddha Bakery on Irving Street. Thirteen or fourteen years ago, when I was living in Chicago, I'd said was I going to check out a Zen center and she had sent me a newspaper clipping with a picture of the green, big-bellied Buddha painted on the bakery window. I was twenty-five and outraged, and more so because I feared I would be sacrilegious to crumble up and toss a picture of the Buddha. When I flew to New York to sit my first sesshin with Yamana-roshi, Mom couldn't resist a later shot of the Big Buddha, who had lost some of his paint by that time. I had barely moved to New York to become his daily student when a copy of the picture arrived with a note saying, "In case you don't remember! Laugh."

I stepped back onto the path, squishing with each step now, still smiling at the memory—no matter what the letter really was, it couldn't warm me as much—and yet, it left me out of focus. I was here smiling at the thought of Mom and her sweet idiosyncrasies, and at the same time, I burned with the same indignation I had when I was twenty-five. There had been some scandal about the bakery but Mom had only mentioned that in passing, because what amused her was the big-bellied olive green Buddha painted on the window of the bakery. Mom had remarked, dryly, "That shade of green is an unfortunate color for an eating establishment."

I washed out Roshi's and my dishes in the kitchen, amidst students slipping in for shots of caffeine before the afternoon sit.

"Did you find your letter?" Amber whispered as I was putting the bowls away.

"No, but I can imagine what it was."

"What?"

I could see in her face what Roshi must have seen in mine, the letter taking intriguing form in her mind. But his teaching was for me, not necessarily for her.

I said, "A reminder about the Big Buddha Bakery."

"You mean the poisoning?"

Chapter Sixteen

O

"Poisoning in the Big Buddha Bakery?"

Amber leaned toward me and grinned in a way that reminded me she wasn't much older than a teenager. She looked about to divulge a really really cool piece of gossip about the scuddiest geek in the class, a piece of gossip her friends had already yanked and pulled in every direction till it was too old and thin to taste. But now, here was I, a new audience.

"Yeah. It was in all the papers. Thing was it was a long time ago. I was in, lemme see, seventh grade, I think. 'Cause when I heard it I was so freaked I dropped all my books and that was the year I had serious Spanish and world history, and that history book was so big I could've been carrying the whole world around and when I dropped it it just about broke my toe. It was sprained and I had to wear sandals for a month and this was January. I mean my feet were soaked. I mean I didn't eat peanuts for a year after that."

"Peanuts?"

"Shhhhh!"

It must have come from as many directions as Amber's answer was

139

taking. Barry was tapping his mouth in the other end of the kitchen; Maureen was at the door, glaring; one of the cooks held his wooden spoon clear of his pot and stared, another chopped louder. Work period wasn't quite over. Amber had no business being in the kitchen at all now, much less gossiping there. I put my palms together and bowed an apology to all of them. They were right. I nudged Amber and she bowed, too. But her heart wasn't in it.

"Outside," I whispered to her and she followed me around the corner of the kitchen, onto the muddy thatch of weeds. Her face was flushed with excitement.

"You didn't eat peanuts for a year?" I prompted. "Tell me about the Big Buddha Bakery."

"Now?"

"Quickly."

"You dragged me away from a chance at coffee for *that*?"

"What else?" I said irritably.

"Well, I mean, you know, you've got connections and all here, I figured, well, that you'd have something for me, I mean, like chocolate."

Frustrating as she was, she was such a little kid I had to keep myself from smiling. And yet, I could see her point. I'd felt just like that about my letter.

Amber hissed, "I'm tired of standing in the mud here when I could be—"

I grabbed her arm.

"The Big Buddha Bakery?"

"Look, I told you what I know. I don't remember anything else, except that peanuts grossed me out after that and I must have told my boyfriend and he must have told his friends because all the boys kept throwing peanuts at me in the halls and—"

"Amber!"

"Hey, stop bugging me. We're supposed to be quiet here," she said with such a tone of righteousness that I couldn't keep myself from laughing. She started to giggle.

"Amber, you must remember something."

She shook her head.

"What about Justin? Or somebody. Somebody must know something."

"Ask Barry. He's from San Francisco. He'll know."

It was so obvious, I felt stupid for having missed it. Of course, Barry would know what happened, ingredient by ingredient. Dessert cooking was a small world, and word of whatever happened would spread fast. The bakery might well have no connection with Buddhism but its name. But friends of Barry, a Buddhist, would have made sure he was kept current on the affairs of the Big Buddha Bakery, particularly if they were silly or scandalous.

But *poison*! I did not want to associate poison with Barry, even the idea of him knowing about another cook who had something to do with poison years ago.

The clappers clacked on their third and final roll-down now. I ran to the zendo, crowded up onto the porch, and, like everyone else, balanced on one foot while pulling off the other boot and scanning the shoe rack for an empty space to store the pair.

Inside the zendo, the sweet smoky smell of incense welcomed me. I bowed to the altar and walked to my seat, bowed to it, and to the room. Across from me, Gabe's cushion was empty. This was the afternoon I'd given him permission to sleep, and even angry as he'd been in the shed, he'd probably be snoring by now. I glanced at the altar where the Buddha sat serenely, as if he had never been stolen. But it was Gabe's use of the zendo that taunted me: He sat in here thinking about his story. I was sitting in the zendo thinking about Aeneas, about Barry, and the Big Buddha Bakery poison. I was no more sitting zazen here than he was. The zendo was a bit warmer now from the body heat. By tomorrow the bite of the cold would dissipate and only the early morning sittings would be icy.

The tea servers walked smartly to the front of the zendo. One bowed to the sesshin director and held out a tray from which he could choose a cup. Other servers bowed to pairs of us, extending their trays to one and then the other. We chose among the small handleless mugs, and bowed with the server as she left to move on. She returned with the teapot, and finally, a tray of cookies, of which we were allotted one each. The cookies were warm, rich with chocolate chips. Here, in the silence, I nibbled, letting the warm chocolate coat my tongue with its lush sweetness. The batter I rubbed between tongue and roof of mouth, savoring the coarseness, the salt of the butter. Even the tea—green—I sloshed in near silence around my teeth. On my left, Marcus, a curly-haired guy in brown wool, sighed. Outside, leaves scraped against leaves, something tapped on the roof. For that moment I didn't think about Aeneas or Mom or the Big Buddha Bakery or Leo or me. For that moment I was just aware of the taste and sounds, the air on my skin, the smell of damp wool. It was an unimportant interlude, but I did think of mentioning its clarity to Roshi as I went out to check on him in the walking meditation period that followed. But he was still asleep and I merely stoked the fire and headed back to the zendo, skirting a couple of guys coming out of the bath house.

"Psst!"

A ladder was leaning against the zendo. Hissing down at me from halfway up the ladder was Rob, black robe billowing out behind him like a pirate flag fluttering in the gray sky. Rob was pointing to the zendo roof.

"Branches caught under the shingles. Flapping. Heard it in zendo. Can't have it banging all afternoon and night. Use the broom. Stand on the third rung so you can reach the top." An odd smile flickered on his mouth. "Be careful and you won't fall. It's only twelve feet up. It'll only take a few minutes."

If it's so easy, why don't you do it yourself? Why the smile before "you won't fall?" I wanted to ask. But in sesshin we do what we're asked to. So I flashed Rob a smile, trotted up the ladder, and onto the roof.

"Don't—"

His wary tone jarred, and it reminded me who he thought I was—the terrified woman he'd pulled out of the cab yesterday. I took a step down the curve of the dome and I glanced down to savor his surprise.

Rob was almost to the top of the ladder. He was wide-eyed, but not from shock; he was terrified. It was the same look that had passed across Kelly Rustin's face when she'd first seen the depth of the canyon she'd be sailing across in the wire gag, before she knew the wire would snap. It must be the same rigid expression I had when I looked down at her from above the trees, the look I had every time I saw the woods. Before I had time to think, I had braced my feet, thrust out a hand and yanked Rob up onto the zendo roof with me. Too taken aback to resist, he lunged and landed on all fours, quite safe. He sunk to his knees, shaking. I could only wonder what people doing walking meditation in the zendo below imagined.

Wedging the sides of my feet, I walked to the top of the dome. Rain sprayed. Wind blew it against my face. Leaves swirled up from the branches stuck in the roof; branches snapped at my legs. Rob cowered just beyond the top of the ladder. Everything was inside out. A week ago, when I was hanging onto the canyon wall staring down at the trees, my skin had gone clammy; sweat had coated my face, my neck, my back, I couldn't breath, could hear only the deafening drumbeat of my heart. Now I was dead calm, but the panic swirled outside me, in the rushing wind, in the desperate thump of the trapped branches, in Rob's blue-white face. I felt it, but it wasn't mine. Here, on this curved roof, I was on my turf. I reached a hand to Rob.

"Hey," I said in a voice that sounded foreign to me, "we've both got rubber-soled shoes. If the branches stick, so will we. Shift your feet like this. Come on, up to the dome where it's flat."

He didn't move, looked like he couldn't, like the twelve-foot drop was a hundred. The wind snapped his robe; in his mind it had to be on the verge of carrying him away. His taut face was sepulchral; in the afternoon light the sweat on his skin glowed. There was nothing I could say. I had no answer for him or for me. And yet I had to say something. This whole situation was mine to deal with.

I said the first thing that occurred to me. "The photos of the opening, six years ago?"

His head jerked in what I took to be the smallest of nods.

"I recognized you, of course"—I was trying to keep my tone conversational, despite the snapping of the branches against the roof, the hiss of the wind. "You haven't changed. But Aeneas looked so much like the Japanese roshis, it was like he was already in Japan."

"He was . . . in his mind."

"Really?"

Sweat dripped off Rob's nose and chin; the wind carried it off. His legs twitched spasmodically. The ladder was right behind him, but in his mind it could have been on the far side of Roshi's cabin. Thoughts swirled in my mind. If I could show him how to walk down the ladder he would be free, *I* would be free. He knew about Aeneas; facts that could help me save Leo. Needs knotted my stomach: him, me, Leo, Aeneas. How ludicrous it was that we were standing on top of the zendo, right over the Buddha.

Words left my mouth as if by their own accord. "Rob, about the opening? The Buddha? Who took it?"

"Aeneas."

"Aeneas stole it?"

"No, he didn't *steal* it. He just assumed it was his."

"How could he—?"

"Because—" Rob lifted himself like an arthritic cat, fear compressing each move, the straightening of a knee an inch by inch process, the moving of a foot requiring virtually an Environmental Impact Report, "—Aeneas figured he *was* the Sixth Patriarch." He stood, leaning so far forward toward the curve of the roof he had to bend only a few inches to pick up one of the brooms. "But you knew that all along."

Knew that? "Rob, what makes you so sure Aeneas took the Buddha?"

"I found it in his luggage, where I knew it would be."

"Wha—"

He had the broom; he was standing, swinging it like a cudgel.

"Watch out!" I yelled.

Too late. My feet flew out from under me and I went flying off the roof. I grabbed for the ladder and held on; my momentum sent it sailing away from the zendo into the open grounds. Below, someone screamed. I shot a look down; the ground sloped away sharply. If the ladder flipped, it would fling me like a pea in a shooter.

"Help her!" someone yelled. I twisted, pulling back. The ladder jerked. My other hand was on it now and I shifted forward. People were running toward me.

"Get away!" I yelled.

If I let go, the ladder would fly up into my stomach. In one last burst, I flung myself backwards. The ladder jolted; I slid down, landing hard on the ground, barely keeping the ladder from banging on top of me. Suddenly people were all around me, grabbing the ladder, asking if I was all right. The splatter of words resounded after the day of quiet, and for a minute the sense of aloneness that pervades sesshin transformed into a mesh of concern.

It was another minute before I stood up, turned around, and noticed Rob, still standing on the zendo roof, still holding the handle of the broom. I couldn't tell if he was shocked, sorry, or just too terrified to move. His expression revealed nothing. And when someone propped the ladder back up and held it for him, he clambered down so fast he jumped the last steps. He hurried over to me.

"Are you okay?"

"Sure."

His hands were on my shoulders, he was looking me in the eye. I expected him to say how sorry he was, that he had lost his balance, grabbed the broom, and in his panic flailed. He said not a thing, merely clapped my shoulders, turned, and strode off.

I started to walk, like I do after a stunt, heading to the second unit director to see if it was a take or not, focusing totally on the mechanics of the shoot. But now, suddenly, reality doused me. Without my stunt training I'd have broken my neck, or landed on my head, or broken enough bones in arms or legs to leave me laid up for weeks.

Like Roshi! Like Roshi, I could be not dead but conveniently out of the way. So much more acceptable to those who take vows not to kill.

"Are you okay?" Maureen asked from behind me, just about jolting me off my feet.

"Fine," I snapped, shifted the ladder free of the zendo and headed to the shed, making a show of balancing the ladder in the middle lest anyone else intrude with their help. I must have been curt enough to make my point. Maureen backed away and no one else came near me.

I tried to replay the seconds before the broom hit me. Had Rob really swung at me, or had he panicked on the roof, grabbed the handle for balance, and swung wildly? Had he meant to apologize and couldn't handle that either? Or were things exactly as they looked?

My stomach went queasy; I was shaking. The ladder rattled. I shifted my hands so its weight would settle them. What kind of place was this where a senior student throws a woman off the roof? What kind of lunatic was Rob?

The ladder smacked into something and slapped me backward. I staggered along, intent on avoiding hitting people as I maneuvered the ladder toward the shed, trying to calm myself with the pretense that I was on a movie set, after a gag, merely moving a prop. If this had been a movie, the shove off the roof would have been a diversion; the important focus would have been the revelation right before: that Aeneas took the Buddha and Rob retrieved it from Aeneas's luggage where he knew it would be.

CHAPTER SEVENTEEN

S uddenly, the ladder went light at the back. Gabe had come out of nowhere; he was shifting it for two-person carry. I was still shaking from the roof, but I was so relieved to see Gabe, the one person I could trust, the only one who hadn't been here when Leo was poisoned, I could have hugged him. The rain was heavier; the afternoon wind water-picked my face. Talk from opposite ends of the ladder was impossible, but Gabe called out directions. He was moving at a half run, pushing me from his end of the ladder. I was happy just to move.

But as soon as I stepped into the dark shed and put down the ladder all the thoughts I'd blocked out flooded back. Roshi's earlier comment about the disappearance of the Buddha, that nothing was irretrievable, except what someone didn't want to tell you to begin with. Had Rob really swatted me off the roof? Why did he want me to know Aeneas took the Buddha as Rob knew he would?

Gabe propped the ladder against a wall.

"You okay, Assistant?"

"More shocked than anything. Did you see what happened?"

"Rob swatted you off the roof."

"Intentionally? Did he really intend to push me off?"

"Well, it looked that way, but hey, no! Not even the Asshole would pull something like that. Look, Rob's a lawyer, always thinking three steps ahead. He wouldn't attack you in broad daylight."

"Big comfort," I muttered, trying to sound a whole lot calmer than I was. "And what was with Rob and Aeneas?"

"Aeneas?"

Gabe looked as if he was about to question my shift of focus but reconsidered. He inhaled deeply, leaned back, arm on the self, posed like a professor about to pontificate. "Here's the thing was, Assistant, Aeneas was golden. Rob worked his tail off. He studied sutras, sat sesshin after sesshin, didn't move when his knees were killing him. You know I'm not Rob's biggest fan, but I gotta give him this: he's committed his life to Zen practice. He could have been a seven-figure lawyer in San Francisco. He was shrewd, cleaned up good, knew people; he could have had whatever he wanted. But you can't keep telling the judge to postpone trial so you can go sit in front of a wall. Even back then, when this place was just starting, he had arranged to sell his practice and buy a way smaller one in town up here. He'd made his commitment to this place. But, look, the key to him is, he's still a litigator; he still plans ahead and definitely still intends to win. He didn't come here to be second banana forever. He signed on at the ground floor of a new monastery with a teacher not likely to go the distance. Odds were good that he could sit, study, succeed. He'd already done that in law; why not here?"

Zen is not statutes and motions, but I didn't divert Gabe with that, not when I'd be diverting back to the issue of the Buddha in a minute.

"And Aeneas?"

"Aeneas outstripped him in everything. And Rob couldn't figure out how. He'd watch Aeneas, trying to catch him studying texts he didn't have, practicing intonation of Japanese chants in private, meeting secretly with Roshi. Aeneas was a resident, and Rob was here only on weekends; he figured he was falling behind every week. It drove him crazy. He was obsessed. Plus, he was sure Aeneas was putting the hit on Maureen."

"Was he?"

"Not from Maureen's reaction. But, Rob couldn't see that, because the thing was *he* wanted to put the hit on her, but he didn't want her to blow him off because she was with the first string guy." Gabe snickered. "Here's the real hoot: she didn't want either one of them, but no way either of them got it."

"Really?"

"Well, she's had plenty of time since. I've been to sesshin pretty much every other year here and I've never seen a sign. Believe me, I've looked."

Gabe shifted to about-to-pounce posture.

Before he could speak, I said, "When Aeneas took the Buddha, Rob searched his luggage because he knew it would be there. Why is that so important that Rob make a point of telling me even when he was shaking with fear up on the roof?"

Gabe started, and even in the dim light, I could see things clicked in for him. He knew what it meant, but he said nothing.

"Goddamn you, Gabe, you're hoarding this for your big story, aren't you? That story that's going to save your career, right? You've come to how many sesshins every other year, but always as a reporter, right? And you're still here as a reporter!"

He shrugged.

"What could possibly be a big enough story to keep after it all these years, for all these sesshins? Rob's jealousy? Aeneas thinking he was the

rightful successor? Aeneas's disappearance? I mean, who cares? What is
the big story?"

He put a patronizing paw on my shoulder.

"Assistant, if I gave away that, you'd know I was no reporter."

"Well, are you? Still?" I hissed, "Or are you just desperate to resurrect a dead career?"

His mouth dropped open—my attack was a low blow, particularly to
him, the paste diamond schlimazel—but before I could say anything he
snarled, "Oh, right, Assistant, like you came here to sit zazen and save all
sentient beings!"

He pulled open the door, just about knocked into an old guy headed
inside with a bucket, and left the door banging after him. I cleared out of
the shed quick. Once I was outside, the light or the fresh air or something
gave me perspective on what had just happened in the shed. I'd learned
by repetition with Gabe, and this time it didn't take me as long to realize
that this blowup with Gabe wasn't about his flagging career or whatever
story he was after here to make up for his big story years back that got
rejected because he couldn't produce the research. That was all smoke
thrown up to cover his reaction to Rob telling me Aeneas stole the
Buddha and Rob knew it would be in his suitcase.

That silly little incident should have been nothing. Why was that so
important? To both Rob and Gabe?

I made it back into the zendo just as the bell was ringing to start the
afternoon sittings. I bowed, sat on my cushion, and turned to face the
wall. There was a lot to think about, but here in the zendo I wanted to sit
zazen. I wanted to recapture that luscious moment in the wide unhurried
present that I had so enjoyed minutes earlier. I wanted to prove Gabe
wrong about me. But the exhaustion from the travel and the early wake-
up and the worry over Leo engulfed me. I nodded slowly forward, feeling

nothing but the release of sleep, until suddenly I jerked awake, straightened my back, took a deep breath, and felt my breath flowing in, flowing out, jerked awake. The pattern repeated time after time. I slept, dreamed, jerked awake so suddenly I couldn't remember more than that I *had* dreamed, and that the dream had been clearer than this reality in the zendo facing the wall, but the content danced beyond the edges of my mind and I was too tired to draw it back.

The second zazen period was much the same. I tried to focus on my breath, but slipped into dreams, jerked awake to recall images too fuzzy to give name to, and Amber saying—

I jolted in my seat, awake now. Amber wasn't in my dream. She was outside the zendo window. What was Amber doing outside? Students are expected to be in the zendo for scheduled sittings.

I glanced to my left. Her cushion was empty. I strained to make out whispered words. But all I could catch was the flirty tone and the familiar cadence in Gabe's voice. Without thinking I let out such a disgusted sigh that Marcus jerked in his seat. Even Amber and Gabe must have heard, for now there was silence outside. Damn Gabe Luzotta! I'd stuck my neck out to let him nap and here he was trotting around the grounds chatting up women like he was at a cocktail party. Soon he'd be in the kitchen demanding cheese puffs and prosciutto-and-melon hors d'oeuvres.

I sat, viscerally aware of my annoyance in the clench of my teeth, the lift of my shoulders. When the final bell rang I walked stiltedly to Roshi's room.

Leo was lying on his side, his head propped with a hand. He looked gray in the dusky gray of his ill-lit room.

"Don't hover."

"Excuse me?" I said, confused. "This is suppertime. We agreed I'd come by now—"

"But not earlier."

"I didn't, earlier."

"Darcy, I *heard* you on the porch. I heard the door open and shut right away."

"Open and shut quick? Well, it wasn't me. I've been in the zendo all three periods." Now I was worried. Open and shut: a quick getaway for someone who'd been spotted? "Someone else was on your porch. When?"

"Help me up."

I lifted him, appalled by how shaky he was. He sat crossed-legged, back propped against his one thin pillow, blankets stuffed around him like a baby bird not quite cracked out of the egg. He was so helpless here. I wanted to wrap my arms around him and keep him warm. I compromised.

"Is this one of those endless Zen silences?"

He laughed, weakly, but it was definitely a laugh. It almost made me weep. Was it only yesterday we were in the truck laughing?

"Yes and no," he said.

"Yes?"

"Yes, it was an endless Zen silence. And no, it probably was during zazen, not kinhin. I think I did hear three bells before the scuffling on the porch. I owe you an apology."

"I'll just use that as credit against the next time I speak out of turn." *Scuffling!* I poked at the insipid fire. "So the person was on your porch while the rest of us were in the zendo?" I paused and it was a moment before I realized I was waiting for him to protest about innocent motives and overreactions. But he maintained the Zen silence, and this time I could see its point. He wasn't creating his own illusions about the porch; he knew he didn't know. "Leo—Roshi—this is serious. I can't watch everyone out there. Gabe and Amber were both outside during zazen. It's partly my fault about Gabe, but I didn't mean for him to be wandering around chatting up girls—"

"Gabe!" he said, shaking his head. The familiar grin passed over his face. He was more in control now that he'd been sitting up a minute. "Hot for the ladies, Gabe. He's never made it through a sesshin without a flirtation. Before the opening he was in San Francisco interviewing a woman from the Asian Art Museum who was leaving for China, so he rode up here with the San Francisco contingent. By the time he arrived, six hours later, he had three dates set up with three different women. If the curator hadn't been leaving the country he'd had dinner scheduled with her on the way back."

"Still—"

"Right. Yes. We can't let people wander when they are to be sitting. Bad for everyone, particularly them. And Amber?"

"The thing is," I said slowly, "for Amber, sitting is torture; she's grasping for distractions—"

"—shouldn't have let her come," he mumbled.

A cluster of replies crowded my mind—*Don't blame yourself, there must always be applicants you aren't sure about.* And *Why shouldn't you have?* And *Damn right.* But he was still talking.

"It's asking too much for a first sesshin."

"She hasn't sat sesshin before at all?" I said, amazed.

"No."

"Then why—"

"I thought she needed it. I thought having Justin here would help her."

"Au contraire."

He arched an eyebrow questioningly.

"I don't understand." I could hear the frustration in my voice. But dammit, Leo cared about his students. It didn't make sense that he would let this kid come up here to go bonkers for two weeks. And come to loathe Zen practice in the process. "She doesn't want to be here. You don't think you should have let her. What's the point of her being here at all? It's driving her crazy and she's looking for trouble."

He listed to the right. I grabbed him.

"Help me down."

"Can I get you—"

"No."

He looked exhausted. His eyes were already closing. I should have let him alone, but the prospect of spending the rest of the evening and all night trying to protect him, trying to figure out what and whom to protect him from, and knowing so damned little was more than I could bear.

"My point is that I can't protect her. I can't protect her, and I can't protect you, because, Leo, I don't know what's going on here."

He seemed to pull himself back from sleep by will alone. "What do you need . . . in order to protect her?"

"I need to know about Aeneas. Like why was it such a big deal that he stole the Buddha off the altar, and that Rob knew it was him."

Leo may have raised an eyebrow or maybe I just imagined it. I thought he was going to answer my question, but I did just imagine that. He sank back and his eyes closed.

I stoked the fire, made tea. He didn't drink it, but it seemed right that it should be there waiting. This morning the oil lamp had given the room a Spartan air, but tonight the added light of the fire gave the cabin an eerie, unsafe safe feel. When the bell rang in the zendo I pulled out a cushion here and sat. I wasn't facing Leo, but somehow I had a clearer sense of him than when we were talking. I had thought he'd slipped into exhausted quiet sleep. But he wasn't asleep; he was thinking. And that was the answer to my question. He hadn't thought about Rob's knowing Aeneas stole the Buddha as being important, but now he was. He was thinking about it a lot.

Chapter Eighteen

O

By the time I got back to my cabin after my final check on Leo, Amber was snuggled so far down in her bed that only a thatch of her golden hair revealed her presence. I shone my flashlight around my bed, but there was still no sign of my letter. The cabin was icy, the floor carpeted with our bags and clothes. I undressed like a November tree in the wind. The only sounds were the soft thud of my feet in thick socks and Amber's wheezy breathing, each exhalation a great sleepy sigh of one happy finally to be in bed. All the time she'd been sitting cross-legged in the zendo, she'd have been yearning for the moment when she would crawl into her warm bed, stretch her knees straight, and let her eyes close without having to jerk herself awake. I hoped she'd held off sleep long enough to enjoy it.

Next to Amber's raincoat by the door I stashed my boots, ready for me to slip quietly back into them in the dead dark of 4:10 A.M. From the look of her, though, there wouldn't be much danger of waking her when I crept out. I stepped back to turn off the oil lamp. It was then that I heard the telltale squish, felt the spreading cold, and knew the awful truth. My sock was wet. An arctic pool was soaking ever-wider in the wool, turning my cold foot into an iceberg that wouldn't thaw at all tonight. I'd stepped in the puddle from Amber's raincoat.

I think—I know—that's what tipped the balance. A dry-socked woman would have let her roommate sleep. I shook her.

"Amber?"

Digging around in my duffel for another sock, I hissed, "Amber!"

"What? Is it morning already?"

"No. Night."

She turned over.

"Amber!"

"What?" she snarled sleepily. "I don't have your damned letter. Gabe left it in the wrong cabin."

"When did he tell you that?"

"Dunno," she mumbled after one of those pauses that screams *Lie!*

"It was him you were talking to when you weren't in the zendo during zazen this afternoon."

"So! What're you going to do, report me to Rob? Is he going to tie me to my cushion?"

As furious as she was, she still wasn't really awake. If I stopped prodding she'd be back asleep in seconds. And, in a few days she'd be strolling through the woods, poking into buildings, and chatting up anyone she could find.

"Why did you come to a sesshin as hard as this? Why one this long?"

"Leave me alone!" she wailed.

"You've never sat a day of sesshin."

"So?"

"So why not join the Olympic Ski Team?"

"Huh?"

"What are you doing here? Just tell me."

Her eyes closed. I couldn't decide whether she was trying to crank her mind up for a decent lie or going to sleep in spite of me.

Finally she muttered, "Roshi called."

"What do you mean, *Roshi called!* Roshis aren't stock brokers; they don't make cold calls to round up business for sesshins. Students apply for sesshin and just hope they're lucky enough to get in. What do you mean, Roshi called you?"

Unleashing a great sigh, she heaved herself over onto her stomach and plunged her arms under her breasts.

"When he found out Aeneas had never gone to Japan he called to tell my parents. But they don't answer the phone anymore; I do that for them. Even if they did they wouldn't have talked to him."

"Aeneas is your brother?" I said, astounded.

I stared at her huddled in her red sleeping bag like a kid on an overnight. How could she have a brother who had walked off into nothingness? I thought about my own brother. How could she bear this enormous grief? Just hours ago she was giggling about boys throwing peanuts at her. I was still staring, expecting her to transform, to age before me.

"Yeah, my brother," she said as if commenting that she was considering lavender nail polish.

I swallowed my amazement. In a lavender nail polish voice I said, "What did Roshi want?"

"To know if Aeneas had called us, of course. Well, of course, he hadn't. Aeneas didn't use the phone."

"After he disappeared, you mean?"

"Well, ye-ah."

I pulled a dry sock from my suitcase. Still standing I pulled it on. "Your parents blamed Roshi for Aeneas's disappearance?"

"Not entirely. I mean, they did and didn't. You know, they wanted to blame someone, and so sometimes they did, but the thing is Aeneas had gotten strange before he ever came here. The last couple years he lived at home he wouldn't touch the phone." Her sleepy face quivered; I thought she was going to cry. She was looking down at the floor beyond her pillow and when she spoke I had to strain to make out her words. "I adored him . . . when I was little. He was the best big brother, he always took me with him everywhere and he was, like, happy to have me there, like I was some special expensive gift he'd been given. He was always happy."

Her face had gone pink; her voice was shaky. I dropped down beside her on her futon and sat rubbing her shoulder, willing myself not to think of my own family. She smelled of cream and peppermint from either muscle ointment or a stash of sweets.

"And then," she said, "I guess he was about fifteen when he started getting strange. He was ten years older than me."

"Strange? More than with the phone?"

"Quiet. At first that's all it was, just quiet. I had started to school, so I didn't care so much that he didn't want to have me with him all the time. I mean, I didn't realize that it was that he didn't *want* me, I just figured . . . I don't know what I thought. I mean, I was six years old. But first it was the phone, then he started staying in his room more—most of this I got from what my parents said later, you know? He started making rules. I mean, my mother would say, 'Don't brush your teeth with hot water.' And he'd say, 'How cold does it have to be?' And she'd say, 'Well, just let it run a minute.' Then that was law for him, and he had to do it for sixty seconds, not"—she started to swallow and ended up gulping back tears—"not sixty-one."

I rubbed her shoulder softly, giving her time to pull herself together.

"When you're quiet, people don't always notice your strangeness, right?"

"Yeah," she said, surprised. "How'd you know that?"

I shrugged. "No wonder Aeneas made such a great facsimile of a Zen student. Sits quietly; adores rules. He must have been in heaven here."

"He was," she said, and despite the irony of my question she spoke of him in the soft tone of pride. "When I saw him that weekend the Japanese roshis came, he was, like, walking on air. He knew every line of every ceremony. He could do all the chants in Japanese. I mean, he always was really really bright anyway, and a better mimic than anyone I ever saw. But here he was a star. And Roshi really liked him, and the Japanese were really impressed."

"Amber," I said slowly, hating to bring up the stains on this cherished memory of him, "I have to ask you this. The Buddha on the altar at the opening, did Aeneas—"

A guffaw exploded from her. The shock of it threw me back, and I watched as she turned toward me, still laughing. She pulled the bag around her shoulders. "The Buddha the Japanese brought, did he lift it right off the altar? Yeah, of course. He liked it. So he took it." She was staring at me now, and my shocked expression made her laugh all the more. "Darcy, it was funny. I mean, I knew the minute the Buddha disappeared that Aeneas had snagged it. It's what he did. He had no sense of boundaries. He used to pocket things in stores in San Francisco. Little Buddha statues, staplers— for some reason he adored staplers—pens, other odd things. At first it really scared me; I mean, I was still a little kid and I knew you shouldn't steal. It could have been a big problem, but the thing was Aeneas didn't want most stuff. But when something attracted him, he just figured he should have it."

"How did you handle that?"

"Luck. We were really lucky. Part of the not-wanting thing was that once he did pocket something it slipped out of his mind. You know, as if he wanted the 'wanting' more than the actual thing. So when I saw him pocket something, I'd distract him. Then I'd borrow his coat, take the thing out, and return it. I got so I could do it all in under a minute. Even in shops, we never had a problem; I always got stuff back before we left the stores. But I had to watch him all the time."

"Didn't your parents—"

"They couldn't have handled it. I just made sure Aeneas never went to a store alone."

"You were in grammar school?"

"Yeah. I was in junior high when he came here."

"That's a huge responsibility for a kid. You must have been so relieved when he came here—"

I just caught myself before speaking the last two words: *and died.*
When he came here and died.

Suddenly the sadness of it was too much. Sweet Amber's sweet, helpless brother. How could he have died, here, in this place where he should have been safe? I wanted to clasp Amber to me, to ease the gnawing around the hole, to fill her emptiness.

Her round sweet face tightened like an apple suddenly dried, as if all the life had gone long ago.

"It was a miracle; that he found a place he could fit in, where he could shine. A miracle. My parents said that all the time. When I told them how central he was to everything at the opening, it was like their son had graduated from Harvard. They loved it that the important Japanese teachers focused on him. Like he wasn't crazy, didn't have a tumor or some weird disease; he was just in the wrong place before. But now, in the monastery, with the Japanese masters, he was a star." She took a breath, and her face relaxed back to normal. "So, like, when we heard that he'd gone to Japan we weren't surprised. My parents were worried about him being in a foreign country, but they were proud of him, and really, really relieved."

I had to swallow before I could say, "But your parents didn't really believe Aeneas went to Japan, did they?"

"Why'd you think that?" she demanded. But before I had to answer, she slumped back on her stomach, face propped on forearms, gaze into a neutral distance. "Yeah, okay. You know, the Japanese taking him, it was too happily-ever-after to really accept. And then when Roshi called and said Aeneas didn't go to Japan, it made sense."

As I listened to her twisting what had been said and what might have been, a cold dread filled me. Roshi had said Aeneas never went to Japan. He didn't say he'd gone anywhere else. But Amber was hanging onto that belief. I knew I should ask her, but I couldn't, not yet. Not yet by far.

I swallowed hard, and again, and forced out, "How'd your parents take what Roshi told you?"

She shook her head and when she looked up at me it was with a different, far less innocent expression. "They didn't. Why would I tell them? It wasn't like that changed anything. It'd only be a new obsession for them. That's what they've got left of Aeneas; now *they* obsess."

I was impressed, and not a little shocked that she could be so controlled.

"So you came to sesshin to find out, right?"

"Yeah."

"And Roshi let you."

"He didn't want to, but I guilted him into it."

I was about to protest that Zen masters don't act from guilt, but in this case, maybe Leo did. Guilt would explain why he let a novice come and why he put his assistant in the cabin with her. Why he introduced this sesshin with the question of Aeneas. Why he was doing exactly what Yamana-roshi warned him against.

I sat in the dim light, looking at her in a vague half-seeing way, thinking about long-gone family, a brother vanishing, and feeling sad, knowing I shouldn't let her go on hoping for a brother who was dead, and being unable to yank away that hope—

And then words burst out of my mouth in such a flurry I only half heard them. But I did hear Amber's reply. She cocked her head and stared at me as if I had asked where the nail polish bottle was, the one I had in my hand.

She said, "Aeneas isn't dead. We never thought Aeneas was dead. He sent us postcards every couple years."

I sighed so heavily she actually laughed.

"From where?" I asked.

"A temple in Kyoto, and later a temple in Seattle, one in Vancouver, the Japanese garden in Portland. My parents were hurt to think he'd gotten back here on trips or vacations and hadn't called, and I actually had to remind them about him and the phone. Someday he'll send a card with a return address, and then I'll go get him."

Tears glistened in her eyes, and mine. I felt a huge wave of relief as if my whole body had been frozen in tension and now the sun had come out. I exhaled long and luxuriously. Only then did I feet the backwash of suspicion. "But the postcard from Japan? How do you explain that? I mean, he never went to Japan with the Japanese masters."

"He must have had one of them send it for him. They liked him; they would have done it as a favor." She pulled her arms back inside her sleeping bag, and snuggled down on her side, her unclasped blond hair spread over her head like a fluffy kid's blanket. "I only had to think about that now, after Roshi's call. Because, see, it was easy to imagine Aeneas charming the Japanese masters. When I was a kid he'd take me downtown to Union Square or Coit Tower. He'd listen for tourists, and soon he'd be 'talking' to them. He was such a great mimic he could almost pass himself off as anything. He picked up sounds, just enough words in their language to make them wonder. But it was more than that; he stood like them, gestured like them, his face was their faces. When he was doing it, he was one of them. It sounds like he was mocking them, but that wasn't it at all—Aeneas would never be cruel; he just wanted to mirror them. Like stealing the Buddha; he just wanted to steal who they were for a minute. People were never offended. They were charmed. It was like they had met the one really tasteful person in all of San Francisco."

I swallowed; even the thought of the question I was about to—*had* to—ask, filled me with a cold no shiver would ease. "Amber," I said, "did he eventually become only that? A mirror of other people?"

She nodded. Then she bawled. I pulled her to me, let her sob on my shoulder until the cold and wet forced us both back into our sleeping bags. It must have been the first time she had really wept for Aeneas, the sweet brother who became no more than a mirror. I thought of the tale of the Sixth Patriarch, the first student's poem:

> *The body is the Bodhi-tree*
> *The mind is like a clear mirror standing*

And the Sixth Patriarch's retort:

> *The body is not like a tree,*
> *There is no clear mirror standing,*
> *Fundamentally nothing exists*

Fundamentally, Aeneas did not exist, except as a mirror. People see through their own eyes, Yamana-roshi had said. With Aeneas it must have been so easy for them. And the descriptions people had given me of Aeneas were not of him at all, but of themselves.

Eventually, I blew out the oil lamp, sure that I would lie awake in the cold dark, wondering about Aeneas who lost his self, and about Rob and Maureen and everyone who mistook a mirror for a man, and were afraid. And Amber, who admitted her brother didn't go to Japan after the opening, but nevertheless believed he was in Japan.

Chapter Nineteen

O

WEDNESDAY

R ain came sharp and hard, and worse, the wind was blowing. It was the kind of night to be tucked in bed, curled around a lover. But at 4:15 A.M. the kitchen was warm and bright in that cozy way of rooms lit when the world still sleeps. The winy bouquet of cocoa mixed with the aroma of coffee. Barry's winnower rattled companionably as it did its part to bring us cocoa. Best of all, Barry was alone in here. I stood for a moment, inhaling luxuriously. I was operating at capacity. One look at Barry told me he was, too. He looked as jumpy as a great bald bear startled out of hibernation. He wasn't even in his black robe yet, but still in sleep-rumpled gray sweats. He stood over the sink splashing water on his face again and again and again, inadvertently spraying the counter and a good bit of the floor.

"Barry, it's not going to help. You could step outside and douse your whole body and it would still be four-fifteen in the morning."

He jerked up. "I didn't realize— Oh, it's you, Darcy." He lurched over to the stove, rubbing a paper towel over his scalp like he was drying the outside of a bowl. "Oh, Roshi's cocoa. Oh, sorry, I was up till, till, uh, I don't know, uh, late."

I gasped. It was too early to control reactions. But another lethal cup of cocoa anywhere near Leo—no way. "That's okay. I'll just make him some tea."

"Didn't he like the cocoa? It was the old batch. Around too long? New batch . . . tomorrow. But I could, uh, make . . . He didn't like it?"

He stood there in his wrinkled water-stained sweats, his big feet bare on the floor, his thick hands open-palmed and held out as if begging for a redeeming answer.

"He didn't complain to me," I said truthfully. "But he said he's got a fever. 'Starve a fever,' right? He's better off with tea."

"A fever? Oh, I better make him special broth. I can . . ."

His worried gaze shifted to the steel table that had reminded me of an autopsy site. It was covered with yet another a layer of cacao beans. I wondered how many times during the night Barry had covered the table with criollos and sorted them, bean by bean. He had the stiff walk of one who'd spent the night bending over. I noticed a staircase behind him, which led to a loft. "Barry, do you *live* in the kitchen?"

It was a big kitchen, a warm, bright room, with access to food, drink, fire, and light. But it was still a kitchen.

"Huh?" Barry said, still rubbing his eyes. "Oh, yeah. I mean, I could have a cabin, but what's the point? I'm always here. When it's not sesshin, I haul in an armchair from the shed. But nights like now, I wouldn't get to bed anyway, not with the rain."

"The rain?"

"It's the chocolate. It's conching." He nodded toward what looked like a clothes dryer. "This is the key part, mixing the nibs with the sugar and lecithin. Too fast and it's grainy; too long and the volatiles float off and you end up with"—he looked revolted—"bland brown paste. It's the aromatic compounds that give chocolate its 'vive.' Time! Time is so short. I've got to finish conching, and the tempering, the cooling, and give it time to set, all finished so I can get down to the city by the weekend. No second chance. No *time*. But the way it's raining, I'll be lucky if the road holds till tomorrow."

He was scanning the room frantically, as if his precious time were hiding in cupboards and under pots. Reliable Barry had disintegrated. Suddenly I realized even this distracted Barry was going away. Tomorrow! That would leave me with only Gabe, and I trusted him only because he had arrived too late to poison Leo. I couldn't let Barry leave tomorrow.

"What are you doing with the chocolate in San Francisco?"

"The Cacao Royale, the international chocolatiers' tasting. The Royale comes only every seven years. It's vital for new entries."

"But you already sell your chocolate, don't you?" Maureen had said he supported the monastery.

"I do, but this batch will be a whole different class. The butterfly compared to the, uh, uh . . ." The simile was too much for that hour of the morning.

"Worm-like thing," I put in. "So you'll be down there with lots of old chocolate friends, huh?"

"Yeah. It's fun." The creases in his forehead eased, his whole face relaxed and he smiled. "That's if you don't mind eating like a pig."

I laughed. "Right, Barry, I'll be pitying you all weekend, particularly at dinner when I'm eating gruel."

I relaxed too. Barry was going to spend the weekend with his old cooking friends. If he had been involved with the Big Buddha Baker who poisoned his wares he wouldn't have been accepted back into the food fraternity, him or his chocolate. But here he was, rushing around to get his fine new chocolates down there to show them off. In fact, while he was there, maybe he could ask if anyone remembered the bakery scandal and if they recalled Aeneas hanging around.

"Barry, about the Big—"

A rush of icy air slapped my face. Rob hurried in and over to the coffee table. With his gaunt, drawn face, with his black robes hanging out from under his black slicker he looked like the Grim Reaper dropping in for a cup of java before his first kill of the day.

I picked up Roshi's tea and took a warm, wonderful sip of my own coffee. Rob stood drinking his slowly, as if tasting each drop separately.

"Barry," I whispered. "You were in San Francisco. What *did* happen at the Big Buddha Bakery?"

The beans dripped out of his hands back into the unsorted pile. He didn't seem to notice. He braced his two big hands against the edge of the metal table, and stared down. The table shook from the quivering of his hands.

"Barry?"

I don't think he would have answered me anyway, but at that moment Rob walked over shaking an empty milk carton accusingly as he veered to the fridge for a replacement. The outside door opened and Maureen stumbled in wiping her eyes. My moment had passed and I took the Roshi's tea and my coffee and lurched out in the blackness, not knowing what to make of Barry. I could only fear the worst, and hope the Roshi would tell me truths to clear this up.

Rob Staverford glared at the empty milk urn. Already things were out of hand in this sesshin, and it was only the third day. You can't run a sesshin for twenty-six people and have the cook up all night making chocolate, for commercial purposes yet. He'd told Roshi that Barry couldn't handle his precious chocolate and his responsibilities as cook; and he was right, as he knew he'd be, as Roshi should have known. Dogen Zenji himself said in the *Tenzo Kyukun*, "Put your whole attention into the work, seeing just what the situation calls for. Do not be absent-minded." If Dogen walked into this kitchen, the thirteenth-century master would be appalled. Do not be absent-minded, indeed. A mind could hardly be more absent than Barry's.

Students needed their days to start quietly; they shouldn't be forced into chatter about absent milk. Sesshin was a precious opportunity, not to be spoiled by the cook's personal preoccupation. Rob's jaw was clamped so tight flesh bulged at either side. His shoulders clenched at the very sight of Barry blithely making tea while the milk urn sat empty.

In the meantime, he poured milk into the container, checked the sugar and honey, and realized there was no bread put out for students who couldn't make it two more hours till breakfast. He grabbed a loaf, and made himself stop and take a deep breath so he wouldn't slam it down on the table. His practice was to do what needed to be done, not to condemn Barry or to remind Roshi that he, Rob, had been right, even though he certainly had, as any idiot could see.

When he stood up, he spotted the jisha, Darcy, still here in the kitchen. He flung back the sleeve of his robe and checked his watch. Four-twenty-two. She ought to have that cocoa in Roshi's hand by now. *He* always did. He'd really have to tell her—

But then he spotted Maureen. She looked more out of it than the other two.

Rob sighed and shook his head.

Maureen Heaney ran a finger across her tight forehead to free the tendrils of blond hair that hung flaccid over her eyes. This morning she had made the mistake of failing to avoid the mirror that accented her ashen skin and the dark circles under her eyes. She squinted against the glaring light in the kitchen. She hadn't slept at all, worrying about Roshi. She could barely focus. She had tried to act normal, especially with the new jisha, but that was yesterday. How was she ever going to get through the day today?

She stared across the kitchen. Barry was tense, too, but of course he would be. The Cacao Royale was a huge deal for him. He hadn't had his head more than six inches from his beans since they arrived; no wonder he wasn't worrying about Roshi. And Rob? Busy pouring milk. If she hadn't been so exhausted she'd have laughed. There was Rob pouring slowly so Barry had ample time to see his unvoiced censure. He could pour till Monday and Barry wouldn't notice, not unless he was pouring it onto the beans.

She didn't laugh—couldn't. Maybe Roshi had the flu, but always before she'd been the one he'd counted on. Now . . . what? What did this mean? What was he thinking? She filled her cup with coffee and gulped it black, even though she knew it would burn her tongue. All the coffee she'd drunk here—seventy-two months of coffee, coffee held in thick mugs to warm her fingers before she and Roshi walked to the office, or the garden or his cabin. Was Roshi making himself sick with indecision, with fear, with guilt? What ever possessed him to bring up Aeneas again? Hadn't they suffered enough over him? How could he think he could resurrect Aeneas and then just walk off ? And what about this place, was he planning to turn the place over to Rob and his ayatollah version of Zen? Was Roshi saying the last years had been a lie?

The cup bobbled in her hands. She just got it onto the table; the coffee splashed, scalding, on her hands. She shook it off, not bothering to see if it had stained her sleeves.

If Roshi denounced the last six years, what did that say about her Zen practice? She had stayed for him, trusted him as her teacher. If he was a fraud, what did she have? She had nothing.

She took another swallow of coffee, not tasting it, drinking it for the heat. She had to get in Roshi's face and find out what was going on; she had to do it today.

When I unlocked the Roshi's door, he was sitting on his bed, with his shoes on.

"Help me outside, Darcy. Quick, before people are out."

I pulled his parka over his back, grabbed a towel and hoisted him up. He was almost a dead weight. His ribs pressed sharp into my arm as I guided him down the three steps and around the side of the cabin so he could brace his arm against the wall and throw up. He did it just once. I wiped his face with the towel and then he said, "Bathhouse."

How we got there and how he got back out of there before the first student trudged in, I don't know. Even with them still dead asleep in their bags until four-twenty, Leo and I had cut it close. But when I got him back to the cabin, I could see the toll it had taken on him. He crumbled on the bed, wet parka and all. I had to roll him over to get it off and then roll him back to deal with his boots before I could get him back under the covers.

"I thought you'd prefer tea," I said pouring him a cup. "Barry made this for you."

I watched his face, but exerting the energy of reaction seemed beyond him. He held the cup with both hands, letting the steam warm his chin, the cup warm his hands. It was only then that I saw how wan, sweaty, how fragile he looked. Small and thin as he was, he had no reserves to fall back on. I had been so sure last night that he'd be better today, walking around on his own, maybe stopping in the zendo. But he looked worse now than any time since yesterday morning, when I assumed he was dead.

"Leo, you are a sick man. I've got to get you out of here."

"Can't."

"What do you mean, can't?"

"Rain." He sighed.

"Barry said the road would hold till tomorrow."

"For him."

"It's the same road for everyone!"

"No, Darcy, it's not."

"Leo!"

"Roshi."

He lifted the cup to his mouth. The china clattered against his teeth. His fingers press against the round surface; I watched, alert to jump forward if they slipped. I was focusing on the cup to keep from seeing how panicked I was, and how sick Leo was. He was my teacher, but he was also a sick, stubborn man.

"Leo—Roshi—my father had a heart attack when I was in high school. It was during the last Forty-niners game of the season, against the hated Rams. He'd eaten a lot of junk and he thought he had indigestion. He thought the pain in his arm was from hauling in the Christmas tree. The division championship was on the line and the score was tied. Dad was sure there was nothing the matter with him. He told my older brothers to leave him alone, he was their father and he knew his own body, dammit. He was still telling them he was their father, when Mike, my youngest brother, hauled him out of the chair and into his truck and to the emergency room, which is why Dad could tell that story later."

"Not your father . . ." Leo forced out in a voice barely audible. ". . . your teacher."

I stood where I was, halfway between the bed and the fireplace, just staring at his cup. It was the same cup he'd used for the cocoa. The cocoa that poisoned him, and the cocoa he poured onto the floor.

Suddenly I knew what that meant, him pouring the cocoa onto the floor Monday night. I knew so certainly I didn't have to ask him for corroboration. In the cup that luscious cocoa was cocoa. But when he poured that liquid onto the floor it was mess. The brown liquid was the same but utterly different. I looked up at him and I had the sense he could see the difference in me. What I knew, and did not say to him, was that he was my teacher, but at some point he would shift into a sick man. He'd be the same but utterly different. And when that moment came, the relationship between us would be utterly different and I would be responsible for him, just as Mike had been with Dad. I hoped that moment wouldn't come, but if it did I hoped I would recognize it. It hadn't come yet.

I turned and started on the fire-building. I didn't ask him about the road. I knew what he meant about that, too. It wasn't the same road for everyone. For Barry, tomorrow it would be a messy, jolting nine miles that would take him over an hour. For Barry, the ride would be cold because he'd want to keep the chocolate cold, and it would be tense. His mind would be half on that and half caught in worry about the rest of the drive south, the contest, his arrangements, and his friends. But for Leo, sick as he was, an hour's drive in the front seat of an old pickup with a poor heater and miserable springs would be torture. He was right: his road had already washed out. Yesterday, I had promised him my silence for forty-eight hours. One more day could be eternity for him, literally. But it didn't matter what shape he was in in twenty-four hours; he wouldn't be going anywhere.

When I finished the fire, Leo was sleeping fitfully. His face was blotchy and flushed and he was breathing like a locomotive on a too-steep incline.

I wanted to stay with him. I knew he'd want me in the zendo, sitting the schedule, supporting the normalcy of sesshin. His snore caught; he gagged. I lunged toward his mat. But before I reached him he had relaxed and was breathing normally. But that gag was enough. He had shifted from Roshi to sick man and I couldn't let this go on any longer. I'd send someone into town for the doctor whether Leo wanted one or not. If my decision was wrong, I'd just take the consequences

I stepped outside and smacked right into Rob. He pointed to his watch, and when I looked blank, he snapped, "Incense."

I'd forgotten about offering him the incense before he made the morning bows in Leo's stead.

I followed, automatically, my mind on the road. Already the road was muddy and the truck would have to maneuver the ridges and gullies, chugging along slow enough that anyone familiar with the grounds could race through the woods, get to a spot on the road first, and sabotage the trip. If I was going to send the truck into town, I needed to get it out of here before dawn, before breakfast. And most importantly, I had to decide whom I could trust.

176

CHAPTER TWENTY

O

I held the smoking stick of incense before me and followed Rob from the Roshi's door to the altar. Yesterday, I had held it for Leo. Since then the world had changed.

Rob completed his circle back to the far end of the bowing mat and began his three full bows before the altar. I walked to my seat, bowed, and sat facing into the room for this first period.

I should have used that first period to sit in the clear, fresh silence of the morning zendo. But the question of whom to trust was too urgent. Once I chose and handed over the keys to our one vehicle, that was it. If I guessed wrong Leo could die and we wouldn't even have a way of telling the world he was dead. No word would go out or any person come in until the end of sesshin. Whom to trust? Amber? No way. Not driving an old unreliable truck like that over a swampy road.

Did Rob and Maureen and Barry know she was Aeneas's sister? None of them had made any overture to her, nor were they giving her wide berth. They hadn't asked the basic questions about him. That meant that Roshi hadn't told them . . . because? Because he was afraid to . . . because . . .? Because he couldn't trust them.

Not Amber, not Rob, not Maureen, not Barry. Shit.

Gabe was sitting across from me. He looked as if he'd been there all along, his legs crossed in half lotus—right foot on left thigh, hands in mudra, left hand resting in right, thumbs together, and his head slightly bowed so that his dark curly hair hung like a thatched porch roof over his already stubble-darkened face. Even here in the zendo, his lips twitched as if he was just about to say something he shouldn't. I liked Gabe, but only an idiot would call him trustworthy.

Not Amber, not Maureen, not Rob, not Barry, not Gabe. Deep shit.

The bell rang, ending zazen, beginning *kinhin*, walking meditation. On cushions, we bowed, untwisted legs, and stood to begin kinhin. I had been checking on Leo so much I'd hardly been in the kinhin line. But now I turned left and walked behind Marcus, a virtual wall of brown wool. My hands were folded over my solar plexus, my gaze lowered, feet moving half a foot-length every breath. The intent of kinhin is to allow movement while continuing meditation. But breath lengths and foot lengths vary and lines do not flow smoothly at times. Now the line was barely moving at all. My nose was an inch from Marcus's bear of a jacket. Instead of moving half-steps forward I was swaying from foot to foot. As a meditative tool, it shouldn't matter which direction the feet go, but this kind of line hold-up, created by one person setting his own standards, oblivious to the crunch behind him, drove me crazy. In the bank, the Grand Union, the post office, I had to wait, but in the zendo I was not about to!

I stepped out of line, hell-bent for the miscreant.

I spotted him—Justin—just inside the door. Justin! It hardly surprised me. The stoicism of Zen is appealing to a certain group of ascetic young men. They are the ones who yank their legs into full lotus—right foot on left thigh, left foot on right—long before their hip joints have stretched enough to allow for the torque. If their knees burn with pain, that's their focus. If they can barely stand after each zazen period on feet gone numb, that demonstrates their ardor. If they require minutes before they are able to move forward in the kinhin line and others stack up behind them shuffling from foot to foot, they have no need to notice. And when, finally, they do move forward in the line they are scrupulous to move no more than the prescribed half foot-length per step.

Justin. Of course.

I tapped him and motioned him outside. He tottered out the door, hands still over his solar plexus. By the time he reached the far edge of the porch, he dropped his hands, and leaned down as if expecting to be given an important Zen task.

I whispered. "Can you drive a stick shift?"

He looked like I'd asked if he knew how to shave. "Yeah."

"Get your driver's license."

"But there are two more periods of zazen!"

"Meet me at the old yellow truck."

His face froze, then, as if the reality of the offer struck him, a grin spread across his cheeks.

"Hurry!"

I ran through the rain to the kitchen for a thermos of coffee. Barry was at the far end leaning over the side of his conching machine. If he noticed me at all, he must have assumed I was filling Leo's thermos.

As I hurried down to the truck I began having second thoughts. I was trusting Justin because I didn't trust anyone else. What did I know about him, except that Leo let him to come to sesshin to make things easier for Amber? And Leo had been wrong about him. Still, he wasn't an old-timer. He hadn't been here at the opening. That made me breathe more easily.

Justin was already behind the wheel when I arrived. I climbed in beside him and handed him the thermos. The overhead light blinked, turning Justin's shaved head into a beige light bulb with deep-set eyes and long narrow nose that threw his mouth in shadow. The truck smelled of damp and of cacao beans and in the dark it seemed filled with Leo in his knit cap, talking about his plastic forks collected from truck stops all the way to Canada.

In the driver's seat Justin was pouring coffee. I had guessed black for the coffee—he was a no cream, no sugar guy if I ever saw one—and when he unscrewed the top he gave a brisk nod of approval. He poured a bit in the cup, handed it to me, and took a swallow from the thermos.

I'd paid no more than cursory attention to him before, but now I surveyed him: Late twenties, average height, but short-waisted so that sitting he appeared smaller than he was. His lean body looked to be not the result of exercise or even heredity but of a predilection for self-denial. His clothes, though, fit well and were not the second-hand garb of those who disdain Mammon. The anorak looked new, and too warm an item for the mild winters of San Francisco. But, although he'd obviously bought it for this fortnight, it was a mite snug. There would be no room under it for an extra sweater to insulate against the cold, no chance of his stoic form being overlooked. This type of garment always came in olive, khaki, and navy, but he had chosen a dark burnt orange that suited his Nordic skin and set off his blue eyes. Stoic on the outside; but what on the inside?

I sipped the coffee he'd shared automatically. There was no one else to trust with our only vehicle *and* Leo's health, and yet . . . What was he inside?

"Justin, have you been here before?"

"Not since the opening."

Oh, rats!

"The opening? When the Japanese roshis came to open the monastery? *You* were there? But you weren't in the picture."

"I *took* the pictures. Because I wasn't a real Zen student."

After six years, his bitterness came through. I clutched the truck keys tighter. Who else was there to ask—

"Someone had to drive Amber," he was saying. "She wasn't old enough, and her dad had just had heart surgery. I didn't think they would let Amber come all this way with me—my wheels were even worse than this." He nodded at the truck. "I thought if they agreed at all, they would make us take their Oldsmobile, regardless of what a goon I would have looked like behind the wheel. I mean, there is a reason those rolling couches were called *Old*smobiles. But they didn't blink; they were so hot to see how Aeneas was doing up here, they would have let us come on a scooter."

"Because they were worried about Aeneas?" I repeated.

The only people I knew up here I couldn't trust. To find another driver I'd have to start plucking guys from the zendo on faith. Who looked like a car nut? Who was strong enough to push a truck in the mud? Who!

"Yeah, I mean, before Aeneas hooked up with meditation it was like he'd been dropped on earth from another dimension. Like he knew he was in an alien society. Our rules had no meaning to him. He could see Reality, of course, but no one knew that. To his family, to everyone, he was a guy going wacko."

"But when he was up here, he fitted in?"

"His parents couldn't fucking believe it. It was like a miracle. I didn't realize then how desperate they were to be reassured. They didn't blink at the pile of tin I was driving. That tells you how frantic they were, because a month later when I wanted to come back they wouldn't let Amber come with me, even though I had a Jag."

"You don't think that's the reason?"

From San Francisco to here was five hours, ending in miles of sharply curving two-lane blacktop that was the Switchback of Temptation for the sports car driver.

"The thing is," Justin was saying, "Amber was just a kid. It was not like there was anything between us. I was seventeen. In a year I would be away at Cornell on the other side of the continent, and she'd still be in junior high school."

"But she wanted to drive up here with you in your Jag."

"Yeah. Maybe it was the car; maybe it was just getting away from her parents for a couple days."

Maybe it was already him? But I was too—too what? sorry for? angry for? ashamed for? Amber to suggest that possibility if it hadn't occurred to him. If I hadn't been so worried about Roshi, if it hadn't been six in the morning, I would have had trouble fighting off the urge to shake him silly for not seeing that he'd been the only stable thing in Amber's young life, little as that had been.

Yet, he had driven her here when she needed it. And now, six years later, he was still around. So, despite anything else, he was responsible, right? That was the important thing—a responsible guy who would fetch the doctor for Leo. Right? The end justifies the means, right?

Wrong! In stunt work you learn pronto that the end definitely does not justify the means. Sloppy means can kill you.

Justin twisted the stopper back in the thermos and held his hand out for the keys.

What *was* underneath his shaved head and stoic garb? *Why was it so important to you to come back here now?* I wanted to say. *Did you do it for Amber? Do you care more about her than is apparent?*

He turned to face me for the first time, leaning in toward me with sudden eagerness. The last time I'd seen that ilk of posture was when I'd made the mistake of asking, "Just what are the twelve steps?"

"Aeneas was the most amazing Zen student I'd ever seen," he said in a voice high with excitement. "Before the opening there was a three-day sitting, tangario. In tangario students sit nonstop—no breaks, no kinhin, three days. Maureen and Rob sat a lot of it. Roshi sat more. Amber and I and a bunch of other people sat a couple periods. But Aeneas sat the entire thing. I mean the *entire* thing. It was amazing, inspiring. I would have followed him to Japan—"

"*If* he'd gone to Japan," I put in.

Ignoring my comment, he said, "Aeneas was Enlightened, like the Buddha. No one understood that. He didn't need to be like ordinary men, to waste his time in school learning unimportant things so that he could spend the rest of his life selling his time for money. He already knew what Life was."

Oh, rats! A fanatic!

"Here, he was like a prince walking among beggars. People here were so ignorant they didn't realize what they had in their midst. The Japanese roshis saw it though. That's why they took him back to Japan—"

"But they didn't, Justin! They didn't take him to Japan."

His head gave a quick shake and he looked toward me as if for the first time.

"Aeneas didn't go to Japan, Justin," I repeated.

"He didn't go to that specific monastery, the one Leo thought he'd been at. We don't *know* he's not in Japan."

"We don't know he's not on Mars."

Automatically my fist tightened over the keys. How could I possibly trust Leo's life to this fanatic?

"The postcard service is bad from Mars."

In the dim light I could make out the suggestion of a smile. I gave him major points for that, took a deep breath and reminded myself: fanaticism does not mean you can't handle a pickup. Au contraire. A knowledgeable fanatic is better than a sane person who can't drive off pavement.

I quizzed, "Justin, the road's muddy. What if you get stuck?"

"There're boards in the bed. I'll slip them under the back wheels, I'll rock 'er." He turned, and in the foggy predawn light looked to be staring me in the eye, "Trust me, I've kept that old Jag running for years. I can drive this thing. I've been through the town. What do you need?"

I sighed. He had passed my test, albeit with a D minus. I trusted him, in theory. Still, I held out the keys tentatively, as if I was offering Roshi's stricken body.

"Get a doctor for Roshi."

"Done! There's a drugstore in town. They'll know the doctor. I'll catch him before he's got a chance to leave home. I'll have him back here by lunch."

Justin snatched the keys, stuck them in the ignition, and started the engine on the first try. The old yellow truck that had grumbled along the road with Leo now hummed eagerly. As I jumped out, the overhead light showed the face not of a fanatic but of a car-guy off on an adventure. Justin whipped the truck back, turned it toward the road, and headed out, gliding from high point to high point as he skirted the potholes.

It was like the truck had been reborn, reincarnated into a new, four-wheel drive model not to be fazed by wind, water, rock, or tree. The question was not whether Justin would snag the doctor, only how soon he'd get him back to Leo. It was twenty after six now. By lunch Leo would have a stethoscope on his chest.

For the first time since I'd arrived at Redwood Canyon Monastery I breathed in deeply and felt my shoulders relax. I smiled.

CHAPTER TWENTY-ONE

O

I glided back to Roshi's cabin, feeling the soft rain on my face as if it were sunshine. He was asleep, but that frantic thrashing had ceased and he lay curled on his side snoring like a little pink piglet. Even the fire required minimal stoking. It was as if the cosmos was trying to make up for the miseries of yesterday. I smiled at his safe, sleeping, soon-to-be-healed form, walked out his door and was back in the zendo for the last zazen period before breakfast.

"When sitting zazen, be alert! Hear the farthest sound," Yamana-roshi often said. He meant it as a way to keep from getting carried off by the maelstrom of thoughts, to sit in silence just listening. In the Ninth Street Zendo with trucks rattling and cabs screeching, buses groaning and cars slamming on brakes, listening to sounds was a given, but hearing the distant sounds behind the traffic noise was a challenge. Here, now, it was no problem to listen beyond the rain on the roof, to the swish of leaves, the creak of a branch, to cock my ears for the first, distant sound of the truck on the road bringing the doctor. It was way too soon for Justin to have made it to town, much less back again, but still I sifted every sound.

At breakfast hour, Roshi woke up long enough to swallow four spoonfuls of watery oatmeal, and I could have cheered. I was beginning to wonder if I had panicked sending for the doctor and if Roshi would chew me out. It would be a small price to pay.

At the after-breakfast break I slept the sleep of the relieved. And when it came time for the lecture, I found I was actually looking forward to hearing Rob.

I don't know what I expected him to say, but it definitely wasn't what he did.

He sat in the front seat, on a raised platform, a *tan*, like the rest of us. Just like Roshi, he adjusted his robes, pulling, tucking, shifting the layers as the ashy-sweet smell of incense wafted through the room. Each skirt had to be spread over his crossed legs and tucked in under his knees. The flap of his okesa, the black outer robe that went over his shoulder sari-like, needed another pull. Then the whole thing had to be checked again. Finally he rocked side to side, eyes shut, finding the center of balance. He did exactly what the Roshi had done, but he did it more precisely. What surprised me was that the effect was not persnicketyness, but rather that of an attentive performance.

I glanced across the zendo at Maureen. Her brow was wrinkled as if she was judging the aesthetics. All robes and no heart?

Barry sat next to her, eyes closed, head drooping, either on the verge of sleep or caught up in thoughts of criollo beans. Or maybe the Big Buddha Bakery?

Rob said, "Good morning."

"Good morning," came the scraggly reply led by the old-timers. The words seemed to echo as new students realized they were expected to respond aloud.

Rob's head bobbed diffidently in response and when he spoke it was in a low, easy tone.

"This is the first of our sesshin talks. Maureen will be giving the one tomorrow, and Barry later on. The purpose of a lecture is to help us get through the hard work of Zen practice. You've been here three days now, and I don't have to tell you how hard it is getting up hours before dawn, in the cold, waiting in line in the bathhouse, waiting for your food—food you didn't choose—sitting on your zafu hour after hour after hour, until you run out of story lines in your mind and you have to face silence. We all ask ourselves—and other people definitely ask us—'Are you crazy? Why did you seek out this practice? Why settle on something so foreign?' Not only is Zen Buddhism from Japan, by way of China, by way of India, but its basic teaching is beyond words.

"Roshi asked me to speak on the tale of the Sixth Patriarch, which is one of those stories that came from China to Japan to America, and here to this obscure monastery in California. Here's the story: The *Fifth* Patriarch was the head of a large monastery in ancient China. He was an important man. The monastery included a school for young monks, pretty much like a strict boarding school. You can picture it. The Fifth Patriarch was getting old, and he realized he had to choose a successor from among these student-monks of his. So he set them a test. Anyone who figured he had grasped what life really is—traditionally that's called enlightenment—could write a poem to show his understanding. Poetry was a valued art, and monks were given training in it."

Rob paused, letting his eyes close a moment, giving all of us time to see the Chinese monastery in our minds. I was just relieved he believed it was Roshi, and not me, who had chosen the topic. Rob shifted forward.

"The test put the monks on the spot. Not only were they being asked to stand up in front of all their friends and fellow students and say I'm the best one, but they were going to have to read out their poems in public. So, as soon as the Fifth Patriarch left, the students batted the prospect back and forth among themselves. 'You do it!' 'No, you, you're always saying how smart you are!' '*I'm* not reading my poem in front of all you guys!' You can just imagine these boys. Finally, they all agreed that the best student would stick his neck out first. He was the senior monk; his name was Shen-hsui. Everyone had assumed all along that he would succeed the Fifth Patriarch.

"But, Shen-hsui wasn't about to read his poem in public in front of all the monks. Shen-hsui knew that even though he had done his best, worked hard, studied hard, he hadn't made the final leap of understanding. But he *was* the best student, the senior monk. So what could he do? No matter what he did he was likely to be humiliated. You have to feel sorry for the guy."

I stared at Rob. Rob feeling sorry for anyone hadn't struck me as possible. Nor had it crossed my mind he could be so congenial a speaker. Around the zendo people were leaning toward him, smiling in the way of children at story hour. It was hard to believe this affable guy was the tyrant who yanked me out of the truck. I had sure assigned him the right topic.

"For Shen-hsui," Rob said, "the poem was the equivalent to taking the SAT or the state bar exam, except that only one person was going to pass. So he slaved over that poem. Finally, when it was as perfect as he could make it, he still didn't have the nerve to read it aloud in front of everyone. Instead, he crept out in the middle of the night and wrote his poem on the wall where the Fifth Patriarch would spot it first thing in the morning. Then, if the Fifth Patriarch approved of it, he would step forward and say it was his. If not, he could slink away unnoticed.

"So morning comes. By this time the other monks have spotted the poem. They figure it's Shen-hsui's. There's been a buzz throughout the monastery. Everyone's hanging around the wall waiting for the Fifth Patriarch to come by. They're discussing the poem; they're thinking it's pretty right-on.

"Suddenly, someone sees the Fifth Patriarch, an old man, walking slowly down the path, probably leaning on a stick. The tension mounts. The Fifth Patriarch stops. He reads:

> The body is like the Bodhi tree
> The mind a clear mirror standing
> Clean the mirror without ceasing
> So not one speck of dust obscures it.

"The Fifth Patriarch considers. The tension is almost unbearable."

Rob raised a hand, palm out. "I have to tell you now a couple things. This poem has been translated many times and my 'poem' is my paraphrasing. For those of you who are new, the Bodhi tree is the tree the Buddha sat under while he meditated and became enlightened. It was almost like an outer skin, protecting him while he sat there."

Rob paused, looking slowly around the room, deliberately letting the tension build. Maybe it was his courtroom experience, but he was a good storyteller, as the eager expressions on faces across from me attested.

"The students watched the Fifth Patriarch consider this poem that had already impressed them. Finally, the Fifth Patriarch signaled for incense and lit a stick in front of the poem. And everyone figured Shenhsui had succeeded. He was in! Things were as they should be, as everyone expected all along. Off they went to celebrate.

"But, the Fifth Patriarch held Shen-hsui back. He told him that they both knew Shen-hsui was a very good student; he'd worked hard, but he still hadn't *seen*, he wasn't enlightened. He told Shen-hsui to keep at it, to try again.

"Meanwhile, the rest of the monks, Shen-hsui's friends, figured he'd succeeded. What's poor Shen-hsui going to tell them? You *really* have to feel sorry for this guy!

Rob paused again; this time his striking blue eyes remained open, but his gaze went opaque, and I wondered what he was thinking about Shen-hsui. Rob exhaled deeply.

"And that would seem to be the end of it. But . . . along came another monk, not an educated student like Shen-hsui but an illiterate kitchen helper, really the lowest of the grunts in the monastery. No one expected anything from this guy, except to scrub the pots out. But earlier, in fact, he had heard one of the sutras, the scripture poems, and he had become enlightened. And now when he heard Shen-hsui's poem, he knew it was wrong.

"So he got a friend to write another poem—his poem—on the same wall, next to Shen-hsui's:

> The body is not a bodhi tree
> There is no mirror standing
> Fundamentally nothing 'is'
> So what is there for dust to cling to?

Small gasps came from around the zendo, even though the tale was familiar. Rob smiled.

"Exactly. Even in my paraphrasing, you heard the certainty in this pot-scrubber's poem, the arrogance.

"And so, when the Fifth Patriarch read the poem, he anointed the pot scrubber his successor, the Sixth Patriarch."

Rob leaned down, picked up the teacup at the corner of his mat, and sipped slowly, as if to let the point settle in. But the tension from the story persisted and the payoff had been inadequate to relieve it. Rain splatted on the closed windows, the air seemed close, and the incense smoke thick. I remembered my momentary panic when Rob had demanded a topic. But this one hadn't come from nowhere. There had been some reason it had been in my mind.

Rob tilted the cup to his mouth, but the tea was already gone. He pretended to drink and replaced the cup.

"There are many points in this parable. The one most valuable for us, in the beginning of a long sesshin is not the obvious one, the Sixth Patriarch's show of his sudden understanding, but the more subtle one which is the Fifth Patriarch's treatment of Shen-hsui.

"What the Fifth Patriarch said to Shen-hsui was that he had not made that leap to understanding *yet*. But that all the work he had done was an essential base from which his leap would be made. That's why the Fifth Patriarch encouraged him to keep trying. Maybe—probably—if no one else had come along he would have succeeded. We'll never know, and that's not important. What is important for us is to understand that all the waiting in line, the taking tiny half-steps in kinhin, the sitting on the cushion without moving, the letting go of thoughts and coming back to silence, doing it over and over and over and over again; this is what we do, so that when a flash of understanding comes we are capable of seeing it."

He sat back, reached for his cup, reconsidered, and drew his hand back.

When it became apparent that Rob was through speaking, Maureen raised her hand. Rob jerked toward her, as if he hadn't planned on entertaining questions. He glanced at his watch. I knew the schedule; it was too soon to cut off discussion.

He nodded.

Why *had* I given him this topic? Something had happened before I stepped out of Roshi's cabin and smacked into Rob.

Maureen leaned forward, almost off her cushion. She had a black shawl pulled tight around her shoulders but her hands poked out the bottom. Rather than resting in the mudra—right hand on left, thumbs very lightly touching—they were braced as she spoke.

"Like you said, there are a lot of ways to look at his tale. There's poor

Shen-hsui, the guy who's so busy following the rules he has no room left for inspiration."

Rob's lips started to curl, but he caught himself before they could reveal anything.

"But," Maureen continued, "there's also the Fifth Patriarch, the roshi. What this tale makes clear is that the roshi is the total authority. He knows his students; he cares about them. But in the end, he makes his choice for the dharma. In the end, friendship, loyalty, investment—I mean of time—don't matter."

Her voice did not drop to indicate the end of her sentence. She merely ceased speaking, leaving her words dangling, and to those of us who knew, dangling from the pronouncement was: no investment, of time or all Rob's money, would get him Leo's job when Leo was gone. *You're the rejected poem, don't you get it? What do you have to say about that?* she was tacitly demanding.

Still looking at Maureen, Rob stiffened. He opened his mouth, but Amber cut him off.

"But the whole point is that it's the pot scrubber who gets it, right? He, like, *sees*. He's the one old roshi chose to take his place. Because he gets it. Like Aeneas, right?"

The room had seemed silent before, but now it was dead quiet. No swish of fabric, no hiss of breath; even the wind outside was silent. Amber's demand hung as in a void.

"Aeneas was an exceptional student," Rob said, in a dismissive monotone.

I shot a glance at Amber, expecting to see shoulders hunched in fury. But she didn't look angry at all; her whole expression was eager, expectant.

"Rob," Gabe said, in a languid tone that was so out of character I did a double take. "Was there a reason—?"

But Rob must have realized he was about to be sandbagged. He signaled the bell-ringer that the question period was over. The woman struck the gong while Gabe was still speaking, and the post-lecture chant cut off Gabe's final word midway.

Gabe raised his voice, but only those of us straining could have made out the rest of his question: "Was there a reason *you left off the end of the tale of the Sixth Patriarch?*"

The end of the tale was: After the Fifth Patriarch read the pot-scrubber's poem, he called the lowly monk to him in secret, and anointed him his successor. But he warned the pot scrubber not to mention his succession. In fact, he sent the pot scrubber away that very night, to travel in distant lands for twenty years, because had he stayed in their monastery the other monks would have killed him.

Now I remembered why the Sixth Patriarch had been on my mind yesterday. The book was open to it on Roshi's floor. As he began this sesshin dedicated to Aeneas, this was what Roshi had been pondering.

I followed Rob out of the zendo, onto the tiny porch through which the roshi enters and leaves, as was my job. Rob slid his feet into his boots, and kept moving. I couldn't bring myself to follow. Like Maureen said, there were a lot of interpretations of the tale of the Sixth Patriarch, but one struck home: the old Fifth Patriarch sent the Aeneas-like monk away, and he kept the senior student in the monastery where he could guide him, and, to make sure he didn't kill his rival when he returned.

The rain had almost stopped. Pale slits of blue sliced the sky and were squeezed away by big-momma clouds. Buddhist precepts of nonviolence aside, if Shen-hsui realized he was merely a placeholder for the anointed one, wouldn't he have been wise to kill the old roshi and take over before the upstart returned? To protect traditional Buddhism from upstarts, he would have said.

I pulled on my shoes, but still didn't leave the tiny porch. Had Rob heard of the postcards Aeneas sent his family? Had Leo? Was it possible Aeneas was coming back?

I stayed put another minute, then walked around the side of the zendo to move my shoes to the shoe rack in front. Inside, the zendo students were walking in kinhin, but on the porch three tall dark-parkaed men and two shorter young women formed a half circle around Rob. Despite their height he towered above them like the tallest steeple in a Russian Orthodox cathedral. As Rob spoke—whispered—he glanced at each of the five and lastly at the zendo door, perhaps to remind them the bell was about to ring for the next sitting. They all nodded but were clearly reluctant to leave this new inner circle. A man in a dark green slicker, the guy I remembered from the first night, who had rushed desperately back to his cabin as if he'd forgotten the single thing he couldn't survive without, eased closer to Rob.

"You're set on preserving the monastery, aren't you? Leaving the road like it is, right? Keeping out hoards of casual students? Keeping this as a traditional teaching monastery, not making it soft, right?"

Rob nodded agreement.

Shen-hsui . . . But we were Zen students here, not killers. What was I thinking?

And yet, someone had poisoned Leo.

Shen-hsui.

More than ever I was relieved that the doctor would be here soon, and Leo would be safe, and everything would be all right. Otherwise, I would have agonized about Leo, worried about Amber poking at Rob, colluding with Gabe, about everyone discovering she was Aeneas's sister. There was no way I could protect her.

Moving past Rob's group on the porch I headed to Leo's cabin. He was asleep. I stoked the fire and was back in the zendo when the bell rang.

But the instant the service that ended the mid-morning sittings was over, I was out of the zendo, ear to the wind. It was ten to noon now, ten minutes to my arbitrary time of arrival! Four servers were carrying huge pots onto the porch, preparing to take them inside and begin the formally choreographed meal—*oriyoki*. There was no chance of hearing the truck over their clatter. I slipped into shoes and hurried down the steps toward the kitchen for Roshi's lunch.

I was almost to the kitchen when Barry burst out the door, robes flying, apron untied and sailing out to one side. The man was clearly in a panic and he was looking for me.

CHAPTER TWENTY-TWO

O

"The truck's gone!" Barry hissed, grabbing both my arms. He loomed over me, the wind whipping his black monk's robe and snapping the strings of his untied apron against my arms.

"It'll be back soon."

"No one told me!"

He was shaking me.

"Barry! It'll be back any time now."

"Who took it?"

"Justin."

"Justin?" he said blankly. He'd been so caught up in his cacao beans, it was no wonder he didn't know people's names. "This Justin, does he know anything about trucks?"

Then I realized the cause of his panic.

"Barry, the truck will be back in plenty of time for you to get your chocolate to San Francisco. Justin's a car guy. When he first drove up here he owned a vehicle older than this truck. The next year he had a Jaguar. Relax."

Relax! Has that advice ever worked? Certainly it was useless now, to a man with his oeuvre in chocolate to deliver.

"Do you want me to tell you when it gets here?"

"Nah," he said, backpedaling from his frenzy and offering me a smile of apology. With his shaved head, big round body and flapping robes, he reminded me of Pu-tai, the Laughing Buddha good luck charm sold in bazaars, the figure on the window of the Big Buddha Bakery. "I can hear the truck from the kitchen," he added.

"Good," I said. "I'll wait there with you." And, pulling myself together to make use of this opportunity, I added, "You can tell me about the Big Buddha Bakery."

I hurried into the kitchen after Barry. The servers were still running in and out of the sesshin half of the kitchen, hauling big silvery serving pots by handles held with potholders. The food had to leave the kitchen steaming if there was any chance of it being near-warm by the time the servers carted it across the paths to the zendo, served it to all twenty students two at a time, and those students chanted the meal verses prior to taking their first bites. Thus had congealed oatmeal and cold rice become staples of the Zen diet. Now the servers were returning the empty rice pots and readying the kettles of boiling water to take to the zendo and pour into students' bowls for cleaning.

I glanced out the tiny window under the staircase, hoping in vain for a first glimpse of the truck. The window was so shaded by brambles and bushes I hadn't realized it was there before.

I moved into the arena of chocolate. The chocolate scent here was not what you'd find in a chocolate shop, even a fine establishment. It was a dryer, duskier aroma, and not quite mouth-watering. Barry stood over the conche, which resembled a giant washing machine. He had apparently finished loading the chocolate and was now hoisting a bag of vanilla beans.

"Barry," I said as he started to pour, "what happened at the Big Buddha Bakery?"

"Shh!" he muttered, his focus never leaving the bag. "Conching can take three days. I've got just one. Less than one, and I've still got to add the rest of these beans, and the lecithin and the sugar."

"White sugar?"

"White, yes. But large grain. There's less ash and moisture content that way and the taste is more natural."

He emptied both bags, the vanilla beans and the sugar, but he might have been distributing the contents bean by bean and crystal by crystal, and I had the ludicrous feeling that had I asked he could have accounted for the position of each bean and crystal when it joined the paste at the bottom of the conche. By the time he put down the last bag, the servers were gone and the green-aproned dishwashers were clanking big spoons against pots, shifting excess food to containers, drying utensils and serving bowls, and only one was scrubbing away at the bottom of the huge rice pot. Brillo pad scraped on metal as if scratching off the thin layer of civility between Barry and me.

Barry looked up from the conche.

"The Big Buddha Bakery?" I prompted.

He sighed. "I've been at this nonstop since Monday. I need to sit down. Come on upstairs."

He walked to the far corner of the kitchen and started up the staircase by the window. Half-hidden behind piled cardboard boxes, it was a narrow necessity, clearly a later add-in. There was room for only one person to climb, and no railing. I followed him to an attic room that covered the entire kitchen. The walls sloped in on both sides, leaving a narrow passage for anyone, but one that had to be a balance test for a man his size. At the far end—over the zendo kitchen sink where the dishwashing crew was still sweating—was a bed, not like the futons Roshi and I had but an actual, extra-long bed with box springs and mattress, and two extra-thick pillows and a French blue quilted bedspread. The head of the bed touched one wall, the foot the other. The floorboards were polished; the eaves held built-in bookcases, a desk with a laptop computer, and a boom box. And, I realized with a start, there was a lamp. A lamp in this monastery that had no electricity or phone!

"Wow!"

"Yeah, Rob's a generous guy."

"Rob remodeled this loft for you? How come?"

"He had the money. I think he felt wealth was unbefitting a Zen student who plans to be the abbot some day. So he spent it on the monastery. He paid for the flush system in the bathhouse and the generator for the kitchen."

"And the big stuffed chairs in the common room, too?"

"Oh, yeah." He gave a grudging nod, similar to the one Maureen had given in the office yesterday. Again it struck me that it's not only more blessed to give than to receive, but a whole lot more satisfying. But condescending beneficence can buy a load of resentment.

Barry motioned me to sit on the bed beside him, but the sloping walls would have forced us shoulder to shoulder. I chose an old black canvas chair by the stairs.

"Barry, about the Big Buddha Bakery—?"

He shook his head. "I really hoped never to hear about it again."

"Did you work there?"

He tapped his fingers on one knee, his head hanging, gaze down.

This was worse than I'd thought. "Okay, you did work there. Cooking, right?"

He stared down, shoulders tightening.

Much worse. "Oh, jeez, you didn't just work there, did you, you *were* the baker."

He stood abruptly, as if shot up by nerves, and began walking toward me, slowly, stiffly, as if fighting for control. His hands were clasped over his stomach; his feet dragged with each step. The floorboards under his feet were worn down from pacing. When he moved past me, his hips were level with my shoulders and I knew one swat of one of those solid arms could send me slamming headfirst down the stairs. At the far wall he turned and started back. Before I could order "Sit," he pulled the desk chair in front of me and sat.

"The food at the bakery—"

"—was fine," he snapped.

"But?"

He took a deep breath and squeezed both hands into fists. He looked at me, his face quivering. Then he cried.

I was up with my arms around his shoulders before I realized it. He was the Barry of Monday, the big kid so excited about his criollo beans arriving. He bent his head down to his knees and wiped his eyes on his robe.

"I didn't do anything at the bakery, but I was their confection chef and I disgraced them. I left, but even that didn't help. No one wants to buy food from a place that hired a poisoner."

"But you said—"

"It wasn't there. It was at the Cacao Royale, like the one I'm going to this weekend. It's *the* chocolate contest here; only comes every seven years. I was so excited about being accepted there, so nervous. I never intended to endanger anyone. Everyone knew that. I was so ambitious. I just had to win. I couldn't see anything but winning. And then, all of a sudden in the 'without' competition there's this guy from Virginia making a vanilla tart that was the buzz of the whole place. There's no excuse for what I did. I didn't intend to harm him, not physically, just professionally. But that's no excuse."

I nodded, waiting.

"Vanilla is a subtle taste. When he turned his back on his pan, I squirted in a dropper full of peanut oil. I distracted him just long enough for it to settle beneath the surface. I thought all it would do would be to adulterate the taste, but . . ."

"Someone was allergic?" I was sorry as soon as I'd said it. And when Barry nodded, I watched him closely to make sure there was no surprise in his reaction, that I hadn't given him an easy out. "What happened?"

"One of the judges; anaphylactic shock; paramedics. He was okay the next day. I don't know if he would have sued me, or the guy from Virginia would have, but before that came up, I realized what I had done, what I had become. I gave the Virginian all my recipes—he's won a few contests with some of them since then. I don't pretend I'm glad for him, but it's what I deserve."

"But no police or—"

"No. Know why?"

I shook my head.

"Because Roshi stood up for me. The chocolate world is a small community. The police don't patrol confection competitions. Someone would have had to press charges. The newspapers were bad enough. But when Roshi trusted me enough to make me his cook up here, even they backed off." He leaned back, sighed deeply and then focused on me anew. "You know, Darcy, I thought you were my friend. But this is a hell of a time to hit me with questions about this. I haven't slept in days, I'm just going to make it to San Francisco. And you broadside me like this."

He looked so drained, so confused and so very disappointed . . . in me. There was no reason *not* to tell him, not with the doctor almost here.

"Barry, I had to ask. Someone poisoned Leo. He's okay," I added immediately. The sudden horror on Barry's face lessened, but only momentarily.

Then he demanded, "Poisoned? You think I poisoned him, don't you? I'm a known poisoner. You think I did this, don't you?"

I wanted to scream, No, of course not! It took all my control to keep eye contact and say, "Did you?"

"NO!" His shout was so loud it must have echoed all over the grounds. I was amazed the dishwashing crew didn't come running. Now it was Barry keeping our eye contact. "No!" he insisted, but in a normal voice. "Roshi took me in when I was at rock bottom. He didn't ask questions. He stuck by me; he didn't toss me out when I wandered off for weeks at a time. He didn't turn me away when I banged on his cabin door at three A.M. and needed to talk. He gave me space and he gave me guidance, and most of all he gave me time to get to this point where I can go back to the Cacao Royale and get some notice in the extra fine specialty chocolate field. Six years ago I thought my life was over. Without Roshi it would have been. But those years were just retooling. I would give my life for Roshi." He slumped back shaking his head. "Why would anyone—?"

"You've been here way longer than I have. I was hoping you'd—"

"How could anyone poison him? We all eat out of the same pot and—" He stopped, mouth open. "Oh no, was it in—" He swallowed hard. "—in my cocoa? The special blend I make for him!"

I nodded.

"How could anyone—?" He took a deep breath and another, as if trying to control his emotions enough to think straight. "I made you a cup of cocoa from his special batch, that first day. It wasn't poisoned then. But doesn't matter. The cannister's right out on the counter, labeled, like an invitation. Anyone could have adulterated it."

"You live here; you know people, so who would poison Leo? Why? Did it have something to do with the opening of the monastery?" When he shook his head in bewilderment, I tried "Or with Aeneas?"

"You're sure it's poison, not flu? Nobody would hurt Leo—okay, listen, let me think." His gaze fell on his watch. He jumped up. "I've got to get back to the conche." Then he sat back down, as if realizing for the first time the danger to Leo. "Listen, Darcy, I'm so exhausted I'm barely computing. I'm terrified I'll make some careless mistake with the chocolate and—But that's beside the point. Poisoning Roshi—it's beyond sense; I can't imagine. I can't deal with it. But I'm going to tell you what I know; I can do that much for Roshi. This is how things are with him. Roshi's gift is that he opens possibilities for people; then he steps back. He lets them swim or sink. He's a great teacher and he can show them how to swim, but he doesn't force anyone. And, Darcy, some people want to sink."

"How did that play out with the people who were here at the opening?"

It was a moment before Barry nodded in comprehension. "Rob? Well, Rob's an ambitious guy. He's used to winning. Roshi lets him cherish his ambitions. Maybe he'll learn from that, but if he has he sure hasn't shown any signs of letting go. See, Darcy, to you this place looks like a hump of dirt in the woods, but the residents here have a lot invested in it. Their lives."

Their, not *our*, lives.

"Maureen?"

"Roshi let her think she could live here forever. He let her plant trees she'll never see mature."

I almost said: like the red maple. But, of course, Barry meant much more than that.

"Gabe he lets wander into sesshin whenever he wants to and pretend he's here for zazen. And this guy, Justin—I'd forgotten about him till you gave him our truck. But, he's a strange one. Kept eyeing my melangeur—it was the first piece of serious equipment I had. Built at the turn of the century—He kept muttering about antiques. If the melangeur wasn't the size of a small elephant I would have worried. Strange guy. When he was at the opening he was mesmerized with the romance of Japanese monastic practice. Anyone could see Aeneas wasn't all there, but Justin didn't want to. Then when Aeneas went off, Justin just upped and left."

"With Aeneas?"

"No, no. An hour or two after. Someone asked him to do some menial task, and he got all huffy and stormed off. But, you know I've seen these high-strung types cooking; I know them. Justin was just waiting for an excuse so he could storm out of here. He's one of those guys who does what he wants and then twists things to justify it."

A shiver shot through me. "Like what?"

"Like taking off with the truck."

"He did that?" I squeaked out.

He gave a great sigh. "Not back then. But he's been gone how long now? He could be near San Francisco by now."

"Do you really think—"

"We'll know soon enough, won't we?"

He shoved himself up, the sluggish move of a man almost out of gas. But his fingers snapped against each other as he walked. I followed him down the stairs to the conche where the cocoa, vanilla, lecithin, and white sugar were mixing.

"What about you, Barry? What does Roshi let you think?"

Barry looked up from the brown mixture. "Me? Darcy, if I knew my illusions, they wouldn't be illusions. But I'll tell you this, whatever they are they're in this conche, not in the monastery grounds. I don't intend to be here next year. Whatever Roshi decides to do with this place is fine with me."

"So, this contest you're going to this weekend, it's the same Cacao Royale?"

"The first time I'll have been back since . . . the incident. But it's entirely different now. And all I have to do is to see that it is entirely different. Roshi encouraged me."

"But what about—"

"You mean the other competitors? Aren't they worried I'll stab them with my spatula?" Barry actually laughed. "Chocolate's a strange world. *I* was appalled at myself. But the way everyone else looked at it, any judge with a food allergy has a death wish. And to something as common as peanuts! It was a cooking event, after all. It didn't hurt my case that I had a lot of friends there and the judge was a jerk. But the real thing is that slipping the odd ingredient in a competitor's dish, well, it's done more than you'd think. And laughed about afterwards. It's like . . . well, Maureen said, it's like cooking class in a boy's prep school. Except we didn't actually throw food."

I could feel a small smile moving my lips. It was easy to imagine Barry in a prep school, living, in fact, just like this.

"How'd the rest of the students here take it?"

"Huh? Oh, no, Maureen didn't say that here. We were in the city then, right after the contest."

"You knew each other before you came here?" Why hadn't that possibility occurred to me?

"Yeah. We'd been together for four or five months then. In fact, I'm the reason Maureen is here. She rode along with me the weekend I drove up to ask Roshi to take me in till I got my head together. That was

October. I stayed the weekend, then even after Roshi said I could come back, there was a bunch of stuff I had to take care of and I didn't get up here proper till the next April. Maureen didn't even have winter clothes, that's how little intention she had of staying here. I mean, for her, a weekend here was the same as three days at the Monterey Aquarium, or Hearst Castle. I had to send her clothes."

"The thing was," he said over his shoulder, "she'd had a big disappointment professionally—the director of the ballet company was a pig. Much worse than the run-of-the-mill casting couch and starvation bully. He'd betrayed her. She was a wreck when she left. I was glad to get her out of the city then. That's half the reason I brought her with me that weekend. So, *she* was surprised she stayed, but I wasn't. I mean, I knew her. But I never dreamed she'd still be here when I got back in April."

"Did something happen at the opening that made her stay?"

He grabbed my arms, but this time imploringly. "Don't make her deal with that again. It was torture for her then."

"Why? I mean, why more for her than the rest of you?"

"I don't know. She wouldn't talk about it, even to me. But, Darcy, Maureen is fragile. Don't push her." He was still holding my arms. "Darcy, promise me you won't upset Maureen now."

I kept quiet. There was no way I could ever make that kind of promise.

A bang resounded outside. I ran for the parking lot.

Chapter Twenty-three

O

The clappers were sounding when I stepped out of the kitchen. *Drop what you're doing. Come to work meeting!*

Fat chance! I ran for the parking lot, almost falling over roots and skidding on loose gravel as I raced down the path. My eyes were on the outlet of the parking area into the road, the spot where the yellow of the hood would first be visible as the truck turned in.

The clang I'd heard had not been on the road, but in the parking lot. I didn't think about that, not until I reached the empty lot, till I had to admit there was no vehicle there except the wheelbarrow still shaking from a crash into a metal storage box. And behind it, Amber, planted, arms crossed, legs apart.

"Where is he?"

"Who?"

"Justin, of course. He's been gone all morning. I thought maybe he was sick—I *know* he wouldn't skip zazen if he could haul himself out of bed. I mean, he did an entire sesshin when he had the worst flu of his life."

That must have delighted the people sitting next to him.

"I didn't want to burst into his dorm. I mean there are *guys* there and all. But when he didn't even come to lunch, well, I knew something happened. Where is he?"

"Checking out the truck."

"The truck's not there!" she snapped. "You knew he was gone! Why didn't you tell me?"

Without waiting for an answer she started glaring around for her next target. I hoped she was the only one who had noticed Justin's absence. Lucky for me it was her and not Rob. He would be furious, and rightfully so, and for the third time in two days. If he hadn't been wound up in his lecture, diverted by the flock of admirers afterward he'd have registered that same zafu empty period after period. I just hoped that Justin's name wouldn't come up in work meeting. Today most people would be continuing their jobs; for them a general announcement would do. A few would be called by name for new jobs. If they weren't there everybody would know.

After work meeting, it would be smooth sailing. Justin would be back by afternoon zazen. The doctor would be here then and he would protect Leo and everything else would fall into place. I looked down and realized I had crossed my fingers. I felt better about Justin, but nowhere near certain.

"Amber," I said, "do you remember the Jaguar Justin had after the opening ceremony?"

"Oh yeah, it was a great old car. Black, with, like, wood on the dashboard and lots of gauges and stuff. It was way cool. My mother just about had a hissy fit when I wanted to come back here with Justin in it. Damn, it would have been such a cool, cool drive. I mean it was such a pisser, you know, like suddenly I wasn't responsible enough to drive all that way with him and—"

She would have gone on grumbling with pleasure had I not interrupted.

"How did he happen to get that car? That must have been quite an expensive set of wheels for a seventeen-year-old."

"Yeah. He really lucked out. He had this uncle, see, his father's younger brother. The guy was a loser and when he scored like his third DUI his wife told him like either you get rid of that car or I'm walking. So he gave it to Justin."

"He didn't sell it? He just gave it to him?"

"Justin figured his uncle hoped his wife would change her mind."

"Did she?"

"Maybe, but not for a long time. He had it when he went to college."

The clappers sounded again. Amber started to turn, but stopped and eyed me.

"Darcy?" She paused, a malicious smirk enlivening her face. "What makes you think Justin's coming back?"

"What? What do you mean?"

"Well, why would he? He can sit cross-legged anywhere. You gave him a cool old truck? He's probably halfway to San Francisco with it."

I didn't believe that, *couldn't believe* it, even though it was the second time I'd heard it, but still my stomach felt like it had dropped to the ground.

"Amber! Stop!"

"Okay, have it your own way!" She laughed and strode back into the kitchen.

The wind wrapped around my neck and its clammy fist dug into my chest. Why *wasn't* Justin back? Leo and I had made it from the highway in an hour. Surely it wouldn't have taken Justin more than two to get there, even with swampy hollows in the road, even if he'd had to get out and slip the boards under the tires. He'd left here before seven. Now it was one-thirty. Maybe the doctor had appointments? Maybe Justin had had to wait till noon or even later. It was still okay.

Barry hustled past me toward the circle of hunched figures in knit caps, canvas jackets, jeans, and work boots.

Maureen was holding the clappers now. The rest of us formed as much of a circle as we could manage and still stay out of the mud. Maureen clacked; we all bowed.

"Gabe will be leading a wood clearing crew, with, uh, Jim Washburn and Monica Donikki. Those of you assigned to crews report back to your crew leader. If you complete your job before the end of work period, see your crew leader for another assignment. If the leader has no assignment, see me." She glanced around the ring. "Ah, Darcy. Your job today is . . . newspaper collection. Has Roshi explained that to you?"

I gasped! I'd forgotten that completely. Leo's newspaper in the meadow a mile through the woods. She expected me to go walking into the woods, walking farther than the point I'd balked at Tuesday. I couldn't do it when I thought my being jisha depended on it, but that was then, before I had stood on the roof and felt the swirling outside of me. Maybe now things would be different, totally different. Now the woods might not be demons but just trees. My heart was pounding against my ribs, fear and eagerness drumming together.

But I couldn't leave Leo, not with the doctor on his way. I felt like I'd been yanked back by the collar.

In a minute the meeting was over and only a few people were clustered around Maureen. I said, "About the paper, I can't go for it. I—"

"I'll go!" Amber grabbed Maureen's arm. "I can handle it. It's no problem. I'll go."

Amber was all but dancing at the prospect of getting free of the sesshin for an hour's unsupervised walk. Her face was flushed with hope. Even her hair was bouncing.

Maureen hesitated. Had Rob been in charge, he would have been reminding Amber that tasks are not assigned for pleasure and shushing her at the same time. But Maureen looked at Amber, and I had the sense she saw her own agitation reflected in Amber and knew the yearning to escape even if it's escaping to nothing but more of the same. Just the thought of an hour on her own could carry Amber through the day.

An hour on her own, alone, exposed. She was Aeneas's sister, the one person Roshi expected me to watch over. Whatever led to Roshi's poisoning, Aeneas was still key to it. I couldn't let her traipse out into the woods alone. No matter . . . no matter, anything.

"Maureen. It's my job, I'll go."

"But Roshi needs you." Amber all but pushed me out of the way.

"I can deal with this."

"No you can't! You're terrified of the woods!"

I know I flushed as red as my hair. A couple people let out laughs. Maureen looked from Amber to me, a smile twitching on her thin face. I couldn't tell whether she was tickled at this little squabble over this little job, or at my wimpy fear of the woods, the fear that maybe I didn't even have anymore. It's bad enough to be humiliated but ten times worse being dinged for something you've overcome, maybe. And there was not a thing I could say.

"You go, Amber," Maureen said. "Darcy, check to see if Roshi has things for you to do."

Maureen had barely finished before Amber was racing away. She had to be called back and given directions. In the end Barry said he'd take her to the path. When they left everyone laughed, but it was a been-there laugh and I wondered if maybe the laughs about me had been kinder than I'd credited. At least with Barry she'd be safe for a while. I followed her as far as the road, and stood watching till she disappeared and Barry walked back. He turned and stared at the empty, silent road.

"That truck's our lifeline. It's our only connection to the outside."

My whole body went cold. I had known it, but hearing Barry say it gave it an ominous reality. I thought of my own cell phone, frustratingly far out of range here. "Why, dammit? This is so stupid. Why didn't you all run in a phone line at least?"

"Costs a fortune."

"But surely some kind of cell phone access—?"

"I'm not the likely successor here."

"You mean Rob doesn't want a phone?" I asked, sidestepping the big issue. "How come?"

"They didn't have phones in traditional Japanese monasteries."

"So?"

Barry just shrugged and stalked away, leaving me to wonder how long and deep the issue of succession had been smoldering. No wonder Barry was planning to be gone in a year. When Leo was gone things would be done Rob's way. And there'd be no room for Barry.

O

Barry clumped back to the kitchen. He hadn't slept more than a couple hours at a time in days, couldn't think of sleep now. So much to do. Was the chocolate conching fast enough? Had he ground the nibs long enough or should he scoop some back into the melangeur and prolong the conching? The mixture in the conche had to be perfect and ready for tempering tonight. He'd have to use some of the tempered chocolate from the last batch—only half criollos—to speed the process. No way to avoid it! Damn! A small amount . . . but still . . . Damn!

It'd all be wasted if the truck wasn't here.

Calm down! Years of facing the wall and this is how you react in a crisis? He forced himself to breathe deeply, to focus on his feet hitting the ground with each step. By the time he reached the kitchen he had a patina of control. He poured coffee, the eighth or twenty-seventh cup of the day.

Maureen! He couldn't let Darcy sideswipe her with questions about that awful weekend of the opening. Maureen was already on the thin edge; they all were. If she had to think about that, even enough to fend off questions . . . he didn't know how bad it would be.

He flashed on her in their two-room flat in the Mission District after she'd been shoved out of the ballet company. Shoved off the edge of her world, left to wander without goal, rant and babble without censoring. Right before the peanut oil fiasco. The worst months of both their lives.

Grief doesn't bind people. Grief is a solitary thing. People say you share your grief. Bullshit. Only in the sense that a hostess shares her box of truffles, offering the guest her pick of one. No guest eats the whole box. One is plenty. The bone-deep dull pain of lost acclaim, never again to hear the audience stunned into silence, then thunder their applause for an adagio she had raised to a new level of perfection, that loss he'd understood. But he could only imagine the prospect of life without dance, and the impotent rage of one who had studied and practiced and lived dance since she could reach the barre. As he'd curled around her sleepless, shivering body, she had tried to explain the longing to move into the transcendent roles reserved for lead dancers, to *be* dance. Then to—finally—be given the title role in Giselle, and the week before the season opened, to be yanked out for an understudy the maestro was screwing; for that she had barely had words. That he had learned from friends: "Guy's a pig. The girl's good; but she's not Maureen." "Nothing Maur can do. She bitches; she's toast. It's his kingdom."

"My body is my instrument," Maureen had said another night.

"Without the stage, the company, the orchestra, I can't play it. Without dance, I'm like a musician using his cello for a crutch."

He could still see her standing at the living room window, her colorless face framed by the thick San Francisco fog outside. She, walking flat-footed back and forth in the night, growing thinner as purpose drained out of her. He had tried tempting her with his best, the torte of crushed pistachio on a bed of bitter chocolate (65 percent cocoa) and drizzled with a sharp raspberry liqueur that had taken him months to perfect. She had taken one bite. *Could* not swallow another, she had insisted. And he had had nothing more to offer, nothing to keep her from walking flat-footed in the night, and worse, in the days, talking nonstop, blurting anything, everything, oblivious to its relevance, or to the listener. She'd been so erratic he had taken the knives to the bakery and been relieved they didn't own a car. Had it been a nervous breakdown? Would she have pulled herself together in another week? He didn't know. He'd been sucker-punched by the Cacao Royale Tasting debacle and the horror of being called a poisoner.

Bringing her here had been pie in the sky; he'd never imagined she'd stay permanently. A shot of guilt stunned him as he remembered how relieved he'd been when she said she wasn't going back to the city.

A month ago he'd have said she was a different woman now, solid, grounded, capable. He'd almost forgotten that ninety-nine pound wraith—until this sesshin. Now he could see the dark circles of sleeplessness under her eyes, the hollowness in them. Look at her leading the work meeting; she'd forgotten to make the announcements, mixed up two men, sent the guy with the bad back on the wood clearing crew. Soon she would be walking at night and words spilling out as if she were pacing with her mouth. If Darcy made her relive that opening weekend . . . He just couldn't let that happen.

He found himself in front of the tempering machine, remembering when it arrived. Maureen laughing, asking if he'd burgled Frankenstein's lab. He tapped the pipes through which the 105-degree slurry would flow to cool and heat again till the cocoa butter crystals turned the liquid to a smooth, fruity solid. Allow too little time and— He shook his head at that thought of the possible gray, crumbly disaster.

O

I walked back through the empty parking lot, trying to reassure myself that Amber was safe, that somehow Barry having walked her to the path would keep her safe on the entire length of that path, past a mile of bushes in which the poisoner could be hiding, a mile of trees he could pop out from. As I passed the zendo, I spotted Rob on the porch, wagging his finger at someone inside. One down. Then I caught sight of the waggee— Gabe. Two down. Maureen would be giving detailed instructions to new crew leaders; she'd be hard-pressed to find time to light out after Amber. And as for Barry, no matter what had happened with Aeneas, or what Amber knew, it wouldn't be enough to drag him away from his conche.

The clouds had split. There was a hint of sun. I took that as a good sign, rounded the bath house, and trotted down the path to Roshi's cabin to see what I could do for him.

When I opened the door and saw him I was appalled I'd waited so long.

CHAPTER TWENTY-FOUR

O

"Leo, you're boiling," I said, hand on his forehead. His face was damp and red.

"Off and on," he muttered.

"What do you mean?"

"Comes and goes. It'll pass."

There was no thermometer, not that knowing his numerical temperature was going to help me. It would just suggest how panicked I should be. Cold compresses, wasn't that the treatment for fever? I'd heard of people being packed in ice. Damn it, where was the doctor? Justin ought to have had him back here hours ago.

But there was also "sweat it out." Oh shit.

"Leo, how long—"

"It'll pass. Go to bed."

Two o'clock in the afternoon, and Leo thought it was nine P.M.!

"I'm not leaving until your fever is down."

He protested, but briefly. After stoking the fire I made a tea run to the kitchen, straining to catch the rumble of the truck, trying to assure myself Justin hadn't really lit out for San Francisco. But had he indulged himself with a side trip to Willits, or a few beers, or a big steak lunch? Or all three?

In the kitchen the cooks were chopping celery and breaking up cauliflower. Someone had moved the tea bags and I had to ask three of the cooks before one of them plucked the box from behind a stack of drying clothes. Every portion of the trip took longer than I had expected. When I got back to Leo his fever had abated some. His forehead still felt hot, but not alarmingly so.

"See," he said, with a watery but still smug grin. "I told you it would pass."

"'Comes and goes,' was what you said," I grumbled, covering my relief. If I'd even known what all was in that cup of cocoa—cyanide and what else?—I might have had some idea what to expect and what should strike panic.

"Help me up."

I propped his pillows against the wall, and helped him sit cross-legged. He had slept so much his internal clock might as well be set for Istanbul. I poured the tea—his into a cup with a thick handle—and let it cool before holding it out to him. He took it in both hands, so carefully I thought of the commentary on Dogen Zenji's *Tenzo Kyokun, Use the property and possessions of the community as carefully as if they were your own eyes.*

Leo looked at his cup and winked. He was on such a high, such a fragile high, I hesitated to ask, but, of course I did ask.

"Roshi, Aeneas was something of a mirror, wasn't he? Was there more to him? Something that triggered events at the opening?"

"The opening?" he repeated in a hazy way that made me wonder if he was tracking.

"For instance, Rob looked at Aeneas and saw an ambitious competitor—Aeneas, who sat so motionlessly that the Japanese roshis were impressed."

He inhaled slowly, but the movement seemed to focus him, and when he answered he sounded as if he hadn't been ill at all. "Aeneas was the only one who impressed them. Abbots in Japan have spent almost their entire lives in temples, leading services, performing ceremonies. They are paid for those ceremonies and doing them beautifully is important. To them, my students looked like a troop of monkeys. They squirmed, they galumphed in kinhin, and worst of all, they questioned everything."

"Not Aeneas?"

"Oh, no. He sat still, walked slowly, and kept quiet. He was focused, tidy, and obsessive about whatever job he was given. In their eyes, he was my one success. I wondered, at the time, would they have consecrated the temple, had there not been Aeneas."

He looked up and I thought maybe he shrugged but the movement was so slight I couldn't be sure. His fragile high was disintegrating. I reached out to help him lie down but he waved me off.

"Ironic," I said, "because Aeneas was what—brain damaged?"

"Probably. No clear diagnosis, but . . . my guess. His condition . . . didn't change here."

"But what could he have gotten out of zazen?"

Leo looked up at me. Something shifted as if he had channeled all his remaining energy into what had to be said. When he spoke his voice was as steady as his gaze.

"Who can speak for someone else? Maybe he just sat and heard the birds and felt the wind, and found his inhalations wonderful."

We sit to sit, I've heard it explained. We sit zazen to experience being inseparable from the wonder of the moment.

"But if your mind is short-circuited," I insisted.

"I don't know the answer, Darcy. Back then I was arrogant. I figured what was the point of Aeneas sitting drugged up in a locked ward. Wasn't he better off here where life suited him? What was the harm?"

"What about Maureen? To her he was the devil who had to be watched every moment. And Rob, he—"

"That was my arrogance. Their reaction was their practice, I thought. Maybe with a teacher with a better practice of his own, that would have been true. But . . . but, I failed them. And when I heard Aeneas was in Japan I assumed the Japanese teachers felt they could not abandon such a promising student to me."

"But why did you think that—that Aeneas went to Japan rather than just off somewhere?"

"His postcard."

Just one? He'd sent his family at least three. "From Japan?"

He pointed to a low chest in the corner by the fireplace. "Bottom left."

I opened the door, anxious to see this card from the man who proscribed using the phone, sent from the country where he presumably had never gone.

The postcard's corners had rumpled with time. One edge had been ripped in two places. It must have sat on Leo's dresser for years, where he could be chastised by it. The pictured Japanese temple garden had faded to pale blue.

"Turn it over, Darcy."

The address was printed in neat letters, in the message side, nothing but a large *A* with the bar scooped down like a smiley mouth and two dots for eyes above it.

"Is that how he—?"

Roshi nodded. "I insisted he write his family. He sent them postcards like that."

"Couldn't he write?"

"He could. He didn't."

"But that mark, anyone could have made it!"

"Yes, anyone."

What color there was in his long face drained away, leaving those too-big features of his ludicrously bright. Poor Amber.

We sat there, he canted slightly to his right against the wall, me cross-legged on a cushion by the fireplace. I hadn't paid attention to the fire before but now the crackling sounded like fireworks and the smoke hung in the air. Somehow it seemed important to sum it up aloud.

I said, "Aeneas never went to Japan with the Japanese abbots. He didn't send that postcard. There is no reason to think he sent the post-cards to his family later. Since he left here no one has heard from him at all. *If* he left here."

"If he left here."

Leo was still holding his tea mug. He sipped, though the tea had to be very cold by now. He looked so gray and empty I kept expecting him to ask me to help him back down, and yet I knew he wouldn't. He had stepped too far into the question of Aeneas.

"He's dead, isn't he?"

"I don't know."

"But you suspect."

"I fear."

"And you fear he's buried right here." I didn't need to make it a question. He didn't disagree. "You fear it's one of your students who killed him, right? The same person who poisoned your cocoa?" When he didn't respond, I insisted, "Right?"

"Yes."

"Leo, you're the Roshi, for Chrissakes, why didn't you just ask them?"

He didn't respond to my outburst. In his same flat, sick voice, he said, "I am."

The Fifth Patriarch sent the pot scrubber away to distant lands and kept Shen-hsui in the monastery, maybe to protect the pot scrubber, maybe to save Shen-hsui. Leo had failed his student, the poisoner, six years ago. Now he was giving him a chance to face himself.

I helped Leo down and he slept, fitfully at first, then more easily.

It was as if he had handed his agitation to me. I sat watching him sleep, listening for the sound of the truck that didn't come, and feeling the cold, solid weight of knowledge of a killer. One of us. Leo's acknowledgment made everything different. Before, I had worried about the killer, but there had always been a safety net of maybe I was wrong. Before, it had been like doing a high-fall gag off a five-hundred-foot cliff, but knowing there was a padded catcher basket out of sight ten feet down. Knowing it was all a stunt. Now it was real. No padded catcher. A real murderer. One of us.

Outside Leo's cabin nothing had changed. In here everything was different.

When I looked at the clock again it was nearly three P.M. Work period would end in half an hour and with it my chance to catch Maureen and force her to tell me what she'd raced away to avoid twice before. Next to Roshi, maybe even more than Roshi, she knew what had happened here. Repeating silently that outside the cabin nothing had changed, I tucked the covers around Leo and slipped out, veering first toward the parking lot, as if that would draw the truck to me. I peered into the bathhouse and kitchen. Barry was stacking boxes; I had the feeling he had seen me and slipped out of sight, but maybe I was imagining that.

Leo's poisoning stemmed from that weekend of the opening. Why hadn't Leo called the sheriff last month when the Japanese teachers wrote that Aeneas had not left with them? But what would he have reported? *An adult man disappeared six years ago. His family doesn't believe he's missing.* No sheriff would investigate that.

But why hadn't Leo or anyone else followed up on Aeneas when he "left?" Leo said he was too abashed to write to the abbots in Japan. Still, the group hadn't flown out of San Francisco till Monday or Tuesday. Why hadn't anyone driven into town and called them? Aeneas had lived for months here. Rob was jealous, Maureen felt put upon, Leo drank. But they weren't unkind people. Weren't they even curious? Didn't they find it odd that Aeneas should have a passport? The normal thing would have been for the four of them to sit on the overstuffed chairs Rob had bought, drink their cocoa, and chew on Aeneas. It didn't make sense that he just slipped from their minds.

Or he was pushed out of their minds.

Or something, that weekend—something more important than the briefly missing Buddha—pushed out everything.

I was at Maureen's cabin now. I climbed the steps, waited a moment—not nearly long enough for good manners—and pulled open the door.

Chapter Twenty-five

O

It was Maureen's cabin I'd barged into, but it wasn't Maureen kneeling on the floor hunting for something under her futon. It was Gabe Luzotta.

"What are you looking for, Gabe?"

He bounced up, grinning with obvious relief.

"Darcy!"

"Didn't you have time to search Maureen's cabin yesterday when you were 'napping'?"

A shock of fear froze his face; then it was gone and he shot me the grin again. But it was too late; I knew it and he did, too.

The first time I saw him he had made me think of a cat, sneaky but endearing. Now the feline he brought to mind was the one who turns belly up imploring you to scratch his stomach. You hesitate, but he's begging you, and he's so cute. Against your better judgment you give in and scratch. In an instant his claws are in your wrist. But I wasn't hesitating, not now.

"What happened to Aeneas, Gabe? Is he alive or dead?"

"I don't know."

He looked ashamed, as if he knew better than to sink those claws, as if he really wasn't the type of guy to be poking under Maureen's mattress. Then I realized I'd been had once more.

"Jeez, you are really something, Gabe. You're not embarrassed to be here rooting through Maureen's stuff, or making use of Leo while you do it. You're just ashamed that you haven't dug up the facts yet, right?"

He laughed. "Well, yeah."

I wanted to kick him hard as I could, see him splat into the wall. I surveyed the room till I got myself under control. It resembled mine and Amber's, except that the clutter here was all one person's. The place was a nest of colors, cushions, books, and CDs, a place to squirrel oneself away. No guests, no lovers, it said, just me safe on my thick red Persian cushions, under my green and purple comforter, protected from everything. It was the other side of Maureen's emaciated body and inadequate garb.

The one rigorously clear spot was her dresser top, a pale polished oak on which stood a startlingly graceful jade statue of Kuan-yin, the female icon of compassion. A hint of sandalwood hung in the air. I would have expected a ballet barre, or at least a photo of a principal dancer, perhaps herself, in beaded bodice, back arched till her extended leg touched her thrown-back head. But there was no memento, nothing to draw her back to the bittersweet comfort of memories. It was the room of a gardener, not a ballerina.

Seeing this room made Maureen's life more understandable to me. And Gabe's invasion even more offensive. He was shifting foot to foot, as if ready to spar. Automatically he grinned.

"You were here that weekend of the opening," I said. "What happened?"

"I told you before—"

"I know. The dignitaries arrived. Just before the ceremony the Buddha disappeared. Aeneas ran through the grounds dressed in Leo's robes and waving a bottle. The Buddha reappeared. And then everyone left."

"Right," he snapped. "So what's your question, Assistant?"

"What makes you think Aeneas ever left here? Or—wait, do you? That's the story you're after, isn't it?"

He had been holding a long saffron scarf. It dropped from his hand and he bent to gather it up.

I grabbed his shoulders. "The truth! Now!"

He turned his hands palms up, left the scarf in a yellow heap, and popped up, his smug grin back in place.

"This is just a byline to you, isn't it, Gabe? An expose! Have you been planning it the whole time since the opening? Coming back here every year or two 'for sesshin' so you can poke under Maureen's futon? Do you take notes every time you have dokusan with Roshi, in case you can get a juicy quote? One more clue to whether Aeneas is buried under the bathhouse?"

"He's not."

"What? Sheesh, Gabe, you're serious? You checked that out?"

"Well, yeah, of course. It's obvious. But there were too many outside workmen involved. You couldn't hide anything under there."

I just stood shaking my head.

"Look, Assistant, this is a big story. Why shouldn't it be exposed?"

"Why shouldn't *what* be exposed? Death? Murder?"

He shrugged again but this time even that motion looked forced, protective, and I had the sense I hadn't gotten to his secret.

"What, dammit?" I was almost shouting.

"Hey, hold your voice down! I don't know if Aeneas is dead or in Seattle. Or Atlanta. Or Kobe. That's not my story."

"Tell me another one!"

"No, honestly. I'm not saying I wouldn't jump on it. You bet I would, but I don't have anything. I can only go at it from the other end. That's why it's taken me so long."

"The other end?"

"The asshole's hypocrisy!"

"Leo?"

"No, not Roshi. The *Asshole!* Rob." He leaned back against Maureen's dresser, resting his buttocks an inch from the Kuan-yin. "Lookit, who shelled out for everything here? Our boy Rob. Money for the dome kit, plus what it cost to haul it nine miles along a road so terrible that cars get stuck. Money to build the bathhouse. That's not chump change out here in the middle of the woods. Just the technology for flush toilets here is big bucks! And the generator for the bathhouse and the kitchen. The chairs and rugs are small stuff. But altogether he's spent a couple hundred thou on this place. And that's what I know he spent. I don't know about incidentals."

"Exposes are supposed to expose secrets people *don't* already know. Everybody knows about Rob's gifts—"

He put a hand on my shoulder and sighed, as he would dealing with a simpleton. "Expose *start* from what everyone knows. It's what you do after that that makes the story."

"Like?"

"Like Rob came here one weekend—one!—before he shelled out for the dome. Dome's don't cost a fortune, but by the time he had it carted here it must have run him close to a hundred grand. He'd met Roshi once. He was a lawyer making three times that per year, but a third of your income ain't peanuts."

I must have looked insufficiently impressed. He pushed on.

"He was a lawyer, in San Francisco. He knew the lawyers for the Zen establishment there. He checked with them, not about Leo but about the title to the land."

"Because he cared only about the land," I tried.

"I'm not at the point of drawing conclusions. I don't limit myself. But if I was I'd be screaming *Yeah*. And . . . *and* . . . then he bought the chocolate equipment. All of it. He got it used, because it's almost antique. But it was not cheap." Softly, smugly, Gabe added, "And then there's the property our boy bought."

"Property?"

He sat down on Maureen's futon and patted the spot beside him. I understood the symbolism, but it didn't matter.

"See, that's the really interesting thing. Rob bought twenty acres on either side of the monastery. His land loops around to the road on both sides. The two plots almost meet in the back. So he's got the monastery surrounded."

"The property is in his name, not the monastery's?"

Gabe nodded emphatically.

"Why would he do that?"

"Well, now, that's the big question, isn't it? Why do you think, Assistant?" But Gabe was on a roll. "The Asshole's got his followers, guys who would love to turn this place into a strict, traditional training monastery, up at two A.M. for sesshin, seating by order of seniority. No heat in the cabins. No paving the road, so the monastery stays isolated."

"No women priests?"

"He probably couldn't get away with that, but he wouldn't relax any rules for people with kids."

Maureen's futon was folded in thirds, creating a low, narrow, lumpy bench against the wall. On it Gabe and I were sitting side by side, knees bent in front of us. I shifted to the edge and turned to face him.

"Would they toss Leo aside?"

"Not everyone in the Zen community here. But Rob's supporters? In a flash. They're a crouching minority, ready to spring."

But they hadn't sprung yet, not in six years.

"Not until Leo gives them reason, right?"

He nodded.

"Or he leaves." In a traditional monastery Rob would have worked his way up. But even traditional monasteries read the tale of the Sixth Patriarch. "What if Leo says he's bringing in, say, a priest from San Francisco. Would Rob's people support Leo or Rob?"

Gabe guffawed, big, hearty bellows, much louder than my outburst he'd so righteously shushed just minutes earlier.

"What?" I demanded.

"Well, Assistant, it's damned hard to be the guy hoisting the flag of traditionalism and organize against the roshi's chosen successor. It'd be like the Queen of England coming out against primogeniture."

Another time I might have laughed, had I not seen where that predicament led. Trying to keep my voice light, I said, "Suppose Leo died? I mean, does he own the monastery land?"

"The monastery is an offshoot of the greater Zen Buddhist community in this area. They gave the land into Leo's care. They're not up here checking on the number of toilets, but if he tried to give the land to the circus there would be a battle."

Gabe hadn't seen the logical outcome of Rob's predicament because he didn't know Leo had been poisoned. If Leo died, control would bounce back to the Zen bigwigs. They'd be forced to take charge. But if Leo was merely sick, there'd be no event to force them to spend a lot of time dealing with matters in this outpost in the woods. If Leo was too sick to attend meetings or make plans, Rob could "speak for him." Then Rob would have free rein to influence the unsure, consolidate his power, cast doubt on Leo's judgment, and there would come a point when it would be very hard for Leo to oust him. It all depended on Leo being too sick to interfere—too sick, but not dead.

For Rob, that wasn't a great plan or a flawless one, but the best he could do on the spur of the moment. Because, I realized, he hadn't needed a plan at all until he was sitting in the truck with Leo driving and me peering through the back window. Until then there had been no threat, not until Leo dismissed him as jisha. I had seen his face lined in anger, seen him wagging his finger at Leo, leaping from the still-moving truck and striding furiously across the quad. The first time he'd spoken to me, his replacement, he'd tried to arrange secret meetings for me to tell him about Leo's plans.

Surely Leo never dreamed Rob would poison him. But, here in the woods, Rob didn't have many options. Had Leo set up this sesshin for Rob? Did he think Rob had killed Aeneas? The Sixth Patriarch—

Suddenly cloth covered my face. Gabe's jacket. His face was against mine. He was kissing me, hard, like an assault. I pushed at him but my arms were out of position. I tried to speak, but his mouth was covering mine. I could barely breathe.

I almost didn't hear the door open. But I did hear the footfalls on the bare floor and out of the corner of my eye saw the boots beside us.

Rob was dressed in low slip-on boots, loose brown wide-wale corduroys, and a thick sweatshirt that smelled of incense from the zendo, but he might have been garbed in purple vestments, holding the papal miter, and eyeing two clerics fornicating in Vatican Square.

The three of us made a tableau, Rob glaring down the length of his long body, Gabe and me huddled like part of the decorative base. We were silent; not even our breath broke the void. Outside feet trudged by, rubber clumping onto macadam; something banged, perhaps the ladder against the zendo roof, and for an instant I actually thought I heard the truck engine, but I knew I was fooling myself.

Then the tableau broke, Gabe sprang back, grabbed my shoulders, planted a loud kiss on my lips, leapt up, and, before Rob could speak, gave him an even louder mouth-to-mouth. Despite everything, I had to mentally applaud Gabe. The man never lost his verve. Rob was still wiping his wrist across his mouth as Gabe whipped out the door.

Leaving me to deal with Rob.

My inclination was to leap up. Instead I shifted slowly, and eased myself up, wishing I could have leaned casually against the dresser as Gabe had, but was unwilling to disregard Maureen's altar there. Instead, I rested an arm against the wall and looked straight ahead at Rob's chest and decided to make the most of this chance to fact-check this story of Gabe's. For Gabe, of paste diamond schlimazel notoriety, meticulous research was essential, so he'd be easy to double-check.

"Rob, what's your total cash investment in this place?"

His shoulders shot up protectively in a way that made him seem smaller rather than taller. When he finally demanded, "What?" he all but confirmed Gabe's accusations.

"Did you assume your purchases were a secret, Rob?"

"Hardly," he snapped. "Maureen probably told you about the bathhouse before you had a chance to wash your hands."

His shoulders had dropped and without shifting anything else he seemed to have shifted himself back into control. He had, of course, been a trial lawyer trained to handle unpleasant surprise.

"She didn't tell me about the zendo. You paid for that when you'd only met Leo one time. You tossed nearly a hundred thousand dollars into the woods with a stranger who'd already screwed up big-time! That's a real pig in a poke, isn't it? You might as well have invested in Nigerian Internet scams."

"Hardly! The council said . . ."

"Of course, the council," I said, knowing zip about any council. "The great Zen council guaranteed your investment."

He didn't move, didn't react. I took that for a yes, a big-time neon flashing red yes. Had Leo known about that arrangement? What choice would he have had anyway? But the surrounding land, in Rob's name only—

"What the hell are you doing in here?" Rob demanded, as if the previous interchange hadn't existed.

"I came to see Maureen," I said, kicking myself for musing when I should have been on attack.

"She's blond and shorter than Gabe," he said sarcastically.

"Well, I found Gabe interesting."

"I could see."

I was still looking straight ahead, at his neck, rather than giving him the advantage of his height. I waited until he inhaled, and demanded, "What about the other twenty acres, the land that encircles this place? Did you work that out with the council, too? Or is that your private deal?"

He grabbed for my shoulders but caught himself just before he touched, as if shocked by his own violence.

"What about the chocolate equipment, Rob? Is that another private deal? How many private deals do you have going here? Private deals, side deals?"

His throat pulled in hard, tendons bulged.

"Who the hell are you to accuse me?" he yelled. "You don't know how things work here!" Getting control of his volume, he said, "Do you think Barry would have come here, just to get out of the city? Are you that naïve?

He's a class A chef; he could have gone to Boston, New York, New Orleans. What do you think lured him here? The woods? A chance to meditate? A teacher he barely knew? Hardly. I busted my butt to find that equipment. It cost a fortune. But the monastery has had a great cook. When times were tough, he kept people here, he drew students who wouldn't have tackled the woods. This place would have fallen apart without him."

"You're quite the patrone, aren't you? You sit in your fine apartment in San Francisco, spend your excess money on the dome for the zendo so Leo can build it. You buy the chocolate equipment so Barry can cook in obscurity. And what about Maureen, what was your great contribution to keep her here digging out a garden year after year? Getting the place in decent enough shape for you to deign to come live here?"

"Nothing! She—" but he was almost choking.

I jabbed. "And, that expensive chocolate equipment, what's going to happen after the Cacao Royale this weekend in San Francisco; what's going to happen when Barry leaves!"

His chiseled face had gone dead white with rage. His fists were jammed together in front of his gut and still he was shaking. I had never seen a man in such controlled fury.

"Someone else—" he squeaked, gave up, and slammed out of the cabin.

Sweat poured down my back. Now I was shaking as hard as Rob. I was desperate to get out of here, to be outside, safe with people. But I made myself stop, bend down, pick up the edge of Maureen's futon where Gabe Luzotta had been looking.

What was under there was a newspaper. I took it.

CHAPTER TWENTY-SIX

O

The newspaper I'd snatched out from under Maureen's futon was still stuffed up under my sweater when I eased open Leo's door. The closing door sent a chill breeze through the cabin. Leo was shivering when I helped him up. But he managed to sip half a cup of tea; I took that as a very good sign. The clappers hit, announcing the beginning of the afternoon block of sittings. I fluffed Leo's extra zafu and prepared to sit zazen in his cabin and wait for the doctor.

"Go sit in the zendo." They were the first words Leo had spoken. When I hesitated, he said, "You can hear the doctor from there."

"How did you—?"

"Know?" He smiled, a weak copy of his grins in the truck two days ago. "Not magic. I heard the truck leave. Barry didn't take it; he would stop in for blessing or luck or because he's afraid to break the ritual. He'll do that before he leaves. So, Darcy, what would necessitate this emergency trip? What else but you deciding I need a doctor?"

"Well, you do. You're not getting better. Look at you, you can't sit up without help. Of course you need a doctor."

I thought he would be outraged at my ignoring his decision, but he gave what looked like a shrug.

"We'll see."

O

Leo was right; it was remarkable how much I could hear from the zendo. Leaves rustled, wind snapped branches against the bath house. Someone slipped out during the second period and I heard the zendo door shut, leather-soled shoes go down the steps, slap on the macadam, and the bathhouse door open. Maureen's newspaper, still under my sweater, crackled so loudly I was sure everyone heard it. Near the end of the third period the kitchen door slammed and the servers' clogs tapped the macadam as they carried the pots to the zendo porch for supper.

But I did not hear the truck, and I couldn't help remembering Amber's jibe: *A cool old truck like that? Justin could be halfway to San Francisco by now.*

I gave up any attempt to just sit and be aware, to do zazen. Desperately, I pulled my attention back to Rob, considered his ambition and Gabe's. Somewhere in that eternity of time between the almost-supper signal of the servers' footsteps and the actual end of that last sitting period ten minutes later, the two men's ambitions contrasted with Leo's statement about the doctor, "We'll see." What Leo had been saying was that since I had agreed to postpone a decision about his health till Friday, things had changed. They had changed not because of his health but because I had sent for the doctor. Our agreement was history—it didn't exist any more; the doctor's imminent visit was reality. Rob and Gabe were still anchored to the future of their dreams; those dreams blocked out reality.

The bell rang once to end the afternoon sitting periods. Beside me, Amber stretched like a dog waking from a long nap. People swiveled around on their cushions to face the room and positioned their eating bowls—three stacked, and wrapped in a white cotton rectangle twelve by twenty-four inches that would be used as an individual tablecloth in front of their knees.

I bowed and left the Zendo to assemble a tray for Leo and myself. When I got to the kitchen, bowls of gruel and salad were waiting on the tray. *We'll see.* The doctor and the truck, which had filled my thoughts and beckoned my ears all afternoon, were illusion. Reality was Roshi's food: poisoned or not?

Barry was not in the kitchen. I dumped the food. It would be a few minutes before the serving pots were back from the zendo and I could ladle out safe food.

Everyone was either in the zendo eating or hurrying back and forth serving and removing dishes. This was the one time the bathhouse would be empty. Maureen's newspaper article crackled under my sweater. My hand was already inching toward it as I raced across the path.

And almost smacked into Maureen!

I know I flushed red. But she didn't notice, not my face, not me at all. She was moving in that feet-barely-touching-the-ground way, as if her balance was off and she might lurch out of control any moment.

"Are you sick, Maureen?"

She came abreast, recognized me, went dead white, and rushed on ahead of me into the bathhouse without a word. Did she know I'd been in her room? That her newspaper was crinkling under my sweater this very minute? I flushed redder yet with shame. I had been so caught up in dealing with Gabe, in worrying about Leo, that the sense of invasion Maureen would feel once she discovered we had been in her room hadn't occurred to me. I stopped, inhaled, tried to come up with something to say, failed, and walked into the bathhouse after her. The newspaper thundered in the silence.

"Maureen?"

No response.

I waited. Wind crackled the door; the plumbing gurgled. Finally, I peered under the stall doors.

She must have come in one door and kept moving out the other.

Relief mixed with the shame, but it would have been crazy not to read the newspaper article after all this. I pulled out the paper. An arrow in blue ink pointed to the final entry in a column:

City Updates: Ballet Harassment Suit Settled.

Ballet-Metropolitan of San Francisco, in a surprise move, settled the sexual harassment suit brought by ten female dancers, presently or formerly with the company. The settlement included the forced resignation of the company's long time director/choreographer, Raul Jeffers.

In the casting couch milieu of ballet, to force a director's resignation for a bit of pinch and tickle is unheard of. Smart money assumes that BalMet and former Director Jeffers had a lot more to hide than that.

Said soloist and plaintiff Alicia Quinteras, "The ballet was our life. We thought we were interpreting the most exquisite art and Raul was the great creator. He made it a sham. Art for sex's sake."

I squinted to make out the handwritten note by the arrow: *Your quote, Maureen. Hope you don't mind. Bastard's gone! Yeah! Alicia.*

Quickly, I refolded the paper, as if to shield it from my own prying eyes. Poor Maureen! I could imagine only too well what she had endured. The stunt world was different from ballet in many ways, but not all. We had our casting couches, too. But you don't run through a wall of fire, even wearing Kevlar head to toe, then cringe at a hand on your ass. It pisses you off, makes you worried about your job, but it doesn't crush you at the core the way betrayal of art does. Art for sex's sake; no wonder Maureen walked out and into the safety of this monastery and Leo.

When I pushed open Leo's door five minutes later, the cabin was dark. I lit his oil lamp and the room looked merely dim. But Leo looked like a dead baby bird. Holding my breath, I felt his forehead—clammy, but cold.

"I've brought you some soup. Can you eat?"

He nodded, and I lifted him, tucked the blanket around him, made sure he was steady before I handed him the soup. I did it all, pushing away the dread that would drown me if I let it. I couldn't even let myself think about the doctor.

"What happened?" he asked.

"When?"

"Just now. You look awful."

"I could say the same for you."

"I asked first." He smiled. "Darcy, the jisha's job is to assist the Roshi. Part of that is to keep him informed about what's going on."

He sounded stronger, as if fortified by his responsibilities.

"I ran into Maureen," I said, busying myself with settling on a cushion. "She turned pale at the sight of me. Like she did when I ran into her in the office yesterday."

"Oh."

It was a small, dead word. I had the feeling he, too, would have gone pale had he had any color left to lose.

"Leo? The opening? What happened to Maureen? Yesterday, when I asked about Aeneas, she mentioned the story about the devil in the cage roasting the neighbor children. What did Aeneas do to her? Attack her? Grope?" I hesitated, barely able to make myself ask. "Did he try to rape her? Was that what she was afraid of? In the picture you were all packed together with nowhere to move, but she looked like she was trying to get away from him."

"Not him."

"Not him? Who?" My throat was dry; I could barely get the words out. I didn't want to hear the answer, didn't want to think of her then, right after the ballet betrayal.

Leo was still holding his soup mug. He had barely eaten from it, but he held it out and I put it on the floor between us.

Behind me the embers crackled softly, needing stoking or shoveling out entirely. A draft shot down the empty chimney onto my back. Leo shivered but made no move to pull the blanket up higher. He looked as if he was gathering his strength. Finally, he turned and looked directly at me.

"I'm going to tell you about the opening."

He hadn't said, I should have told you earlier, or I didn't want you to be burdened with it, or I shouldn't be telling you. I nodded.

"I had screwed up before. I was lucky to be given another chance at any Zen center. This place was my penance. No old students came with me. I walked down that road from the highway alone. I spent the first month alone here in a tent, in the woods, with nothing but the land. And then Rob heard about me; he drove up one weekend. He bought the dome kit; we built the zendo. A few others came, more to get away from their lives than to be present here. But I was grateful for them. And Barry. And Aeneas."

"And Maureen?"

"Maureen." He spoke her name as if gazing at an alabaster bowl. "Maureen." The oil lamps drew long shadows down his face, transforming him into a charcoal drawing. "Everything changed when Maureen came. This place was so hardscrabble, so endlessly dirty, cold, slogging. But she was delicate, exquisite, so very beautiful that it transformed everything. In Zen we do the next thing and then the next. But it's hard, particularly for novices here, to escape. They would never have made it through the winter without Maureen. I don't know that I would have.

"There were three men and a woman resident then. They were all in love with her in their ways."

The wind had stopped momentarily. The silence resounded. Leo's voice hadn't dropped as it should have to end a thought. He had simply stopped speaking.

His unspoken clause hung between us.

I swallowed and said, "And you?"

"And me. I was in love with her, too, in my way." He took a deep breath. "But I was the teacher, and I had taken vows not to abuse sexuality. Sexual scandals had threatened to destroy Zen in America. Priests turning from guide to predator had done violence after violence to students: the assault itself, the loss of trust, and finally it had denied them the solace of their practice. I looked at Maureen's allure and I knew the dangers.

"And yet, I did not tell her to leave. Instead, I told myself I could handle the situation. I drew the group together and talked about the dangers of abusing sexuality, of unrecognized greed. I listened for hints in private discussions. I kept my eyes open. I watched them all. And I watched myself.

"Mostly I watched Maureen. I knew she had been in a prestigious ballet company, and that they had let her go, and she was devastated. I expected her to be like a whiff of incense, there and gone. I was surprised at how strong she was physically, how hard she worked, at how little she revealed. That reticence, the mystery of it, was part of her allure. She was like a poem, half created from the memories of the reader. I saw that in the eyes of everyone here.

"No matter how carefully I watched, the situation was kindling waiting for a match."

"Was that what drove you back to drinking?" I asked.

"Not back to. I drank. I suspect everyone had their escape. I pretended that I could drink and still keep watch. Maybe I could." He gave his head a shake as if annoyed with his introspection. "By the time of the opening, the tension had ground into our cells. It was like the mosquitoes buzzing around us."

He reached for his cup, lifted it carefully, sipped, and replaced it.

"The opening itself was a huge event for us, and mostly for me. It was my acceptance back into the Zen community. All those who had discussed my disgrace—had spoken against trusting me with even this remote piece of land—were coming to acknowledge my success. There were some who would have been pleased to watch me fall on my face. I should have been sitting in meditation, seeing my thoughts, my reactions to all that, but I had been too busy building, worrying, drinking. In my mind the ceremony had to be perfect."

"Was it?" I asked, unable to stand the tension.

"Until Aeneas took the Buddha. That delicate, porcelain Buddha. He might as well have grabbed Maureen and run off with her under his arm. Every bit of pent-up tension every resident had suppressed exploded. Even after Rob retrieved the Buddha all the residents were out of control.

I got them all in this cabin, had them sit, talked, let them talk—I'm sure the guests heard the yelling. And in the end I did the worst thing. I told them it was us against them, and we couldn't let the guests see us fall on our faces like they expected." He looked me in the eyes, but I didn't know what he was looking for. "I discarded the practice for the appearance of practice. I betrayed my students, to save the opening. You see that, don't you, Darcy?"

I ached to ameliorate, to comfort him, but there could be nothing but the truth between us now. I nodded.

"They knew it then, that they were attending the inaugural blessing of a sham. They went through with it . . . for me. And I thought that was the end of it.

"Afterwards, after the guests had all gone, I went to Maureen's cabin to try to explain. I had been drinking but I wasn't drunk. I was in that in-between stage where you think you're in control of your observations. You act on what you think you see."

I sat unmoving; the draft fingered its way down my back inside my sweater.

He lifted the cup, held it next to his lips as if he had forgotten its purpose, as if he had shifted into the past, was facing Maureen's cabin door. I reached to take the cup from his hands. He jolted. Then he looked at the cup, but made no reference to his action, and put it down without drinking.

"She opened her door. I shifted to step inside. She didn't move; she was looking at me not just with fear but with dread. She gasped, moved back away from me. She didn't raise her hands, didn't try to fend me off. But I could see in her eyes the horror, the betrayal of every woman who has ever discovered her teacher just wants a piece of ass. I thought I had hidden my want of her; I'd been so careful. But I'd failed; all that time she had been walking in fear of me, of this moment, knowing it would come, knowing I would betray her." He paused, stared directly at me, and said slowly, "I did not come for sex, but my betrayal that afternoon laid the groundwork for her to make that assumption."

In the zendo the clappers hit twice, echoed by another set a half tone higher. The two pairs wove back and forth until one took the beat and clapped faster and faster and a bell marked their end. Feet slapped on the wood of the porch, rubber and leather smacked the steps, and then, muted, the macadam. The bathhouse door creaked open, thudded shut. Leo was still sitting in the same position, cross-legged, braced against the wall, gray blankets tucked around his still, gray form.

I shifted, about to ask if he wanted help to lie down. But he wasn't through speaking.

"Maureen and I never spoke of that. I made opportunities over the years, but I had intruded once and I didn't feel I could do that to her again. Not on that. For a long time she avoided me. Not easy out here. But possible. She made sure we weren't alone. Every time I saw her make a sharp turn and take a different path, it reminded me of my betrayal, and my responsibility to deal with the consequences. And so . . . and so we've gone on here, year after year, because neither of us could leave."

We sat there, Leo and I. It was as if we were not in Leo's safe little cabin. The slap of shoes as people passed did not enter our ears. The clappers did not call to us. We were with Maureen, walking on the shard-strewn ground of betrayal, each with our own contribution to it. Inside my sweater the newspaper cut into my breast. I remembered hearing of Leo's words after Aeneas had taken the Buddha: There's nothing that can't be replaced, except what someone didn't want to tell you to begin with. But he'd been wrong there. Trust can't be replaced.

And yet something didn't fit. Something . . .

Leo coughed. His face was scarlet; his skin clammy, his breath suddenly ragged.

"Take me to the bathhouse. Quick."

I scooped him up and into a coat, steadied him while he aimed feet into moccasins inadequate for soggy winter weather and steadied him as he moved across the path faster than he had any business doing. I listened to him retch, then I went back inside the men's bathroom.

"Help me brush my teeth," he said in a thin, raspy voice.

I held him by the sink as he brushed. Watching him struggle with this mundane and messy task would have been the capping intrusion and I looked away, my arm around his ribs, listening to the scratching of the toothbrush.

He moved so slowly on the way back I was almost carrying him. He felt flimsy, as if he had vomited up all but this shell. How could he make it through the night?

From behind us metal rattled.

"The truck," he said.

The truck! The doctor!

Leaving him on his futon I ran as if I were flying. It was there! The old yellow truck, more mud-laden than ever, pointed its round yellow bumpers, its round snout of a hood right at me. Dusk was passing into night now, but the yellow truck shone like the sun. I slammed into the front of it, pushed off to the left, and pulled open the passenger door.

The truck was empty.

I turned back, but the path was empty. Then I heard the men's voices behind the truck. I leapt forward, ready to grab the doctor by the arm.

Justin was propped against the rear bumper. His new winter jacket was spackled with mud, his hair was wet and stuck to his forehead, and even in the dark I could see his hand trembling. The man beside him was Barry.

"Where's—"

"He never made it to town, Darcy. The truck gave out. He tried to fix it—"

"Right tools; didn't have," Justin forced out.

"He did well to hike back here on that muddy puddle of a road and get me. We were lucky the truck gave out near the path; at least I could get back there and check under the hood before dark. Justin did the best he could," he said, slapping the boy's shoulder. "It's an old truck; tricky. There was no way Justin could know the engine well enough. I had a devil of a time getting it back in shape."

Never made it to town. No doctor. I stumbled to the edge of the parking lot and for a moment thought I would throw up, too. But even that didn't happen. Finally I walked back to the truck and asked Barry the most ordinary question I could think of.

"Is there dinner to heat up for Justin?"

Barry nodded and the two headed up toward the kitchen. Barry hadn't said if I had asked him to check the engine this morning, instead of sending Justin out without telling him, the doctor would be here.

I walked back to the cabin where Leo was sleeping now and built a huge fire, not that it made any difference. He woke up only once to growl at me to go sit in the zendo. I went for the last period when we sit facing into the circle. Normally in sesshin that is my favorite period of the day, when, after a long, hard day alone facing the wall, facing the thoughts I don't want to see, feeling the fears I'm afraid to touch, all of us have turned and look toward the center of the zendo, toward the whole community, each person sitting still, calm in appearance, with an apparent serenity that wasn't there in the morning. Physical pain is manageable because the end is in sight. The lights are soft for the last period; the small flames of the candle and the oil lamps bring a coziness to the altar.

The incense has burned all day and, by the end, whiffs no longer startle me; it has spread to a gentle spice that fills the air between us. When the final bell rings we bow to the altar and to each other and find ourselves holding those bows an instant longer, as if our fingers were touching across the room.

Tonight it all seemed a mockery.

When the alarm woke me at 4:10 A.M. after another night of prodding dreams I understood what had niggled at me about Maureen's years here. Leo had said neither of them could leave. Him, I understood; this was his place, and he had to prove himself here. He had to provide a place for her in order to overcome his betrayal. But Maureen was the victim; why had she stayed year after year? Depression, inertia? It wasn't enough. Leo's story made no sense for her. Either he was seeing through his own eyes, or he wasn't telling me everything.

Chapter Twenty-seven

O

THURSDAY

Roshi was already awake when I arrived with his tea at 4:20 Thursday morning. I helped him outside, trying to judge his state of health by his walk, his stance, his gargle. Yesterday, when I had thought I could save him, my judgment seemed crucial; today, with no choices to make, it was just opinion. He sipped the tea, shifting the hot little mug from stiff hand to stiff hand, his breath steaming in the icy room. When the fire caught, he said, "Get yourself coffee, Darcy. Go on to the zendo. Hold the incense for Rob. And then leave me to sleep. Don't come back till after breakfast. You sleep till then; you need it. Leave my door unlocked."

"No." The word had just popped it. But it was the right one. "I can't."

"I *said*, leave it unlocked." He had swallowed the last of the tea but was still holding the mug, drinking in the warmth. The steam from the cup meshed with the his breath, and blended into the cold air. "I have put a great burden on my students. I have to keep my door open for them. This is what I do."

A jisha does not contradict the Roshi. I looked down at his sweet gray face and said, "No. Not in the dark. After breakfast."

I was out the door and had it locked before he could object, and hurried to the kitchen to obey him, at least about my coffee. Barry was peering into the cooler where trays of shiny brown rectangles lay waiting for their trip south. Behind him were piled four white boxes the size of center desk drawers. Barry stared into the cooler, out and at the boxes, and back to the cooler. His movements were jerky and he looked like a man too exhausted to make simple decisions about transferring. It was already Thursday and he was cutting things close, but if he blamed me for taking the truck yesterday, he was too polite or too tired to mention it.

Foregoing preliminaries I asked the question that had woken me up at 2:45 A.M. I needed him to confirm it. "When the Japanese roshis were here there were no buildings, were there? You were all sleeping in tents, and the zendo half finished, right?"

He nodded, too tired to question my question.

"Yes. Even the kitchen was a tent. The bathhouse was a shell."

I took the coffee outside and drank it in the safety of the darkness. If Aeneas never left here six years ago, if he had been buried here, there was no building to bury him under. Six years ago there was only one convenient, camouflaged place to bury anything.

When the clappers sounded I went to Rob's cabin, lit incense, and followed him in silence to the zendo. I held out the incense for him at the altar, bowed, and walked right past my seat and out the front door.

Which meant I had to go splashing through the cold mud around the zendo to the back door where I had followed Rob in. Where my shoes still were. And then, because my socks were covered in mud, I couldn't put them in my shoes, and I couldn't sit there on the back porch fiddling with my shoes, reminding everyone in the zendo that I was outside, so I ended up socking it back around the zendo to the bathhouse, shoes in hand, which made no sense whatsoever, and only highlighted my exhaustion.

I yanked off one soggy sock, grabbed some paper towels, wrapped them around my foot, and stuffed my foot into my boot.

"Oh, good. I found you."

Maureen stood panting at the door. I was wrapping paper towels around my second foot. I was too cold to stop.

"Uh-huh?"

"I have to see him."

"Roshi?"

"Yes! Roshi."

"Why?"

"Wha—?"

The wad of paper towels was keeping me from getting my foot all the way into my boot. I stood, trying to cram my foot down enough to walk. The towels stuck, creating enough of a lift under that heel that I'd be hobbling, but it would have to do.

I stood up, and realized Maureen was still there. It took me a moment to remember what she was asking.

"Oh . . . Roshi. He's not seeing anyone now."

"But I have to."

For the first time I really looked at her. The circles under her eyes were so dark they looked like theatrical makeup. She was twisting the opening of her sleeve. All I could think of was the abusive ballet master, and Leo at her cabin door. She looked so strung out that I hated to tell her no.

I hedged, and asked again, "Why do you need to see him? What about?"

"About? About, uh, uh, the garden."

That wasn't the issue. I wished I could have wrapped an arm around her, or gotten her old boyfriend Barry to do it. She needed someone calm. And she needed sleep as much as I did. Maybe more. There was a wild look about her; she really did need to see Roshi. But sick as he was I couldn't expose him to someone in this bad a shape.

I felt terrible, but I said, "Not now. He can't see anyone till later."

"But I need—"

"Maureen, you of all people know he wouldn't keep you out without a good reas—"

She slammed out of the bathhouse.

Another time I would have gone after her, but exhaustion brings down the final curtain fast. She could pound on Roshi's door, but she couldn't get in. And she wasn't likely to carry on about her "garden" through the door. Still, I veered past his cabin to make sure it okay, and before I stumbled into my own cabin. My feet were icy. I thought they would keep me awake. Life is illusion!

I didn't wake up till Amber poked me after breakfast break, three luscious hours later. Her poke had been no gentle nudge, more like her skiing into me, but even with that I could have turned over and gone back to sleep for a day or two.

"Get up! Zazen's in fifteen minutes!"

"Roshi told me—"

"Shh!" she hissed, bending over me and looking ridiculously righteous about the whole thing.

It wasn't till I kneaded my eyes and sat up that I remembered this was the time I had agreed to leave Roshi's door unlocked. Too soon! Way too soon. I couldn't stand the idea of Roshi lying in his room at the mercy of whoever tromped in, whoever murdered Aeneas. If Roshi didn't mention the lock, I was set to forget it.

I peeked in on Roshi—sleeping—and almost smacked into Rob as I hurried across the path from Roshi's cabin to the zendo.

"Sorry," he muttered.

I stopped where I was, surprised that he would break stride for that minor courtesy—to me, yet.

"Roshi wants me to follow the same schedule as yesterday?"

I nodded, even more surprised. I had told him that yesterday; there was no reason for him to expect change.

"If the weather holds we can do outdoor kinhin," he went on, I realized, talking to let off steam. "That'll take up the slack."

"Slack?"

"Maureen!" he said, with a show of exasperation. "She can't be bothered to plan. She isn't even a good gardener if it requires planning. Look at that red maple!"

My stomach quivered with guilt. My nap had erased all thought of Maureen and how unstrung she had looked in the bathhouse.

"She caught me before breakfast. She hasn't prepared her talk. No notes, no sources, nothing. I told her yesterday, but she did nothing. Now she's going to ramble. Still, it's going to run short."

I sighed.

"That'll be fine. People always get something from learning about senior students' practices. Hearing that she's screwed up will be a comfort to most of the new people. 'If the work leader can mess up her talk, then maybe there's hope for me.' This should be the worst thing that happens to any of us," I said, and actually patted him on the arm as I headed for the zendo.

Each block of sitting periods has its own feel. There's a dark, mysterious cozy feel of promise when you enter the zendo for the first time at dawn. In the afternoon, there's an ease, a re-quieting from the diversion of work period, and often it includes feeling your reactions to some illicitly spoken comment during that period, some hurt hugely magnified in the silence. The last block before bed when your knees ache from being bent, your spine has a dull pain and yearns for a chair with a back, is just endurance. But the mid-morning sitting, the one starting now, feels fresh, professional in its way. The *jikido*, assigned to straighten the cushions and do a quick sweep of the floor during the break, has given the zendo itself a fresh look. You've been fed, had a break in which to nap, had two or three cups of coffee, and you are as alert as you're ever likely to be. There's only one sitting before the lecture, and you're ready to make the most of it.

At the end of the zazen period, we did kinhin outdoors, at a good clip. But when we got back in the zendo and settled on our cushions, this time facing into the room, the front seat was empty. We waited, eyeing the door. It didn't open. Five minutes passed. Rob announced, "We will stay as we are, and just sit zazen."

I knew the present zazen period was no longer than the previous one, but this was a glimpse of eternity. Since I was facing into the room, I managed, without moving my head, to eye Roshi's door, and the front door alternatively, as if that would draw Maureen in here.

When the bell finally rang, she still hadn't come. I hurried out of the zendo, put on my boots, and thought I was heading for her cabin, till I realized my feet were carrying me to the place I was most worried about, to Roshi's cabin.

"Roshi," I said, bursting through his doorway, "Are you okay?"

"Was, till you woke me," he grumbled, smiling at me.

"Maureen's missing. Rob was looking for her; and then she didn't show up for her lecture."

"Pour me some tea."

"Did you hear what I said?"

"Yes."

He pushed himself onto his side and tried to sit up. I grabbed and hoisted him. My hands were shaking. As soon as he was up, he attacked his unshaven face with both hands, shaking the skin under his fingers as if he was massaging the bones beneath. He nodded toward the teapot.

"It'll be cold," I said.

"Still tea."

"Right."

I reached for the pot, annoyed. There was a point when this roshi business went too far. Had he missed what I was saying entirely?

"Roshi, Maureen was desperate to see you this morning."

His gaze rested on the door. He meant that if I had left it open as he'd wanted she could have walked in, talked to him, and this crisis could have been averted.

"But then she ran into Rob and told him about not preparing for her talk," I countered, trying to control my voice so the high pitch didn't let him know how pissed off I was getting with him.

"Interchangeable?" he said, holding his hand out for the teacup.

"I didn't mean you were!"

He made no response, verbal or otherwise. I turned my back to him to fuss with the tea, to get myself under control. I squeezed my hands into fists. Maureen was gone and he was blaming me. Dammit, what was I supposed to do?

"Was I supposed to let her in here to have another go at you?"

I had spun to face him and I was shouting. His hand was still out. I grabbed the teacup and poured, and it was all I could do to keep from slamming it into his hand. I took a deep breath, then another, and handed it to him exceedingly carefully.

He jostled the cup. I started to grab, but he shook his head.

"If I spilled it, it could be a mess."

Then, in perfect control, he lifted the cup to his mouth and drank. But in my mind the room was morning dark, the day was Tuesday, and I was scrubbing up the cocoa off the floor. Now the room was light, the day was Thursday, the liquid was tea, and it wasn't on the floor. The only thing the same was my fury. It burst through me, smashing at my skin from the inside. My hands shook, my head ached. I wanted to scream—again. I wanted to—

I glared back at him. I knew this was a lesson, like the cocoa. I knew if I let go of my anger I would see his point and learn something. But I didn't care. I was too furious.

"If she'd walked in, you could be dead. Would that make things better? Not for you; not for her."

He looked down at the tea.

"Could *not* be a mess."

"Yeah, maybe you could have handled her fears. But you haven't in six years. What makes you think you could now? You know what the Achilles heel of the roshi is, Leo? It's arrogance."

I'd gone too far. His features barely changed and yet his face was entirely different. He looked as if I'd punctured him. I hadn't meant to hurt him, not to the core like that. I wanted to grab his hands in mine and tell him how sorry I was.

"Close the door on your way out. Leave me the key. Tell Rob he'll have to double as jisha."

He lowered himself to the bed and turned away.

Oh, right, kill the messenger! Tuesday I had been excruciatingly careful not to give him the satisfaction of slamming the door. Now I didn't care. I plucked the key from my pocket, tossed it on the dresser, and slammed out.

I turned and walked across the muddy ground away from the cabin. I didn't know what had come over me. I wanted to cry, to kick. Emotions swirled through me with no mooring. I felt like I didn't know who I was anymore.

"Darcy Lott," I muttered, "stunt double, the woman who overcomes danger."

Not one who becomes it. I wanted to run, but I couldn't in the mud and in the boots. I wanted to scream, but I couldn't in the middle of sesshin. I couldn't even just keep on walking because the damn trees walled me in. Bile gushed into my throat; up was down, green sky pressing the air from my lungs. I was lost.

Then I did the last thing I would have guessed. I stopped dead, turned around, walked at double-time to the zendo, bowed to my cushion, bowed to the room, and sat zazen. I was still so angry, so shocked, so desolate, so lost there was no way to think about anything, and I just sat, feeling the anger burst into my stomach and then my chest, realizing my teeth were clenched so hard my ears were ringing. Some number of times I was on the verge of leaping off the cushion, furious that I might be giving Leo the satisfaction of doing what he would have told me. There was no way out.

But after a while something changed, the fire of my fury died, and I just sat and listened to the wind on the windows, Amber's little high-pitched wheeze next to me, the sound of my own breath. I realized then that I had stepped through a door, on my own I had trusted my Zen practice. I had, as we chant, *taken refuge in the Buddha.* I wasn't lost; I was right here.

I also knew I needed desperately to find Maureen.

The bell rang. I thought it was to end the lecture period, when Maureen should have been giving her talk, but, in fact, it marked the end of the entire midday sittings. I had sat through the whole thing, including the kinhin walking meditations, and marked none of it in my memory. Now I could hear the servers racing up the porch steps with the lunch pots. My first impulse was to bow, leave, and find Maureen. But in my new clarity I knew that part of the reason I had snapped at Leo before was hunger. I had missed too many meals here. Cold, tired, and hungry were never a felicitous trio. Still, it was torture to know Maureen was out there somewhere, fragile and on the verge of I didn't know what. And Roshi's door was unlocked.

I should have beckoned Rob outside and told him he was now jisha. I . . . couldn't.

CHAPTER TWENTY-EIGHT

O

aureen's cabin was empty. The office, too. I hurried out, under the overhang and into the shed, and stood looking at the bottles lined up in front of the garden poison. It was cold here and damp. The earth floor sloped under my feet, and the place smelled of mold and chemicals. Even with the door half open the small room was so dark that bottles looked fuzzy and labels were merely colored paper on them. Just yesterday Gabe had startled me here. He had chosen this unlikely spot for a nap. It hadn't struck me then, but now I looked around this unadulterated outbuilding and wondered what made him even imagine he could curl up and sleep in here. It sure wouldn't have been my first choice. But he had been to the monastery before, and this time he made a beeline for this shed. That meant not only was there a big enough space for him somewhere in here, there was a known nook.

If the space was big enough for him, it would be ample for Maureen. I looked around for a flashlight. You'd think, in a place like this . . . You'd be wrong.

"Maureen?" I called softly.

No reply.

"Maureen?"

Nothing.

The wood was piled three logs high in the front and four in the back. I braced a foot, and leapt into the dark. Onto something soft. Forcing my hand down I felt beside me. I was on cloth. A sleeping bag. Ah, the soft thing. I could have laughed. Gabe would have been hiding out in comfort here if he didn't mind spiders and whatever country critters inhabit outbuildings.

My eyes had adjusted but the shadows were still close to black. All I could tell was that my space was very small—high enough to stand up, but not wide enough to lie full out. That, and that I was alone. Then my hand hit something hard and smooth. A flashlight. Automatically I pulled it toward me. It stuck, then, with a snap, gave.

I flicked it on and flashed the light back to the spot where it had hung. A good-sized nail protruded from the wall, and when I looked closely at it I could see the clean line the metal loop of the flashlight had made on the nail. The flashlight had been there a while. Perhaps this was its permanent home.

I shone the light around the back portion of the shed. The space was akin to a monk's cave, in size and accoutrements. Besides the sleeping bag I was on, there was a small trunk. It creaked like a horror-movie sound effect as I opened it. Inside was a floor pillow covered in tan print cotton, and a wool blanket; nothing else. I shone the light over the walls. In front of me the logs created a room divider of sorts. On either side were bare studs, and the back slanted out and down.

This part of the shed was a hideaway where Leo or Maureen or Barry or even Rob could come when he had to get clear of the rest of them in those long months when they were alone here; that's why the flashlight was not in the front part with the cans and bottles, but back here to accommodate the user.

This last-ditch hideout, but Maureen wasn't here!

I could so easily picture her standing here just as I was.

I understood how central Maureen was to everything here. She had come here as Barry's girlfriend. She'd seen him through the Big Buddha Bakery affair. She was the one they all loved in one way or another. She knew about Rob's ambition. She was closest to Roshi. When we outlanders arrived for sesshin it was Maureen who was in the kitchen weaving people into the preparations. She was the one who had made sure I knew how to find my cabin.

But her centrality was more than the result of being the only woman on the permanent staff. The key was not her position, but herself. What I had seen as a sort of sprightliness and Rob viewed as ditzyness, was more basic than either. There was a porous quality to Maureen, like the lightest of sponge cakes that a cook yearns to ice or to fill on the way to making it his signature confection. She was a helium balloon waiting to be tethered, with a quality that led everyone to think they were the proper tethering post. Her porousness, her lack of protective skin, made her alert to the danger in the air here.

Oh, what I would have given to change my decision in the bathhouse this morning. Instead of telling her no, if I had only taken her to Roshi. I wouldn't have left her alone there, of course. But Roshi was right. He had needed to see her, to keep her from cutting her tether altogether. Again I thought of Aeneas in the only convenient, camouflaged burial place, and wondered if Maureen was close to joining him.

A cold finger of wind traced the side of my neck. Pales stripes of light shown between the boards, but rather than light the shed they made the dark darker. I had never been in a ramshackle shed like this. We don't have outbuildings in Manhattan, nor did we when I was growing up in San Francisco. Locations where old dirt-floored sheds were common were spots I had avoided. And yet something felt familiar.

It wasn't the shed, I realized, but Maureen. Maureen was like my second sister, Janice. Not in appearance. Janice had coal-black hair like most of the family. Like Maureen, Janice was the one the others confided in. "The nice one," aunts called her. She was the second girl, the fourth child, and, more importantly, the central one of the three middle children, there to hear year-older Gary's exploits, there to comfort, protect, and often have to find excuses for year-younger Grace. Because they were all so much older than I, I probably wouldn't have made the connection had I not stumbled in on Janice, scrunched in the back of the closet behind the stairs. I was five, so she'd have been fifteen. She'd put her finger to her lips, made me promise not to tell, and proclaimed our secret a sacred bond. It was the importance of sharing that secret that etched her words in my memory. She had said, "Sometimes I can't take it any more. Nice people pay a price. Other people would be hurt to know how big that price is. So you can't ever tell."

What Janice didn't say, and I learned only much later, was one time when Gary and Grace got to be too much and Janice couldn't hide out she had attacked them with a shovel.

I had to find Maureen before . . . before?

She hadn't taken the truck. Was that a good sign, or a terrible one? She'd still be somewhere around here. Barry was already worried. He'd know where she'd be.

I ran along the paths, skirting the trio of women friends walking slowly, silently savoring their after lunch break. At the chocolate kitchen I flung open the door, and nearly fell over the packed boxes.

"Barry!" I panted.

"Wish me luck," he said lifting another large, insulated box onto the counter.

He looked so different it stunned me. He looked like he'd stepped from the Redwood Canyon Monastery to the L.L. Bean catalog. Gone were his plain black monk's robes. Now he sported loose wide-wale tan corduroy slacks, light-blue work shirt, and navy V-neck sweater. All he needed was a pair of tassel loafers.

"You're leaving now?" I said, horrified. I'd forgotten all about his chocolate contest.

"I know, I should have been on the road an hour ago. I had to spend an hour making sure the truck wouldn't conk out again. Now it's going to be dark before I get as far as Santa Rosa. I've got the chocolate in cooler boxes; it *should* be all right. But I'm skirting the edge. I should be transporting it in a temperature-controlled truck and—"

"Barry, Maureen's gone!"

"Maureen?" he said blankly. *He'd* already forgotten about the monastery here. It was a moment before he pulled his attention back from his packed chocolate and road worries and demanded, "Where's she gone?"

I shook my head. "Don't know. Just gone. I checked everywhere here."

As cook, of course, he wouldn't have been expected to be in the zendo in the mornings. He was too busy to be at lecture so he wouldn't have noticed Maureen's absence. And nobody would have thought to tell him.

"She was pretty unhinged this morning. She wanted to see Roshi and I said no."

"Good decision. That's why you're the jisha."

"*Was* the jisha. He fired me."

The words came out squeaky. I realized I was shaking.

He put down the box, walked, over and put his arm around my shoulder. "Don't let all this get to you. This is sesshin. Everything is magnified."

"But Maureen! I can't just leave her wandering."

"She does that, goes off. She's lived here six years; she knows her way around."

"Where would she go? She's not in the shed."

"You know about the shed?" His arm stiffened on my shoulder.

"What about the fire tower?"

Suddenly, Amber was standing across from us. I hadn't heard her steps or seen her moving into view. For the first time I glanced down at the lower kitchen and noted Justin and two women drinking coffee.

"Break must be just about over, if all of you are up and drinking coffee. It can't be long till zazen begins?" I asked, to sort things out in my mind.

Amber seemed to be the only one of the three of us fully here. "Maureen could be in the fire tower, right, Barry? You said she'd go there to get off by herself, right?"

"Let her be. Look, she does these things. Don't worry."

"But—" Amber was bouncing on the balls of her feet.

"Don't you have coffee getting cold?" he said.

"Yeah, but—"

"Coffee?"

She turned and stomped back to the far end of the kitchen.

Barry turned so his back was to her and said, "Look, the thing is Maureen needs down time. It's been tense here and, well, Darcy, it's not your fault, but she feels left out. Roshi's always leaned on her. It's important to her to be the one who saves his bacon. To have him pick a stranger—"

"And have that stranger turn her away when she needed to see him—"

"Exactly. But that's her practice; she has to deal with it."

He started to turn back to his boxes.

"But Barry, Maureen is key to everything that happened when Aeneas di—when whatever happened to Aeneas happened. If she'd talked to Roshi—"

He grabbed my shoulder and stared down at me.

"Are you thinking she killed Aeneas? Well, don't. I know Maureen. That's not possible. Believe me."

"I never said she killed him! Why did you jump to that conclusion?"

He muttered something about being sure but it was one of those responses that just fill space with words. I *hadn't* put that thought into words before, even in my head. But now Maureen and that convenient hole she dug for the red maple the day Aeneas vanished, screamed: Look at us!

I just couldn't imagine Maureen poisoning Leo . . . unless she was really flipping out . . . which she was. I had to find her, even if she was in the fire tower, in the woods. But that meant leaving Leo unprotected. Things were swirling out of control. It was all I could do not to beg Barry to stay. I looked at his boxes and wished there were a magic way Leo could take their place.

Then I made the one decision I could for Leo. Leo would object, but I wasn't his jisha anymore. And there wasn't going to be another chance to get help.

"Barry, when you get to town, send the paramedics."

"Roshi?"

He drew back and then his eyes widened as we both realized what bad shape he was in—he hadn't questioned why Justin had taken the truck yesterday, hadn't thought about Leo.

"I don't know how sick he is. It comes and goes, but he's too weak to walk on his own. Too weak to ride in with you. Maybe he's getting better; but maybe not. The paramedics, they can get here, can't they?"

It was a bit before he said, "Yes." Then after another silence he said, "I could stay—"

I yearned to say: Yes! Please, please stay! But this contest was about so much more than cooking better-tasting chocolate than the next guy. It was about his life. I had already made a bad decision about Maureen, I couldn't bear to stand in Barry's way. I knew Roshi wouldn't.

"No. Go. But, give me some advice before you leave. Roshi wants Rob as his jisha. But, well, I don't trust Rob," I said in great understatement. "Would you leave Rob alone with Roshi now?"

Barry stepped back, inhaling slowly through his teeth. By the time he exhaled, I didn't need more for an answer.

"Then who would you trust? I can't just go on leaving Roshi's door unlocked and hoping no one notices. I have to find someone I can trust."

"Darcy, face it. If Roshi trusted anyone he wouldn't have made you jisha."

I sighed. He sighed. Then he said, "I've got to get going. I'll call the paramedics when I get to town. Don't worry. Roshi will be okay for a couple hours."

But I was worried, about Roshi and about Maureen. And letting Barry go was the hardest thing I had ever done.

When Barry hoisted a box and headed outside, Amber reappeared at my side. "I know the cut-off to the fire tower. I can take you there."

"It's off the path in the woods, isn't it?" I said, feeling my stomach drop to the floor.

"Yeah," she said gleefully. "But listen, you can keep your eyes closed the whole way. I'll lead you like you're a blind person."

CHAPTER TWENTY-NINE

I sent Amber for heavier sweaters. "It'll be dark before we're back."

    She bounded off like a kid about to be taken to the park, passing Barry as he strode, all-business, back from the truck.

"Barry," I said, quickly to cover my anguish about his leaving, "are you going to say goodbye to Roshi?"

He wiped the sweat off his bald dome, then a smile widened his face as if he'd been given a gift. "I'd like that. He said he wasn't seeing anyone, so I didn't want to ask. But, yes, that would mean a lot to me."

"You don't mind me coming with you? So I can make sure he's okay?"

"I could check him out for you—But, no, of course, you want to see him yourself, check his progress. Of course."

"Thanks."

"Let me take the last box to the truck."

I waited outside, trying not to think about the woods. Fear is thoughts and feelings in the body, nothing more, I reminded myself. I had been afraid of the woods so long that whatever thoughts I had originally had were too blurred to read. They had hardened into a knot in my throat that threatened to choke me. I stood feeling the afternoon wind with its warning bite of night, feeling the corrosive cold in my chest, but not the knot. I couldn't bring myself to do that.

When he came back out Barry had added a hat and wool scarf to his garb and was holding a red padded box the size of a pizza container. It *was* a pizza container.

"From Roshi's newspaper delivery?" I asked.

"Yeah. They stack up till Giles, the newspaper supplier, drives in for a day-long sit, or one of us drives to town."

"When the road floods, do the boxes keep coming?"

"I had them four deep in the kitchen one winter."

"Pity you can't use them for insulation. Nice red padded boxes covering the walls would make my cabin a whole lot cheerier." I was chattering about inanities like a kid asking for a glass of water, a bedtime story, a kiss—anything to put off the dark.

Barry strapped the boxes in the truck's passenger side, creating a nest that would make any ornithologist proud. Beyond him, the scarred and cracked dashboard sat empty—gone was Leo's fine display of plastic forks, the ones he had collected at truck stops all the way to the Canadian border. Despite the sunless sky, the truck seemed to glow from the warmth of my memory of that moment, right here, when Leo had admitted he was Roshi, and I had let out a whoop bigger than Amber's.

The sweetness of that memory made the walk back to Roshi's cabin all the harder. I watched Barry knock and then followed him in, me the unwelcome intruder. Barry stopped right inside the door. He gasped, then dropped to the floor in a full bow, I think to cover his shock. There was something about huge, city-dressed Barry that made the cabin and Roshi himself look smaller and grayer than ever. He reached out a bony hand and tapped Barry's head. If wasn't a blessing but a kid's rap, as if he was saying to Barry, *Don't make too much of this. It's just two guys saying good-bye for the weekend.*

Barry looked up and he must have smiled, for Roshi's smile looked like a response. Barry sat back on his heels, easily, even in shoes. Roshi propped himself on his elbow. Was he weaker? I couldn't tell. The two of them sat in silence, then Roshi cleared his throat and said, "How's this head?"

"Fine," Barry said, but in an unsure questioning tone. "Oh, you mean my head *now*."

"Where's the pain?"

"Gone."

He bowed, and I knew the pain they meant was the last Cacao Royale. As Barry stood up I stepped back, opened the door, and—

"Darcy," Roshi said, "where is Rob?"

"I don't know."

"You know what I mean: did you tell him he was jisha?"

"No. I don't trust him."

Barry eased back out of the way.

"Barry, get Rob for me."

"Roshi, I have reason—"

"Barry, now! Take Darcy with you as you go."

My eyes teared up. I turned quickly and hurried out, hurt and furious with Leo and not overly pleased with Barry. It wasn't his job to support me, but still . . .

Barry walked out, pulling his scarf tighter around his neck.

"Don't let it get to you. He's tossed me out a couple times. But like he said, the past is past. He'll still be your teacher tomorrow."

"Yeah!" I snapped. "If he's right about Rob."

"Rob won't hurt Roshi."

"Even if it's for the good of the monastery?"

It was a moment before Barry said, "It isn't." Then he added, "I've got to go," and strode back along the path to the bath house and around toward the zendo.

He wasn't the one Rob had knocked off the zendo roof. Likely he didn't even know Rob had done that, much less why. Loss of control, or intent? Which was more dangerous?

I stood outside Roshi's cabin, tempted to go back in, but Amber burst out of the bathhouse, waving my thick green sweater like a flag. I had no choice but to believe Roshi—and Barry—knew what he was doing.

"Come *on!*" Amber was bouncing from foot to foot, reaching over, all but unzipping my jacket and pulling the green sweater over my head. "It'll be getting dark. You don't want to go into the woods at night, little girl." She giggled.

All the rage I'd felt with Roshi flared and was doused by that giggling. Amber was right; this was just a walk in the woods. I started across the path, wriggling out of my coat and into the sweater and back into the coat as I walked. At the bathhouse I slowed, and turned toward the zendo.

"Come *on!*"

I hesitated.

"Darcy, what are you waiting for—Rob to explode out the zendo door and chew us out for cutting out of work period?"

"Right. Okay, we're off."

When I was a kid we'd had a big, young, male golden Retriever. For him, "Heel" was a momentary trick. The joy of a new person, smell, or piece of food sent him bounding off, jerking me along. More than once I had to grab a phone pole light to stop us. Walking with Amber had that familiar feeling.

"I'm glad you're not on leash," I said, but fortunately she had bounded out of range.

I raced to keep up with her, barely noting the old yellow truck standing alone in the parking area big enough to hold twenty vehicles. The surface was mud over gravel and had that crackly quality of brittle skin over moist flesh.

When we reached the road the wisdom of the parking area gravel was clear. The road was like walking on a brownie, and not one of those too-dry brownies either. I kept my head down, looking for solid spots, staying on the rise between the tire trenches. Amber was actually bouncing between rise and rim. I got so caught up in watching that I missed my footing on the rise and slid into the trench with a splash. The wind wasn't strong yet, but it rustled the fronds on the redwoods and the pine needles and the branches of the leafless trees, the arboreal fingers of the dead.

"Yeow!"

Amber slid across the planks of the bridge and smacked into the low stone wall.

"Amber! Be careful. You could have sailed over that wall. It's meant to sit on, not to keep you out of the water."

"This, from you?" She laughed. "Wow, look at the water down there. It's way higher than Monday."

I had to take her word for that. When I passed over this bridge Monday I had been in the bed of the truck, staring for dear life into the cab, watching Rob shake his finger at Roshi, as if he was already in charge. And now he was in control of Roshi. With us gone, the only person on the grounds who might watch him was Gabe Luzotta. I reminded myself why I trusted Gabe; that, at least, was something.

I had been tempted to pause on the stone wall, but I moved right on over the firm if slippery bridge. I skidded to the end, looked up to find Amber, and instead found myself an inch from the red maple. All I could think of was: this is where Aeneas is buried. It had to be. There'd been no buildings to be buried under six years ago. And this tree had been planted the day he vanished. The hole was here and waiting. This tree was planted too far into the road and never moved. I swallowed hard and, despite my heavy sweater, the chill penetrated my bones. Aeneas was buried right here. He wouldn't have had the protection of even a body bag. He wouldn't have been laid out formally, of course, merely dumped, a huddled ball at the bottom of the hole and the damp brown earth thudded down on him. And the tree, had it sipped from the liquids of his body? I turned away in horror and came face to face with Amber and almost choked.

"You're worried about the woods, aren't you?" she asked more solicitously than any time before.

I nodded, suddenly terrified that she would read my thoughts about her brother. I turned toward the woods. The knot clogged my throat. My stomach went oily. The terror that had clutched me Tuesday grabbed again, only it was worse now because of Tuesday. I'd spent an entire hour here then and couldn't force myself into these woods. Why did I think today would be different? If dealing with the woods was just a matter of stepping into it, I wouldn't have avoided it for thirty-five years. I wouldn't have abandoned Kelly Rustin in the crevasse. Nothing had changed. My head felt light, floaty. I—

I jumped. A horn, I realized an instant later, had beeped, maybe more than once. Amber was waving in big sweeping arcs like a kid in a car window. I turned. The truck was right behind me. I had to grab the fender to stop my spin. Barry was waving back at Amber but he looked like the adult giving the obligatory wave to the wound-up child.

He motioned me to him.

"Everything's okay." He nodded toward the monastery. "Rob knows how to take care of Roshi."

Before I could mutter *That's what I'm afraid of*, he said, "He's running the show now. He doesn't have time to be offing the roshi, too. Trust me, Darcy."

Grudgingly, I nodded. I'd already made my decision. It didn't matter what I thought now.

"Go!"

"She's afraid of the woods," Amber announced, in case there was one person in the monastery she hadn't already informed.

"I know. So I'm going to sit here in my truck until you're out of sight. If that makes me late for the contest, it's on your head."

I smiled and said what Roshi hadn't.

"Good luck, Barry. Come back with the . . . what? What's the prize? A silver, uh, stomach?"

I could tell he was forcing his smile, and that he was using all his control to cover his nerves.

"A bowl. Porcelain."

"Well bring it back here," I said, giving him time to recover.

"Okay, off you go. Now! I'm watching. Don't make me start beeping the horn again."

I reached in, took his face in both hands, and gave him a quick kiss. Then I turned, and before I had time to focus on anything, Amber had grabbed my hand and pulled me forward.

"Keep your eyes down," she said, emphasizing each word with a pull on my hand. "Concentrate on the path."

"Okay, okay. But let go. At this rate you're going to yank me into the river."

"Hurry up. Barry's still back there."

"He's not really going to wait."

"The truck's not moving. No, don't turn around, keep going."

Despite myself, I had to stop and laugh.

The horn beeped.

"Okay, okay," I grumbled, and placed foot before foot on the muddy path, watching for tree roots and stepping over rocks.

"See, there was nothing to be afraid of."

I didn't reply. I knew the truth, that this was a fake situation, with Barry behind us, with me looking down, walking like I was a neophyte gymnast on a balance beam six inches off the ground, and with Amber there to distract me. It didn't mean anything about my fear of the woods, but I supposed it did mean something.

We were still on the flat path before it forked to the upward tine Roshi had joked about. I glanced down at the stream. The bed wasn't wide, but surprisingly deep. The flow ran fast but still low in the rocky bed as it headed back under the bridge and around the monastery knoll. If I had the Cacao Royale bowl, if I dropped it in the stream, would it float back past Aeneas? Or would it get stuck in the dark under the bridge, under the red maple to catch the seepage— I shook off the gruesome thought and said the first thing that came into my mind.

"On the last set I worked on, the director had an entire wall of waterfall in his trailer."

"Jeez, you really are a city girl."

"Yeah, I guess. If you'd call me a cab now I'd be a happy city girl." I glanced up at her, saw the green waving behind her, leaves. I swallowed and looked back down at my safe brown path. "Amber, talk to me."

"What about?"

"Anything. Uh . . . Aeneas. What did you expect to find here?"

Slick dead leaves covered the path as if a river of leaves had flowed down the hill. They were dark, maybe from desiccation, maybe from dusk. I didn't dare look up and see how quickly night was closing in here in this deep, narrow canyon. I stepped gingerly, moving before my feet had time to slide. The flood of leaves ended abruptly and the footing, no better than it was ten minutes earlier, now seemed like pavement.

"Amber, what did you think you'd find out at the monastery?"

"No. You talk. What are you afraid of?"

Oh, God, that was what I was trying to forget about. "This isn't the place for—"

"Uh-*huh*, it is."

"It's all I can do to get through this without talking about the past."

"Well, you talk, or we're quiet. I'm sick of being the one to spill. You spill for achange. I mean, I'm doing you a favor, a big favor here. The least you can do is talk about what I want for a change."

"You're not doing me a favor; you're getting yourself out of sitting cross-legged facing the wall."

"Yeah, well. You don't want to talk, I'm outta here."

"Just what the fuck do you need to know, Amber?" I was braced, listening for a rewarding little gasp, but Amber merely slowed her step, said, "It's a long walk. Gimme everything."

"Don't you . . ."

But there was no point lecturing about privacy or manners. She *didn't* have any sense of privacy, not out here. I stomped after her, feeling the breeze on the heat of my face. A branch slapped my shoulder. Leaves began to crowd in from both sides. My throat tightened. I focused blinder-like on Amber's back, but the trees still pushed in, squeezing out my breath. I could have tried to face my fear, feel the sensations that comprised my panic; it would have been the Zen way. The hard way. I took the other.

"You win, Amber. I was the youngest kid, a toddler when my sibs were teenagers. We kids went to Muir Woods, or maybe Tilden Park in the

Berkeley Hills, I don't know. We went to woods. I must have wandered off and they forgot about me."

I had given this explanation before, said it just as matter-of-factly, but now, here I felt nowhere near blasé. The thick woody air pressed in on me. The brook gurgled beside me, but it was as if its sound no longer entered my realm.

"There must have been some reason you were so scared. I mean, lots of kids get lost."

"In the woods? In the dark?"

"The dark? Were you lost overnight?"

"No, of course not."

We were moving again. Beside us the stream crashed and gurgled. The damp smell of leaves and bark and mud thickened the already heavy air. A glimmer of sun broke the clouds to sparkle off Amber's blond hair and then die away.

"I don't remember it being really dark in Muir Woods or Tilden," Amber called back to me over the splash of the brook. "More like dappled. Did your family go somewhere dark in there?"

I had to think. Of course I hadn't been back to either place.

"I doubt it."

"But you remember it as being dark."

I did. I had always remembered the dark. Nothing more, just dark. Branches hung over us, turning the muted afternoon light to dim stripes. Dead, wet leaves covered the mud. I had to plan each step, watch for leaves, for roots, for hidden roots, things that can grab you, smack you down. The air was so thick I was breathing through my mouth.

"So, either," Amber said, shoving past a fat shrub, "either it was night, or you fell in some deep hole or steep canyon or something, right? Not like the kids down the well stuff, probably, right? But deep, under lots of trees, you know, like here, once the sun drops beyond the hills and—"

"Amber! I don't know! I was four years old."

She muttered something, but the blood was surging in my head, my ears ringing and I was about to break into a sweat and I had no idea what she was saying now. I just walked, focusing on her legs, one lifting, swinging forward after the other. After a bit I heard the river gurgling and sometime later I felt the breeze on my face. I didn't look up.

"So, who are your siblings?"

Amber had taken pity on me; I grabbed.

"Gary and Janice and Grace would have been—let's see—fourteen, fifteen, and sixteen. And John'd been nineteen. Kathleen's older but she was away at school then. And Mike must have been about eight, so he was just another nuisance to be watched."

"Who watched over him?"

"Janice, my middle sister. She was always the nice one, the one who could deal with an eight-year-old all day."

I flashed on them, walking ahead of me somewhere in the city, sunlight turning Mike's red curls pale next to her long coal black hair. I don't know why I even remembered that insignificant moment, but now I clung to it, with its safe, citified background, and the memory eased my panic.

"And you? Who watched out for you?"

"John. John was in charge, always. He was careful, a good planner. A rock climber . . . knew how important it is to plan."

"There's a rock climbing wall in Tilden, right?"

I tried to inhale, but couldn't, not enough. The air was too thick. I knew what she was thinking and she was wrong. Wrong.

"Yeah, there's a wall, but John wouldn't have been going climbing that day, not with all of us there."

"But he could have gotten distracted, spotted the wall, seen it was empty, grabbed the chance—"

"No he wouldn't!" My breath came fast, my shoulders were jammed tight against my neck.

"Okay, okay!" Amber picked up the pace.

The light was fading and I had to watch the ground for roots and rocks. Maybe silence was better than dumb questions. John was a police officer; he'd always been a future police officer. He would never have abandoned his sister on a whim.

"What about your other brother and sister? What did they do on these trips?"

I hesitated; I didn't trust Amber anymore, but I didn't dare not answer. I felt too much like a four-year-old here, desperate to hold the hand of someone bigger. I took a deep breath and tried to calm myself.

"Grace. Grace was into herbs even then. The joke was she'd never notice if it rained because she never took her eyes off the ground. And Gary was, you know, the second son."

"The funny one? The one who sneaks beers underaged?"

"Exactly. Gary had a million friends."

"So neither of them would have noticed if you wandered off."

"Not if I wasn't their responsibility. But if John had told them to watch me, they wouldn't have—"

"Darcy, they were kids! Maybe they ran into friends? Maybe your sister saw a cute guy the family didn't like? Maybe your funny brother ran off to meet friends and you followed him without him realizing. Maybe—"

"No! They left me, and the trees closed in on me, and there was no way out!" Sweat coated my face and back. Bile gushed into my throat. I stood shaking in that dark, dark place with no way out.

"Don't tell, Darce."

"What?"

Amber had said something, but *Don't tell, Darce* had been whispered in my head, in my memory, in a tone too hushed to recognize, too scared to ignore. I saw the dark woods as I had back then, felt my four-year-old scaredness, and my relief, my head bobbing as I promised not to tell, and a hand wrapped all the way around mine to lead me out of the dark place as if there had been a way out all along.

I breathed in, deeply, more easily, oddly proud of myself for not telling all these years. For blocking out the memory so completely I could never tell. "Mom would have killed anyone who let me wander off."

"Huh?"

Amber must have been talking about something else. Relief washed over me. It was so simple, so small a thing to cause all my panic all these years. In a wave of bravado, I looked up at the trees . . . and almost puked.

"You okay?" For the first time Amber sounded panicked.

"Yeah, as long as I don't see the trees. This fear thing is too engrained in my body to disappear by thought alone."

"So much for shrinks, huh?" She laughed. "Listen, we gotta move.

I moved along behind her, squinting to make out the vagaries of the path. The chill breeze cooled my face. Tension flowed out of my shoulders. I felt ridiculously relieved, as if everything was back in its rightful place again.

Amber stopped, turned.

"What now?" I demanded.

"Hey, don't take my head off. I'm the one leading you! Here's the path to the fire tower. It's steep here. You're going to need to grab onto these saplings here. See? If I hadn't stopped you, you'd have missed it altogether. You'd have gone on walking in the woods to who knows where."

"Okay," I said, relieved.

I breathed in as shallowly as possible, to avoid the smell of the earth and the leaves, as if they were girding up for one last desperate go at me.

I focused on the climb, silently describing each intended move: Now grab this branch, pull, now this one. Brace your foot, push. At some point the words stopped and I was just climbing, hand over hand, foot bracing for foot. After a couple minutes the path leveled off, still steep, but a walking path.

Panting, Amber turned back to me. "You okay?"

"Yeah." I said, still looking down at the damp safe earth. Now that we'd stopped I could hear the wind snapping the leaves. If I looked up I would see trees. I stared at Amber's shoes.

"It's a switchback from here on," she said, shifting her feet to turn.

She started up the path, pulling herself by branches. I followed, feet sliding, head down. I climbed, reaching for steadying branch after branch. I looked only ahead, zeroed in on Amber's back. I climbed but I didn't look up. Someone had made steps from old railroad ties. Some were firm, some were not, some were gone entirely. By the time we got to the top of the mountain it was nearly dark.

The fire tower stood like an erector set creation, a square room atop long support legs, reached by a staircase three stories high, one that did not inspire confidence.

"Oh no," Amber said, "I'm not going up there."

"Why not?"

"I'm just not."

"What? Afraid of heights?"

"No!" Which meant yes.

"Here. Sit on the step. And listen, thanks. Thanks. You know that, right?"

"Yeah."

I moved around her and started up the steps. They were wide, planks that turned at right angles at the corners of the structure. I kept my eyes aimed up at the small square room as I climbed eight steps, turned, eight steps turned, thirty-two steps per story. It was almost dark and I had to concentrate on the steps, seeing nothing but them as I climbed, but I was relieved to be out of the woods proper and on man-made stairs, even decrepit ones that creaked in the wind. I climbed and turned, my breath coming faster. The moon was already out and for a while I thought that it was reflecting off the tower window, but as I neared the top of the stairs it was clear I was wrong.

I stopped with three steps to go. "Dammit! Dammit to hell," I muttered inadequately. Then I climbed the last three steps.

The lookout room here was a square box, three yards long, three yard wide, windows on all sides to let the watcher spot a fire in any direction. There was no chance of a surprise visit. For the person inside, no chance of hiding. I peered in.

The first thing I saw was a candle flame.

The second was a skull.

CHAPTER THIRTY

O

"Aeneas?" I gasped, staring in through the window.

On a low cabinet a candle flickered next to the dry white skull. The light twitched its cheekbones and winked through the holes where eyes once had gazed.

Wind smacked my back as I stood on the widow's walk surrounding the tiny room. High up here, unblocked by trees, the air current was cold and sharp. It shook the whole structure. I braced myself, hands flat on the glass and peered inside the ten-foot-square room. In front of the cabinet and the skull was a black mat and cushion but no one was sitting cross-legged on them. Meditating on the skull of the dead is a revered practice in some Buddhist sects. It is a reminder of the brevity of life and the importance of the moment. But it's not a Zen practice. And certainly not appropriating the skull of a dead friend.

What kind of people had they become here? I thought for a moment I was going to throw up. But I just stood with my roiling stomach and the biting cold.My hair slapped my face. Curly strands stuck on my sweaty skin, and I stood peering as through a hurricane fence, shivering. The door was halfway down the walk; the knob was stiff, but it did turn. I stepped inside the room.

Then I saw her.

Maureen sat clutching knees to chest, her back to the wall by the door. Her fine blond hair hung so limp her ears stuck out, as if the hair could no longer be bothered covering them. Her bare arms rested on her knees and despite the muscling of years of gardening the skin seemed to hang as limp as her hair. Her gaze was straight ahead; no part of her body was moving. She didn't look up.

For a moment I thought she was dead. But when I touched her shoulder she turned toward me, slowly, as if she'd forgotten how to move. The wind rattled the windows and slithered through holes in the molding and the boards. In here it was barely warmer than outside and I was glad of my sweater and jacket. But despite her thin T-shirt and goose-bumped arms, Maureen didn't shiver. The first time I'd met her she seemed impervious to the chill wind, but she was racing around then. Here there was nothing to keep the cold from pooling in her marrow.

"Maureen?" I squatted beside her and waited for her reaction to tell me what I was dealing with. She didn't move. Instead of me drawing her out, I felt as if I was being pulled into her stasis. Had the cold seeped into her organs, her brain?

"You've got to walk around, warm up."

She seemed to consider replying, but didn't.

I planted my feet, grabbed her arms, and pulled her up. She was so light and limp the momentum sent her past my shoulder and I had to brace my legs to keep us both from sailing into the windows behind. She was standing, but shakily. I shifted behind her, pulled her against my warmer body, and held her icy hands in mine. She felt like clothes held up by memory. I don't know how long we stood like that, she leaning into me, me braced against the window, the windows thinly separating this bare room from the cold bare darkening sky. When she took a step I released her, unzipped my jacket, pulled off my heavy green sweater and held it out. "Put it on."

"I don't need—"

"I brought it for you."

"It hardly seems worth—"

"Maureen, put on the damned sweater." I smiled to cover my fear and frustration. She didn't return that smile, but she did don the sweater. It was only then that I glanced around the now-dark room. Fire towers are always sparsely furnished, but this one held only a nylon sleeping bag, wadded in one corner, an office swivel chair that must have been a bear to get up here, the low cabinet, and the skull.

"Aeneas?" I asked, returning to my original question.

"Oh no," she said, and uttered a sound that could almost have been a laugh. "I don't know who she was. She was a woman." She walked, still shaky, across the small room and stood in front of the cabinet, which I now realized to be an altar of sorts, and looked down at the skull as she might have at a favorite aunt with whom she'd spent a lot of time. "There are differences in a male and female skull, the ridge over the eyes, for instance. She was a Caucasian. I wanted a Caucasian . . ."

"Because?" I prompted.

"I wanted her to be as much like me as possible. So I could never delude myself by thinking she had died in a massacre in a foreign land that would never happen to me or from Ebola I'd never be exposed to, or malaria I could handle with quinine." She was talking half to me now, half to the skull, almost-animate in the flickering candle light. "I wanted to— I have—thought that she sat in a room like me, probably here in California. They said she was in her forties. I've thought she walked along an unpaved road when she was thirty-six like me, never imagining that in ten years she would be dead. Never picturing a truck racing over a rise, the driver drinking a beer and arguing with his girlfriend. Or the doctor saying, 'If you'd only come in sooner.' Maybe never imagining things would get so bad she'd pick up a knife and draw it across her throat. Never dreaming she . . . would cease to be. Never imagining . . ."

Beyond her, beyond the skull, a wisp of cloud drifted east. Silently I mouthed the possibility she couldn't bring herself to consider: Never imagining the teacher she'd trusted would be like the ballet director she'd just escaped, at her door wanting a piece of ass.

I didn't dare bring that up, not here. Break the mood, that was it. I moved beside the chest into her line of vision.

"But really understanding you're going to die in a short time gives you a whole different take on life, don't you think? I mean, if you're only going to live another year or ten years or even twenty years, you'd better enjoy things now, 'cause there's not going to be much more."

She looked at me, appalled, as if I'd suggested we take the skull out to hit the hot clubs with us.

"We need to walk. Circle for circulation." I reached for the sleeping bag, draped it around her shoulders, and started us on a slow circumambulation of the room. Anyone who hadn't spent thousands of ten-minute periods in the slow half-steps of kinhin would have balked, but when I slipped my arm around Maureen's waist she moved compliantly.

"Maureen, if this skull isn't Aeneas, then where is he?"

She shifted unsteadily foot to foot as if they had frozen into rounded knobs. The nylon bag swished and our feet clacked stiltedly on the wooden floor. I couldn't decide if she was considering my question or was unwilling to answer. Finally I said, "You were planting the red maple. You buried him, didn't you?"

She gasped, her little intake of breath almost lost beneath the rustling of nylon and the clattering of the currents on the window panes. But she didn't deny my accusation. I wished she had. I didn't want Aeneas's killer to be her. I hated to think of her being a killer, having been a killer all these years.

"Why?" I forced out.

"What else was there to do?" Her tone was both plaintive and defensive. "It was the only place. The Japanese roshis were due to drive past . . . Fitting in its way. The maple was a gift from the Japanese roshis."

I struggled to keep my tone neutral, to reveal neither my shock nor sorrow. "Did you bury him by yourself?"

"Yes."

"It must have taken a long time."

"Yes. The robe, it was silk, it kept slipping; I had to keep wrapping it around his body, so the dirt didn't get on his face. The soil's very hard."

"And no one offered to help you?"

"Who would have? Only Roshi."

"Leo?" I stopped. She took another step, and the sleeping bag slid off her into my hands. I moved in front of her. "Leo! Why?"

"After he killed Aeneas."

Leo? I dug my fingers into the slick fabric of the bag. It couldn't be Leo. Not Leo. Finally, I pulled myself together enough to ask, "What makes you think Leo killed Aeneas."

"I saw him."

"You *saw* him kill Aeneas?"

She looked like I'd slapped her. It struck me that this was the first time in all these years that she had heard aloud the accusation which must rarely have left her consciousness. I had thought it was the melding of the ballet director and Leo that had paralyzed her, but it was this.

Softly, I said, "Tell me what happened."

She stood a moment, reedy body outlined by the wispy cloud passing behind her. Then she motioned me to the single chair. I held out the sleeping bag but she shook her head and began to pace, walking to the south windows by the skull, back past me to the north window, and back south. The room was ten-foot square. She moved slowly, placing a foot, pausing, and moving the other, an unsteady thin figure made thinner, shakier by the flickering candlelight. The dark beyond turned the windows to dim mirrors and her spectral shape glided like a soft echo beside her. I was about to ask again when she sighed deeply, and I realized that rather than reconsidering her decision to explain, she was relieved to be forced to talk about the secrets she had protected all this time.

"Where to begin?" she mused as she paced. But her steps were firmer, as if she was already relieved of her burden. What she was about to tell me was old news for her. It was not she who was quivering with shock now, but me. I was desperate to ask about Leo, to exonerate him, but it only made sense to start at the beginning.

"You came here because Barry wanted to?"

"Mmm. You know about the chocolate contest?"

"Yes."

"It devastated him. He needed to get away, emotionally . . . geographically. When we got here there was nothing but a couple tents. Not even the zendo. Barry was a city chef. This was definitely not his kind of place." She gave a small, unsteady laugh that belied her tone. "But it was what he needed. So I stayed for him, to draw him back here." She glanced toward me, as if for confirmation of her decision. "Not entirely, I'm not saying that. I had, uh, a career problem; I was not in great shape. A summer in the country; it sounded good. He couldn't get out of the city and I knew if I went back we'd both get onto other things and forget about this idea of a monastery in the woods. So I stayed. It was to be just for a while, you see."

Her arms hung loose, swung gracefully; each of her steps seemed both relaxed and considered. I could see her as a dancer. When she continued speaking, her voice seemed unnaturally calm and steady, as if she was in a coffee shop chatting with friend. "We didn't think things through," she said. "There can be a boy's camp quality to a place like this. That first year Leo and I and others—never more than four or five—worked all day every day, hard physical work. Everything was a trial. We were sleeping in tents, trying to cook in a tent, building the zendo, trying to sit zazen when it was too cold to sit still. And then it rained hard for a solid week and we talked about going to a motel, and when we finally gave in and decided to go, we all squeezed into the truck cab, and found the road had washed out."

"Was one of those people Aeneas?"

"Not then. He showed up at the end of the rainy season, when we were desperate to get the zendo built, so we could live in it. So then we worked like crazy again. And Aeneas was great for that. He seemed like a quiet city boy—didn't know shit about building, but he had a good sense of geometry, which is what you need to construct a dome, and he would do anything you asked, cart loads up the hill all day, hold the other end of boards, stand patiently while one of us figured out a problem." She paused and looked at me. "You're going to say, we should have spotted his disorder. Yes, we should have. But, you know, it's hard to spot a problem when you're overworked and exhausted and it doesn't seem like a problem at the time. Maybe it occurred to each of us that Aeneas was strange, but, if so, it was the last thing we wanted to mention, not and have him leave. We needed him."

Carefully I pulled the sleeping bag in closer around my legs. Cold as it was in the tower I'd have liked the bag around my shoulders, but I didn't want to chance diverting her. She still walked as if inured to the cold, but her steps were steadier, as if each admission was a weight removed.

"And then when other people came, to them Aeneas was one of the 'old guard' and it wouldn't have seemed their place to criticize him?" I guessed.

Maureen nodded. "But when the construction binge was over, the same qualities that made Aeneas valuable to us became a problem. He was erratic. Most of the time he would sit quietly, but there was his compulsiveness, his following you around—"

"By you, do you mean yourself?"

"Yes, me, definitely. But everybody. He was like a lost kid who will follow whoever feeds and comforts him. If Leo hadn't been drunk none of this would have happened. The thing is that Leo can drink a lot and look okay. When we were building, we were too busy to require judgment calls from him; it was easy for him to slip under our radar. So when Aeneas had one of his outbursts or got odd, we assumed it was okay with Leo."

"Odd?"

"Well, he followed me too close, too often, like an adoring toddler. He'd pick up things that weren't his and put them down somewhere and the person who owned them would assume they were lost, or worse, stolen. He ruined our first big pot of stew by tossing in coffee grounds. We were mad enough then, you'd think that should have alerted us. But we were too busy building or clearing or hauling and we didn't have time to fuss about Aeneas. It all came to a head . . ." she stopped, one foot still well in front of the other. She swallowed and then seemed to force herself to go on. "It was the last full day of the Japanese roshis' visit to this country. They had been to a conference of Zen dignitaries of some sort in San Francisco and the trip to our monastery opening was an afterthought, a courtesy to some roshi they knew in New York."

I gasped. The roshi in New York had to be Yamana-roshi, and these events six years ago were the crisis that kept him from for his long-awaited trip back to his family temple in Japan—the trip he had had to cancel, forever. He had said he'd vouched for Leo, but this was more like sponsoring him, linking their names, melding their reputations like black paint into white. Outside, the wind snapped something against a window. Leaves, ripped from their moorings, swirled and were gone.

But Maureen had been pacing away from me. She hadn't noticed my reaction. Now she turned and began the steps back north.

"Something sparked Aeneas that night. If I had to guess, I'd say liquor, maybe one of the visiting roshis was drinking sake and poured him a cup, or maybe he came across Leo's—Leo would never have given him liquor; he knew better than that. But the result was Aeneas went out of control. He put on Leo's robes, and ran barefoot through the quad, screeching. The Japanese just heard him and saw the robe and, of course, they assumed Leo was on a drunk. Aeneas tore through the zendo, knocked over the oil lamps—it took Rob days to clean the kerosene off the floor and we were lucky the building didn't burn, after we'd spent months building it. He'd picked up a manila envelope somewhere and he was waving it around. From the zendo Aeneas looped down, broke the roaster Barry'd managed to bring with him from the city, and knocked Gabe flat on his back and smashed his laptop.

"Leo must have heard Gabe swearing. He came racing out and after Aeneas. Everything was chaos. Rob had discovered the kerosene on the zendo floor. The Japanese roshis were trying to get into the zendo for some kind of departing ceremony and not understanding why Rob was keeping them out. They didn't speak much English, and it was clear they just thought he was being rude. Gabe was carrying on about losing irreplaceable records. Barry was probably in mourning—he was just about broke and the chances of getting another roaster were nil."

"And you?"

"Well, what I'm telling you is what I heard. I wasn't there. The Japanese roshis had given us the maple, and I wanted to get it planted so they would see it on their way out. So I was down by the road getting ready to plant. I had the hole dug almost deep enough. I'd realized I needed some B-one liquid to ease the shock of transplanting when I put the tree in, so I started toward the shed. I was walking along the side of the road, in the shadows, when I spotted Aeneas running, arms flailing his manila envelope like a flag. It had been an exhausting weekend and the last thing I wanted was to have to deal with him, so I stepped back into the trees where he wouldn't see me.

He ran by, still in Leo's brown robe, and Leo came after, yelling like I'd never heard him. He spotted me, started toward me, then veered back after Aeneas. But he was so crazed it terrified me. I moved farther into the woods and stayed still, hardly breathing for—I don't know—ten, fifteen minutes, maybe longer. I could hear shouting, but it was all mooshed together with the wind gusting and rattling the leaves. It was getting dark and I needed to get that tree in. And enough time had passed that I was more curious than frightened, so I started back. The road was empty, the shadows almost black by then. I got all the way back across the bridge to the tree without seeing anyone.

"Leo must have made some sound, something that drew my attention. I don't remember hearing anything, but I must have. I walked back onto the bridge and looked down over the stone wall. Aeneas's body was lying face up on the rocks below and Leo's gin bottle was a few feet away."

CHAPTER THIRTY-ONE

O

The night currents sprayed the windows with leaves and pine needles. There was an odd groaning outside, as if from rusty cables being pulled beyond endurance. The fire tower seemed flimsier than ever, and colder.

I could picture Maureen six years ago, standing at the edge of the bridge, blond hair blowing like wisps of smoke, peering over that odd stone-wall railing that was wide enough to sit on in a place no one was likely to sit, but not high enough to protect one leaning over. Its width gave the illusion of safety, tempted the high-spirited to prance across it, denied the danger of the rocky stream bed thirty feet below. A fall would be lethal, even now, with the water providing some cushion over those sharply piled stones.

Maureen had been planting the tree, so she'd have been in a T-shirt, probably sleeveless, khaki work shorts, and work boots. The opening had been in April, too early for her to be tanned. The sallow white of her legs would have been tinted only by dirt from her dig. She had stopped working almost half an hour earlier. It was dusk then. Even she would have been shivering. Even before she saw Leo, and Aeneas's body on the rocks below the bridge.

The creaking of the stairs jerked me back to the present.

I wanted to wrap the sleeping bag around Maureen. But I sensed that she needed not merely to tell me what had happened, but to *be* back in it. So I left her cold.

"What happened then?"

"The bottom dropped out of the world. I felt it then, though I didn't think about it or understand it. But I did know it, you know?"

I understood in the general way one does, but I said, "How?"

"Well, it was odd that I came here at all. The idea of sitting still in meditation was the antithesis of anything I could have imagined as a dancer. When I was dancing I'd have been afraid that sitting still would tighten my psoas or gluteus medius muscles and inhibit my arabesques. Then, my life was arranged to prepare me to dance, to dance, to cool down after dancing, to think about dancing again. I came here for Barry, but I never thought I'd stay. I stayed not because of Buddhism or meditation, or Leo really, except in that he allowed one as unconnected as me to stay. I thought I was being an anchor for Barry, but the truth is I stayed because I couldn't think what else to do."

The world was full of places to escape to, ninety-nine percent of them more comfortable than this. If she had endured even a month here to hold a spot for Barry, I would have been amazed. Six years' exile in the woods was too much for love, fear, or escape. Something about Buddhism or meditation or Leo must have hooked her. Now I watched her walking even more slowly, placing her right foot down, heel touching a beat before sole, moving south away from me, impervious to the sound of the wind, to the metallic creaking, the wavering light creating expressions of its own on her face as she continued on.

"But during that winter Leo talked about working for work's sake, and that made sense to me. It was the dance of work. In dance your spend twenty-three hours a day preparing for the one glorious hour you're dancing, and if you're in rehearsals, even during those hours you stop and wait, you watch and think how you're going to change to get the effect you want, and try and stop and try again, and maybe you get ten minutes max of the dancing that transforms you.

"But here everything we did was dance. Or it could be. I don't want to romanticize things. There were a lot of days I didn't manage any more than ten minutes of dancing here, either, but I knew what Leo meant. I knew I could have that kind of life. I knew I was home, and living with a master. And then Leo did the unimaginably vile."

"He killed Aeneas?"

"He killed Aeneas."

She was in front of the makeshift altar. She stared at the skull. The candlelight shone upward under her chin, her nose, her eyebrows, and up under her hair like a spotlight on the bottom of clouds.

"Why did you stay here after that?" I asked.

She turned and for a moment, before her face was in shadow, the candlelight revealed the desperate longing in her eyes. "Because I had been charmed with the concept of Zen rather than really understanding it. I had taken to heart what Leo taught about making everything dance. But it wasn't mine yet. And when Leo was unveiled as a phony, you understand what that meant, don't you?"

"Tell me."

"That all that he said he 'knew' he didn't know. He was just parroting things he'd read, or heard from other teachers who maybe didn't know either. He was . . . nothing." She moved on, not more slowly now or faster, but with a relentlessness to her step and her voice. "And I was less than nothing. I had failed at dancing. Oh, maybe I could have succeeded if I'd gotten the right manager and gotten into the right company, but I hadn't been able to do that, and that's all part of the dance, too, isn't it?"

I nodded.

"Then I came here and embraced this place and Leo, and it all crumbled to nothing. And I hadn't the sense to see that coming at all." She reached the north window and stopped, talking into the darkness. "So I stayed because I had nothing to take anywhere else."

She turned and stood facing in my direction though not facing me. "You understand that, don't you?"

"Yes."

Maureen walked to the altar, turned back, poised to begin her pace back toward me, her gaze downward. She still hadn't looked toward me, and I knew she wouldn't until she had said all she needed to. On the low cabinet to her right the candle flickered, winking one eye socket of the skull. And behind—oh, my god!—was something round. The top of a head! In the candlelight I could barely make out blond hair, but in another moment that became unnecessary. The rest of the head appeared—Amber! She stared wide-eyed at the skull and then at me. I shook my head. Amber didn't move. Maureen was still looking at the floor, still garroted by her past. I made a downward movement with my forefinger. *Sit down!*

Amber plopped down with such a thud that even Maureen started, though she didn't turn around. Had she, she would have seen nothing, unless she stood at the window and looked down. I felt bad about Amber, who had fought her fear of heights in a climb that must have been stomach-churning. It was cold and miserable out there.

But . . . but Maureen had resumed and was saying, "'That doesn't explain *six* years,' that's what you're thinking, isn't it? I suppose you're right," she went on without checking to confirm her opinion, "but in a place like this time melds and this week is no more pressing than next year. The first winter, there was the excitement of building the zendo and the opening ceremony. After that, I might have left, but Leo fell apart. He had always drunk, but not noticeably. After he killed Aeneas he just drank and sat, though god knows what good sitting did him, except to keep him from stumbling off the bridge himself. No one but me understood the horror he was going through or trying to escape, or trying not to escape. Who knows? The one thing that was clear was that if I left he would have died, from a fall, from a gunshot if he'd managed to come up with a gun—that's not hard to do in these parts— or most likely from neglect."

"So you felt you had to stay?"

"It took me years to admit, but I was glad of something necessary to do. And I loved him, but that took me years to realize, too."

She was still walking, talking, but not looking at me. And now I appreciated the depth of anger and abandonment she must have felt when, at this key time of this last sesshin, the last one she would ever sit with him, Leo chose a stranger as his assistant. How she must have resented me. Must *still* resent me. And him.

"He's taken *six* years of your life and tossed it away."

"Yes. And no." She let out a small laugh. "But isn't that the Zen answer?"

It was clear that reminiscence was over. But there was still the final question. I knew the answer, but I needed her to put it into words. "What did you do after you found Aeneas's body?"

"What? Oh. Nothing. Well, I just stood there. I mean, what could I do? I couldn't ask Roshi. I was terrified of letting on I knew. I couldn't just leave Aeneas's body there and go see if I could find someone to tell, and I understand now that I was so horrified about Roshi that I couldn't bear to admit what he'd done. But I didn't understand that then. Then, well, I must have been working with a tenth of my brain. All I could think of was the Japanese roshis and the other guests here for the opening ceremony and how upset they'd all be. I know how irrational that was, but it's what I thought.

"So I buried him, under the maple, just like you thought. He was still in Leo's robe. The manila envelope was wedged under his body in the stream. I did open it, but the ink had already run in places. I couldn't make out a single word. It was just a few sheets, handwritten, like a draft of a speech, or a long recipe—a *recipe!*—but it was signed, I could tell that. I dropped it in the hole, and then . . . then . . . I dropped Aeneas in. It was awful beyond words. I'm surprised no one ever made the connection. I wasn't thinking linearly or I would have assumed people would miss Aeneas, figure he was dead and focus on the one fresh hole."

"So you didn't start the rumor of him going with the Japanese roshis?"

"No. The first time I heard it I nearly laughed. But I caught myself. Leo must have started it."

"That would be a cruel thing to do to Rob."

The words were out of my mouth before I saw their ludicrousness. Maureen merely shrugged, as if to say one among many. She stopped walking. She was in front of me, and she turned to me for the first time. I thought she was going to add something else but she simply held out her hands and I gave her the sleeping bag, which she wrapped around herself and then she slid down and sat on the floor. She looked like it was taking all her energy to keep from crumbling down head onto floor. She looked like . . . Leo. She needed to get back to her own room, to eat, and mostly to sleep in peace. But the ends had to be tied up here first.

"Maureen, in six years, didn't you and Leo talk about this?"

"No. Oh god, I know how odd that sounds, but like I said, time takes on a sameness in an isolated place like this. Years don't matter, only seasons. He came to my cabin that night to talk about it, but I couldn't face it, not that soon. The sight of Leo terrified me. It was all I could do not to slam the door on him."

No wonder she'd reacted that way. Had Leo really assumed she thought he was like the ballet director, that he was only there for sex? Or had he been lying to me, too?

"After that," Maureen went on, "I waited for Leo to make an announcement. The next morning was the first morning zazen of just us residents and I assumed he would explain and ask forgiveness for bringing shame on us all. His guilt, of course, would be his own; no one can absolve someone else. But he didn't. Then I thought he needed time to sober up. But he just drank more. I kept expecting him to at least say something to me, you know?"

I nodded.

"He folded in on himself. It wasn't just that he didn't talk to me about Aeneas; he didn't talk to any of us about anything."

"But didn't you—"

"Didn't I press him? Yes. We were alone. I said point blank, 'Roshi, you killed Aeneas.' He looked at me like I'd made an esoteric statement about transcendence that he didn't quite understand. Then he changed the subject."

"Didn't you ask again?"

"I . . . I couldn't. It was like with that response he'd pulled the rug out from under me. Then, when I could think straight again, I was filled with a weight of terror. Maybe he really didn't remember killing Aeneas. Drunks forget. There was only my word he had killed him. I was the only witness. He could say I killed Aeneas. *I* was the one who buried him. If fingerprints on cloth last that long, mine where on his.

My hairs, whatever. It was me Aeneas followed around. I spent a lot of time being wary."

"And then?"

She shrugged. "Time passed."

"But you couldn't leave."

"Initially, I couldn't. I couldn't have moved to Seattle and wondered every morning if this was the day someone would dig up the maple. Even so, I felt like I was just waiting for the end and there was nothing I could do about it. So I just did what I had to to get through each day. I got to living like there was no tomorrow, like I wanted to experience everything about this day that could be my last here. And then even that passed and I just lived here."

"Until Leo announced that this was the last sesshin?"

"Yeah. We all knew something was coming, but nobody knew what." She pulled the nylon bag tighter around her. It didn't look to be making her any less cold. "It was like the whole thing started all over again. I thought when he gave that opening talk in the zendo that he was going to admit killing Aeneas. But he lied, outright lied; he said he had believed Aeneas went to Japan. Then he holed up in his room, and I was getting more and more panicked and he wouldn't see me, and then you wouldn't let me in, and—"

Her breath caught and then she just sobbed, great loud cries that shook her whole body and made the nylon slither against itself. I had to stop myself from going to her, pulling her close to the comfort of another body. Hers was a solitary sorrow and she needed to cry alone with it. I let her be till her breath was easier, then I moved down beside her, put my arm around her, and tucked the sleeping bag around her feet. I found myself reacting just as she had, not facing the question of Leo's guilt—unable to face it—but rather dealing with the immediate problem of how to get her out of here, shaky as she was. Fortunately, Amber was sitting right outside.

I waited till Maureen stopped crying and said, "I'm getting help. I'll be right back. Okay?"

She nodded absently, and I hesitated to leave her alone even that short a time. I was tempted to ask if she had a knife, to pretend I needed it, but in the end I decided not to bring the subject to her mind. I'd just be a second.

Chapter Thirty-two

O

Barry yawned and guided the old yellow truck with both hands on the wheel. He wasn't worried about veering off the road, the ruts were too deep; he might as well be driving a trolley. But those ruts were like great brown canals, the mud covering who knew what?

Great rain-soaked branches of redwood swayed in the wind. Water crashed on the windshield. He jumped, flung out his right arm to protect the stack of boxes on the seat next to him. All he needed now was the chocolate sailing into the dash, his perfect bars coming up scraped or gouged! *Ah, Appearance, sub-standard,* that prissy judge from L.A. would sneer. What was his name? Grummond? Gundersen? Whatever, all he'd need would be an excuse to score down someone like him, the peanut-adulterer.

Barry wanted to ponder every facet of the weekend, to transport himself to San Francisco now, not have to endure the six-hour drive. He could almost smell the first whiff of chocolate as he crossed the threshold of the Salle de Cacao, and the aromas as he walked along the aisle, the hint of wine, the touch of almond, maybe the stunning bouquet of a new crop of cacao beans never before processed. He ached to be down in the city, meeting Carlson from Seattle, Milchisi from Tucson, Tsunaka from L.A., deciding which hot new South of Market restaurants to try, to spend the meal not in silence, not spooning gruel, but forking ahi tartar with radicchio and taking apart the sauce, ordering pineapple tart with kirsch ice cream and grumbling about the over-sweet liqueur.

The truck hit something. He braced the wheel, braced the boxes of chocolate, and forced himself to focus back on the road. Had he slept at all since the beans arrived? He must have but he couldn't remember when his eyes had closed—before now. He jerked himself awake and stared at the road.

CHAPTER THIRTY-THREE

O

I walked to the south end of the room, next to the cabinet and peered out the window ready to beckon the freezing Amber in.

Amber was gone.

I let out a great sigh. Of course, she got fed up. Maybe she was at the bottom of the steps waiting. Maybe pigs will fly in packs.

"Maureen," I said, and waited until she looked up. "We have to go now."

Outside, a crate on pulleys groaned in the wind. It must, I thought, have been what they used to get that one chair up here. I looked from Maureen's slender body to the crate. She'd be an easy fit.

"Where does the pulley crate go down to?'

"The river, a bit beyond the fork that leads here."

There had to be a means of controlling its descent; I'd choreographed stunts in way worse than that. If I tucked the sleeping bag around her . . .

"The carriage goes all the way at the bottom?"

Maureen pushed herself up. "I'm not going downhill in that thing! I'm fine; I can walk down."

"But it's—"

"Wait, you're the one who freaks out in the woods, right? Okay, for you, the walk down'll be hell, but I'm okay. I may have to help *you!*" She slapped the sleeping bag into folds and ignored it as it slithered out of them. "Okay, let's go," she said, and before I could answer she blew out the candle. We left the skull alone in its aerie.

I stepped outside, and a gust of wind knifed through the seams in my jacket. I could just imagine how easily it cut between the stitches in my heavy green sweater that Maureen was wearing. Suddenly the steps down from the tower seemed flimsy, the footing slippery, and the railing unsafe. I never would have okayed a stunt on them, not without checking every board and joint. The steps were wide enough for only one person. It went against my grain to expose Maureen, but in the end I decided it was safer for her to go first: if she slipped I could grab her, rather than her missing a step behind me and sending us both tobogganing into the river. When I suggested she lead, she smiled, and said, "You just keep your eyes on me and you won't have to deal with the woods at all."

"I'm okay."

"Uh-huh," she said sarcastically.

I felt such a burst of indignation—unreasonable, shaking outrage—that it was all I could do to clamp my teeth together to hold the words back. I had been afraid coming up here, but dammit I had managed it, and managed it for her! Likely, I'd be afraid again when we got down from here into the woods. It would have been annoying to be derided for that fear then. But right now, up here, I wasn't worried about the woods, and it was exponentially more insulting to be scorned for a fear that I didn't have. I rapped her shoulder and pointed down. Maureen flipped the switch, sending the empty carrier clanking down the hill. She took off at a distressingly fast clip. If I'd had any question about whether her emotional distress affected her balance or fortitude this romp down the stairs stuck the answer in my face—a face that was well behind hers. That made me madder yet.

Rage is encompassing. It focuses its full attention on sustaining itself, stoking its fires with replayed insults and expectations undeservedly denied. It aerates the blaze with speculation on the vile motives of the offender. If the fire dims, it rekindles with recalled offenses. It fosters sulking and shouting, allows no entry to kindness, comfort, or logic. In a well-nurtured rage, even an apology can be an affront. Rage lets nothing in.

It's rare that anger benefits the one seething, but it did now. I was too furious to be afraid. I stoked and nurtured that fury. I'd made this long trek into the last place I wanted to be and what thanks did I get from Maureen? Zip. Less than zip. And more to the point, I had traveled across country to sit a sesshin with a master, and was I getting any teaching? Ha! I'd been replaced as his jisha and thrown out of his cabin. *You got more teaching than anyone here*, a voice reminded me. I shoved that thought away. I'd come here to face my fear—*Well, you are in the woods, girl*. What about sitting zazen? This is where I was supposed to learn to sit in meditation without escaping. I sure hadn't done that.

But two out of three wasn't enough; I could feel my rage slipping away and the trees closing in. *One* out of three.

Then, in a burst it came: *If you look a man in the face and shove him off the bridge so he lands on his back, and go on, mouthing the dharma, sitting in the zendo hearing the sounds, feeling the air on your face, seeing your own thoughts for six years, what value is Zen practice, Leo? Can you fucking fake it that long? And what about the lessons you gave me with the cocoa, was that all fake, too? We trust you to show us how to open the lock and you can't even recognize the door. What you did to Aeneas, you do to us all.*

"Damn you!"

We were on the hillside, stopped. Maureen was standing in front of me, her face open with fright. "I'm sorry," she murmured.

It took me a moment to realize she assumed I was still stewing about her condescension. "Wasn't about you," I said, lamely.

"Him?"

"Yeah."

"Yeah," she said, and squeezed my hand, and I felt the odd, empty bond that joined us.

And I wondered how much stronger, how much deeper was her rage than mine. She had harbored Leo's secret for six years and he'd rewarded her by tossing her aside, and tossing the secret aside. He'd undermined her practice and her being.

"Maureen, if you poisoned Roshi, I can understand."

"Someone poisoned Roshi?" Even in the shadowy moonlight here in the woods I could see the horror and distress on Maureen's face. "Is he— omigod—is he . . ." She didn't even seem able to form the word.

"No, he's not dead. He's had spikes of fever and he's weak."

"Why didn't he call me?" Her voice was almost a whisper but it held within it a wail she couldn't completely suppress.

Above us the wind whipped the redwood and pine branches. Below, the stream smacked the rocks as if to make sure neither of us forgot how Aeneas died.

She wrapped her arms around her ribs. It was the only time I had seen her actually admit cold. Her eyes shut and her breath became shallow. She looked as if she was tightening smaller and smaller, becoming more and more compact till she reached a solid, lightless ball of energy. It exploded in one word.

"You!"

She grabbed my shoulders and gave one sudden shake that knocked me off my feet. The cold air shot under my arms and legs; I was wind-milling, grabbing, my hand on something round, abrasive, my feet hitting, slipping, wet. And then a thud and a yank on my arm socket, and I was down the bank, the water rushing over my feet. A wave of panic shot through me. I grabbed onto the tree trunk with my other hand and pulled my feet out of the water, scrambling for purchase on the steep bank.

"Darcy!"

Maureen was reaching down. There was a branch to her left and I took that and pulled myself halfway up. Her hand was still out, as if she hadn't processed my move, but I wasn't about to trust her. I bypassed the hand and grabbed her elbow. She let out a small gasp of surprise. She felt solidly braced and I locked on with the other hand, managed a couple quick steps on the slippery bank and was back on the path, shaking with cold, shock, and anger.

"What is the matter with you? You could have killed me!"

"Darcy, I'm so sorry. I don't know what . . . I just lost it. Omigod. I'm so so sorry. I never meant to—I know you didn't keep me away from Roshi on your own. He told you to, right? It's just that after all those years . . ."

"Never mind," I said and meant it. "I'm thinking of Aeneas and how easy it must have been to knock him off the bridge. Just a burst of anger . . . and wham!"

I wanted to tell her how bad I had felt when I'd blocked her from seeing Leo, but I couldn't speak the words, not after her outburst here. I'd been sorry then, but more right than I'd realized. But I was also remembering sitting in the zendo after Roshi first spilt the cocoa and how amazed I was at the fury he lit within me. How very dangerous was that trait? Maureen was the most volatile, but everyone was on edge now. And Leo's door was unlocked!

"Come on. We need to move."

Maureen nodded and moved fast. I raced after, my hands no longer on her shoulders. Maybe, I thought, the paramedics would already be at Leo's cabin when we got there. I knew I was fooling myself but I clung to the hope as if it were real. I tried not to think about how bad the road was, how far Barry might have to go to find a phone, or if the paramedics would be on a call, or if they even came this far into the woods at night. I thought instead of Barry kneeling down by Leo's side and Leo wishing him luck. And I wished with all my being that Barry was back here by Leo's side giving that luck back to him.

Before I realized it we were at the end of the path, over the bridge, and half running up over the quad. The grounds were empty, the dark broken by the spots of light from the kitchen, the twinkling glow of the oil lamps through the high zendo windows. It had to be one of the evening zazen periods. I'd lost track of time. Ahead of me Maureen was panting, her feet hitting heavy against the macadam, pushing hard to thrust her forward. She'd was running on emotion alone. I was panting, too, but I passed Maureen as we rounded the bathhouse and veered onto the path to Roshi's cabin.

The light coming through his open door was dim, but against the dark night it glowed like neon. Silhouetted by it was part of a standing figure, the part not hidden by the half open door. A leg from knee to boot.

"Boot," I hissed back to Maureen.

Her breath caught. She understood the danger. No one coming to see his roshi enters his cabin with boots on. Socks, yes. Shoes, rarely. But muddy boots, never. Only someone who doesn't care, or can't stop himself would charge in there with boots on.

Chapter Thirty-four

O

arry was dreaming. He knew it was a dream, like when he fell
asleep in zazen. In a minute he'd jerk awake. But right now he
was in town, in Doctor Jeffers' examining room, pulling the
short blond doctor away from the old man clutching a blue paper sheet
across his gut, and insisting, "I said go take care of Roshi. Now!" Darcy
was smiling at him, though she wasn't there. But that's how dreams were.
He could still feel the warmth of her smile, but something was wrong. He
shook his head, focused on the muddy, unpaved road.

He was in the Chocolate Hall behind his display, the chill of the
over-air-conditioned room seeping through his sweater, watching Gundersen or Grummond and a plump red-haired woman judge he'd never
seen as they took in the sheen of his perfect bars. *Seventy-two percent
cocoa.* He couldn't keep the pride from his voice. Gundersen and the
woman each picked up a bar, sniffed. The woman smiled, but Gundersen was poker-faced. They snapped the bars in half and the woman
smiled again at the crisp cracking sound. They cut slivers and, closing
her eyes, the woman placed a sliver on her tongue. She smiled and
sighed orgasmically. All around people gasped. Barry held his breath.

Now Gundersen put his chocolate on his tongue. Barry went tense. Gundersen puked.

Barry jolted awake. "Just a dream," he said aloud. Sweat coated his face and back. "Focus on the road, dammit!"

He had the window open wider than was absolutely safe for the chocolate, but the vent kept the draft from hitting the boxes. No choice. He had to stay awake. He stared ahead, eyes open wide. This had to be another dream, it couldn't be real! He shook his head hard, and stared back at the road. Nothing had changed. He hit the brakes. The boxes were halfway off the seat before he caught them.

In the middle of the road was a car! A new, metallic green number, one of those American jobs made to the specs of a Honda or Toyota. Who the hell . . .?

Jeez, this was the last thing he had time for. Some stupid tourist "exploring!" Jeez! And now he was stuck. The guy'd better be ready to do some heavy pushing.

Banging open the door he lowered himself onto the ridge at the edge of the road and slogged toward the car. He was a couple yards away when he could see two things. The mud was over the hubcaps, like the car had been sinking for days, and, there was no driver.

He braced his arms on the hood and pushed. The car didn't budge. It might as well have been sunk in cement. He pulled open the passenger door, surprised it was unlocked. A rental contract lay on the seat. Rented to Gabriel Luzotta! Shit! That fuckup Luzotta! What kind of jerk abandons his car in the middle of the single lane halfway to the coast road and can't be bothered to get a crew to trot out the path from the monastery to shift it? Luzotta'd been here before; he knew the layout, and the fuckup knew it rained, what kind of . . .

Barry stalked back to his truck. His shoes were thick with mud. He paid no attention, but swung himself into the truck, started the engine, and inched forward. The truck's bumper slid over the little green car's low and useless excuse for a bumper.

Knuckles white against the steering wheel, Barry looked ahead at the ten-foot rise on the north side of the narrow road, at the line of trees to the south. He got out of the truck and looked behind him, knowing he would see nothing different, knowing even if he could somehow jack the car up enough to get the truck's bumper under it and front tow it, there was no space big enough to push it off the road. No space ahead, no space behind.

The picture of the Chocolate Hall flashed in his mind, replaced by Luzotta's green rental car. Barry swung himself hard into the truck, turned on the engine, and gunned it. He backed up, floored the gas, and rammed the car again.

Then he took the lid off the top chocolate box, lifted the mold with his 72 percent criollo bars, and slammed it into the mud.

Chapter Thirty-five

O

I was about five feet from the door when I heard Leo's voice.
"No! Wait! Don't!"

What I did next came from kindness, not fear. I stepped aside and let Maureen go to him first. Then I leapt up his stairs, and hit the porch as she burst in. The door banged hard. Inside, everything was a flurry of color, the green of the sweater flying right then left around the charcoal brown of the other coat, the green disappearing under the brown as they fell to the floor; the yellow wisps of Maureen's hair rising like steam as she pushed and scrambled and clawed on top and ended up staring down at Amber's golden brown hair and flushed face. And on the other side of the room, gray like a movie not yet brought to life, lay Roshi, mouth open, his eyes wide in anguish.

It was another moment before I spotted the fire poker on the floor by Roshi's futon, its sharp end inches from his face. Before I could ask him if he was okay, Roshi nodded and looked toward Amber, who had started struggling under Maureen.

"Bastard," she hissed. "You fucking bastard."

"Let Amber up," he said.

Maureen didn't move. "Roshi, she would have killed you."

"Maybe," he said. "Probably not." His voice had the same detached and yet wholly concerned tone I had come to expect from him. He might have been eyeing his cocoa cup and saying, *This should taste great.*

He pushed himself up with more vigor than he'd shown in the past two days. But when he looked down at Amber there was no detachment in his gaze. His eyes were creased with concern.

"Maureen?"

With a show of reluctance that didn't quite mask her exhaustion, Maureen eased herself off Amber's wriggling form.

"Take this cushion." He pointed Amber to a large, almost luxurious zafu in the corner next to the fireplace. It was, I noted, far from the door. To me he said, "Make us tea?" as if he had never fired me from jishahood. "Maureen, you need to sit right there by the fire."

A surreal few minutes followed, as if we were not here to cast blame for the murder of one woman's brother, one man's student. As if Maureen's life had not been derailed by it. The fire had gone out and even the ash was cold. I brought in wood but ended up creating a blaze mostly from newspaper and twigs, and hung my wet socks in front. The three of them sat in silence, while I poured the pale tea, not quite steeped, into four small glazed handleless cups. The cups, as always, were too hot to hold and the tea steamed between us four like the unanswered questions.

I sat in the only place left, in front of the door, a flesh and bone blockade against escape.

Roshi picked up his cup and sipped, his eyes closed. When he opened his eyes, it was clear he was ready.

"Amber," he said, "your brother is dead and I am responsible. No words can alter that. If I could undo anything from the moment he thought of coming here to the day he died—"

"The day you murdered him!"

He gave a slow nod, of acknowledgment rather than agreement, and went on.

"What I'm going to tell you will be small comfort. No one dies without his death changing everything and everybody."

"Don't! Don't you dare start lecturing me!"

Her hands were around her cup and she slammed it hard on the floor, slopping tea over the side. Her whole body was in angry motion, legs jiggling, torso rocking, teeth tapping impatiently, as if it was all she could do not to lunge at him.

"Bear with me just a moment, Amber. You have lived with questions about his death for many years. I want you to have answers."

She nodded, suspiciously.

He was talking to Amber but he wasn't looking at her. In someone else that apparent rudeness might have been from nerves or habit. But when a roshi speaks to a student on serious matters he gives her his full attention. Amber was getting merely the fringe of it. His gaze was on Maureen. That seemed natural; she was sitting directly across from him, in front of the fire. But he had placed her there.

I shifted a bit toward him so I could watch her reaction, too.

"Amber, Aeneas's death changed everyone here. Even those of us who assumed he went to Japan—"

"What are you saying? You killed him!" Amber was on her knees halfway to him.

Maureen's face went pale. She started to shake and had to clamp her hands together to control them.

"Leo," she said, so softly I had to lean forward, "you killed Aeneas. I saw you there."

He sat silently, unmoving, his gaze never shifting from her. An entire minute passed slowly, as if each second were moving individually across our consciousnesses.

Still looking at Maureen, he said, "I am responsible for all that happened here. I should never have accepted Aeneas. That was greed and laziness on my part. We needed the help, and so as questions about him came up I pushed them aside. I wanted to believe he was a serious student, a bit strange, but strange in a way that would prosper here. If I hadn't been dwelling in the past, reliving events that happened before I came here, and planning for the future, I might have seen him more clearly. If I hadn't allowed myself the escape of liquor I might have seen the problems before they came to . . . death."

"Dammit," Amber slammed both hands on the floor, "don't beat around the bush. You put your hands on my brother and you threw him off the bridge. Admit it. Just admit it!"

Despite Amber's outburst, he was still looking at Maureen. "It wouldn't have happened if I had been aware. But, Amber, I did not throw him off the bridge."

It was Maureen who gasped. "But I saw—"

"Saw what?"

"He was running down from the quad. He was wearing your robes, waving a manila envelope and a gin bottle. He was—" She swallowed, and again, and took a deep breath, and even with that it was a moment before she could go on. "You came running after him. I was in the woods beside the bridge. I saw you. I heard you yelling at him. You were calling him 'a miserable self-centered lout.' You said, 'How could you do this to me?' I heard you say that."

Roshi nodded slowly, but this time it was the sign of agreement.

"I accused him of selfish ambition, but I was the ambitious one. That weekend meant everything to me. Fujimoto-roshi and Ogata-roshi were esteemed teachers in my lineage. They didn't come to this country just for the opening of this little country monastery, but they did extend their stay for an extra five days; they came a long way into the woods and they put up with primitive conditions."

He paused, picked up his tea cup with both hands and with deliberation sipped twice, as if offering a tribute to the two roshis. As he put the cup down, Amber eased back onto the cushion, though she still looked able to spring.

"Their coming to the opening was a great honor for all of us, but particularly for me. Many of you were so new you didn't realize it was an honor." He was talking to Maureen and now he waited for her to give a sign of agreement, but she stiffened and held her gaze steady. "But I knew. And I knew that their coming signified that I was accepted back into the fold. The long months of work we had done here, the hardships we had endured without complaint—" His wide lips curled in an ironic smile. "I mean, complaint to *them*; it all added up to a monastery under the guidance of a responsible teacher." He nodded at Maureen and said, "As you could have told me, I was on shaky ground."

Maureen's only response was to shiver more visibly. Even with her hands planted together in her lap her quivering arms shook the sleeves of the green sweater. Why was he tormenting her? He was playing directly to her, touching her most tender memories. With each shared memory he was beseeching her to trust again, to open to him the wound that hadn't begun to heal.

His smile faded and left a sadness in its place.

"I had been drinking a lot the whole time I was here. You probably never saw me entirely sober until then. Getting myself sober was about the hardest thing I'd ever done, and I was still shaky when the Japanese contingent arrived. But I was sober because I was so intent on everything going perfectly. I fussed at Barry to make food that would have required a hotel kitchen, at you to produce flowers when it was way too early for this climate. I checked and reorganized the seating in the zendo, spent hours making everyone practice the ceremony. I think now it was an alcoholic reaction, that brittle, almost superstitious need for perfection. Whatever, I needed it. And on the day of the opening everything was perfect, the weather, the food, the ceremony, everything, remember?"

A small miserable sound escaped Maureen's mouth. She lowered her gaze, then with obvious force of will made herself look back at him.

"And then, after all that, when the ceremony was over, I sat on the cabin steps, high from the success, still on pins and needles and desperate for a drink." He inhaled slowly and said in a tone of disgust I hadn't heard since our drive in here in the truck, "I could not have handled things worse. Instead of sitting zazen with my fears and my needs, that whole year I walled them out. I had no business passing myself off as a teacher. You can sit facing the wall for decades and learn nothing if you try hard enough not to. I was a fraud, but a fraud who knew all the right words."

Amber's angry intake of breath startled him momentarily, then he nodded to her.

"Right. Get on with it. Just when I thought everything had gone perfectly, I heard Aeneas. He was whooping, like kids do playing cowboys and Indians. I *heard* him first and then there he was loping past the zendo in my robes, waving a gin bottle. What did I think? I didn't think. All the tension of planning, all the suffering of drying out, all the anguish of my hopes came together. Something burst inside me. I ran after him, screaming. You remember what I said, Maureen; I don't. I was just in a rage. When I caught up with him by the bridge he turned and gave me that sweet, guileless look of his. You remember that expression, Amber," he said, looking at her for the first time. "That must be how you see him in your mind."

She bit her lip. She was shaking as much as Maureen.

"My bubble of rage popped and was gone. Or so I thought. I remember what I said to him then. 'You'll have to wash that robe and iron it before you give it back to me.' Then I told him to stay there a few minutes and consider how he had insulted the visiting teachers, and me. I would leave him alone for ten minutes to think about what he had done, and then I would go with him to apologize to Ogata-roshi and Fujimoto-roshi. I walked up the road, five minutes up, five minutes back—I timed myself because I knew how literal Aeneas was. When I got back, he wasn't there. I thought he had gone on back to the zendo or the quad. Maybe he was already apologizing."

He picked up his cup and sipped very slowly, glancing at Maureen between sips.

"Suddenly, I was angrier than ever. I thought: Aeneas is bowing in apology. Maybe he is explaining, maybe not. The Japanese barely know any English—so, same difference. What they see is Leo Garson's best student apologizing for the behavior of his teacher. You know how it is when you're angry: you don't want logic; you just want to be right."

I had felt just like that climbing down the hill. I nodded, not that Leo noticed. But Amber's hands clenched into fists, her wide, smooth jaw clenched, and she looked on the verge of shouting: Don't give me this crap about anger!

Maureen I couldn't read at all. She was still shivering; she hadn't touched her tea. Her gaze was locked on Leo's but in an unfocused way, as if she was watching his words more than his face.

He put down the cup, moved his hands back to his lap, and said, "With a great force of will I kept myself from running up to the zendo, finding Ogata-roshi and Fujimoto-roshi and explaining. But I didn't want to appear foolish, see? So maybe ten minutes passed, and when I got halfway there I saw the two old men walking toward their van. I'd been so caught up in my anger I'd forgotten they were so close to leaving. They had to get to San Francisco for ceremonies before their flight home, so there wasn't much leeway.

"So I bowed to them, spoke carefully in what little Japanese I remembered so they would have to see I was sober, gave them the kind of formal farewell that was called for. I was thinking: I should have had everyone here for their send-off. They're noticing that. They're thinking I'm rude or incompetent. They bowed and I can't recall what they said because I wasn't 'there.' I was in my own thoughts. And then they were gone.

"Afterward I remembered Aeneas, dressed in my robe, and it made perfect sense that he had waited for them on the road and that they took him because they couldn't bear to leave him here, with me. And based on that thought, I went back to my room and drank till I passed out."

Maureen said, "But Roshi, I *saw* you come after him. I heard you threaten him. "

He nodded. Now they were staring eye to eye.

"You planted the red maple in a hurry and too close to the road."

He said no more but their faces changed together. It was Maureen's I watched as the fear gave way to welcome shock, to belief, and then a flash of outrage.

"You suspected *me* of killing Aeneas?" she demanded in a wavering voice.

"Well, after I realized he was dead I did *think* . . ." And then he smiled.

I said, "And that's why you set up this last sesshin with the pressure of remembering Aeneas, right? For Maureen, to force her to face killing Aeneas?"

He acknowledged my comment with the smallest of nods. Maureen didn't react at all. So much had to be shifting in her mind now—Roshi *hadn't* killed Aeneas. He *hadn't* lied. His teaching *wasn't* tainted. Her practice *was* valid. The color was seeping back into her face. She had been given her life back. Her teacher whom she doubted, who she thought had replaced her with me, had rearranged this whole sesshin because he cared so much for her.

Their relief and joy filled the room. I sat basking in it, and at some point came the realization that I, too, had gotten life back, my life here with my teacher here. I had gotten back the Leo in the truck, the Roshi with the cocoa. The fire crackled; it was almost down to embers, but still the room seemed warm and safe and full of promise. Maureen and Roshi were still sitting silently, no longer staring eye to eye, but looking toward each other. They needed time alone. I braced my hands to push myself up and ease out.

"Hey!" Amber shouted. "This is all sweety sweety, but my brother is still lying dead under that fucking maple. And somebody here killed him."

Chapter Thirty-six

mber's words were like a bucket of cold water on the rest of us. In the relief about Roshi, we'd sidestepped the point that if he hadn't killed Aeneas, then someone else had.

"Roshi," I said, "once you realized Aeneas hadn't left here, you figured he was dead, right? And you assumed Maureen killed him. Did you wonder about anyone else?"

But even as I asked it I knew the answer. If he had set up this practice period to allow Maureen to come to terms with her supposed guilt, he would do no less for his other students. He certainly wouldn't blurt out his suspicions in a group of four.

"Maureen? What about you? Who else—?"

But Maureen was in no condition to answer anything. Her hands were not merely quivering, they were shaking. She held them out, watching the fingers wriggle like worms. She had been near to emotional collapse in the fire tower hours ago. Of course, she had no reserve to deal with the idea that one of her other friends was a killer, one of the people she had assumed was safe.

"Amber, Barry's gone. Take Maureen to Barry's room above the chocolate kitchen. It'll be warm there. Get some food for her and stay with her. No one will know you're there. I'll show you where it is."

I motioned her out, leaving Maureen and Roshi their time together.

The wind had picked up, moist with fog. I glanced up at the California night sky—dark, murky gray. Then, for the first time, I checked my watch and was shocked to find it was 9:25 P.M. In fifteen minutes people would be pouring out of the zendo, Aeneas's killer included.

"You haven't answered me. What about my brother?" Amber demanded as we came abreast the bathhouse.

I motioned her inside. "Use it now. While no one's here."

She froze. My commonplace comment had brought the danger home to her in a way that Roshi's description of her brother's death so long ago couldn't. I put my hand on her back and led her into the bathhouse.

"Amber, do you know anything that puts you in danger? Anything Aeneas told you? Anything you found out here?" She shook her head, but there was a tentative quality to the movement. "What about Justin? You were both here that weekend Aeneas died."

"That weekend?"

She eased her buttocks against the edge of one of the sinks and looked nervously at the empty stalls a few feet away. The white tiles on the floor were muddy; the room cold. The chalky soap made it seem like any girls' room in any elementary school.

"You know what surprised me that weekend? That Aeneas was just the same. I mean, I thought, well, I hoped, that after he'd spent so long in a meditation center he would be, well, normal, you know? But there he was, still wandering around, picking up things like everything was his. Still in his own solitary world, except when he got obsessed and had to have something in the big world."

"Something as mundane as a manila envelope?"

319

"I suppose," she said tentatively. "He didn't just choose stuff for no reason. I mean, if it was pretty, or interesting, or important—"

"Important?"

She fingered a blob of pink soap hardening on the sink, scooping it onto her nail, looking at it without seeing.

"Well, you know, if someone treated it like it was valuable. Like the Buddha. He might have taken it because it's pretty, but definitely because it was on the altar."

"Rob found the Buddha in his suitcase."

"Yeah, but that doesn't mean anything. Just that that's where Aeneas was when he lost interest in it."

"But," I said, thinking aloud, "if Aeneas picked up something, like that manila envelope, and the owner chased him, then Aeneas—"

"Right." She flicked the soap off her nail, and turned to face me straight on. "When he was still at home, mornings were like chaos. My parents had to hide the car keys. I couldn't lay my homework down or he'd grab it. Anything any of us cared about was fair game, even Mom's shopping list, and umbrellas! We went through so many umbrellas that winter the guy in the store must have figured we were running a shelter.

"It's sad, really sad, but once he left for here, we all relaxed. My parents set their alarms for half an hour later. And when I came for the opening, I had a term paper due Monday. I'd actually gotten it done, but I'm a lousy typist and I absolutely had to read it over, even if it meant doing it in the car, with Justin. I did, and it was fine, but I was so nervous about Aeneas getting hold of it, I stuck it in the glove compartment and made Justin lock it and the car. Justin thought I was crazy. I mean, he had his college entrance essays with him—we figured things would be so boring at the monastery we'd have plenty of time to work. I told him to put them in the glove compartment, but he didn't believe me, not then."

She shrugged. "He thought I'd lost it. I could see that he thought I was going wacko, just like Aeneas."

Her hand tightened on the sink. "Oh, god, it's so sad. I wish I never came to this miserable place. I wanted to learn about Aeneas but I didn't want to remember again. When I was with him I was a kid. I adored him; then I hated him; then he was a pain in the ass. But now, now that I can think what it was like for him, Oh, god, I just don't want to think about him actually dying."

The small sweet bell pinged in the Zendo, ending the last sitting period. People would unbend their stiff legs, fluff their cushions, and prepare for the final three bows. In five minutes they would be in here.

"Amber," I said, "The things that Aeneas snatched, can you be sure they were important to the owner? Aeneas could have misjudged, couldn't he?"

"No." The sound was closer to a squeak than a word; she shook her head as if to amplify it. "No, never once in all the months he took stuff, never once did he take anything that didn't matter. You know what idiot savants are? Well, Aeneas was one when it came to knowing what was important to people. I mean, Darcy, it used to drive me crazy, the thing about my homework. So I tried to divert him by making a fuss over my coffee mug or a magazine. But it was like he *knew*, you know? I ended up thinking that his focus was so narrow that he was a master of what was in it. So, no, he never made a mistake. He only took what mattered."

"And it went on for months?"

"Well, yeah. We hid stuff, my parents got locks. I mean, we weren't fools. Toward the end our house looked like we'd moved out. There was nothing personal around. It was only when company came there was a problem, and by then we didn't have . . . much company." She swallowed hard, and hurried into the stall. She flushed twice, I'm sure to cover her sobs, and when she came back she stood at the sink, not washing, only letting the cold water run over her hands. "Whatever Aeneas took here, that day," she said, "wouldn't someone have missed it?"

"Maybe," I said.

But I didn't tell her Aeneas had fallen on top of the manila envelope, or that Maureen had buried it with him. I didn't explain that anyone chasing after Aeneas would have assumed that envelope was washing downstream.

I didn't tell Amber any of that. I just watched her reflection in the mirror, and mine. I looked awful, like I did after the worst hangover, my skin yellowy except for the dark circles under my eyes, my hair a tangle of greasy red curls clown-like against my deathly skin. But the shock was Amber. She looked like all the moisture had been drained from her cells. The plump promise of youth was gone. She squeezed her eyes shut against another onslaught of tears, and muttered, "I'm so scared."

"You aren't a danger to anyone. You don't know anything, right?"

"Aeneas wasn't a danger. Whoever killed him, how can he be sure I don't know anything?" She took a breath and glared at me. "How do I know Maureen didn't kill him, and you're sending me to hide out alone with her?"

"She didn't."

"Prove it."

"Prove you didn't kill him."

"What?"

"You could have. You were there. My point is you can't always prove someone didn't do something, you can only prove that they did. You're going to have to trust me." Two bells sounded in the zendo—the final bow. I gave her a final squeeze and said, "Come on. We've got to move."

We finished in the bathroom and hurried across the still-empty quad to the kitchen. As we reached the door, I heard the wooden clappers in the zendo, signaling people to turn and file out of the zendo for the night. To the students in there this was the end of the third rigorous day of sesshin, the turning point from days of exhaustion to days of calmer awareness. They would be relieved to finish it less tired than yesterday and thankful for that; in their perceptions life was slowing, like down-shifting the truck. I envied them that moment when it happened, that clear, noticeable downshift, after which they would notice sounds of wind and birds and rustle of cloth unheard before, the comforting awareness of breath ebbing and flowing, the first inkling of freedom from the chatter of thought. Despite all that had happened Leo—Roshi—had pre-served that for them.

I did a whirlwind check of the kitchen and Barry's room, recalled that I hadn't seen food in Roshi's room, and slapped some peanut butter and jelly on bread; it's hard to be too sick for peanut butter and jelly, and, in fact, he had seemed much stronger when he was talking to Maureen than he had hours earlier. I made two sandwiches and managed to down half of my own before Amber and I got back to Roshi's cabin.

Maureen was standing by the door. When I walked in she and Roshi merely bowed to each other before she left with Amber. It was a simple move, done in unison, but like a kiss, it said more than words could manage. I could guess what passed between them, but I would only have been guessing. I shut the door and when I looked at Roshi there was no telltale smile or drooped eye of sadness. The moment with Maureen was gone and I thought he was focusing on me. But when he put out his hand I realized the attraction was the peanut butter sandwich.

"Didn't Rob bring you dinner?" I asked while he wolfed.

"No," he got out between bites.

He was eating with such gusto I was both relieved and afraid the sandwich would be too much after his near-fast of the last couple days. But there wasn't a chance I would deter him. The mundane quality of that cheered me a bit. And Rob's failing at the basic jisha duties made me feel downright smug. With relief I watched Leo devour the brown bread, and, with a snakelike flick of his tongue, catch an errant squirt of jelly before it fell to the floor. His skin had a flush of pink; he was sitting normally. He looked like a man who had not merely stepped back from death's door, but leapt back.

"Roshi, I hope Maureen will be okay with Amber. You know this has been really hard on Amber. She's lost her memory of her brother."

I half expected him to comment that that memory was illusion, but he nodded sympathetically, and finished the sandwich. "I told her it would be hard. She didn't believe me. I thought she might need this last chance to know about her brother. But I didn't know her. Still, we'll see."

I could still feel the quiver of Amber's back as it had been against my hand, feel her shaking from anger and fear. What was the matter with Leo? Was he off in some Zen cloud? "Leo, this isn't a regular sesshin. Of course, she's scared. Somebody pushed her brother off the bridge! There's a murderer here!"

"No one is after her. Only I am the target."

"Maybe. But she doesn't believe that."

He took a deep, controlled, but angry-sounding breath. For a moment I thought I'd gone too far and, no matter how deficient Rob was as jisha, I'd be fired again. From the zendo came the slap of the door shutting and almost immediately soft-soled shoes splatting down the steps. It surprised me how clearly sound carried at night in the country. It was not quite ten o'clock. Barry had left hours ago. The paramedics should have been here hours ago. "Roshi, did the medics come and go already?"

"Medics?"

"Barry called them when he got to a phone."

He was looking at the spot where Maureen had sat, his face scrunched in the kind of indecisive worry roshis were supposed to be beyond.

"Surely the medics would come here, even though it's night, wouldn't they?"

"Let's see." He pushed himself up, and nothing I said dissuaded him from putting on his robes, his parka, and his boots and heading out across the quad amid the students hurrying to the bathhouse or their cabins, and down to the road. The only choice I had was whether or not to follow.

CHAPTER THIRTY-SEVEN

O

L eo was in full Roshi mode. He was moving slowly in his long
brown robe, but in such a stately fashion he seemed like a brown-
masted schooner in full sail as he proceeded along his path to the
bathhouse. One of the advantages of being roshi is not waiting in line. But
that doesn't mean not having to wait till the stalls empty.

I stood outside, shivering in the fog-chilled air, wishing there had
been a gracious way to ask Maureen for my sweater back since she was
headed to spend the night under Barry's blankets, and trying to decide if
it was worth the effort to confront Roshi with any of the sixteen
supremely sensible reasons for not heading down to the road in the dark
to wait for the paramedics.

It felt so good to be back worrying about Leo in this familiar way,
as his jisha again, worrying if he'd be warm enough outside waiting for
the reliable paramedics, and most of all to know he wasn't Aeneas's
killer, that I hadn't really focused on Amber's question. If not Leo, who
had killed Aeneas?

Someone acting on impulse, from anger or necessity or both. Aeneas
wouldn't have discerned anything, exposed anything, repeated anything.

He only snatched things. Like a dog, he snatched and ran, teasing the owner with whatever was in that manila envelope. I could imagine him jumping up on the ledge-rail of the bridge, all part of the game. And I could imagine the chaser, desperate for his envelope, making a grab for it, and shoving Aeneas. It wouldn't have been planned. No premeditated murder would have culminated with the victim's body abandoned in the stream in a spot two people passed within minutes.

Planned or not, dead is dead. Someone murdered Aeneas.

But why stay at a monastery in the woods near Aeneas's body? Was it from fear that Maureen would transplant the maple and uncover the body? Was there evidence on the body? The killer's skin under Aeneas's fingernails? Something else? Or just the killer's fear of it? Was he waiting, wondering how long it took for the evidence to deteriorate? Each year he would have felt safer. The body was being eaten away, the maple growing larger.

What had Leo said about the red maple when we almost hit it driving in here? *When we get the road paved, we'll take out that maple.* Not *if, when.*

The bathhouse door swung open and this time it was Leo. One look at his face—eyes narrowed, those bushy brown brows lowered, wide lips pressed hard together—confirmed his determination. I followed him silently.

One of the paths led from the bathhouse to the parking lot, but he didn't take that. Instead he veered to the right and steamed toward the kitchen, his robe beneath his parka catching the wind. A student, possibly the path-sweeping lawyer from Vermont, passed him and nodded in half-recognition. Otherwise the way was empty. Students were permitted to go to the kitchen for tea after the last zazen period, but by then bed was too inviting. I did wonder if we would find Rob there and what explanation he would give for ignoring Roshi all afternoon.

And then the obvious struck me. If he'd poisoned his long-time teacher, his supposed friend, of course he couldn't face him. Nor could he kill him, not at the time when he was the one known to have access to him. So he let him lie there unattended, a sick man who could have had a crisis, and who did go hungry all afternoon. I didn't like Rob, but I had credited him with relentless responsibility. It infuriated me to think he could switch it off like that, like tossing a kitten in the river. I hoped now we did find him in the kitchen. When Roshi walked up to him, I wanted to see his face.

Documents are kept in manila envelopes. Deeds to the surrounding land; bills of sale for construction; correspondence with the hierarchy in San Francisco about Leo, mutual assumptions Leo would be edged out in a couple years. Rob was a lawyer; he would have preserved copies of everything, including both sides of correspondence. There were plenty of documents he wouldn't have wanted made public that day, at the opening, in front of the roshis and priests and Buddhists from all over the West Coast.

Leo strode into the kitchen. But there was no one else there, no illumination but two plug-in night lights in sockets by either door that made the room seem larger. He flicked on the overhead light in the chocolate kitchen. The click resounded in the silence. The bright bulb shone off the white paint. The still, red melangeur was no longer mixing cocoa with lecithin and large-grain sugar; the white conche pipe was not tumbling chocolate till its texture met even Barry's standards; the silvery metal table that looked like something out of an autopsy room was bare and shiny. Whatever warmth there had been from heating the gruel for dinner had dissipated, and the smell of cocoa that had given this kitchen its homey appeal was all but gone. It was as if Barry had taken it with him.

Roshi shook the kettle, lit the flame underneath, checked the height as he must have done every time he'd heated water. He walked to the cupboard, pulled out two plain white cups—not the sturdy little handle-less mugs students used in sesshin, but the kind of delicate cups that rest on saucers. He set cup on saucer with no tinkle of china, foot on tile as silently as if on carpet. Moving almost as if in slow motion, he reached for the cocoa shelf.

I braced, poised to snatch the Special Reserve canister out of his hand. No way would I have him put that cocoa in his mouth again. But then he did the oddest thing of all. He bypassed the tin of cocoa Barry had made for practice period, ignored the Roshi's Special Reserve tin, and plucked a packet of commercial cocoa. How had Barry let that packet sully his cocoa cabinet?

The hiss of the kettle blew like a steam engine in this silent room. I jumped back, but Leo took the noise in stride, poured a small bit of cocoa in each cup, and added half a cup of water. He returned the kettle, found a spoon, stirred and handed me a cup. "Smells good, huh?" They were the first words he'd spoken since we'd left his cabin.

I looked from him to the cocoa. I understood this was a lesson. I didn't want to be fooled. I wanted to understand. And yet, beyond whatever symbolic meaning it had, it did smell good. It smelled delicious. I thought of that first wonderful cup of cocoa I had gotten here, the one I'd taken outside Monday and sipped as if I were drinking in Heaven. I inhaled deeply and I smiled.

"Drink."

I smiled and sipped. "Yuck! It's awful. Worse than awful." I plunked the cup down and picked up the cocoa packet. "It's still half full. Roshi, you have to use the whole thing. Even then it can be weak. But this, this is ter-rible. I can make you a decent cup. We've got good cocoa here and the water's still hot. There's no need for us to drink this swill. It'll only take—"

"Drink this," he said, and sipped his own.

Frowning, I picked up my cup and prepared to down it in one big gulp. He caught my hand. It was the first time his hand had touched mine, and it seemed a very personal thing. His fingers and palm were calloused but they felt soft. Perhaps it was the way he cupped his hand, or maybe even his intent coming though the flesh. I remembered him— Leo—in the truck looking at me and me wondering if he was staring a mite longer than strictly necessary and thinking of the affairs nurtured in isolated places like this, like flower bulbs forced in tight vases.

"Drink," he repeated. He released his hand. It may have lingered a moment, but more likely I was imagining that so I didn't feel so foolish about the memory.

Whatever his intention, the result was I did drink the miserable cocoa slowly, tasting it, trying to treat it like instant coffee, as a brown liquid with no connection to its decent cousins. I didn't get to like it, but I did drink it. I took the cups to wash, and when I turned back he was making two more cocoas, this time with Barry's good cocoa, and in good-sized mugs. As he poured, I inhaled and smiled. He smiled back that wide kidlike grin. He turned off the overhead light, leaving the kitchen in the dim glow of the night-lights. Then he lifted the mugs, walked across the kitchen and up the stairs to the loft to Amber and Maureen, the aroma lingering behind him.

I stood in the half-dark, fuming. I'd understood his lesson and *this* was my reward! The aroma of the good cocoa teased me. I'd barely eaten all day, because I was taking care of Roshi then, taking care of Maureen, and now *she* got the good cocoa.

But, the water was still hot, and the good cocoa was in the cabinet. I strode over, feet rapping the floor, yanked out the good stuff and helped myself to a heaping spoonful. Righteously, I poured the hot water, stirred, and defiantly drank. The cocoa was good, very good. But when it was gone, I missed my pique.

The door opened behind me. I nearly dropped the mug. It was only when a whiff of cold air brushed my cheek that I realized the noise wasn't Roshi coming back downstairs. I turned slowly, cup still in hand, expecting to see Rob heading deliberately for the kettle and a final cup of tea after a hard day of directing.

But the figure wasn't moving deliberately, and it wasn't Rob. It was Justin. I sank back into the shadows and watched Justin move furtively, almost soundlessly from the door to the stove, pause long enough that I wondered if he had sneaked in for tea. Getting an extra cup of tea wasn't a hanging offense. Why didn't he turn on the light and grab a cup?

I stood for a moment in the shadows. Justin moved on toward the stairs, placing each foot soundlessly. I was barely breathing. How far could I let him go? I couldn't let him creep up the stairs and take Roshi by surprise. And yet I had to give him time to expose his intentions. Amber all but said Aeneas had stolen his college application essays. He'd have spent days, maybe weeks on each one. The opening was in March; the deadline for the essays must have been almost immediate. No way Justin could have reconstructed them in time. And he could hardly send in applications with notes saying: The dog ate my essay. Of course he'd chase after Aeneas. Of course he'd be enraged enough to shove him off the bridge.

He was almost to the stairs. At least, I thought, he didn't grab a knife. He's not planning on attacking. He was moving so slowly he paused on each foot, like he was walking in kinhin. No, wait! He was testing the floor, listening with each step. The envelope? Did he figure it was hidden in here? Did the kitchen have a trapdoor or some facsimile of loose floorboard? It doesn't take much to hide an item none of the residents care about. But why would he bother about his college entrance essays all these years later? Nothing could be of less value to him now.

Unless there was something else in the envelope, something he was sufficiently loath to discuss, admit, focus attention on, that he had lied about to Amber.

I was speculating, but he was working on some thesis, and I wanted to let him follow it as far as he could. He moved around the far side of the melangeur and its great round red tub blocked him from view. I inched forward, faster than he had, but every bit as careful not to reveal myself. The boards under his feet may not have been squeaking enough, but to me those under my feet were screaming. I stopped, waited, but Justin didn't turn.

Bent over, I moved forward.

I was beside the morgue-like metal table the beans had been on. Under its flat metal surface was two feet of empty space and then a bottom shelf. No protection from view. I peered through the opening just as Justin reached the bottom stair to the loft. He reached up, unhooked a foot-long rod from the wall. I couldn't make out what it was.

No more time.

I sent the morgue table shooting across the room at him. He jumped onto the stairs. For a moment I thought he was going to do exactly what I was heading off—run upstairs—but the noise must have startled them up there and something banged overhead. Justin leapt off the stairs, sprinted across the kitchen, and out the door.

I raced after him out the chocolate kitchen door. In the few minutes I'd been inside, the fog had wrapped the kitchen. Now I couldn't see anyone. Couldn't even spot movement. The path forked below the sesshin kitchen door. Surely Justin had taken the left tine toward the zendo, not stayed straight to the parking lot. There was no reason for him to go there. I turned and hurried down alongside the kitchen, my feet slapping into the silence.

A hand grabbed my arm.

CHAPTER THIRTY-EIGHT

O

Before I realized what happened I was back in the kitchen, the sesshin-half this time, and staring at Roshi. The strength of his pull on my arm shocked me. His illness had lightened him physically but not emotionally, and this "save" came straight out of emotion.

"What was all that, Darcy?"

"Justin, creeping across the room. When he got to the stairs I shot that cart at him. I couldn't have him wandering on up the stairs to find you and Amber and Maureen."

I glanced toward the stairs expecting to find Amber headed down, but despite the racket she hadn't come looking for the cause.

"Justin," he mused. But he looked not as if he was thinking but something deeper was going on, as if he was sensing something within himself that had been there all along but he had avoided seeing.

I washed out the cups. The splat of the water resounded through the emptiness of the room. "Roshi, just who is Justin? Amber didn't need him to drive her here this time. He didn't come to study with you. So what's he doing here now? He still thinks it was Aeneas who was the enlightened being; still acts like Aeneas went to Japan even when the truth is smacking him in the face."

Roshi leaned against the counter.

"So he said."

"But why would he say such bizarre things if they weren't true?"

He shrugged.

"People do, Darcy. I know that's not the answer you're looking for right now. You want something beyond a reasonable doubt. There's a lot I don't know about the students here. We are a small monastery, not like Zen centers with renowned teachers and waiting lists. We schedule our sesshins and we take who comes."

"But how do you know what you're getting?"

"We don't," he reiterated. "This is a monastery in the woods in a cold, rainy climate. We have no electricity; we are nine miles from the road. It's not Puerta Vallarta here. If someone wants to come to spend two weeks in silence, facing the wall, with knee pain, back pain, shoulder pain, not to mention mental pain, I assume he is serious about his practice. I figure if he's not; he's in trouble. So far that's been true."

"But someone killed Aeneas."

My words hung between us. I was thinking of Justin's college entrance essays sitting invitingly in the car, despite Amber's warnings. Was Justin the one she meant when she said it was only guests who became Aeneas's victims because they didn't protect their belongings? Next to original research documents, college entrance essays top the "can't do without" category. If Justin spotted Aeneas with them, of course he'd chase after; of course he'd be furious enough to shove him.

"Did Justin say anything—"

"Darcy, no one said anything definite. Do you think I would have let this go on for years if they had?" His face went slack. He nodded, slow, minuscule movements. "It's time to go."

"Go where?"

"You, to bed."

"And you?"

"That's not . . . I don't know."

There had been a change in his voice during that pause; the last sentence seemed to surprise him as much as it did me. It scared me more than Justin had. He didn't know where he was going because he didn't know if he'd be coming back. He didn't know if he would be killed.

My whole body quivered and I knew if I didn't hold tight I would sob. I breathed in, staring at the counter next to him, feeling the cold of the air, forcing myself to concentrate on this moment and not the future without him.

I leaned on the counter next to him and said, "This is my first job as jisha. I've let you get poisoned. I've let you go all day without food. I'll be damned if I'm going to let you get yourself killed."

A grin twitched on his face; he looked like he was about to wink, maybe to make some joke about his fork collection. Then, as quickly as it had come, Leo was replaced by Roshi, and it was Roshi who said coldly, "You are not jisha. You have ten minutes to get to bed before lights out."

"Roshi—" I was desperate to ask him . . . something, anything. I didn't know if it was to keep him or, failing that, to keep a part of him. He looked so fragile. I grabbed him by the arms. "You are my *teacher*."

"Each moment is your teacher. Be alert." He removed my hands. He may have given them a little squeeze; I can't be sure if he did or if I so wanted it that I imagined I'd felt it. He opened the door, paused and said, "Check on Maureen before you go," and stepped outside into the dark, leaving me more alone than I could ever remember feeling.

I stepped outside and watched him go. The fog fuzzed the light in the bathhouse and meshed the dark figures moving on the paths with the trees and buildings behind them. Almost immediately, I lost track of which one was him. I walked across the path toward the bathhouse, passing a tall man in a thick Peruvian sweater. The bathhouse looked like a temple on a foggy Japanese lake, ridiculously romantic with its rectangles of dim yellow throwing just enough light to outline the curlicued corners of the roof. I was ten feet from the building, on the path from the kitchen, when the door from the men's side opened, backlighting a robed figure as it emerged into the night.

I recognized Roshi from his deliberate gait. But that wouldn't have been necessary. He was carrying a lantern; it lit his face, throwing a grotesquely large shadow of his head onto the side of the building. Slowly he walked to the zendo, up the steps, and without removing his shoes opened the door and peered around inside. Then, satisfied in whatever his purpose, he closed the door, hoisted his lantern, and moved down the stairs, back along the path to the bathhouse, and turned right toward the parking area. He hadn't looked around as he passed my path or at any other time in that walk. He hadn't looked because he was not being alert to danger. He was a well-lit invitation to danger! The killer wouldn't have to worry about finding him to attack. And in case the chances of his being saved were too great here, Roshi was moving down the path to the parking area and the road. And the woods. He was all but daring the killer to get him. In this fog anyone could come up behind him and he'd have no warning. If he wanted warning.

I flashed on that moment his face had gone slack and he had said, *I don't know.* He hadn't meant merely that he didn't know what would happen in the next hour, he'd meant, I was sure, that he didn't know anything, not the logic of his original plan, nor the safety of his student he had assumed he was protecting, nor whether his new, more dangerous plan would work. Was he on a suicide mission? Was he spurred by guilt about Aeneas? Or was this a last, desperate effort to protect the rest of us?

His slight figure grew smaller in the fog till I couldn't distinguish him from the shadows beyond and could barely see his light.

Then I dug my hands into my pockets and hurried after him.

Chapter Thirty-nine

O

Roshi's walk had the quality of meditation, a slow, steady, deliberate moving of the weight onto one foot and then the other so that the progress was steady, unbroken, ineffable.

Coastal fog in California is different than the gray, downy comforters that smother the Atlantic coastline. It blows in from the Pacific at night and is cranked back in morning like an old awning. There are small tears in its canvas through which the moon blinks and is gone. The moon blinked on Roshi as he crossed the bridge. He slowed and for the first time his gait was shaky, the uncertain steps of a sick man. At the middle of the bridge he stopped.

I moved closer, trying not to crackle twigs underfoot. His face was drawn and the moonlight bleached out any color, leaving it garishly white. He made a small bow toward the stone wall railing, lifted the hem of his robe, stepped up on it and gazed down over the edge to the water and the rocks.

I broke into a run.

I don't know if he heard me or if he had intended all along to climb back down, but he stepped back onto the bridge, walked on across to the

Japanese maple, and paused before it as he had on the bridge wall. I could see him bowing as the fog sealed up the tear and he faded under it.

He turned onto the path beside the stream. My stomach lurched. *You've been in the woods twice today, once going, once coming back*, I reassured myself. But the first time I had been all but blindfolded as Amber led me along, and coming back I'd had my hands on Maureen's shoulders most of the way. Neither time had been in the same thick fog that coated woods of my childhood. Not for a moment had I been alone. Now, my body felt light with fear, as if any gust would blow me off. I swallowed hard and forced myself to keep moving. Roshi's lantern was growing dimmer in the distance.

At the Japanese maple I paused, as Roshi had. The rain had washed off its leaves and just the skeleton remained. Surprising myself, I bowed, walked around it, and stepped onto the path, into the woods.

My feet went numb; I could barely feel the ground. My breath stopped at my throat. My mouth turned sour with bile. I thought I would faint, or slip into the stream, or die. I couldn't move, couldn't go forward.

Just pretend you're in Central Park, Gabe would have said.

"Central Park," I murmured. "The boathouse. This is just a path to the boathouse."

The bile welled. I was going to retch and keep retching till I chucked all my guts into the stream. This wasn't Central Park; it was *here*. The fog swirled in, around me. Roshi's light was almost invisible.

I was going to pass out.

Roshi was walking to his death alone.

His light was a speck far onto the path.

I grabbed onto it with my eyes and followed, looking neither right nor left, feet shuffling along the ground for balance. On my left the stream sputtered and sloshed; below, leaves and twigs crackled; above, leaves swished against other leaves. It all blended to one sound not as loud as the draw of my breaths. Ahead, the tiny lantern light flickered and was gone. I broke into a run. Then it reappeared, as if Roshi had swung the lantern in front of himself and back.

He moved ahead steadily, but ever more slowly, and I was afraid his own gait would falter. He only needed to lose his balance once to tumble down the embankment onto the rocks, into the river. Yesterday he had been too weak to sit up without help; this burst of strength couldn't last. It was all I could do not to grab him and drag him back to his cabin. But he'd just have set out again when I wasn't looking.

My brief run brought the feeling back to my feet and I walked more steadily, my gaze toggling from the light to the ground and back with every step. Condensed fog dripped off leaves and tapped on my forehead, and made a pungent potpourri of pine and damp earth. I may have walked for half an hour, or maybe it was five minutes. I was so intent on not losing Roshi and on staying on the path I didn't think about anything else, didn't see leaves, or trees, only the dot of light in the darkness.

The light went out again. Roshi was about thirty yards ahead. I walked on, feeling a great draft of aloneness, waiting for the comfort of the light to return. It did not flicker back on. Something banged, wood on wood. A gruff groan sawed through the still air.

"Roshi," I yelled. "Leo, are you all right?"

There was another bang—wood on wood—louder, sharper.

"Leo!" I ran, batting branches out of my way. My boot caught against a root or something. I lunged, grabbed a branch and twisted, landing on one knee.

Leo didn't answer.

Had he fallen in the river? Like Aeneas?

Oh, God, like Aeneas? The killer? Had the killer managed to get ahead of us? "Leo, answer me!"

The only answer was a metallic sound. An irregular clanking and the grumbling of a small motor, like the wee electric mowers New Yorkers use to mow their wee back lawns. Like a hedge clipper. Or a motor bike.

I stopped. The grumbling was steady, but the clanking seemed more distant. Two sounds? What did that mean?

The clanking was growing softer. But it was all I had. I ran toward it. "Leo!"

Still no answer.

I almost fell over the source of the noise. If I'd come this far on this path earlier with Amber, I surely would have noticed the bottom of the pulley lift up to the fire tower. It was a big metal cube—a generator, maybe—with heavy wires leading upward. I squinted into the dark and thought I could make out the carriage box lurching upward. Maureen had been insulted at the idea of taking it down from the fire tower. Leo had to be in it now . . . unless it was a decoy to lead the killer uphill and let Leo get behind him. But Leo wasn't devious. He had staged this walk to draw the killer's attention. He was in that box, moving slowly up the hill, marked by his light and the rattle of wood and metal resounding through the forest. He couldn't be more exposed. All the killer had to do was cut the cables. They were sturdy wires, but hardly indestructible.

Or, easier yet, he could race up to the fire tower, tip over the arriving cart, and fling Leo down the hillside to what would look like the most unequivocal of accidental deaths: Sick Man Falls to Death Exiting Awkward Carrier.

"Oh shit!" That could be true, murderer or not. It would be one thing to stand at the edge of the widow's walk up there and haul a desk chair out of that cart, but a different and way more dangerous project getting yourself out of that swaying crate onto the deck with the wind gusting, smacking you and the cart.

I raced back till I found the cut-off up to fire tower, the tine, as Leo had called it when he told me about the fork in the road.

This was the steep part, I remembered that. I clambered up grabbing branches, yanking myself over bulging rocks, my feet slipping on leaves and twigs and loose pebbles. Fog floated down the hillside like gray paste, thicker with each foot I climbed ; it caught on the outcroppings, sagged wet on my shoulders. It pressed the branches and fronds into my face as it had done in Tilden Park or Muir Woods. My face was against the mountainside. I could barely make out the dirt and leaves and vines. I grabbed a branch, hoisted myself up, feeling for footing, finding none, sliding back down, hanging by my hands, my nose scraping against rock. I was going to throw up. I was going to scream.

No! I was not four years old, not now. I clamped my mouth shut, forcing myself to stare down at the ground, to stay in the present. Had I missed the path entirely? I couldn't bear that thought. I climbed again, grabbing, yanking, planting my feet and grabbing before they had time to slip. Bile filled my throat, sweat coated my face; I saw the walls of the canyon in Tilden Park the day when I was four; I heard my brothers laughing while I screamed and screamed and screamed. They laughed, softer, softer, and then there was nothing but the cold fog and the side of the canyon and the dark.

My tailbone slammed against something, slamming me back into the present. The pulley scraped louder. The carriage banged high above my head.

I could hear Roshi groaning.

"I'm coming," I yelled.

I scrambled hand over hand, feet barely touching the hillside, not thinking, just moving. When I reached the uphill path, I ran, slipping on the scree of pebbles, leaves, and twigs. I grabbed branches and kept pulling myself forward. My breath was short, shallow, my lungs banging against my ribs with each gasping breath. I rounded a switchback, and another. Everything looked the same. Was Roshi still calling, moaning? I couldn't hear anything over the branches snapping underfoot and my own gasping.

Where was the carriage? I looked up, squinting into the foggy night for wires, for the box. I smacked into a branch, something sharp piercing the corner of my eye. Blinking madly, I rushed on. The danger would be at the top.

I was gasping for breath, my throat raw, my mouth dry as incense powder. I couldn't go another step.

I had to keep going. Just take this step. This step. This step.

The stairs to the fire tower erupted out of nowhere. I almost flung myself down on them with relief. The cable screeched next to me. The clanking of wood on wood sounded like a hundred pairs of clappers calling me to the zendo, to the fire tower, on up all four flights of steps.

The carriage was above me, inching toward the widow's walk.

The stairs rose, endlessly. My legs wavered and I could barely breathe. I thought—I stopped thinking and stepped, and stepped. I didn't call to Leo anymore. I had no breath for that.

I lifted my foot for a step that wasn't there and almost toppled onto the platform, the first landing. Grabbing the rail, I muttered, "Keep going. Step!"

My head swirled. I was gasping with every footfall, pressing on feet I couldn't feel. I cleared the second landing and it was all I could do not to collapse across it.

"Step."

Wood thudded above. The carriage hitting against the docking. *Stay where you are, Leo!* I was desperate to yell, but couldn't. I could only keep moving. There was no rush, I told myself; he would let the carriage settle into place before he tried to climb out. Or he wouldn't wait. He would stand up. He would wave his lantern. He would leap over the edge.

I forced myself up, hands shaky on the railing, yanking myself upward. The wind snapped my jacket like a flag, whipped my hair against my face. *Step!* I pulled myself up, and up again.

A noise came from the widow's walk. I shoved my feet down, pressed harder, and climbed. It was only when I cleared the top and looked right over the planking of the widow's walk that I saw the cart waving in the wind and a figure bent down beneath the windows waiting.

CHAPTER FORTY

I froze against the fire tower stairs, my head just about the level of the planking on the widow's walk. The fog was thicker up here, sucking a dimension out of everything, leaving the fire-watch room and the figure huddled beneath its windows flat sketches of grays. I stared at the form, unable to judge size or intent.

A gust shook the stairs as if they were four stories of toothpicks on the top of the mountain. The pulley carriage swayed. I strained, desperate to make out Leo still in it. A second gust jostled me loose. I grabbed for the post.

The huddled figure had moved away from the wall, closer to the pulley carriage.

Covered by the cacophony of sound and shaking from the next gust of wind, I swung around the railing, up onto the walk and in one leap was next to the figure, arms extended, hands clasped like a baseball bat.

"Stop!" Roshi sputtered, and sank to the flooring.

I just caught myself in time. "Roshi! Omigod! However did you manage to get yourself out of the carriage?" My words were lost in the wind. I half lifted, half dragged him around the corner and inside the fire-watch room. The room was almost as icy as the outside. I spread out the sleeping bag, helped him onto it, and pulled the other side over to cover him. Then I pulled off my coat and made a pillow to keep his head off the hard wood floor. It was a sign of how wasted he was that he didn't object.

"The lantern," he said.

It was outside, standing next to the wall by the carriage. The rough trip should have broken the globe or sloshed out the kerosene, but Leo must have focused his whole attention on protecting it. Old and dried out as the wood was up here, that lamp could have sent the whole fire tower up in smoke.

Leo looked spent. Like Maureen he had used every bit of energy on the trek. I tucked my coat sleeves around his shoulders and fussed with squirming nylon sleeping bag trying to create a cocoon for him.

"Oh, Leo," I moaned, wishing for words for the amalgam of love, frustration and fear I felt for this man.

After a while he said, "Put the lantern on the cabinet over there."

"What about the skull?"

"Stick in inside."

I must have gasped or something, because Leo actually laughed.

"Darcy," he said, "it's just a piece of plastic."

"Plastic!" I held it to the light. It may not have been bone, but it was a very good likeness. "Maureen said—"

"Maureen chooses to imbue it with spiritual meaning. That meaning is her illusion, in her head. Not in the plastic."

"Suppose it was a statue of the Buddha, would we still plunk it inside like a disused ashtray? Would it still be just plastic?"

He reached up with his fist and knocked on my forehead.

"Ah, 'There's nothing that can't be replaced, except what someone didn't want to tell you to begin with.' Who said that?" he demanded in a completely different, all business, tone.

"You did, Roshi."

"No, I didn't."

"After Aeneas took the Buddha off the altar. A while after."

"Where did you hear that?"

"I don't know. Someone told me. Why?"

"It doesn't sound like me. What I probably said was that no 'thing' can't be done without. You know why, Darcy?"

I nodded. "There is no bodhi tree, no mirror or stand; fundamentally nothing exists, so there's nowhere for dust to land."

"I was going to quote Suzuki-roshi: Things change. But the Sixth Patriarch will do." He held my gaze a moment and he grinned, a big full grin like I remembered from the truck driving in. "As for the part about what someone didn't want to tell you to begin with being irreplaceable, I don't know who said that."

But I did. And I understood why it had been said, and what was in the manila envelope.

He motioned me to get zafus out of the cabinet and go ahead with placing the lantern.

"But Leo, there's a killer out there. If I put that light up there I might as well hang out a sign, 'The Roshi is in.'"

"For anyone who didn't notice the pulley?"

"Well, yeah."

He maintained the smile. "Pulley was half an hour ago. Only one here besides me is you."

"He could be waiting till I leave."

"Go."

I gave up. I mean, what was I going to do with the man? I couldn't cart him back down the hill, not weak as he was. So I stuck the plastic skull in the cupboard, and replaced it with the lantern. The cupboard

347

held two worn zafus, which I pulled out for us. Roshi was quite particular about his spot against the blank wall. He wasn't looking straight on to the door, he was facing the spot next to it. And that was where he motioned me to sit. I tried again to wrap the squirming sleeping bag around him, as I had with Maureen, and somehow in that effort I understood the sincerity of her practice. Meditating on the skull up here was like a flashy pirouette; her real practice was just the basic steps of being at the monastery, working the garden, storing the cabbages for sesshin, staying out here winter after summer after winter, wrapping herself in the miserable nylon sleeping bag as he was. It was staying here in spite of her fear and suspicion that Leo was a killer, because at gut level she had never really believed it and she loved him too much to leave him unprotected.

I was glad that she was down in the monastery, safe in Barry's room over the kitchen and that, finally, she had her teacher back.

Now Roshi was doing for the killer what she had done for him, giving him the chance to reclaim himself.

The gusts rattled the windows. A steady draft slipped under the door and wound up over the top of my socks under my pant legs. In zazen the gaze is supposed to be downward, but I glanced at Roshi. The lantern threw wavy shadows over his face, emphasizing bushy eyebrows over sharp cheekbones. I don't know whether he felt my gaze on him or if he'd just been worrying about me, but when he raised his eyes and met mine his small sweet smile almost made me cry. It was gone in an instant and his face melted into a fuzzy outline of regret.

A moment passed. His eyes narrowed, his jaw tightened.

"Go, Darcy."

I didn't go. I sat down on the cushion, crossed my legs, put my hands in the mudra, right hand resting in left, thumbs touching lightly. Despite the wheeze of the wind, the windows crackling, and the imminent prospect of footsteps on the stairs, there was an odd uneasy calm here, like being in the eye of a hurricane. I found I was aware of the movement of my breath, the cold air on the bit of shin I hadn't quite gotten covered. My eyes shut. What I saw was the hillside, bracken-covered, fog-dimmed, the meld of this hill and the one in Tilden all those years ago. My throat tightened; my skin went clammy; I was desperate to escape. I breathed. The spicy bite of incense tinged the air. I "heard" my brothers laughing, as they walked away from me. How *could* they? How could they have just left me there? I'd been screaming! How—Roshi shifted. I shot a glance, but he was okay. And when I closed my eyes I was back abandoned in Tilden Park, hearing my brothers, the responsible ones, giggling as they walked away. The incense was thicker; I inhaled.

And then I laughed.

"What?" Leo demanded, grinning himself.

"My very responsible brothers were smoking grass. No wonder they didn't want me to tell Mom." I couldn't stop chuckling. Mom would have taken their heads off.

The light sputtered. I jerked my eyes toward it. It danced and settled.

Leo, Roshi, sitting against the far wall of the fire tower was still looking over at me. "Darcy, you think you're protecting me. But you're not; you're only putting off what has to happen."

"It doesn't *have to*. Not here!"

"Here, is where I have chosen—away from the zendo and the grounds, where it is private—"

I started to protest, but he silenced me with his gaze.

"Here," he said, "where it is dokusan."

"But—"

"There will be two of us involved. I am doing this for both of us. Without this, I cannot go on. Do you understand?"

I nodded. I did understand. But I wasn't leaving, and Leo understood that.

I sat listening to the sounds, feeling the cold on the slice of exposed ankle as if only that small bit of my body existed, its cold smothering the passable warmth of the rest. Drafts stung the edges of the skin where the covering of slack leg stopped; it dug through flesh to bone, icing the fibula, like steel on steel. I felt that small, all-consuming patch of cold, and I thought of the manila envelope Aeneas had stolen.

"There's nothing that can't be replaced, except what someone didn't want to tell you to begin with."

"Darcy!"

Who could have predicted my siblings' secret plan to smoke marijuana on a family hike in the woods would lead to my years of fear? Who could have imagined Aeneas's casual grabbing of a manila envelope would end with him dead? No wonder my brother John had been stunned that my fear of the woods was still a big deal. I was the little kid scrambling to keep up; I had always laughed about it with the rest of them. Right now he was probably berating himself for not checking on me every year after the Tilden event, making sure I was unscarred.

But the killer *had* checked on the red maple, made sure it wasn't in danger of being dug up. When Leo announced this was his last sesshin, he brought it all to a head at this sesshin.

Cloth rustled. I pretended not to hear. I ignored the groaning of the wooden structure. I couldn't deal with Roshi's demand to leave, not yet. If the killer had stayed with Aeneas's body, called for help, said Aeneas slipped off the bridge, no one would have doubted him. But he looked at Aeneas's body which covered the manila envelope, and assumed the envelope with its irreplaceable document was floating away down-stream. He had to choose. He went after the envelope.

A hand touched my head.

"Roshi—"

But it wasn't Roshi.

Chapter Forty-one

O

"**D**amn Gabe Luzotta and his fucking rental car!" Barry yelled. He filled the doorway of the fire tower. His corduroy pants were thick with mud almost to the hip, his navy V-neck sweater was ripped at both shoulders, and his blue shirt sweated through. If he had worn a cap it must have caught on a branch somewhere on the hillside, and there were blood-caked scratches on one side of his shaved head. He was panting, glaring down at Roshi. I could hardly believe he was the sweet guy who had loaned me his anorak. He gasped in air, seeming to swell even larger, and yelled, "I ran the whole way; the path's almost as bad as the road. Damn you, Leo! If you hadn't announced you were leaving, and made this sesshin a big deal, last chance ever sesshin, Gabe fucking Luzotta wouldn't have hot-footed it out here. And his damned rental car wouldn't be stuck in the middle of the road."

The car Gabe had complained about that first day I met him! Of course it would be blocking the road. Gabe had abandoned it and hiked in on the path! All Barry's work, his isolation, his fine imported equipment, to create the perfect batch of chocolate, and now that chocolate was stuck in the front seat of the truck miles from the paved road.

Hot sweat vaporized off his scalp. "I spent six fucking years here to get myself in shape to go back to the Cacao Royale. I sat every fucking sesshin so I could learn to be calm enough to handle the contest. And now . . . now you do this!" His hands were on the doorjambs, as if they were all that restrained him.

I was too stunned to move.

Leo looked up at him, no sign of fear in his face. He seemed to be considering what to say.

Don't! I wanted to shout. *Keep still. Don't set him off!* On impulse he'd tossed the peanut oil in his other contestant's vanilla tart. And now Barry was just waiting for Leo to stoke his rage. He was so furious he could barely breathe; his breaths were like great crackling thunder. How could I have missed him coming up the stairs? Leo must have heard him, why didn't he warn me?

But Roshi had set up this sesshin to help his guilty student. He'd drunk the poisoned cocoa and held his silence. Barry was his student, he wouldn't abandon Barry now. He would do nothing to save himself.

Barry took a step toward Leo, wrenching his hands free of the door. "The Cacao Royale comes once every six years! I can't wait six more years! I'll never get criollos that good again. That chocolate was my *life*."

Leo was all roshi now, as he had been that first night in his cabin when he poured his cocoa on the floor. I remembered how furious that had made me, and it terrified me. I wanted to scream, *Don't! Leo, don't* teach *him now. Don't push him!*

Roshi looked up at Barry, meeting his eyes. What he said was, "Your chocolate is good. It would probably win."

Barry went stiff. He was like a plywood board tottering on its narrow edge. *It probably would win. Your* life *is the illusion of something that might happen.* Leo must have said that to Barry a hundred times. Barry's eyes widened. He saw it now. Then he teetered back and his face tightened against it.

Let him save face somehow. Don't push him! I wanted to shout. But push is what Zen masters do. Losing face totally is the entire game.

How could this be the same Barry who said, *Roshi took me in when I was at rock bottom. He didn't ask questions. He stuck by me?* But I remembered what followed. *He gave me time to find my way, my Zen practice, to get to this point where I can go back to the Cacao Royale.* Was it just about the chocolate, all along?

Barry tapped his foot hard on the floor. Wind battered the windows; the stairs creaked. He was still near the doorway, almost next to me, but he'd forgotten I was there. He was staring only at Leo. I pulled my feet under me. The wind was so loud even I didn't hear them scraping the floor. I started to ease myself up.

"Damn it!" Barry yelled. "Yes, damn it, I would win. I would have won! I would have been . . ."

"You *are*," Leo said.

I froze, halfway up, knees bent.

Leo inhaled slowly. The wind had died momentarily and the rasp of Leo's breathing cut ragged edges in the silence. The rattling of the door filled the void. It sounded like gunfire. The smell of the oil lamp was stronger. Barry didn't move. He knew what Roshi meant; but he didn't want to know, not now.

"My chocolate is sitting in the truck!"

"You are *here*."

"Don't tell me I have a life here. I don't. You've taken even that away, you—"

Barry took another step toward Leo. One more step and he could grab Leo. His breaths were coming fast, thick. "Once you're gone, Leo, and

Rob's in charge, *here* isn't going to be here! The place will look the same, the generator'll still fail four times a year, the lousy road'll still wash out. Someone else will run in on the path because the damn road's a swamp." He took the last step. "It'll all look the same, but it won't be the same, Leo." He was shaking; spraying sweat from his red face over Roshi.

I eased to standing, behind him. I could grab his knee and yank hard. It would land him on his face, but only for a moment. Frantically, I looked for a cudgel, a metal bar. The only things in the room where the oil lamp and the chair. If I rolled the chair hard . . .

Leo sat, legs crossed, the blue nylon sleeping bag still spread on the floor around him. The smoke from the oil lamp filled the room like incense.

"Goddamn it, Leo, I left the Cacao Royale humiliated, in front of my friends, disgraced in front of people who enjoyed laughing at me. Do you know how that eats at you? There isn't a day you don't think *if only*. But dammit Leo, now, after six years, I could have gotten it all back. This was my one chance and it's rotting in the front seat of a truck stuck in the mud!"

Incense filled the air. Leo looked up, locking eyes with Barry. Leo's too-big features seemed enormous against his wan skin. He was a small, thin, sick man, but strength flowed from his eyes. He reached his left hand up to Barry. Barry didn't bend, but loomed lower to take it.

I held my breath.

Barry bent closer and hissed, "My one chance to redeem myself !"

Roshi grinned at him, that same big grin he'd shared with me minutes earlier, and said, "Chance to be a polished mirror on a stand?"

Barry jerked forward.

I lunged for the chair, pulled it into position, braced my feet to send it flying.

Barry bowed. "Roshi," he said softly.

Barry was still shaking. I was shaking. Now that I looked at Barry standing there before roshi, his hands outstretched in his bow as if holding out the illusion that had kept him at arm's length these six years, I knew he couldn't have killed Aeneas. He could have shoved him off the bridge, but before Aeneas hit the water, Barry would have been racing down to the stream, propelled by his remorse. He hadn't killed Aeneas or poisoned Leo.

I felt such a rush of warmth for Barry and for Leo, I could feel it in my body.

The incense surrounded us, all three. The incense rose as if a dozen sticks were suddenly burning, as if—

"Omigod!" I yelled. "Fire! The tower is burning!"

CHAPTER FORTY-TWO

" **F** ire!"

Barry didn't move. He stood, still smiling down at Roshi, and Roshi was smiling up at him.

"Fire!"

Barry still didn't react. Whether from exhaustion or fear, Barry was useless.

Getting out of a burning fire tower was all in a day's work for a stunt double. But stunts were done with Kevlor suits, and fire engines standing by. This was bare skin and trees that would ignite like roman candles.

Pushing away panic, I started shouting orders.

"Roshi, are you strong enough to hang on to Barry?"

Leo nodded, with an expression more of hope than certainty.

"I can carry him down the stairs," Barry said, pulling him to standing.

"Too late for stairs! The flames are halfway up! Knife? Is there a knife, clippers?"

Leo pointed to the cabinet. I grabbed clippers.

"This whole tower's going to crumble. Come on. Fast!" I ran outside. Smoke poured up from the damp wood, flames from the dry. The pulley carriage banged in the wind. Five minutes? Wishful thinking? Arson fires burn faster.

Arson! The killer! Even if we made it down, he'd be waiting, watching us climb, slide, down into his trap. I had to divert him, but there was no time. Nothing to use. The oil lamp—too small in the dark. The chair? We couldn't throw it far enough to draw him away.

Wind snapped my hair into my eyes and I pushed it free. The veil of smoke was closing in. Desperately I looked around. The pulley carriage! "Barry! The rope cable! Loop it over your hands, hang on for your life, all our lives."

Barry set Leo down against the wall. Leo looked up, eyes wide with interest. I cut the cable. The carriage shot down into the spark-filled dark. I grabbed the pulley and cranked like mad, churning the loosened cable up toward us.

"Barry, knot your end. Hurry!" The rope looped onto the walkway. We needed forty feet. No way to be sure. "Cut again, above your hands. Knot the piece beneath."

Barry cut. He was holding the severed length. The forty-foot length.

"Tie it on the corner of the walkway, away from the stairs and the fire. Firm knot. It's got to hold you both. You can't rappel; no time. You've got to slide; brake with your feet. You're going to hit hard. The killer may have gone after the carriage, but he'll see it's empty. He'll be back in a minute. But—"

"I . . . can't."

I was cranking the second rope. I didn't stop. "No time for 'can't.'"

"Darcy. I just can't. Heights. I'll go dizzy."

Waves of sympathy and utter frustration washed over me. The second rope was looped on the walkway. It looked short. A flame shot up where the carriage had gone. The smoke was thicker. "Barry, cut this now!"

He cut. I turned to face him. The man was shaking. Advice was useless. Mere words. Barry's fear was beyond words.

A shard of flames shot up from the stairs. The whole platform swayed. Roshi stood propped against the windows, his black robe crackling in the wind.

I grabbed the ropes, tied the longer one around the far corner post, and made a large loop at the other end. "Here, Barry." I slipped the loop over his arms.

"Darcy, I can't." His face was red with humiliation. The poor guy was shaking.

I pressed his hands around the rope.

"No! I can't—"

I pushed him over the edge.

He may have screamed, but any sound was lost under the crackling of the wood as part of the stairs collapsed. The tower lurched toward the failing stairs. It flung Roshi toward them. I leapt for him, caught his black robe, and skidded my feet against the wall of the tower room. He spun toward me—as if he'd been alert for the right move. Using the taut robe like a rope, he turned and pulled himself close enough to catch my hand.

The tower swayed again. The thick smoke turned the world black. With Leo behind me, I felt along the outer wall of the tower room, around the corner, to the far corner post and looped the last rope over it. The killer could be waiting for us below. I turned to Roshi.

"I know," he said, "'hang on.'"

"Tight. The rope may be short."

He grinned the pickup truck grin. "How sweet is the strawberry."

Tiger at the top, tiger at the bottom, mouse eating the vine. How sweet is the strawberry.

Leo was on my back. I pushed off and slid fast.

Flames shot up beside us. The rope seared my hands. I couldn't feel Leo at all. I squinted through the smoke hoping in vain for an upright to rappel against. Fire singed my cheek; I could smell my hair burning.

Thunder.

It wasn't thunder. The fire tower was collapsing on top of us.

"Hang on!" I let go of the rope and we fell.

I curled into a *C*, landed hard on hands and knees. I was half standing, my hands having slammed against a pile of rocks.

Roshi wasn't on my back. Frantically I peered through the smoke. "Leo! Roshi!"

"Here!" His voice came from a few feet away. "I'm okay."

"Barry!"

"Safe," Leo yelled.

I didn't know why Leo answered for him, but there was no time to find out. The killer was still around here. Flames shot into the sky. The whole tower was crumbling. There was nowhere to go but into the woods toward the path, toward where the carriage must have crashed. Flames turned the trees light. I ran past them, skirting them, squinting for the path. Debris from the falling tower crashed beside me. Smoke clogged my lungs. I kept squinting to clear the ash from my eyes.

Trees canopied the path. I raced down, half running, half skiing, almost falling over the broken pulley carriage. The light dimmed. I held my forearms out, bounced off the trees.

"Could be . . . wrong way," I muttered.

Then I spotted him, thirty feet ahead rounding a curve in the path. In a few seconds he'd be beneath me. I grabbed two saplings, swung forward and leapt. I came down hard on his back.

I'd knocked the wind out of him. He lay gasping, desperate for air.

The impact knocked me back into a tree. I stood, panting, glaring down at him, fury welling so fast I couldn't speak. I wiped the soot from my eyes, and in that instant he rolled over onto all fours, stretched out a hand and forced out, "You okay?"

"Stay where you are, Gabe!"

"I can't," he said trying to push himself up. "No time. Rob, he set a fire! Fire! People up there! Got to get them down!"

CHAPTER FORTY-THREE

O

It took me only an instant to see through Gabe's maneuver, but in that time he was on his feet, above me on the path, where he could see the way down. But I was blocking that way. I swayed slightly side to side like a goalie wary for the first sign of a shot. I had to take Gabe here. If he got past me in the woods he'd be gone, off on some path he'd discovered years before, or back to the road to the highway, or to the monastery, the kitchen knives and the students sitting unsuspecting in the zendo. The wind snapped through the branches, smoke streaked the air. I focused on Gabe.

"Gabe, you poisoned Leo!"

"You're crazy, Assistant. I couldn't have. I wasn't even here yet. My car broke down, remember! You saw me. Trudging up the road." His eyes narrowed. "You saw me there, standing under all those trees. Those big, looming trees, just like the ones here."

Suddenly the trees behind him, on each side of him, leapt into focus as if they were alive. Their branches swayed, leaves crackled. They blurred and I couldn't see them, only feel them in my swirling stomach. They were swaying with me back and forth. Sweat covered my face, my back. If I could shut my eyes . . . but I didn't dare. I focused hard on Gabe, only him, as if he was standing crouched in front of a blue screen. "You fooled me with that," I said. I could barely force out the words; they were not quite loud enough for him to hear. He moved closer. "When I tried to figure who could have poisoned the cocoa, I gave you a free ride because I believed you'd just arrived. But," I kept my gaze on his face, "I forgot about that path, the one that leads from the monastery to the road, to just about where your car is. Gabe, you've been here before, you know the path. If your car broke down, why would you walk miles on the road when the path is much shorter?"

"Gimme, a break, Assistant. It was dark. I'm a New Yorker; I'm not used to driving." He shifted slightly to the left. The trees loomed behind him.

I froze, desperate to regain focus, not to let him see my panic. "You're a New Yorker, you're used to chutzpah. You're a master. Here's what happened. You ditched your car, ran the path, hid outside the kitchen until Barry went to bed. You know about Roshi's special cocoa. We all know where it's kept. You crept into the kitchen, dropped the poison into the container. Outside, no one saw you, because, like you said, it was dark. Did you go back along the path and sleep in the car for a couple hours before your walk along the road? Or did you hide out on the grounds, maybe behind the wood in the shed—"

"But you *saw* me walking toward the monastery!"

"Gabe, please! You could have trotted a hundred yards up the road, turned around, and walked back!"

He was still checking terrain, planning his move. I couldn't risk a look. It was a moment before he said, "Coulda! Assistant, anyone coulda!"

"Anyone" wouldn't have a rental car with a rental agreement signed a day earlier than he'd told me it was. But that clincher I wasn't about to tell him, not here. The smoke was getting thicker. Even close as we were, it veiled his face so I couldn't see his eyes flicker before he made a move.

"Besides," he said, widening his stance, bending his knees, "why would I poison Leo?"

I blinked against the soot. Leo and Gabe were above us, where the smoke was thicker, the flames— "Leo knows you, Gabe. He knows you crashed sesshin; he didn't accept you. He knows Yamana didn't vouch for you, probably never heard of you. You just made use of Yamana-roshi's name after you asked me who my teacher was at home."

His hand inched to the right. Was he reaching for a stick, a loose branch? I didn't dare move my gaze from his face.

"Mostly, Gabe, because you need Leo sick, but not dead, so Rob could get a clear shot at being his successor!"

"Rob! The asshole! Why would I do anything to help him!"

"Because Rob will keep the monastery as is. He will keep the road as is. He won't pave it. He won't widen it. And most important, he won't dig up the red maple, won't find Aeneas's body, and he won't find your manila envelope buried with him." I saw his flinch. "That document was the key to your future. You wouldn't chance it getting wet, would you? You'd seal it in heavy-duty plastic in the envelope. How many years does plastic survive in the ground? How long will it tie you to the murder?"

Something rustled behind him. Barry? Down here, safe? Carrying Leo? Not safe at all, not if Gabe spotted them.

"Oh, Gabe, you are the original hard luck guy. They're right, at home, calling you the paste diamond schlimazel. You couldn't get lucky if luck was for sale."

His knees bent more, like he was ready to pounce.

"First you get screwed for another writer's mistake, then Aeneas steals the documentation that would have saved your story, made your career. You chase him onto the bridge, you grab for the envelope, and he falls—"

"Okay, okay, Assistant. You're right. He fell! I didn't push him, I just grabbed. He just fell. I didn't kill him. He goddamn fell."

"He fell, the envelope went with him. He struck his head. And you, Gabe, did you help him, drag him out of the water, give him mouth to mouth? You didn't, did you? Because your envelope was gone. Gone downstream, you thought. Under the bridge, back toward the zendo. You left Aeneas to die; you went hunting for your envelope, peering under the dark bridge, trying to see if it washed up in there, or did the current carry it downstream while you were looking under the bridge? Was it floating farther and farther away every minute? Which way to go? You never gave Aeneas a thought, did you?"

He didn't protest. It was too late for that game. His body was tensed; he was in full crouch now.

I should have stopped, but I couldn't. "You left a man to die. For an envelope you never did find, because—" I laughed with a touch of hysteria. "—you can't buy luck. What were the chances the envelope would be under Aeneas's body? If you had stopped to help him, you'd have gotten your papers back; your article would have sold; you'd be big time now! Oh, the irony, Gabe. You—"

He pushed off and jumped straight at me, arms outstretched. I leapt to the side. He smashed down, swung hard with both arms, clipping my shoulder.

I fell against a tree. I pushed up. He was running downhill, sending scree flying. In a second I'd lose him in the dark. I lunged, hung onto his back. We rolled till we smacked into a tree.

I do rolls for a living. Gabe Luzotta didn't have a chance. He was bleeding, and panting. Before he could clear his head, I said, "How come you were so sure Aeneas was buried under the maple?"

"When I came back...Maureen...was walking...away with the shovel."

It wasn't till after Barry arrived and found something to tie Gabe's hands behind him that my skin went clammy, my stomach churned, and I disgraced myself.

Chapter Forty-four

O

The moment Gabe had feared all these years came while we were all in the zendo. The sheriff dug up the red maple, exhumed Aeneas's body, and found the plastic-wrapped manila envelope with the signed admission statement from the curator in San Francisco, the paper that could have made Gabe's career but ended up drawing him back here year after fearful year until it testified to his guilt.

After that, sesshin took on a surreal quality. The sheriff questioned everyone individually in a macabre simulacrum of dokusan interviews. Then people were free to leave, but only a few did. Most of the students had barely been aware of the events, much less endangered. I thought Amber would be the first out, but she stayed. I guess she, like Maureen before her, really came for reasons other than what she had assumed.

On Sunday, we had the long-overdue memorial service for Aeneas. We walked slowly in a circle in the zendo, chanting the Heart Sutra, and offering incense. Amber could have spoken about her brother, but she didn't. It was Rob's words that I remember. He quoted the second poem from the tale of the Sixth Patriarch.

The body is not a bodhi tree
There is no clear mirror anywhere
Fundamentally nothing exists
Nothing for dust to cling to.

"Did Aeneas understand there had never been a mirror? I don't know. But he was a mirror for me, and I have more dust clinging than I let myself realize." Rob's wide shoulders slumped, the light of his startlingly blue eyes dulled. He stumbled and caught himself on Maureen's outstretched hand. I had never respected him more.

Roshi, seated on his zafu, his robes tucked neatly under his knees, said what he had in his opening talk three days ago. "Things change." He looked slowly around the room, meeting each person's eyes, then repeated, "Things change."

We all waited for him to go on, but he said no more. Indignation rattled me; I almost cried out, *Is that all, Roshi? A man died here. One of your students killed him. You did nothing for years! Can't you at least give us some closure?* But in the end I decided Roshi was right in giving no final words that would have framed Aeneas's death and Gabe's murdering, would have made it suitable for display, discussion, finished, and done. One of the familiar symbols of Zen is the circle. The circle is never complete; there's always an opening through which life flows.

In the remaining days, we returned to the rule of total silence, and moved in that state of closeness and separation it provided. I thought of the irony of my life, that I had been so focused on being accepted by the big kids I had never let on how scared I'd been and so I spent my life being scared. But even now, I knew I would keep the events of the family hike in Tilden Park to myself. They were still John's to keep or tell.

But as the days passed and I wore out those considerations, I found myself just sitting on my zafu in the zendo. The weather cleared and I felt the sun on my shoulders; it worsened and I listened to the rain battering the windows; I heard the leaves rustle, the oil lamp sputter, Marcus's breathing to my right, the occasional odd glucking noise from Amber, and my own sudden laugh—aloud, there in the zendo.

Fundamentally nothing exists

I had misplaced the emphasis as: fundamentally nothing *exists*. Now I heard it as: fundamentally *nothing* exists. And I sat enjoying those sounds and feelings I had always considered nothing but filler between my thoughts. Momentarily a veil lifted.

After that I spent my breaks learning to walk in the woods, feeling the pounding of my heart as thumps of flesh, catching thoughts of danger that no longer existed, seeing trees as plants. Until Amber popped out from behind a redwood and just about panicked me into the stream.

Barry was different, too, and Maureen. Barry just cooked. Only twice in the remaining days did I see him look longingly toward his big silver winnower or the great orange conche. One day in the second week, when we all came back to the zendo, cold and tired from work period, the servers offered each of us tea and a small block of wonderfully rich chocolate, with a hint of wine, a soupcon of gardenia. I nibbled slowly, savoring each morsel, and shot a glance at Barry in time to see him smile.

Maureen, on the other hand, was more distracted than ever. Had it not been for the silence I would have asked her where she'd be going when Leo left.

Roshi saw each one of us in a dokusan interview. When my turn came, there was too much to say, and no way to focus it and what tumbled out of my mouth was, "I feel so bad for everyone. But you know who I keep thinking about? Gabe. I had liked Gabe."

"We all liked Gabe," Roshi said as if discussing someone who was still here. "We do the best we can, even though sometimes it doesn't seem anywhere near good."

We all do the best we can. He had said that to me on the drive in, as he laughed about my suitcase filled with tubes of shark cartilage ointment for everyone's knee pain rather than the wool pants and socks to make my own mornings here bearable.

"Leo—Roshi," I said slowly, knowing I was on the edge of speaking out of turn—again— "if you had known the killer was Gabe, instead of thinking it was Maureen, would you still have set up this sesshin for him?"

I thought he would ponder that, or tell me *Of course* or *Hardly*. But in an instant he leaned forward and snapped his finger against the back of my hand. He meant that what exists is the present, not speculation about what might have been in the past. He didn't have to say that we had all benefited from this sesshin.

But I wasn't quite ready to give up on the question of Gabe. "It just shouldn't have had to end like this. I mean, someone else was lazy with their research, and he ended up losing his big chance to get his piece in the *New Yorker*. He managed to get an interview with a woman at the Asian Art Museum in San Francisco, an interview that would have clinched his documentation. Then Aeneas snatched the admission she signed, and left Gabe without 'the thing someone didn't want to give to begin with.' Gabe's real good at poking till he gets an answer. I can imagine him getting that curator to say more than she intended, particularly when she had time to think about it afterwards. All for a magazine expose that wasn't going to do her any good. But once Gabe lost the verification, he was cooked. No wonder he was frantic. And now he'll be going to prison and his life is over."

Roshi picked up his cocoa, poured a bit on the floor. Then he looked at me and added, "Or not."

I smiled. Then I bowed and reached for the rag. *Or not.*

I started to leave.

"Darcy, your fear of the woods, you do know it was—"

"A great gift?" I said sarcastically.

He grinned. "A great gift. If you'd never had this fear that so embarrassed you, that you had to keep working to overcome or at least hide, would you ever have been in shape or brave enough to be a stuntwoman?"

"Well, no."

"Or tough enough to sit facing the wall day after day, not knowing what would cross your mind the next moment, if you'd see something you didn't want to know, or if you'd suddenly forget all that and just be."

I nodded. "I guess it was a gift."

At that cliché he grinned and gave me the half-wink I had hoped would pass between us when things got too-too in the zendo, when he was still the funny guy in the old truck, before I had any idea he was the teacher.

"Thanks for sharing."

I bowed and walked out. He was laughing.

It wasn't till I was in the van, looking out the window at Leo standing at the end of the path that led back to the bathhouse, with Maureen and Rob, that I felt the full thrust of missing him.

About halfway along the road, the lawyer from Vermont pulled out an envelope he'd found on his bed. My letter. It was, indeed, from Mom. She had mailed it the day I got my acceptance to sesshin and called to give her the address, in case of emergency.

Darce,

Surprise! The day your Zen sit ends, we'll all be waiting at the coast road to take you to a huge, carnivorous dinner. In a place that allows dogs. (If Duffy's not in China.)

Love ya,

Mom

When the dirt road ended, there they were: Mom, John, Gary, Janice, and Duffy, who forgot all his fine training and generations of dour Scottyness and leapt into my lap.

O

By the time I got home to New York the story of the murder was still ricocheting off its own angles in the New York papers and magazines. Gabe had no remorse about Aeneas, but he came to see plenty about the descriptions of himself: pedestrian wordsmith, shoddy investigator, toothless muckraker, and the most stinging: perennial schlimazel.

Thanksgiving was over and white winter lights sparkled on the street trees as I turned from Sixth Avenue onto Ninth Street. Cabs raced westward, adding their lights to the rush hour array. I walked slowly through the after-workers heading past me to Balducci's for gourmet takeout. I thought of sesshin gruel and how glad I was not to be eating it now. I had expected to find only relief on returning here, but things change. I would have given anything to have avoided going to California and to Leo, but now that I was back here, I thought of him every time I lifted a cup, opened a letter, sat cross-legged alone in my apartment. His words were tattooed beneath my skin, but they weren't enough. I missed his teaching; I missed *him*.

And yet, when I walked into the Ninth Street zendo, gratitude filled me like the incense suffusing the air. The jisha bowed and pointed to Yamana-roshi's dokusan room. I knocked once; he rang his bell and I entered.

Yamana-roshi sat cross-legged on his brown mat. On the altar beside him the candlewick was long and the flame burned high. I bowed to the Buddha and to Yamana-roshi and sat on my cushion. I had already told him about Aeneas's death and Gabe's guilt. Now, here in the dokusan room, the issue was my own practice.

"Be alert!" he said. "Were you alert?"

"I kept an eye open."

He smiled at that Americanism he so liked. "Just one?"

"Just sometimes."

"Hmm. Are you out of the woods?"

"Yes and no. I can walk in them, but I'm not out. I wasn't there long enough to not escape."

He nodded slowly. "Nothing has changed, Darcy. You are still you. I am still me. I cannot help you."

My stomach lurched. I could feel the panic rising up my body. "But"—

He raised his palm. "Garson-roshi called me. He is leaving the monastery. One of his senior students is taking charge. A man"—a smile flickered on Yamana-roshi-s face—"who makes very good chocolate.'"

Tense as I was, I smiled. It was the right choice. Of all of us, Barry was the one who had faced his fantasies and walked on.

"What about Le—Garson-roshi?"

"He said to me, 'I am not a desirable commodity just now.' His words. True. But he is a deep teacher, deeper than before. He has agreed to go to a Zen center which needs a teacher. A center in a very sticky situation."

Yamana looked away for an instant, and I suspected the move was to cover his reaction to the picture of a situation covered in honey.

"Very odd, too good to be true. He needs a jisha he can trust."

I put my hands together, bowed, and said, "Yes."

It occurred to me on the way out that I should have asked where that Zen center was.

Acknowledgments

I am indebted to Scharffen Berger Chocolate Maker for its very fine factory tour, which I took twice. (Life is hard.)

And to my friend Dolly Gattozzi for her wise and gracious suggestions and her knowledge of Zen Buddhism.

A special thanks to my superb agent, Dominick Abel.